DEATH'S
MISTRESS

Terry Goodkind has been a
wildlife artist, a cabinetmaker, a
racing driver and a violin maker.
He lives in the desert in Nevada.

ALSO BY TERRY GOODKIND

TERRY GOODKIND

DEATH'S MISTRESS

SISTER OF DARKNESS

THE NICCI CHRONICLES
1

HEAD
of ZEUS

First published in the UK in 2017 by Head of Zeus

9 7 5 3 1 2 4 6 8

A catalogue record for this book is available from the British Library.

ISBN (HB): 9781786691637
ISBN (XTPB): 9781786691644
ISBN (E) 9781786691620

Printed and bound by CPI Group (UK) Ltd, Croydon, CR0 4YY

Head of Zeus Ltd
Clerkenwell House
45-47 Clerkenwell Green
London EC1R 0HT

WWW.HEADOFZEUS.COM

DEATH'S
MISTRESS

CHAPTER 1

Another skull crunched under Nicci's boot, but she kept trudging forward nevertheless. In the thick forest, she could not avoid all the bones underfoot or the clawlike branches that dangled near her head. The way would have been treacherous even in full daylight, but in the deep night of the Dark Lands, the trail was nearly impossible.

Nicci never bothered to acknowledge the impossible, though, when she had a task to complete.

Piles of moss-covered human remains cluttered the shadowy forest. Yellowing bones stood out in the gloom, illuminated by moonlight that seeped through the leafy vine-strangled boughs overhead. When she climbed over a rotted oak trunk that had collapsed across the path, her heel crushed the old shell of another skull, scattering ivory teeth from a gaping jaw—as if these long-dead victims wanted to bite her, like the cannibalistic half people who had recently swarmed out of the Dark Lands.

Nicci had no fear of skulls. They were just empty remnants, and she had created plenty of skeletons herself. She paused to inspect a mound of bones stacked against a lichen-covered oak. A warning? A signpost? Or just a decoration?

The witch woman Red had an odd sense of humor. Nicci couldn't understand why Nathan was so insistent on seeing her, and he refused to reveal his intentions.

Crashing through tangled willows ahead, Nathan Rahl called back to her. "There's a big meadow up here, Sorceress. We'll make better time across the clearing."

Nicci did not hurry to catch up to the wizard. Nathan's impatience often led him to make rash decisions. She pointed out coolly, "We would make better time if we didn't travel through the thickest forest in the dark of night." Her long blond hair fell past her shoulders, and she felt perspiration on her neck, despite the cool night air. She brushed a few stray pine needles and the ragged lace of a torn spiderweb from her black travel dress.

Pausing at the edge of the wide meadow, the wizard raised an eyebrow. His long white hair seemed too bright in the shadows. "Judging by all the skeletons, we must be close to our destination. I am eager to get there. Aren't you?"

"This is your destination, not mine," she said. "I accompany you by choice—for Richard." The two had trudged through the trackless forest for days.

"Indeed? I thought you were supposed to watch over me."

"Yes, I'm sure that's what you thought. Perhaps I just wanted to keep you out of trouble."

He arched his eyebrows. "I suppose you've succeeded so far."

"That remains to be seen. We haven't found the witch woman yet."

Nathan Rahl, wizard and prophet, had a lean and muscular frame, azure eyes, and handsome features. Although the two men were separated by many generations, Nathan's face, strong features, and hawklike glare still reminded Nicci of Richard Rahl—Lord Rahl, leader of the much-expanded D'Haran Empire, and now leader of the known world.

Under an open vest, Nathan's ruffled white shirt was much too frilly to serve as a rugged travel garment, but he didn't seem to mind. He swirled a dark blue cape over his shoulders. The wizard wore tight but supple black pants and stylish leather boots with a flared top flap and dyed red laces for a flash of color.

As Nicci joined him, he put a hand on the pommel of the ornate sword at his hip and gazed across the starlit clearing. "Yes, traveling through the night is tedious, but at least we keep covering distance.

I spent so many centuries in one place, locked in the Palace of the Prophets. Indulge me for being a little restless."

"I will indulge you, Wizard." She had agreed to take him to the witch woman, but after that she had not decided how best she would serve Richard and the D'Haran Empire. "For now." Nicci was also restless, but she was a woman who liked to have a clear, firm goal.

He smiled at her brusque tone. "And they say prophecy is gone from the world! Richard predicted you might find my company frustrating as we traveled together."

"I believe he used the word 'obnoxious.'"

"I'm quite sure he didn't say it aloud." They crossed the dew-scattered meadow, following a faint trail that led to the trees on the other side. "Nevertheless, I am pleased to have such a powerful sorceress protecting me. It befits my position as the roving ambassador for D'Hara. With my skills as a wizard and a prophet, we'll be nearly invincible."

"You are no longer a prophet," Nicci reminded him. "No one is."

"Just because a man loses his fishing pole doesn't mean he ceases to be a fisherman. And if my gift of prophecy is taken away, I will still muddle along. I can draw upon my vast experience."

"Then perhaps I should let you find the witch woman yourself."

"No, for that I need your help. You've met Red before." He gestured ahead. "I think she likes you."

"I've met Red, yes, and I survived." Nicci paused to regard a knee-high pyramid of rounded skulls, a sharp contrast to the peaceful starlit meadow. "But I am the exception, not the rule. The witch woman likes no one."

Nathan was not deterred, nor had she expected him to be. "Then I will work my charms. So long as you help me find her."

Stopping under the open sky, Nicci looked up into the great expanse of night, and what she saw there frightened her more than any moldering skeletons. The panoply of stars, twinkling lights strewn across the void, were all *wrong*. The familiar constellations she had known for nearly two centuries were now rearranged with the star shift Richard had caused.

When Nicci was a little girl, her father had taken her out into the night and used his outstretched finger to draw pictures across the sky, telling stories of the imaginary characters up there. Only two weeks ago, those eternal patterns had changed; the *universe* had changed, in a dramatic reconfiguring of magic. And when Lord Rahl realigned the stars, prophecy itself was ripped from the world of the living and sent back through the veil to the underworld. That cataclysm had changed the universe in unknown ways, with consequences yet to be seen or understood.

Nicci was still a sorceress, and Nathan remained a wizard, but all the intricately bound lines of his gift of prophecy had unraveled within him. An entire part of his being had now been simply stripped away.

Rather than worrying about the loss of his ability, though, Nathan seemed oddly enthusiastic about this unexpected new opportunity. He had always considered prophecy to be bothersome. Imprisoned in the Palace of the Prophets for a thousand years, considered a danger to the world, he had been denied the opportunity to lead his own life. Now with prophecy gone and the undead Emperor Sulachan sent back to the underworld, Nathan felt more free than ever before.

He was delighted when Richard Rahl sent him off as a roving ambassador for the newly expanded D'Haran Empire, to see if he could help the people in the Dark Lands—a thinly disguised pretext for Nathan to go wherever he liked while still ostensibly achieving something useful. The wizard had been eager to see lands unknown. (And the way Nathan said the words made it sound like the name of an actual country, "Lands Unknown.")

Knowing his intent, Nicci couldn't possibly let the wizard go off alone. That would have been dangerous to Nathan and possibly dangerous to the world. While the battered D'Haran army returned from the bloody battles, and the dead were still being tallied and mourned, Nicci had accepted an important mission of her own. A mission for Richard.

Everyone from Westland to the Midlands, from D'Hara to the Dark Lands, and even far south into the Old World, needed to know that Lord Rahl was the new ruler of a free world. Richard had decreed that he would no longer tolerate tyranny, slavery, or injustice. Each land would remain independent, so long as the people followed a set of commonly agreed-upon rules and behaviors.

But much of the world didn't even know they had been liberated, and there would surely be petty warlords or tyrants who refused to accept the new tenets of freedom. Richard needed to know the extent of his empire, so much of which remained unexplored, and that was a service Nicci could provide, gathering information as she traveled with Nathan.

Nicci believed in her mission wholeheartedly. This was the dawn of a golden age. In the Old World, what remained of the Imperial Order in the aftermath of Emperor Jagang and his predecessors was now a mixed bag of local leaders, some of them fair-minded and enlightened, others abusive and selfish. If any local leader caused trouble, Nicci would deal with the problem. Though she knew Richard would back her up with his full military might, she did not intend to bother the whole D'Haran army, unless it became absolutely necessary.

Nicci would make certain that it did not become necessary.

On a more personal level, although she loved Richard with a depth she had never felt for anyone else, Nicci knew that he belonged with Kahlan, and she would always feel out of place close to them. She didn't *belong* there.

By going off with Nathan to Lands Unknown, she could serve Richard, but also have a new freedom. She could have her own life.

I've heard what the witch woman can do." Nathan strode along with far too much cheer in the brightening morning. He tossed his blue cape over his shoulder with a flourish. "I need to ask something of her, and I have no reason to believe she won't grant it. We're practically colleagues, in a certain sense."

They maneuvered through a dense grove of spindly birch saplings, pushing aside the white-barked trees as they followed the mounds of crumbling bones. Nathan sniffed the air. "Are you certain this is the way?"

"Red will be found if she wants to be found." Nicci glanced down at the staring empty eye sockets filled with moss. "Many people regret finding her."

"Ah, yes—be careful what you wish for." He chuckled. "That should have been another one of the Wizard's Rules."

"Up on her mountain pass, Red left the ground strewn with thousands and thousands of bones and skulls from a great army of the half people she slaughtered single-handedly." Nicci looked from side to side. "But some of these remnants are much older. She has been killing for a long time, and for her own reasons."

Nathan was undeterred. "I shall endeavor not to give her a reason to kill us."

The granite boulders around them grew more prominent, shaded under lush maples and domineering oaks. A tingle crept along the back of her neck, and Nicci looked up to see a muscular catlike thing regarding them from the top of a large, rounded outcropping. The strange creature had green eyes and darkly spotted fur. Seeing them, it let out a sound that was partly purr, partly growl.

Nathan leaned against a birch, unafraid. "Now, what is that animal? I've never seen a species like that before."

"You lived most of your life locked in a tower, Wizard. The world has many species you haven't seen."

"But I had plenty of time to peruse books of natural history."

Nicci had recognized the animal at first glance. "The Mother Confessor named him Hunter. He is Red's companion." The catlike thing's pointed ears pricked up.

Nathan brightened. "That must mean we are close."

Without seeming to hurry, Hunter jumped down from the boulder and trotted off through the birches, guiding Nicci and Nathan along. "He has led me to the witch woman before," Nicci said. "We should follow."

"And of course we shall," Nathan said.

They moved at a fast pace, following the creature through the slatted birch forest and tangled underbrush. Hunter paused every so often to glance over his shoulder, making sure they were still there.

Finally, Nicci and Nathan emerged above a serene, hidden hollow. The outstretched boughs of a gigantic lichen-covered oak spread over the entire glen like an enormous roof. The bitter smell of smoke rose from an ill-tended cook fire that burned in a ring of stones not far from a fieldstone cottage constructed against the side of the opposite slope.

As if waiting for them, a thin woman sat primly on a stone bench in front of the cottage, watching them with piercing sky-blue eyes. She wore a clinging gray dress, and her hair was a mass of tangled red locks.

Black-painted lips made her smile ominous instead of welcoming. The crow perched on her shoulder looked more curious about the visitors than the witch woman did.

Knowing full well how dangerous Red could be, Nicci met the other woman's gaze without speaking. Even though he had seen the countless skulls, Nathan ignored the danger and strode forward with a hand raised in greeting. "You must be the witch woman. I am Nathan Rahl—Nathan the prophet."

"*Wizard*, not prophet," Red corrected. "Everything is changed now." Her black lips smiled again, without warmth. "You are Nathan Rahl, ancestor of Richard Rahl. I have been called a seer and an oracle, but I have had enough visions to last me for quite some time. I foresaw that you would come to me."

The spotted catlike creature sat beside her, blinking his green eyes as he faced the visitors. Still seated on her stone bench, Red fastened her gaze on Nicci. "And Nicci the Sorceress. I'm pleased to see you again."

"You have never been pleased to see me," Nicci said. Part of her wanted to summon her magic, release a flow of destruction, both Additive and Subtractive Magic, anything that might be necessary to blast the witch woman into ashes. "In fact, you commanded the Mother Confessor to kill me."

Red laughed. "Because I foresaw that you would kill Richard." She must have seen the dark edge of Nicci's anger, but she showed no glimmer of fear. "Surely you can understand. I had only the best of intentions. It was nothing personal."

"And I did kill Richard, just as you predicted," Nicci said, recalling how that decision had nearly torn her apart. "Stopped his heart so he could travel to the underworld and save Kahlan."

"See? So it all worked out for the best, then. And I did help you to bring him back." The crow on Red's shoulder bobbed forward, as if nodding. The witch woman hardened her gaze. "Now, why have you come here?"

Nathan stood straight and tall. "We've been searching for days. I have a request to make."

Widening her black smile, Red indicated the countless skulls around her in the glen. "I receive many requests. I look forward to hearing yours."

CHAPTER 2

Without asking permission, Nathan adjusted his cape and took a seat beside the witch woman on the stone bench. He let out an exaggerated sigh. "I am a thousand years old, and sometimes I feel the age in my bones."

Nicci looked at the wizard, not hiding her skepticism. She had traveled with him for many days and many miles, and he had seemed completely healthy and spry. She doubted such an obvious ploy for sympathy would work with Red.

The crow took wing from the witch woman's bony shoulder and flapped up to settle on one of the lower branches of the enormous oak. The bird scolded Nathan from above.

Red shifted her legs and turned toward him. "A thousand years? You must have stories to tell."

"I do indeed, and that is part of the reason I'm here. Since the Palace of the Prophets was destroyed, the antiaging spell has failed, so now I grow old as all mortals do." He looked at Nicci with a twinkle in his eye. "The sorceress is aging too, although she certainly doesn't show it."

"'Aging' is another word for 'living,' old man," Red said with a sharp chuckle. "And I presume you'd like to go on living."

"I've just begun to live." The wizard leaned back on the stone bench as if he were relaxing in a park. "Now . . . for my request. I have heard of a thing that witch women can do, and I'd be curious if you might do me the honor?"

Nicci also listened attentively, just as intrigued, since the wizard had refused to tell her his plans, despite the lengthy and arduous journey here from the People's Palace.

Red tossed her thick braids, making them wriggle like restless snakes on her head. "Witch women have numerous skills, some wonderful, some dangerous. It depends on which ability interests you."

He laced his fingers together over one knee. "The Sisters of the Light possessed journey books, spell-bonded journals in which they could record their travels and also send messages over great distances. But a *life book* . . . ah, now that is something different. Have you heard of it?"

Red's intense pale eyes showed her interest. "I've heard of many things." She paused for just a moment. "And, yes, that is one of the things I know."

Nathan continued, as if he still needed to explain to the witch woman, or maybe it was for Nicci's benefit. "A life book chronicles the journey of a person's life, all the accomplishments and experiences." He leaned closer to her, adjusting his vest with a tug. Overhead in the tree, the crow cawed.

"I would like to have a life book for myself, since I am starting a new phase of my existence, a new set of adventures." He rubbed an imaginary stain from the sleeve of his ruffled shirt, and he looked back at her. "Can you work your storyteller magic?"

Nicci stood apart from them, watching. Once the wizard got an idea in his head, he was very insistent. She had led Nathan through the untracked wilds to find the skull-cluttered lair of the witch woman—all because he wanted to ask Red for a *book*? Nicci said with dry humor, "You lived in a tower for most of your life, Wizard. You think the sum of your experiences would fill an entire book?"

Hunter squatted in the dry oak leaves strewn all around. The feline creature snuffled the ground, nudging fallen acorns, equally unimpressed with Nathan's request.

The wizard sniffed. "Given enough time, the interesting events of even a tedious life can fill a book." Nathan turned back to Red. "I've always been a storyteller myself, and I wrote many popular tales. You may have heard of *The Adventures of Bonnie Day*? Or *The Ballad of General Utros*? Grand epics, and relevant to the human condition."

Nicci made an acerbic observation. "You were born a prophet, Nathan Rahl. Some would say that your very profession was to make up stories."

Nathan gave a dismissive gesture. "Yes, some would say that—and these days, with the great changes in the universe, I'm afraid telling stories is all a prophet can do."

Red pursed her black lips as she considered. "The stories of your life might make a book, Nathan Rahl—and, yes, I do have the magic to extract it. I know a spell that can preserve everything you've already done in a single volume, and that will be the end of its own story."

"Volume one," Nathan said with delight. "And I am ready to start a new journey with my sidekick Nicci."

Nicci bristled. "I am no one's sidekick, Wizard. I am your companion, perhaps, but more accurately, your guardian and protector."

Red said, "Each person is the main character of his own story. That may be how Nathan views you, Nicci—as part of *his* tale."

"Then he would be wrong." She refused to soften the edge of her tension. "Is this life book meant to be a biography? Or a work of fiction?"

Even Nathan chuckled at that.

The crow left its branch, swooped around the clearing, and settled on another bough, as if to get a better view.

The witch woman rose from the bench. "Your proposal interests me, Nathan Rahl. There is much you need to do—whether or not you know it yet." When she cast a glance at Nicci, her ropy red locks swung like braided pendulums. "And I know much of your life as well, Nicci. Your past would constitute an epic. Since I am working the storyteller magic, would you like a life book of your own? It would be my pleasure." Red had an unsettling hunger behind her sky-blue eyes. "And I also know there is an importance to you as well."

Nicci thought of the catastrophes she had survived, the dark deeds she had done, the changes she had undergone, the damage and the triumphs she had left in her wake. She was important? Other than a handful of witnesses and victims along the way, the only one who knew that story was Nicci herself. She gave the witch woman a cold, hard look. "No, thank you."

After a brief hesitation, the witch woman brushed her hands together dismissively and turned with a smile to the wizard. "So, a single life book for Nathan Rahl, then." She left the bench and headed toward her cottage. "First, I will need supplies. There are preparations to make." Red pushed aside the discolored leather hide that hung across the doorway and ducked inside.

Lowering her voice, Nicci turned toward Nathan. "What are you about, Wizard?"

He just gave her a smile and a shrug.

Red emerged with a small ivory bowl: the rounded top of a human cranium. She set it on the stone bench next to Nathan and reached out to him. "Give me your hand."

Happy that she had agreed to his request, he extended his hand, palm up. Red took hold of his fingers, stroking one after another in a strangely erotic gesture. She traced the lines on his palm. "These are your life lines, your spirit lines, and your story lines. They mark the primary events in your life, like the rings of a tree." She turned his hand over, studying the veins on the back. "These blood vessels trace the map of your life throughout your body."

When she stroked his veins, Nathan smiled, as if she were flirting with him.

"Yes, this is exactly what I need." Red snatched a knife from a cleverly hidden pocket in her gray dress and drew the razor-sharp blade across the back of his hand.

Nathan yelped, more in disbelief than in pain, as blood gushed out. "What are you doing, woman?"

"You asked for a life book." She clutched his hand, turning it over so that the red blood could run into the skull bowl. "What did you think we would use for ink?"

As she squeezed his fingers, trying to milk the flow, Nathan was flustered. "I don't believe I thought that far ahead."

"A person's life book must be written in ink made from the ashes of his blood."

"Of course it does," Nathan said, as if he had known all along. Nicci rolled her eyes.

The blood flowed steadily from the deep gash. Hunter sniffed the air, as if drawn by the scent of it.

When the skull bowl was a third full of dark red liquid, Nathan said, "Surely that's enough by now?"

"We'd better make certain," Red answered. "As you said, you've had a very long life."

Finally satisfied, the witch woman released Nathan's hand and took the bowl over to her smoky cook fire. With a blackened femur, she prodded the coals, nudging them aside to create a sheltered hollow in the ashes. She settled the bone bowl into them, so the blood could cook.

Nathan poked at his cut hand, then released enough magic to heal the wound, careful not to let the blood stain his fine travel clothes.

Before long, the blood in the skull bowl began to bubble and smoke. It darkened, then turned black, boiling down to a tarry residue.

The light slipping through the crowded branches overhead grew more slanted in the late afternoon. High above, birds settled among the branches of the expansive oak for the night. The crow scolded them for their trespass, but the birds remained.

Red ducked back into her cottage, where she rummaged around before returning with a leather-bound tome that bore no title on the cover or spine. "I happen to have an empty life book among my possessions. You are fortunate, Nathan Rahl."

"Indeed, I am."

Red squatted next to the cook fire and used two long bones to gingerly remove the skull bowl. The blood ink inside the inverted cranium was even darker than the soot charred on the outer surface.

Nathan watched with great interest as she set the smoking bowl on the stone bench. She opened the life book to the first page, which was blank, the ivory color of freshly boiled bone. "And now to write your story, Nathan Rahl."

She called the crow down from the tree, and the big black bird landed on her shoulder again. It used its sharp black beak to stroke her red braids in a sign of affection. The witch woman absently caressed the bird, then seized its neck. Before the bird could squawk or flail, she snapped its neck and caught its body as it fell. The dying crow's wings extended, as if to take flight one last time. Its head lolled to one side.

Red rested the dead bird on the bench next to the skull bowl. With nimble fingers, she combed through its tail and wing feathers, finally selecting a long one, which she plucked loose. She held it up for inspection. "Yes, a fine quill. Shall we begin?"

After Nathan nodded, the witch woman trimmed the end with her dagger, dipped the pointed shaft into the black ink, and touched it to the blank paper of the waiting first page.

CHAPTER 3

T he life book wrote itself.

Red sat on the stone bench, hands on her knees, not noticing that she left a smear of dark soot on her gray dress. As she worked her spell, a guiding magic suspended the crow-feather quill upright, and then it moved of its own accord, inscribing the story of Nathan Rahl.

Bending closer, the wizard looked on with boyish delight, resting an elbow on his knee. Nicci stepped up to watch the words spill out across the first page, line after line, and then move on to the next page. Each time the ink ran dry, the feather paused above the book, and Red plucked it out of the air, dipped it into the bowl of burned blood, and placed it back on the page. The flow of words resumed.

"I recall how many times I wrote and rewrote *The Adventures of Bonnie Day* until I was satisfied with the prose," Nathan said, shaking his head as he marveled. "This is far easier."

The story flowed, page after page, chronicling Nathan's long life as a dangerous prophet, how he'd been imprisoned by the Sisters of the Light, first to train, then to control him . . . how for years they monitored his every utterance of prophecy, terrified of the turmoil that could arise from false interpretations. And prophecies were nearly always misinterpreted, warnings often misconstrued. Merely trying to avoid a dire fate usually precipitated that exact fate.

"People never seem to learn the lesson," Nathan muttered as he read. "Richard was right to disregard prophecy for so long."

Nicci agreed. "I am not sorry that prophecy is gone from the world."

The words flew past faster than anyone could read them, and the life book's pages turned of their own accord. Nicci scanned back and forth, catching some snippets of Nathan's life, stories she already knew. On the road, he had spent much time telling her about himself, whether or not she asked.

He leaned closer as a new section began. "Oh, this is a good part."

In his loneliness in the palace, the Sisters had occasionally taken pity on Nathan, hiring women from the finer brothels in Tanimura to comfort him. According to the tale as written in the life book, Nathan enjoyed the conversation of an ordinary woman with ordinary dreams and desires. Nathan had once whispered a terrible prophecy in the ear of a gullible whore—and the horrified young woman had run screaming from the Palace of the Prophets. Once out in the city, she repeated the prophecy to others, and the repercussions spread and spread, eventually triggering a bloody civil war . . . all due to Nathan's reckless pillow talk to a woman he would never see again.

The Sisters had punished Nathan for that, curtailing his limited freedoms, even after he revealed that the supposed "mistake" had accomplished his intent of killing a young boy child destined to become a ruthless tyrant, a tyrant who would have slaughtered countless innocents.

"A relatively minor civil war was a small enough price to prevent that outcome," Nathan remarked as he skimmed the black-blood words scrolling out.

When the quill ran dry again, Red dipped it into the skull bowl, stirred the burned blood, and set the feather tip on the page, where it continued to scratch and scrawl.

Nathan's story went on and on—rambling, in Nicci's opinion—and the feather pen wrote word after word. Of course, most of his adventures had occurred only after he managed to escape from the palace: his brief romance with Clarissa and its tragic end, his work with Richard Rahl to overthrow the Imperial Order and Emperor Jagang, his battles to stop the evil Hannis Arc and the undead Emperor Sulachan.

Faster than Nicci expected, the entire volume filled up. When the black blood finally reached the last page in the book, the tale ended with the all-too-recent account of Nicci and Nathan trudging through moss-covered skulls to find the witch woman in the Dark Lands. All of the charred-blood ink in the skull bowl was used up, and the lifeless feather dropped and drifted to the ground.

Nathan was obviously impressed with his own story. "Thank you, Red." When he closed the cover, he was delighted to see that his name had appeared on the leather front and on the spine. "I shall carry the life book with me and read it off and on. I'm certain others would like to read it as well. Scholarly libraries will want copies."

The witch woman shook her head. "That will not be possible, Nathan Rahl." She took the tome from him. "I agreed to create a life book for you, but I never said you could keep it. The volume stays with me. That is my price."

Nathan sputtered. "But that wasn't what I thought . . . that isn't the purpose—"

"You did not ask the price beforehand, Wizard," Nicci said. "After living a thousand years, you should be wiser than that."

Red ducked back into her cottage, leaving the volume on the bench, as if daring Nathan to take it and escape. He did not. She emerged with a smaller, thinner leather-bound book, which was also blank. "I will take your life story, but I give you something that's worth far more. A new life book filled with potential, rather than stale old words." She offered it to Nathan. "I have your past, your old story, but with this book, I give you the rest of your life. Live it the way you would want it to be written."

Nathan ran a fingertip over the smooth leather cover, disappointed. "Thank you, I suppose." He held the book in his hands.

"I happen to know that you, and the sorceress, are both vital to the future." The witch woman stepped uncomfortably close to Nicci and dropped her voice. "Are you certain you don't want a life book of your own? There may be things you need to learn."

"I am certain, witch woman. My past is my story to keep, and my future will be written by me, in my own way, not through the control or influence of you or anyone else."

"I just wanted to make the offer." She turned away with a hint of secret amusement in her eyes, followed by a shadow of unexpected concern. "You may still be required to do things, Sorceress, whether or not you want to hear about them."

Nathan opened his new life book and was surprised to find it wasn't entirely blank. "There are words written on the first page. 'Kol Adair.'" Perplexed, he looked up at Red. "I don't recognize the term. Is it a name? A place?"

"It's what you will need." Red bent over her cooking fire and used the blackened femur to stir the coals and reawaken the flames. "You must find Kol Adair in the Old World, Nathan Rahl." She flashed a glance at Nicci. "Both of you."

"We have our own mission," Nicci said. "Here in the Dark Lands."

"Oh? And what mission is that? To wander aimlessly because you are too much in love with Richard Rahl to stay at his side? That is a pointless quest. A coward's quest."

Nicci felt the heat in her cheeks. "That's not it at all."

Nathan came to her defense. "After our last great battles, I wanted to come back here, to see if I could help the people."

Red sniffed. "Another pointless quest. There are always people who need help, no matter where you go. In the Dark Lands? In the Old World? What is the purpose? Would you rather not save the world and save yourselves?"

Nicci turned her anger into annoyance. "You babble nonsense, witch woman."

"Nonsense, is it? Turn the page, Nathan Rahl. Read your new life book."

Curious, the wizard did as she suggested. Nicci leaned close, seeing other words written there on the second page.

Future and Fate depend on both the journey and the destination.

Kol Adair lies far to the south in the Old World. From there, the Wizard will behold what he needs to make himself whole again. And the Sorceress must save the world.

Nicci said, "I have helped save the world enough times already."

But Nathan was more perplexed. "This is a game for you, witch woman. You planted this joke for us. Why would I need to be made whole again? Am I missing something?" He touched his arm, which seemed remarkably intact.

"That is not for me to say," Red said. "You see what's written, a path established long ago."

"And prophecy is gone," Nicci said. "Ancient predictions mean nothing."

"Truly?" asked the witch woman. "Even pronouncements made when prophecy was as strong as the wind and the sun?" While Nathan flexed his fingers, as if searching for missing digits, Red brushed back her tangled locks of hair. "You of all people should know that it is unwise for others to interpret a prophecy."

Nicci tightened the laces on her traveling boots and adjusted her black dress. She could not keep the skepticism out of her voice. "As I said, there is no more prophecy, witch woman. How can you know where we need to go?"

Red's black lips formed a mysterious smile. "Sometimes I still know things. Or maybe it is a revelation I foresaw long before the stars changed overhead. But I do know that if you care about Lord Rahl and his D'Haran Empire, you will heed this warning and this summons. *Kol Adair*. You both need to make your way there, whether for the journey or the destination. If you don't, then all that Richard Rahl has worked for may well be forfeit." She shrugged, suddenly seeming aloof. "Do as you wish."

Nathan slipped the new life book into a leather pouch at his side and closed the flap. "As Lord Rahl's roving ambassador, my assignment is to travel to places that might not know about the changes in the world." He looked up at the darkening sky through the canopy of the ancient oak. "But the exact route is at our discretion. We could go to the Old World just as well as to the Dark Lands."

Nicci was not so convinced. "And you are going to take her babblings seriously, Wizard?"

Nathan stroked back his long white hair. "Frankly, I've had enough of the Dark Lands and all this gloom. The Old World has more sunshine."

Nicci considered, realizing she had followed him, but with no real goal otherwise. She just wanted to serve Richard and strengthen his new, solid empire, to help bring about his longed-for golden age. "I have my own orders from Lord Rahl to explore his new empire and send reports back of the things we find. At Kol Adair, or elsewhere."

"And save the world," Red added.

She did not believe Red's prediction—how was she supposed to save the world by traveling to, or seeing, a place she'd never heard of?—but the wizard had a valid point.

The Old World, once part of the Imperial Order, was now under the rule of D'Hara. Even those distant people would want to hear of their freedom, to know that Lord Rahl would insist on self-determination and standards of respect. She had to see what was out there, and take care of problems she saw, so that Richard need not be bothered. "Yes, I will go with you."

Nathan adjusted his cape and shouldered his pack, just as eager to depart as he had been to find the witch woman in the first place, but Nicci hesitated. "Before we go south to the Old World, we need to tell Lord Rahl where we're going. We have no way to communicate with him." She didn't want Richard or Kahlan to worry about the two of them if they disappeared for a time.

"We could find a way to send a message when we reach Tanimura," Nathan said. "Or some other town along the way."

Red surprised them. "I will take care of it."

She picked up the crow's limp carcass and cradled the bird in her hands, extending its flopping wings. She adjusted its lolling head, straightened its broken neck, then closed her eyes in concentration.

After a moment, the crow squirmed and fluffed its feathers. Red set the reanimated bird back on the stone bench, where it tottered drunkenly. The neck remained angled in the wrong direction, and its eyes held no glint of life at all, but it moved, like a marionette. The crow stretched its wings, as if fighting the remnants of death, then folded them back against its sides.

"Tear a strip of paper from a page of your life book, Nathan Rahl," she said, handing him the black quill. "There should be enough ink left for you to write a note for Lord Rahl."

Nathan did so, scratching out a quick summary on a thin curl of paper. When he was finished, Red rolled it tightly and bound the strip to the crow's stiff leg. "My bird has sufficient animation to reach the People's Palace. Lord Rahl will know where you are going."

She tossed the awkward crow up into the air. Nicci watched the dead bird plummet back to the ground, but at the last moment it extended its wings, stiffly flapped them, rose up beyond the enormous oak, and flew into the dusk.

Hunter's ears perked up, and the catlike creature sniffed the air before bounding off into the forest to dart among the shadows of the tall trees. Out beyond Red's sheltered hollow, Nicci saw a flash of fur, something as large as a horse prowling through the thickets. Hunter happily bounded after it, frolicking through the underbrush, and disappeared along with the large predatory shape in the deeper gloom.

Red looked up. "Hunter's mother often joins us for dinner." Her mouth formed an odd smile. "Would you like to stay?"

Nicci took note of the strewn bones and skulls and decided not to take further risks. "We should go."

"Thank you, witch woman," Nathan said as they headed into the thickening night. Even alone in the wild, dark forest, Nicci guessed they would be safer than if they chose to stay at Red's cottage.

Nathan strode along, paying no attention to the skulls. "It will be a grand adventure. Once we leave the Dark Lands, we can head south to Tanimura. At Grafan Harbor, we're sure to find a ship sailing south. We will find Kol Adair, and that's just a start."

Richard had told her to go to the boundaries of the D'Haran Empire, and she decided that the far south was a perfectly viable option. "I suppose the rest of the world will be sufficient for our purposes."

After Red watched the two disappear into the forest, Hunter trotted in and squatted by the cook fire. Moments later, his shaggy mother padded in, as big as a bear and bristling with cinnamon fur.

The much smaller son nuzzled her, wanting to play, but Hunter's mother thrust a huge head forward to Red, who dutifully scratched the silky fur behind the creature's ears, scrubbing with the nails on both of her hands. Hunter's mother made a sound that was somewhere between a growl and a purr; then she slumped heavily among the fallen leaves in the clearing.

Red picked up Nathan's hefty life book. Yes, even a quiet and tedious life could add up to significant events in a thousand years. She knew the real chronicle was just beginning for Nathan, and the real mission in store for both of them. Even though Nicci refused to let Red create such a book for her, the witch woman had been an oracle. She knew that the life of the sorceress, both past and future, would fill many volumes as well.

And the Sorceress must save the world.

Carrying Nathan's tome, Red pushed aside the hanging leather flap over the opening and ducked inside her cottage. The low dwelling was lit with the orange glow of guttering candles settled in skull pots. The front room was small and cramped, but at the back wall against the hillside, she pushed aside another door hanging.

She entered the main part of her dwelling, a large complex of wide passageways and grottoes burrowed into the hillside itself. Red stood before shelves and shelves that were filled with numerous volumes similar to the one she held now. She had collected so many life books over the years, over the centuries, that she had lost track.

But oddly, and chillingly, every single one of the books had ended with the strange and previously incomprehensible words:

Future and Fate depend on both the journey and the destination.

Kol Adair lies far to the south in the Old World. From there, the Wizard will behold what he needs to make himself whole again. And the Sorceress must save the world.

The same words in every book. Hundreds of them. Thousands of them. Each one with the same warning.

Red slid the story of Nathan Rahl into an empty slot on the shelf next to another volume. Countless life books, nearly one for each of those skulls buried under the moss. . . .

CHAPTER 4

With their new destination in mind, though somewhat skeptical of the importance Red had assigned to it, the two traveled for weeks through the Dark Lands before reaching the more populated areas of D'Hara. Heading south, they found well-traveled roads and villages, including inns where they could eat home-cooked meals instead of foraging for game or wild fruit, and they could sleep in actual beds instead of bedding down on the forest floor. As a woods guide, Richard Rahl had reveled in finding his own trails in the forest, but Nicci much preferred civilization, and Nathan certainly did not object to comforts.

Along the way, the two gathered news and disseminated their own tales about Lord Rahl's victory over Emperor Sulachan. Most people in the south of D'Hara knew little about the political changes that had occurred, but everyone had seen the stars convulse and shift in the sky, and they listened to the travelers with both wonder and dismay.

In the warm, crowded common rooms of inn after inn, Nathan spread his hands and explained in a deep, confident voice, "Truth be told, the end of prophecy means that you can live your own lives and make your own decisions. I was once a prophet myself, and I speak from experience—such powers were far more trouble than they were worth. Good riddance!"

Many local oracles and self-proclaimed seers, however, were less enthusiastic about the changes. Those with a genuine gift had already noticed the sudden lack of ability, and those who continued to sell their predictions were surely cheating gullible customers. Such "prophets" were incensed to hear themselves denounced as frauds and charlatans.

But chastising frauds was not the mission Nicci had adopted, nor did she consider it "saving the world." She moved ahead with her next goal in sight. She would go to the Old World, scout the new lands Lord Rahl now ruled, and help Nathan find the mysterious Kol Adair, whatever it was. Tanimura would be their starting point. The great port city was one of the northernmost bastions of the Old World, a place where the main overland trade routes converged.

As the two neared the coast, the air took on a fresh, salty bite. Traffic increased on the wide road through the coastal hills. Creaking mule-drawn carts passed them, as well as wealthy noblemen or merchants riding well-groomed horses with expensive tack. Farmers guided wagons laden with vegetables or sacks of grain, heading to the markets in the port city.

While walking along in the warm sun, the wizard held up his end of the conversation—more than his end, in fact, but Nicci saved her energy for the hike. When they reached the top of a hill, the view unfolded before them.

The old, sprawling city of Tanimura had been built on a long peninsula that extended into the sparkling blue expanse of the ocean. To the west, before spilling into the sea, the Kern River had excavated a broad valley. Croplands and villages dotted the countryside, interspersed with patches of dark forest. Nicci's focus, though, was on the whitewashed buildings of the extensive city.

The wizard stopped to rest, shading his eyes. "A splendid view. Think of all the possibilities Tanimura offers." He plucked at his threadbare sleeves, his frayed cuffs, his open vest. "Including fresh clothes."

Nicci said in a quiet voice, "It's been years since I was here." She narrowed her blue eyes, scanning the city, noting what she remembered and what had changed.

The wizard gave a noncommittal grunt. "Once I escaped the palace, I thought I would never come back . . . yet here we are."

Down the sweep of shore, Grafan Harbor was bustling with large cargo or military ships that sported creamy white sails, as well as fishing dhows with triangular sails. Nicci's lips quirked in a small, hard smile. "I see they've managed to rebuild the docks."

In the harbor here, she and her fellow Sisters of the Dark had destroyed the *Lady Sefa,* the ship that had held them hostage. Emperor Jagang had granted the women their revenge on Captain Blake and his vile crew, even encouraged it, and Nicci and her companions were not kind to the sailors who had raped and abused them. The Sisters had found a turnabout pleasure, peeling off the soft flesh of the men, strip by strip. Then, unleashing the full force of Subtractive Magic, they had destroyed the *Lady Sefa,* lifting the entire vessel out of the water, snapping the masts like twigs, crashing the huge ship down onto the Grafan docks, and then wreaking havoc upon the whole harbor, as if the other ships were no more than the toys of a malicious child.

Although that had been one of her darkest times, Nicci still smiled at the memory.

Nathan also stared down toward the crowded city, lost in his own memories. He lowered his voice to a conspiratorial whisper. "We both left such a mark on Tanimura, dear Sorceress, they might not welcome us back."

His gaze was drawn toward the southern end of the peninsula and a large island just off the coast. Halsband Island had once been connected to the mainland by a prominent stone bridge that allowed visitors, merchants, scholars, and Sisters of the Light to pass directly to the Palace of the Prophets. The mammoth edifice had stood for millennia, a place where gifted males were imprisoned and taught. The palace had been shielded in numerous ways, woven with a spell that prevented its inhabitants from aging . . . but Nathan had triggered a light web, bringing down the entire imposing palace so that its magical archives could not fall into Jagang's hands.

Halsband Island looked like a wasteland now, the palace vaporized. From what Nicci could tell, even after six years no hardy souls had returned to claim the devastated land for their own.

The wizard wore a bittersweet expression, but forced a smile. "I spent a thousand years there. What could be a better start to a new life than to erase all signs of the past?" He pushed aside his dark blue cape and patted the leather pouch at his side that held the new life book and its ominous pronouncement. "It's time for a new adventure, before we get too old. You and I are not used to aging at the same rate as everyone else. Tanimura awaits."

Nicci set off down the road to the city. As they walked down the hill, an oxcart rolled past, driven by an old farmer wearing a straw hat. The man stared at the road ahead as if it were the most interesting thing in the world. His cart was loaded with round green melons.

When Nathan asked for a ride, the old farmer gave them a casual gesture. The two sat in the back of the wagon among the piled round melons. Nicci picked up one. "It looks like a severed head." The ox plodded along, not caring whether the road went uphill or downhill.

Jostled by the slow, uneven cart, Nicci watched the approaching city. She remembered the tree-lined boulevards, the tall whitewashed buildings, the tile roofs. Banners flew from high poles, scarlet pennants of the city of Tanimura and larger flags of the D'Haran Empire.

She and Richard had stopped here for a time on their way to Altur'Rang, when she had forced him to play the role of her husband, hoping to convince him to believe in the Order. She had been so passionate, determined, ruthless, and so naive. He had learned how to cut stone here in Tanimura. . . .

Nicci's brow furrowed at the troubling memory. "We will not stay long, Wizard. We'll get supplies for a long journey and find a ship sailing south to the Old World. I'm sure you're anxious to find your Kol Adair."

"And you must save the world, of course." Nathan winced as the oxcart rolled over a large rock in the road, and one large melon rolled over the edge, but he deftly caught it and set it back on the precarious pile. "But why in such a hurry? Dear spirits, we traveled weeks to get to Tanimura. If that prophecy was written down a hundred years ago, there can't possibly be any rush."

"Whether or not the witch woman is correct, Lord Rahl asked us to explore the fringes of his empire and to spread the terms of his rule. Everyone here already knows who he is. Our real work lies elsewhere."

"Indeed it does," Nathan admitted with a sigh. "And I'm curious to find this place called Kol Adair that Red thinks I need to see."

He looked at his shirt, then tried to brush away a grease stain from a rabbit they'd eaten in camp, and a spot of gravy that signified the much better food that an innkeeper had prepared for them the following night. "Before we can go on, though, my first order of business will be to acquire a new traveling wardrobe. Without a doubt, Tanimura has many tailors and garment shops to choose from. I believe I can find what I need."

Nicci's black traveling dress was still in good shape, and she had a spare in her pack. "You worry about clothes altogether too much."

He looked down his nose at her. "I spent a thousand years wearing frumpy robes in the Palace of the Prophets. Now that I am out in the world at last, I am entitled to indulge myself."

Nicci knew she wouldn't change his mind. "I'll make my way down to the harbor and make inquiries with the dockmaster. I can learn which ships are ready to depart and where they are bound."

More carts joined them on the road, and they passed stables on the outskirts of the city, livestock yards where pigs and cattle wandered about, unconcerned with their fates. Charcoal kilns stood like tall beehives, letting a whisper of sweet smoke into the air. Across a meeting square, shirtless carpenters were building a tall tower that so far consisted only of support beams.

The listless cart driver did not speak a word to them, merely drove his ox along. As the city buildings clustered together, the crowds increased, as did the noise. People shouted to one another, merchants hawked their wares, washerwomen hung dripping clothes from lines strung between buildings.

Not far away they saw a large market crowded with rickety wooden stalls featuring good-luck trinkets, bolts of patterned fabric, wooden carvings, fire-glazed clay pots, and bunches of red and orange flowers. The old farmer flicked the ox with a switch to turn the animal toward the market, and Nicci and Nathan slid off the cart, ready to venture into the heart of the city. The wizard called out his thanks, but the old farmer didn't respond.

As he stood to get his bearings, Nathan adjusted the ornate sword in its scabbard, checked the life book, straightened his pack, and self-consciously brushed down the front of his shirt. "I may be a while. Once I secure the services of an adequate tailor, I'll have him make more appropriate attire for me. Capes, shirts, vests, new boots. Yes, yes, if I am to be Lord Rahl's ambassador, I must look the part."

CHAPTER 5

The ancient city of Tanimura was full of wonders, distractions, and dangers for the unwary. Nicci felt right at home.

She was all business as she made her way into the thick of the city, her mind set on finding a southbound ship and a captain familiar with the port cities in the Old World. From what the witch woman had described, Kol Adair might be far out in the sparsely populated fringe lands, not marked on common maps. But they would find it.

During her years serving Emperor Jagang, when she had been called Death's Mistress, Nicci had brought many outlying towns under the rule of the Imperial Order. Although Jagang had been intent on conquering the New World, he had little interest in the less populated areas far to the south of his own empire. He had once told her the land did not hold enough subjects or enough wealth to be worth his time.

Despite the distance, Nicci was convinced that those far-flung people also needed to know about Lord Rahl. She would be proud to tell them of their new life without tyrants and oppression, and she relished the challenge. She would do it for Richard.

Future and Fate depend on both the journey and the destination.

As she headed down toward the harbor, the streets were steep and winding. The crowded buildings were stacked haphazardly, two- and three-story structures that filled any spare patch of ground, buildings erected on top of buildings. Some homes and shops were tilted as if trying to keep their balance on the hillsides. Gutters lined the streets, filled with a brownish slurry of rainwater mixed with emptied chamber pots.

Broad-hipped women gathered and gossiped around a well, pulling up buckets of fresh water, which they handed to glum-looking teenagers to carry away. Scruffy barking dogs ran down the streets in pursuit of loose chickens.

Nicci passed through a fabric dyers' district, where the air was filled with a rich and complicated tapestry of sharp, sour odors. Cloth merchants hung bolts of dripping fabric—indigo, saffron yellow, or stark black—which flapped in the sea breezes as they dried. In the thread makers' district, boys ran down the street pulling long colorful strands, twisting bobbins to tighten the threads.

The tanning district reeked as leather workers cured and processed hides. Taking advantage of the foul smells, enterprising children ran about offering to sell passersby fistfuls of mint leaves as nosegays. A little girl with black hair in pigtails ran up to Nicci, waving the mint leaves. "Only a copper. It'll make every breath smell fresh."

Nicci shook her head. "The smell of death doesn't bother me."

The skinny girl could not hide her disappointment. She was dressed in rags, and her face was covered with dust and grime. She looked as if she hadn't had a good bath, or a good meal, in some time. Noting her industriousness, Nicci gave her the copper anyway, and the girl ran off laughing.

The markets were loud, colorful storms of people, vendors hawking shellfish or live octopus from buckets of murky salt water. Butchers sold slabs of exotic imported meats—ostrich, musk ox, zebra, even a greasy gray steak supposedly from a long-tailed gar—spread out on planks for display, although many of the meats drew more flies than customers. Smoked fish dangled by their tails across wooden racks like succulent battle trophies.

Food vendors sold skewers of spiced meat sizzling over charcoal fires. Bakers offered loaves of knotted brown bread. Two women stirred a steaming cauldron and ladled out bowls of what they called "kraken chowder," a milky stew with thready seaweed, bobbing onions, and rings of tender suckers that had been sliced from some large tentacle.

Nicci walked at a brisk pace, uninterested in the distractions. Jugglers performed in the streets, gamblers placed bets on a game of shells and cups. A musician sat on an overturned pot eliciting caterwauling sounds from a flexible stringed instrument.

In the spice merchants' district, men in long green robes haggled over the price of cumin, turmeric, cardamom. A toothless old woman squatted on a curb as she sorted lumpy roots of mandrake and ginger. When an errant breeze whispered along the street, the spice merchants rushed to cover their powder-filled baskets. One man bent over a clay bowl of red pepper, and the breeze feathered some of it into his face, making him cough and retreat, flailing his hands.

Tanimura was a crowded, vibrant city. Every person here was concerned with everyday living, but few of them considered the larger work of building and maintaining the D'Haran Empire. These people weren't soldiers. They had lived for years under the Imperial Order. They had survived the turmoil of the long, bloody war, and now they might not even realize how fundamentally their existence had changed. If Lord Rahl's rule endured, these people might never need to concern themselves much about it.

As she worked her way into the older, more crowded district just above the harbor, the streets grew tighter and more tangled. The buildings were tall and dingy, and every street degenerated into an alley. More than once, she found herself at a dead end of brick walls and garbage, forcing her to retrace her steps.

Nicci turned down a wider alley between leaning three-story buildings with cracked and stained walls. The buildings closed into shadows redolent of stagnant water, rats, and refuse. She pressed forward, supposing the passageway would open into a broader thoroughfare, but instead it turned along oddly skewed corners, and the passage narrowed.

Ahead, she heard a frightened shout and the sounds of a scuffle— curses, gruff laughter, the smack of a fist striking flesh, then the more muffled sound of boots kicking. She was already running toward the sounds when an outcry of pain joined what sounded like a little boy's mocking laughter.

"That's all the money I have!" It was a young man's voice.

Nicci rounded the corner to come upon three muscular men and a wiry boy, all bunched around a young man of perhaps twenty years. It took her only an instant to gauge the tableau, identify the predators, the victim. The young man cornered by these thugs didn't look like a Tanimuran. He had long ginger hair and pale skin covered with freckles; his hazel eyes were wide with fear.

He swung at his attackers, but the three larger men pummeled him with their fists. It was like a game to them, and they seemed in no hurry. The boy, no more than ten years old, pranced from one foot to the other, clutching a small sack of coins in his hand, obviously stolen from the victim.

One of the thugs, a heavyset man with short but extraordinarily muscular arms, planted a solid kick on the meat of the victim's thigh. The red-haired young man went down, sliding against the slimy, stained wall. Even as he fell, he kept his arms up in an attempt to fend them off.

Nicci said, "Stop what you're doing." It wasn't a shout, but hard enough to draw their attention like an unexpected slap.

The three men spun to look at her in surprise. The curly-haired boy's eyes went as wide and bright as coins, and he bolted down the winding alley, disappearing as quickly as a cockroach revealed by the light. Nicci ignored the child and faced the three men, the real threat.

The thugs turned toward her, ready for a fight, but when they saw only an attractive blonde in a black dress, their expressions changed. One let out a guffaw. They spread out so they could come at her from different directions.

The squat heavyset man called after the boy, who had disappeared down the alleys. "There's no need to run, you little bastard. It's just a woman."

"Let him run, Jerr—we'll find him later," said a second man. He was swarthy with a round face and bloodshot eyes that probably resulted from long familiarity with alcohol, rather than lack of sleep.

"We don't want the little brat to see what we're going to do with her anyway," said the third man, with greasy brown hair tied back in a ponytail. "He's too young for that kind of education."

The ginger-haired victim tried to get up. He was bleeding from his nose, and his shirt was torn. "They stole my money!"

The man with bloodshot eyes smacked him hard across the face. The young man's head hit the alley wall hard.

Although she felt coldness rise within her, Nicci didn't move toward them. "Perhaps you didn't hear me. I told you to stop."

"We're just getting started," said Jerr, the leader. In unison, the three men drew their knives. Apparently, beating the young man wasn't enough entertainment, and they had something else in mind for Nicci. Such men usually did.

Leering, they came toward her. The man with the ponytail slid around to cut off her retreat—but she had no intention of retreating. They obviously expected her to run in fear, but that was not something Nicci did.

"Nice black dress," said Jerr, holding up his knife. "But we'd rather see you without it. Makes things easier."

The young redhead tried to scramble to his feet, pressing a hand to his bruised thigh. "You leave her alone!"

The man with bloodshot eyes snarled at him. "How many teeth do you want to lose before this day is out?"

Nicci regarded the three of them with an icy gaze. "It has been several weeks since I had occasion to kill a man." She looked from one to the next. "Now I have three in one day."

The thugs were startled by her boldness, and the heavyset Jerr laughed. "How do you expect to do that? You don't even have a weapon."

Nicci stood with her hands loose at her sides, her fingers curled. "I am the weapon." From within, she summoned her magic. She had countless ways to kill these men.

The redhead finally managed to stand, and he foolishly lurched toward them, calling out to Nicci. "I won't let them hurt you!" He dove at the legs of the man with the ponytail, knocking him to the ground.

Bloodshot Eyes raised his knife and advanced toward Nicci, waving the point back and forth in the air in front of her, as if she was supposed to be intimidated. Jerr called out, "Cut her, Henty, but don't hurt her too bad—not yet. I don't want her blood all over me when I get between her legs."

Nicci could have unleashed wizard's fire and incinerated the three of them in an instant, but she might also kill the young man, as well as start a fire that could rage through the old town. That was unnecessary. She had other means.

Nicci created a wall of air that slammed into Henty, and he looked as if he had blindly smashed into an invisible tree. As he stood momentarily stunned, Nicci used the magic to fling him up and back fifteen feet above the ground. She was not gentle—she had no reason to be.

Bloodshot Eyes slammed into the high wall, and the impact crushed his head like one of the dark melons in the farmer's oxcart. A splash of red painted a broad round splatter on the already stained wall; then the body traced a long uneven smear as it slid two stories down to the ground.

Unable to believe what he had just seen, Jerr also came at Nicci with a knife. She used her powers to crush his larynx so he couldn't scream; then she pulped the bones in his neck for good measure. The leader's eyes bulged, bursting with a sudden web of red hemorrhages, and his head flopped to one side. When his knees gave out, he sprawled forward.

Ponytail kicked his way free of the scrappy redhead, who had tackled him, and slashed his knife across the empty air, trying to cut the young man, who ducked out of the way. Then, the last thug turned to snarl at Nicci.

She stopped his heart, and he dropped to the ground like a felled bull.

The young redhead looked around the carnage. "We're saved!" His face had gone pale, which made his freckles even more prominent. He gaped at the three dead men lying in the garbage in the alley. "You killed them! Sweet Sea Mother, you—you *killed* them. You didn't have to do that."

"Maybe not," Nicci said, "but that was the most convenient solution. They made the decision for me. Those men would have preyed on others, robbed others—and eventually they would have been caught. I was saving time and effort for the magistrate and the hangman."

The distraught redhead couldn't decide what to do. His lip was bloody, his face puffy and bruised. "It's just—they took my money, but I doubt they were going to kill me."

Nicci ran her gaze up and down his lanky form. The young man wore a loose homespun shirt dyed brown and sturdy canvas pants of the kind worn by sailors. He didn't have any weapons she could see, not even a knife at his side. "You don't *think* they were going to kill you? That is not a gamble I'd choose to make."

He swallowed hard, and she was struck by how innocent and foolish he seemed. If even the bruises and the loss of his money purse had not taught him the necessary lesson, then Nicci would not waste further time on him. "If you keep walking these alleys, unarmed and unaware, you will soon have another opportunity to learn whether or not the thieves around here intend to kill you." She turned to walk away. "Don't count on me being here to help next time."

The young man hurried after her. "Thank you! Sorry I didn't say that soon enough—*thank you*. I was raised to show gratitude to those who do good things for me. I appreciate it. My name is Bannon . . . Bannon—" He paused as if embarrassed. "Bannon Farmer. I'm from Chiriya Island. This is my first time in Tanimura."

Nicci kept walking. "I guessed that much, and it may be your last time in Tanimura if you don't stop being such a fool."

Bannon followed, still talking. "I used to be a cabbage farmer, but I wanted to see the world, so I signed aboard a sailing ship. This is my first time in port—and I came to buy a sword of my own." He frowned, and patted his hips again, as if he somehow thought he had only imagined the robbery. "They took my money. That boy—"

Nicci showed neither surprise nor sympathy. "He bolted off. You'll never find him. That child is lucky he ran, though—I would have disliked killing a little boy, even if he was a thief."

Bannon's shoulders slumped. "I was looking for a swordsmith. Those men seemed nice, and they told me to follow them, led me down here." He shook his head. "I guess I should have been more suspicious." He brightened. "But you were there. You saved me. Are you a sorceress? I've never seen anything like that. Thank you for rescuing me."

She turned to face him. "And shame on you for *needing* to be rescued. You should possess more common sense than to let yourself become a victim. I have no mercy for thugs and thieves, but there would be no thieves if there weren't fools like you to prey upon."

Bannon's face turned a bright red. "I'm sorry. I'll know better next time." He wiped at the blood coming from his lip and nose, then smeared it on his pants. "But if I had my own sword I could've defended myself."

He leaned against the alley wall and struggled to pull off his left boot. "Maybe I have enough coins left, though." When he upended the boot, several coins rained out, two silvers and five coppers. He held them in his palm. "I learned this trick from my father. He taught me never to keep all your money in one place, in case you get robbed." He looked forlornly down at the coins in his hand. "It isn't enough to buy much of a sword. I had hoped for a fine blade with a golden hilt and pommel, intricate workings. The coins might be enough, though. Just enough . . ."

"A sword doesn't have to be pretty to be effective at killing," Nicci said.

"I suppose it doesn't," Bannon replied as he replaced the coins in his boot, and stomped his foot back into place. He looked back down the alley at the bodies of the three thugs. "You didn't need a sword at all."

"No, I don't," Nicci said. "But what I do need is a ship sailing south." She began to walk back out of the alley. "I was on my way to the harbor."

"A ship?" Bannon hurried after her, still trying to adjust his boot. "I'm from a ship—the *Wavewalker,* a three-masted carrack out of Serrimundi. Captain Eli is due to set sail again as soon as his cargo is loaded. Probably with the outgoing tide tonight. He'd take passengers. I could put in a good word for you."

"I can find him myself," Nicci said, then softened her voice, realizing that the young man was just trying to help. "Thank you for the recommendation."

Bannon beamed. "It's the least I could do. You saved me. The *Wavewalker* is a good ship. It'll serve your needs."

"I will ask," Nicci said.

The young man brushed himself off. "And I'm going to buy my own sword so I won't be helpless next time I get in trouble." With an inappropriate display of conscience, he stared at the dead thugs in the alley shadows. "But what shall we do about them?"

Nicci didn't bother to look back over her shoulder. "The rats will find them soon enough."

CHAPTER 6

After the sorceress went on her way, Bannon wiped blood from his lip and felt the bruise. He tried to fashion a smile, which only made the pain worse, but he smiled anyway. He had to smile, or his fragile world would fall apart.

His canvas trousers were scuffed and stained, but they were durable work pants, a farmer's garment made to last, and they had served him well aboard the ship. His homespun shirt was now torn in two places, but he would have time to mend it once the *Wavewalker* set sail. There would be quiet listless days adrift on the water as they voyaged south, and Bannon was handy enough with a needle and thread. He could make it right again.

Someday, he would have a pretty wife to make new clothes and do the mending, as his mother had done on Chiriya Island. They would have spunky, bright-eyed children—five of them, he decided. He and his wife would laugh together . . . unlike his mother, who had not laughed often. It would be different with him, because *he* would be different from his father, so very different.

The young man shuddered, took a breath, and forced his mind back to the bright and colorful picture he liked to hold in his mind. Yes. A warm cottage, a loving family, a life well lived . . .

He habitually brushed himself off again, and the smile felt real this time. He pretended he didn't even notice the bruises on his face and leg. It would be all right. It had to be.

He walked out into the bright and open city streets. The sky was clear and blue, and the salt air smelled fresh, blowing in from the harbor. Tanimura was a city of marvels, just as he had dreamed it would be.

During his voyage from Chiriya Island, he had asked the other sailors to tell him stories about Tanimura. The things they had described seemed impossible, but Bannon's dreams were not impossible, and so he believed them—or at least gave them the benefit of the doubt.

As soon as the *Wavewalker* had come into port and tied up to the pier, Bannon had bounded down the gangplank, enthusiastic to find the city—at least *something* in his life—to be the way he wanted it to be. The rest of the crew took their pay and headed for the dockside taverns, where they would eat food that wasn't fish, pickled cabbage, or salt-preserved meat, and they would drink themselves into a stupor. Or they would pay the price asked by the . . . special ladies who were willing to spread their legs for any man. Such women did not exist in the bucolic villages on Chiriya—or if they did, Bannon had never seen them (not that he had ever looked).

When he was deep in drink, Bannon's father had often called his mother a whore, usually before he beat her, but the *Wavewalker* sailors seemed delighted by the prospect of whores, and they didn't seem interested at all in beating such women, so Bannon didn't understand the comparison.

He gritted his teeth and concentrated on the sunshine and the fresh air.

Absently, he pulled back his long ginger hair to keep it out of his way. The other sailors could have their alehouses and their lusty women. Since this was his first time here, Bannon wanted to get drunk on the sights of Tanimura, on the wonder of it all. He had always imagined that the world would be like this.

This was the way the world was *supposed to be.*

The white tile-roofed buildings were tall, with flower boxes under the open windows. Colorful laundry hung on ropes strung from window to window. Laughing children ran through the streets chasing a ball that they kicked and threw while running, a game that seemed to have no set rules. A mop-headed boy bumped into him, then rebounded and ran off. Bannon felt his trousers, his pocket—the boy had brushed against him there, possibly in an attempt to pick his pocket, but Bannon had no more coins for the would-be thief, since he'd already been robbed. The last of his money was safely tucked in the bottom of his boot, and he hoped it would be enough to buy a reasonable sword.

He took two breaths, closed his eyes, opened them again. He made the smile come back and deliberately chose to believe that the street urchin had just bumped into him, that he wasn't a feral pickpocket trying to take advantage of a distracted stranger.

Searching for a swordsmith, Bannon emerged into a main square that overlooked the sparkling blue water and crowded sailing ships. A heavy woman pushed a cart filled with clams, cockles, and gutted fish. She seemed unenthusiastic about her wares. Older fishermen with swollen, arthritic knuckles worked at knotting and reknotting torn fishing nets; their hands somehow remained nimble through the pain. Gulls flew overhead, wheeling in aimless circles, or shrieked and fought over whatever scraps they had found to eat.

Bannon came upon a tanner's shop where a round-faced man with a fringe of dark hair wore a leather apron. The tanner scraped and trimmed cured skins while his matronly wife knelt at a wide washtub, shoving her hands into bright green dye, immersing leather pieces.

"Excuse me," Bannon said, "could you recommend a good sword maker? One with fair prices?"

The woman looked up at him. "Wanting to join Lord Rahl's army, are you? The wars are over. It's a new time of peace." She ran her eyes up and down his lanky form. "I don't know how desperate they are for fighters anymore."

"No, I don't want to join the army," Bannon said. "I'm a sailor aboard the *Wavewalker*, but I'm told that every good man should have a good blade—and I'm a good man."

"Are you now?" said the leatherworker with a good-natured snort. "Then maybe you should try Mandon Smith. He has blades of all types, and I've never heard a complaint."

"Where would I find him? I'm new to the city."

The leatherworker raised his eyebrows in amusement. "Are you now? I wouldn't have guessed."

The tanner's wife lifted her hands out of the dye basin. They were bright green up near the elbows, but her hands and wrists were a darker color, permanently stained from her daily work. "Down two streets, after you smell a pickler's shop, you'll find a candle maker."

The leatherworker interrupted, "Don't buy candles there. He's a cheat—uses mostly lard instead of beeswax, so the candles melt in no time."

"I'll remember that," Bannon said. "But I'm not looking to buy candles."

The woman continued, "Pass the dry fountain, and you'll find the sword maker's shop. Mandon Smith. Fine blades. He works hard, gives a fair price, but don't insult him by asking for a discount."

"I—I won't." Bannon lifted his chin. "I'll be fair, if he is."

He left the tanners and went off. He found the pickler's shop with no difficulty. The tang of vinegar stung his eyes and nose, but when he saw large clay jars with salted fermenting cabbage, his stomach felt suddenly queasy, and unbidden bile came up in his throat. It reminded him too much of the stink of his old home, of the cabbage fields on Chiriya, of the bottomless prison pit that would have been his life back there. Cabbages, and cabbages, and cabbages . . .

The young man walked on, shaking his head to clear away the smell. He passed the disreputable candle maker without a second glance, then marveled at an elaborate fresco painted on the long wall of a public building. It depicted some dramatic historical event, but Bannon did not know his history.

He found the dry fountain, which was adorned with the statue of some beautiful sea nymph. Tanimura was so full of marvels, he almost didn't want to leave here, even after being robbed and nearly murdered. Was that any worse than what he had left behind?

He had fled his home in desperation, but he also wanted to see the world, sail the oceans, go from one port city to another. It wouldn't be right to remain in the first place he saw. But he was certainly impressed with that beautiful and frighteningly powerful sorceress, who was unlike anyone he had ever met on Chiriya. . . .

After spotting the sword maker's shop at the end of the street, he sat on the edge of the dry fountain, pulled off his left boot, and up-ended it so that the coins fell into his palm; two silvers and five coppers. That was all. He had a blister from the coins in his shoe, but he was glad he had taken the precaution. He'd learned that lesson from his father.

Never put all your money in one place.

Bannon swallowed hard and walked up to the sword maker. *Fine blades.* Self-consciously, he touched his empty pockets again. "I need to buy a sword, sir."

Mandon Smith was a dark-skinned man with a polished bald head and a bushy black beard. "I would imagine that to be the case, young man, since you've come to a sword maker's shop. I have blades of all kinds. Long swords, short swords, curved blades, straight blades, full guards, open hilts—all the finest steel. I don't sell poor quality." He gestured to show an array of swords, so many types on display that Bannon didn't know how to assess them. "What type of sword were you looking for?"

Bannon looked away, wiped at the bruise on his face. "I'm afraid you might not be able to provide the type of sword I need."

Mandon palmed his bushy beard, but the hairs promptly sprang back out into its full brush. "I can make any kind of sword, young man."

Bannon brightened. "Then, the sword I require is . . . an *affordable* one."

The swordsmith was startled by the answer. His face darkened in a frown before he burst out laughing. "A difficult request indeed! Precisely how affordable did you mean?"

Bannon held out all of his remaining coins. Mandon let out a long, discouraged sigh. "Quite a challenge." His lips quirked in a smile. "It wouldn't be right to let a man go without a blade, however. Tanimura has some dangerous streets."

Bannon swallowed. "I discovered that already."

Mandon led him inside the shop. "Let's see what we can find." The smith began sorting flat blank strips of metal that had not yet been fashioned and forged. He rummaged through half-finished long swords, broken blades, ornate daggers, serrated hunting knives, even a short flat knife that looked incapable of anything more dangerous than cutting cheese or spreading butter.

The smith stopped to ponder one clunky-looking blade as long as Bannon's arm. It had a straight, unornamented cross guard, a small round pommel. The grip was wrapped in leather strips, with no fancy carving, wire workings, or inlaid jewels. The blade looked discolored, as if it hadn't been forged as perfectly as the other blades. It had no fuller groove, no engraving. It was just a simple, sturdy sword.

Mandon hefted it, held the grip in his right hand, tossed it to the left. He moved his wrist, felt the weight of it, watched it flow through the air. "Try this one."

Bannon caught the sword, fearing he would drop it with an embarrassing clatter to the floor of the shop, but his hand seemed to go right to the hilt. His fingers wrapped around the grip, and the leather helped him hold on. "It feels solid at least. Sturdy."

"Aye, that it is. And the blade is sharp. It'll hold an edge."

"I had imagined something a little more—" Bannon frowned, searching for words that would not insult the swordsmith. "A little more elegant."

"Have you counted the number of coins you've got to spend?"

"I have," Bannon said, letting his shoulders fall. "And I understand."

Mandon clapped him on the back, a blow that was much harder than he expected. "Get your priorities straight, young man. When a victim is staring at a blade that has just plunged through his chest, the last thing on his mind is criticism about the lack of ornamentation on your hilt."

"I suppose not."

Mandon looked down at the plain blade and mused, "This sword was made by one of my most talented apprentices, a young man named

Harold. I tasked him with making a good and serviceable sword. It took him four tries, but I knew his potential, and I was willing to invest four sword blanks on him."

The smith tapped his fingernail on the solid blade, eliciting a clear metallic clink. "Harold made this sword to prove to me it was time he became a journeyman." He smiled wistfully, brushing his spiky black beard with one hand. "And he did. Three years after that, Harold was such a good craftsman that he created a fantastically elaborate, perfect sword—his masterpiece. So I named him a master." He squared his shoulders and leaned back with a wry sigh. "Now, he's one of my biggest competitors in Tanimura."

Bannon looked at the sword with greater appreciation now.

Mandon continued, "That just makes my point—it may not look like much, but this is a very well crafted sword, and it will serve the needs of the right person—unless your needs are to impress some pretty girl?"

Bannon felt a flush come to his cheeks. "I'll have to do that some other way, sir. This sword will be for my own protection." He lifted the blade, tried it in both hands, swung it in a slow, graceful arc. Oddly, it felt good—perhaps because otherwise he had had no sword at all.

"It'll do that," said the swordsmith.

Bannon squared his shoulders, nodding absently. "A man never knows when he might need to protect himself or his companions."

The dark edges of the world infringed upon his vision. Marvelous Tanimura seemed to have more shadows than before, more slinking, dark things in corners, rather than bright sunlit colors. Hesitating, he held out the coins, everything that the thieves hadn't taken from him. "You're sure this is enough money?"

The swordsmith removed the coins, one at a time, the two silvers then four of the coppers, closing Bannon's fingers on the last one. "I would never take a man's last coin." He gestured with his bald head. "Let's go outside. I have a practice block in back."

Mandon took him behind the smithy to a small yard with barrels of scum-covered water for cooling his blades, a grinding wheel and whetstones for sharpening the edges. An upright, battered pine log as tall as a man had been mounted and braced in the center of a dirt clearing strewn with straw. Fragrant piles of fresh pale wood chips lay around it on the ground.

Mandon pointed to the scarred upright log. "That is your opponent—defend yourself. Imagine it is one of the soldiers of the Imperial Order. Hah, why not imagine it's Emperor Jagang himself?"

"I already have enough enemies in my imagination," Bannon muttered. "We don't need to add to them."

He stepped up to the practice block and swung the sword, bracing for the smack of impact when the blade hit the pine wood. The vibrations reverberated up to his elbow.

The swordsmith was not impressed. "Are you trying to cut down a sunflower, my boy? *Swing!*"

Bannon swung again, harder this time, resulting in a louder thunk. A dry chunk of bark fell off the practice block.

"Defend yourself!" yelled Mandon.

He swung harder with a grunt from the effort, and this time the impact thrummed through his wrist, jarred his forearm, his elbow, all the way to his shoulder. "I'll defend myself," he whispered. "*I won't be helpless.*"

But he hadn't always been able to defend himself, or his mother.

Bannon struck again, imagining that the blade was cutting not into wood, but through flesh and hard bone. He hacked again.

He remembered coming home barely an hour after sunset one night on the island. He had been working as a hand in the Chiriya cabbage fields, like all the other young men his age. He had to work for wages rather than working his family's own land, because his father had lost their holdings long before. It wasn't even dinnertime yet, but his father was already out of the house, surely halfway drunk by now in the tavern. Getting drunk was about the only thing at which his father showed any efficiency.

At least that meant their cottage would be quiet, granting Bannon and his mother an uneasy peace. From his fieldwork in the past week, Bannon had earned a few more coins, paid that day—it was the height of the cabbage harvest, and the wages were better than usual.

He had already saved enough money to buy his own passage off of

Chiriya Island. He could have left a month ago, and he remembered how he had longed to be gone from this place, staring at the infrequent trading ships as they sailed away from port. Such vessels stopped in the islands only once every month or two, since the islanders had little to trade and not much money to buy imported goods. Even though it would be some time before he had another chance, Bannon had made up his mind that he wouldn't go—*couldn't* go—until he could take his mother with him. They would both sail away and find a perfect world, a peaceful new home like all those lands he had heard of—Tanimura, the People's Palace, the Midlands. Even the wild uncivilized places of the New World had to be better than his misery on Chiriya.

Bannon had walked into the house clenching the silver coin he had earned that day, sure that it would finally be enough to buy passage for himself and his mother. They could run away together the next time a ship docked in port. In order to be sure, he intended to count the carefully saved coins he had hidden in the bottom of the dirt-filled flowerpot on his windowsill. The pot held only the shriveled remnants of a cliff anemone that he had planted and nurtured, and then watched die.

Upon stepping into his cottage, though, Bannon had immediately smelled burned food, along with the coppery tang of blood. He stopped, on guard. Standing at the hearth, his mother turned from the pot she was stirring, trying to force a smile, but her lips and the side of her face looked like a slab of raw liver. Her pretense that everything was fine failed miserably.

He stared at her, feeling sick. "I should have been here to stop him."

"You could not have done anything." His mother's voice sounded hoarse and ragged, no doubt from screaming and then sobbing. "I didn't tell him where you hid it—I wouldn't tell him." She began to weep again, shaking her head. She slumped to the inlaid fieldstones on the hearth. "I wouldn't tell him . . . but he knew anyway. He ransacked your room until he found the coins."

Feeling an acid sickness in his stomach, Bannon ran to his room and saw his meager keepsakes scattered on the floor, the straw stuffing of his pallet torn out, the quilt his mother had sewn wadded against the wall—and the flowerpot with the cliff anemone upended, the dirt poured all over his bedding.

The coins were gone.

"No!" he cried. That money should have been a new hope, a fresh life for them both. Bannon had worked hard in the fields and saved a year to get enough for them to leave Chiriya and get far away from that man.

His father had not just stolen the coins, he had robbed Bannon and his mother of their future. "No!" he shouted again into the silent cottage as his mother wept on the hearth.

And *that* was how his father had taught Bannon never to keep all of his coins in one place, because then someone could take everything. It didn't matter how good the hiding place was, thieves like his father could be smart, thieves could be brutal—or both. But when thieves found at least *some* money, then Bannon could make a convincing plea that it was all he had, and they might not think to look elsewhere. . . .

"By the good spirits, my boy!" The swordsmith's voice cut through his dark haze of memories. "You're going to break my testing block, break that sword—and break your arm while you're at it."

Bannon blinked and saw what he had done. In an unconscious frenzy, he had chopped great gouges into the pine log, spraying splinters in all directions. His hands were sweaty, but they squeezed the leather-wrapped grip in a stranglehold. The discolored blade thrummed in the air, but the sword was undamaged, the edge not notched.

His shoulders ached, his hands were sore, his wrists throbbed. "I think . . ." he said, then swallowed hard. "I think I've tested it enough. You're right, sir. It seems to be a good blade."

He reached into his pocket and pulled out the last copper coin. "One more thing from you, sir. Would a copper be enough for you to sharpen the sword again?" He looked at the mangled practice block and suppressed a shiver. "I think it might have lost some of its edge."

Mandon looked long and hard at him, then accepted the copper coin. "I'll put an edge on it that should last a long time, provided you take care of the blade."

"I will," Bannon promised.

The swordsmith used the grinding stone to resharpen the sword, throwing off a flurry of sparks. Bannon watched but didn't see, as his thoughts wandered through a quagmire of memories. Before long, he would have to get back to the *Wavewalker* so he could be there when they sailed out on the evening tide. The rest of the crew would be hungover and miserable, and just as penniless as he was. Bannon would fit right in.

He fashioned a smile again and touched his bruised lip, then ignored the soreness as he imagined everything he could do to the thugs if they ever bothered him again. Now he was prepared. He dipped briefly into his fantasy—no, his *belief*—in a satisfying life, a happy family, kind friends. That world had to exist somewhere. Throughout his childhood on Chiriya, during all the times his father had shouted and struck, Bannon Farmer had built up that picture in his mind, and he desperately clung to it.

By the time he had reconstructed the rosy image of how things should be, Mandon had finished sharpening his blade and handed the weapon back to him. "I give you this sword with my fervent wish that you never need to use it."

When Bannon smiled, this time he did feel the sting in his lip. "That is my hope, too. Always my hope." But he doubted that would happen.

Bidding Mandon farewell, he left the shop and made his way down to the docks and the waiting *Wavewalker.*

CHAPTER 7

Nicci reached the docks in Grafan Harbor after making her way from the darkly cluttered buildings to a more spacious district of merchants' warehouses and administrative offices. The harbormaster's hall was a busy place, with the windows and doors thrown wide open to let in the breezes. Clerks in high-collared jackets bustled along the docks with their papers and quills, interviewing ships' quartermasters to inventory and tax the exotic and ordinary cargo.

Dockside inns and taverns were adorned with garish signs and unappealing names. The Snout and Maggot was unusually busy, filled with people who conversed in shouts instead of normal voices. In front of the tavern, a pudgy boy offered burned meat pies to sailors who lounged on the steps or leaned against the outside wall.

Servicing the steady flow of lonely men in port, rickety-looking brothels were crowded so closely against one another that the patrons of one establishment could hear the lusty activities in the adjoining brothel. Wildly imaginative murals painted on their exterior walls advertised improbable images of the services their women or boys performed. As Nicci considered the murals, she doubted many sailors could manage the intricate, overly flexible positions. She bit her lower lip, where once a golden ring had marked her as Jagang's property. From her unwelcome experience in the soldiers' tents, she knew that while most men believed they had great prowess as lovers, they were usually just brutes who finished quickly and without finesse.

She walked past moneylender stalls, extravagant ones that financed whole sailing expeditions, or smaller and more usurious moneylenders who preyed upon desperate sailors. A forlorn-looking man was locked in a pillory in front of one moneylender's shack. Slumped and scowling in the restraints, he had been pelted with rotted fruit, and he sneered back as passersby jeered at him.

Nicci knew how Tanimura worked. Some supposedly compassionate captain would pay the man's obligation and take him aboard a ship as part of the indentured crew, but such "rescued" men were bound to such impossibly high interest rates that they were practically slaves. Although Nicci despised slavery, she also had little sympathy for any fool who would create such a situation for himself.

Walking along the waterfront, she assessed the ships tied up at the docks, keeping her eyes open for one named *Wavewalker*, which Bannon Farmer had suggested. Those vessels with large cargo holds were clearly trading ships, while narrower-beamed hulls and streamlined construction signified fast patrol ships or warships.

Groups of hairy, muscular men offered their services as porters like human oxen hauling cargo to where shouting merchants held auctions. Laborers pulled thick hemp ropes through squeaking pulleys to raise crates and pallets off the decks.

At one smoke- and grease-stained cargo vessel, the sailors struggled with a block and tackle to lift the severed tentacle of a huge sea creature. The leathery gray skin was covered with slime and adorned with suckers. The heaving workers swung the flopping appendage over the side, and it landed with a thud and a splat onto the dock. Butchers swept in, using saws and cleavers to chop the tentacle meat into smaller steaks, while young apprentices ran up and down the docks calling out, "Fresh kraken meat! Fresh kraken meat for sale!" The smell was so foul and fishy, Nicci couldn't imagine anyone willingly eating the stuff.

She was startled to hear Nathan's voice call to her. "There you are, Sorceress. I am ready to help you find us a ship to carry us on our grand expedition to the Old World."

When Nicci turned to look at the wizard, she nearly laughed at his appearance. Upon leaving the People's Palace, Nathan had worn fine traveling clothes, but during their journey through the Dark Lands and then down to Tanimura, his garments had grown bedraggled, the fabric faded, the cloth frayed around the cuffs, the hem of his cape tattered. Now he sported new brown leather trousers and a white linen shirt with fresh starched ruffles down the front, voluminous sleeves, and wide folded cuffs, each fastened with a golden link. He wore an open embroidered vest, a fine forest-green cape. He also carried a bound satchel, which no doubt held other shirts—probably another few impractical white ones that would become stained and dingy in no time at all—as well as vests, trousers, maybe even a second cape, as if he needed one.

Nathan seemed to interpret her expression as admiration. "Hmm, I may have to reassess my opinion of Tanimura. It is a marvelous city after all, despite my past unpleasantness here. An entire district devoted to nothing but tailors! Shirt makers, jacket makers, trouser makers, cloak makers. The selection is extraordinary!" He lowered his voice to a husky whisper. "Would you believe I found two alleys devoted to highly creative smallclothes for women?" He cocked an eyebrow, and Nicci knew he did it just to annoy her. "I could take you there, Sorceress."

"I think not," she said. "My black dress and my other travel garments are quite adequate, and I am traveling in service of Richard." She had no interest in obtaining lacy smallclothes to entice some unknown man. Nicci had never needed lace, if that was what she'd been after.

Nathan continued with his unflappable exuberance. "And cobblers specializing in all types of boots." He tapped the toe of his new black boot on the dock boards, adjusting the fit. "Belt makers, button carvers, bucklesmiths—did you know that was a profession? Bucklesmiths!"

Nicci could imagine him walking among the shops, fascinated by so many choices, like a child overwhelmed by a sweet shop. "I am surprised you made up your mind so quickly."

"Indeed! After I first escaped from the Palace of the Prophets, Clarissa and I went to a tailor outside of Tanimura, and he took some time to complete the job to my satisfaction. Very meticulous." A wistful flicker of memory crossed his face. "But here in the city, with such extraordinary selection, I merely needed to name the clothes I wanted, and some tailor would find the items, exactly in my size." He made a quick, satisfied sound in his throat, hefting his packs. "I bought several outfits."

He looked along the docks, scanned the numerous ships tied up in the harbor. "So, I am ready to depart. Have you found us passage?"

Nicci thought of the young man in the alley. "I'm looking for a ship called the *Wavewalker*, a three-masted carrack due to depart tonight, sailing south. It may be what we need."

"Follow me," Nathan said. "The *Wavewalker* is this way."

She didn't ask how the wizard could know such a thing or how long he had been exploring the harbor without her. Together, they walked along the pier and found the *Wavewalker* tied up to the third dock from the end. The ship's figurehead showed the face of a beautiful woman with curly tresses that flowed back, transforming into ocean waves— the Sea Mother, a superstition from the southern coastal towns of the Old World.

The last carts and barrels of supplies were being loaded on board the *Wavewalker* for departure with the outgoing tide that night. Sailors carried cages of chickens onto the deck, and the potbellied ship's cook led a forlorn-looking milk cow by a rope up the boarding ramp.

Sailors gathered at the rails, watching the activity on the docks, many of them looking miserable from hangovers or bruised from brawls. No doubt they had spent or lost all their money and had returned early to the ship, having no place else to go.

Nicci and Nathan walked up the ramp, carrying their packs. The wizard waved at an older man in a gray captain's jacket, who rose from a wooden stool on the deck. The captain looked perfectly comfortable on board, liking his own ship better than the amenities in Tanimura. From the corner of his mouth, he removed a long-stemmed pipe from which wafted a curl of greenish-blue smoke, pungent with the smell of dream weed.

"Are you Captain Eli?" Nicci asked.

The man raised his bushy eyebrows and bowed, meeting them as they came aboard. "Eli Corwin, ma'am. How is it that you're familiar with who I am?"

"One of your sailors recommended that we speak to you about booking passage south to the Old World. We wish to depart soon."

Captain Eli removed his flat, gray cap. He had thick, wiry black hair shot through with silver strands. A dark boundary of beard outlined his jaw, but the rest of his face was clean shaven. "If departing tonight is soon enough, then this is your ship. The *Wavewalker* is a cargo vessel, but we have room for a few passengers, provided the fee is adequate."

"We have more than a fee." When Nathan puffed his chest with pride, his fancy new shirt swelled, as if the ruffles were flowers blooming. From the leather bag at his side, he removed a document and extended it to the captain. "This is a writ from Lord Rahl, master of D'Hara, appointing me his roving ambassador. The protection and status also covers my traveling companion."

Captain Eli skimmed the writ so quickly that Nicci knew he wasn't actually reading the words. He did not seem impressed. "This writ and the price of a passage will be enough to pay for your passage."

Nicci felt heat rise to her cheeks. "Lord Rahl's writ should guarantee us free passage."

"Maybe it should." The captain put the cap back on his head and inserted the pipe between his lips. He inhaled a long slow breath, then exhaled. "But such documents could be forged. There are many tricksters out to cheat an honest captain." He sucked again on his pipe. "Surely a powerful man like Lord Rahl, master of D'Hara, has a treasury large enough not to begrudge me the price of your passage."

He gestured toward the adjacent ship, where men in exotic silk pantaloons unloaded crates of spiny fruit. "For most of the captains here, a letter from a ruler they've never heard of will gain you nothing. For me, I'll try to be fair."

The cow let out a low moan as the cook tried to wrestle it down a ramp to a lower deck.

"Informing the world about Lord Rahl's rule is part of our mission," Nicci said. She still placed little credence in the other quest that the witch woman claimed was so important.

Captain Eli returned to his seat on the stool. "And you are welcome to tell every member of my crew about your Lord Rahl's wonderful new empire—so long as you pay for your cabins."

Nicci stiffened, preparing to demand that the captain acquiesce, but Nathan stepped forward. "That seems eminently reasonable, Captain. You're a businessman, and we can be fair." He plucked open the bindings of a small pouch in his palm and dumped gold pieces into the captain's outstretched hand.

Surprised, the man looked at the coins, warred with his decision, and then handed two gold pieces back to Nathan. "This is enough, thank you."

When the captain secured the coins in his own purse, Nathan whispered to Nicci, "We can always make more. Why not keep everyone happy?"

Rather than carrying huge sacks of coins from the D'Haran treasury, Nathan used his magic to transmute common metals into gold, so they never worried about having whatever money they needed. The wild people in the Dark Lands had no use for currency, but here in the civilized towns of D'Hara, Nathan found it useful to carry a fair amount of gold.

"For that price," the wizard added, "my companion and I will each receive a private stateroom."

The captain chuckled good-naturedly. "A stateroom? I see you've never been aboard the *Wavewalker*. In fact, I wonder if you've ever been aboard a ship at all? Yes, I can find a cabin for each of you. Some highborn nobles might consider them closets, but each room has a door and a bunk. After a week or two on the waves, you'll think of them as fine accommodations."

As long as she got to her destination, Nicci didn't care about spacious rooms or padded furniture. "That will be acceptable."

Some of the crewmen lounged on the deck, assessing the new passengers as if they were some strange fish they had drawn up in a net. Since the ship was due to depart soon, a stream of sailors continued to return, some staggering with hangovers, some carrying possessions they had purchased in port. They glanced at Nathan with a curious expression, no doubt wondering about his remarkable clothes and his fine sword, but their eyes lingered on Nicci, drawn to her long blond hair and the black dress that accentuated her curves. Nicci saw no sign of the young man she had rescued in the alley.

Dismissing the scrutiny of the sailors, the captain directed the two guests to their cabins. As she crossed the deck, Nicci noticed five shirtless men whose broad chests sported a waving line of tattooed circles. All five had dusky skin and mud-brown hair pulled back and tied like the tail of a warhorse. Although most of the crewmen turned their gazes away from Nicci's stare, these haughty shirtless men stared at her with undisguised hunger.

Seeing their lascivious grins, Nathan stepped in front of Nicci. "Make way! Don't you know this is Death's Mistress?" The shirtless men grudgingly backed off.

Their cabins in the stern of the ship proved to be just as small and unimpressive as Captain Eli had led them to expect. Nicci could tell that Nathan was disappointed in the accommodations, and she said, "Even a small cabin is better than lying on the forest floor in the cold rain and fog of the Dark Lands."

"You are ever the optimist, Sorceress," he said. "I concur."

For now, as the sun set over the delta of the Kern River and the tide began to go out, they went back up on deck to watch the preparations for departure.

Captain Eli shouted orders as his crew climbed the masts and crawled out on yardarms to unfurl sails. Others slipped thick hawsers from dock posts and loosed the ropes from stanchions on the pier. Hour bells rang from towers along the harbor.

She still had not seen Bannon Farmer aboard, and she feared the young redhead had blundered into another group of cutthroats in an alley and had suffered the fate she expected him to.

Just as the sailors prepared to lift the *Wavewalker*'s boarding ramp, though, a young man with long ginger hair bounded down the dock. "Wait for me, I'm coming! Wait! *Wavewalker*, wait!" Nicci noticed that he was now carrying a sword, which bounced and slapped against his thigh as he ran.

Bannon raced along as merchants and dockworkers scattered out of the way. He bumped into a reeling, drunken sailor who couldn't seem to remember where his own ship was, but Bannon spun past him and ran up the boarding ramp. His fellow sailors laughed, and a few exchanged coins. "I told you he'd be too foolish to jump ship when he had the chance."

Captain Eli gave Bannon a scolding look. "Some of our crew were betting you'd be a one-voyage sailor, Mr. Farmer. Next time don't be late."

"I wasn't late, sir." Bannon panted hard, swiping his loose hair out of his eyes. His cheeks were flushed with the effort. "I'm just in time."

When Bannon noticed Nicci, his face brightened, and the broad grin only emphasized the growing bruise on his smashed lips. "You're here! You came. Welcome aboard the *Wavewalker*."

"It seems we will be passengers. This ship is going where we need to travel." She took a breath, then added, "Thank you for the recommendation."

He held up his plain, unadorned sword. "See, I found a blade. Just like I said."

The other sailors joked. One said, "Some might call that a sword— I'd call it a grass cutter." Another said, "Who do you intend to impress with that ugly thing? A blind woman? Or maybe a farmer who needs to chop down tall weeds."

They all guffawed.

Bannon frowned at his clunky sword, then re-formed his expression into a cheery grin. "A sword doesn't have to be pretty to be effective at killing," he said, repeating Nicci's earlier words. "It's a sturdy sword." He held it up. "In fact, that's what I will name it. Sturdy!"

Captain Eli cut him off. "Enough showing off your sword, Mr. Farmer. Right now, I need your hands and your muscles on the rigging ropes. I want to be clear of the ships in the harbor and out in the open water before night falls."

Standing beside her at the starboard rail, Nathan mused, "Well, we are on our way, Sorceress. To Kol Adair, wherever it is." He gave her a wry grin. "I think I'm already starting to feel whole again."

CHAPTER 8

The sea was calm and dark, and the full moon rose like a bright torch as the *Wavewalker* glided out of Grafan Harbor. The three-masted carrack cruised past the chain of islands that strung out past Halsband Island, which now held only the pulverized rubble of the Palace of the Prophets.

After they had left the glowing lights of Tanimura, the night sky became a deep velvet black. Nicci stood on deck and looked up, trying to find new patterns among the bright stars that had shifted in the universe.

The canvas sails strained tight, creamy white as the full moon shone on them. The ropes glistened with a thin film of night dew. The carved figurehead of the Sea Mother stared forward with wooden eyes, as if watching out for hazards ahead.

Bannon came up to her near the bow, smiling shyly. "I'm glad you decided to come with us aboard the *Wavewalker.*"

"And I am glad that you survived Tanimura." Nicci couldn't tell whether he had learned any wariness or common sense from his time in the city. "It has been a day full of surprises."

He still proudly clung to his new blade. "You were right about the sword, that it needs to be serviceable, not pretty. And sturdy. It needs to be sturdy." He held the weapon as if it had become his most prized possession, turning it back and forth as he watched the moonlight play along the discolored blade. He swept it sideways in a practice stroke. "I can't wait for a chance to use it."

"Do not be so eager for that, but be ready if need be."

"I will. Do you have a sword of your own?"

"I don't need one," Nicci said.

His expression fell as he was suddenly reminded of what she had done to the thugs in the alley. "No, I doubt you would. I saw you hurl that man and smash his head against the wall. It cracked open like a rotten pumpkin! And that other man . . . you turned his neck to jelly! I don't even know what you did to the third one." Bannon shook his head. His eyes were wide. "I was trying to fight him for you, but he just . . . died."

"That is what happens when you stop a person's heart."

"Sweet Sea Mother," Bannon whispered. He brushed his hair back. "You saved my life, no doubt about that, and you were right—I was too innocent. I should never have blundered into a situation like that. I expect the world to be a nice place, but it's darker than I think."

"It is," Nicci said.

"It's darker than I want it to be."

Nicci wondered if the young man had stolen some of the captain's dream weed. "Better to see the dangers in the world and be ready when someone inevitably turns on you. It is a far preferable surprise to find that a person is kinder than you think, than to discover he is secretly a traitor."

Troubled expressions circled the young man's face like eddy currents. "I suppose you're right, and I want to thank you again. I owe you." He fumbled in the pockets of his canvas trousers. "I brought you something. To show my gratitude."

Nicci frowned at him. "That is not necessary. I saved your life because I was in the right place, and because I despise those who prey on the weak." She had no intention of letting this young man fawn over her. "I do not want your gifts."

He withdrew a tiny fold of soft cloth that he held in the palm of his hand. "But you have to take it."

"It is not necessary," Nicci repeated, in a harder voice this time.

"*I* think it's necessary." Bannon sounded more determined. He set his sword aside awkwardly, squatted against the side wall of the ship, and opened the cloth to reveal a pearl the size of a grieving woman's tear.

"I do not want your gifts," Nicci reiterated.

Bannon refused to listen. "On Chiriya Island I was taught manners and gratitude. My parents wanted me to be polite to everyone and to meet my obligations. You were there when I needed you. You saved me, and you punished those evil men. My father said that if I was to be an upstanding man, I had to show gratitude. It doesn't matter whether you expect anything in return. I am required to give it to you."

His breathing quickened as he extended the pearl. It seemed to be made of silver and ice. "This is a wishpearl, an advance on my wages. The captain says we'll have plenty before the end of the voyage, but I wanted it now." He nodded intently. "Right now it's very rare, and I want to give it to you."

A sailor on watch strolled past. "Rare?" His voice had a mocking tone. "That's just a leftover. We unloaded two chests full of them in Tanimura—it's how Captain Eli paid for his whole voyage. Soon enough, we'll fill more chests on our way down south."

Bannon whirled to face the eavesdropping sailor, clenching his hand tight over the wishpearl. "I was having a private conversation."

"This is a ship, cabbage farmer! Think again if you expect privacy anywhere on board."

Defensive, Bannon picked up his sword. "It's worth something now, and it's the last wishpearl. I want to give it to the sorceress, and if you don't treat her well, she'll crush your windpipe and stop your heart. I've seen it with my own eyes."

The sailor laughed again and strolled off.

Though Nicci did not want the offering, she understood the complexities of obligations. She had indeed saved him, although she had not set out to do so. "If you've learned your lesson and taught yourself not to become a victim, Bannon Farmer, then that is demonstration enough of your gratitude."

"Not enough for me," Bannon insisted, and extended the wishpearl again. "Just take it. Throw it overboard if you like, but *I* will have done what was right. I fulfilled what *I* needed to do."

The pearl felt slippery and cold in her fingertips. She rolled it back and forth on her palm with a fingertip. "If I accept this pearl, what does it obligate me to do for you? What are you expecting?"

Bannon flushed, deeply embarrassed. "Why, nothing! I would never ask . . . that isn't what I was thinking!"

She hardened her voice. "As long as you're clear on that."

"It's a wishpearl. Don't you know what a wishpearl is?"

"I do not. Is there some significance other than being a pretty bauble?" Seeing that she had hurt him, Nicci grudgingly softened her voice. "It is a beautiful pearl. I don't know that I've ever seen a finer one."

"It's a *wishpearl*," he repeated. "You should make a wish. It might be just a legend, but I've heard that wishpearls are concentrated dreams and you can unleash one if you wish on it."

"Who would believe such a thing?" Nicci asked.

"Many people. That's why the *Wavewalker* makes such a profit on each voyage. Captain Eli knows the location of a long line of special reefs. He harvests wishpearls and sells them in the port cities—at least that's what the other sailors said." He lowered his voice and ducked his chin. "This is still just my first voyage, you know."

Nicci held the wishpearl, thought of where they were going, of the mission the witch woman had given to Nathan. No doubt it would be a long journey. She looked down at the icy silver sphere under the moonlight and said, "Very well, then I wish this voyage will help us get to Kol Adair." She closed her fingers around the pearl and slipped it into a small pocket in her black dress.

CHAPTER 9

T he *Wavewalker* headed south across open water, beyond sight of
the coastline. Having spent so much time sitting alone in the
Palace of the Prophets, Nathan was accustomed to sedentary
days, but at least now he was out in the fresh air, inhaling brisk breezes.

In the distance, Tanimura was only a memory—a thousand years of
memories, as far as he was concerned. Time to make new memories.
Red possessed the life book of his past, but he had a new volume for
a whole new set of adventures. Now, without the gift of prophecy,
every twist and turn of the future was a surprise to him. Exactly as it
should be.

The captain and his crew knew how to guide the ship even when the
winds did not blow in a favorable direction. The well-practiced sailors
understood the intricate puzzle of how the rigging and the sails worked
together, furling and unfurling canvas to catch any wisp of wind. It
was like magic to Nathan, even though there was no magic beyond a
well-seasoned familiarity with the mysteries of the sea.

Most of the crew had been with Captain Eli on numerous voyages,
and each sailor had a job to do—except for the five shirtless, tattooed
men who lay about and did nothing. Watching their lazy behavior and
attitude, Nathan lost respect for them, and not simply because they
leered so much at Nicci. They displayed no interest in participating as
members of the crew. He supposed the arrogant men must have their
purpose, or the captain wouldn't tolerate them on board. For now,
though, they were primarily useless.

Bannon Farmer was the newest sailor on the *Wavewalker* and thus received the least-pleasant chores, dumping out slops, pumping the bilge, scrubbing the deck with a bucket of salt water and a stiff hand brush. But he performed the drudgery with a strange cheer.

Nathan watched the young man climb the ratlines and stand on the high platform to serve as a lookout, or crawl out on a yardarm to loose a sail. Once Bannon finished his chores, he would sit next to the wizard in the lazy afternoons, asking questions. "Have you really lived a thousand years? What fascinating things you must have done!"

Nathan patted the life book at his side. "I am more interested in what I have yet to do." He gave the thin redhead an encouraging smile. "But I'll be happy to tell you some of my stories, if you will tell me yours."

Bannon's shoulders slumped. "I don't have any stories to tell. Nothing's ever happened to me." Looking away, he rubbed the discolored bruises on his face. "Why do you think I ran away from Chiriya? I had a perfect life there, loving parents, a warm home. But it was too quiet and calm for a man like me." When he forced a smile, he winced from the scab on his still-healing split lip.

"I planted the cabbage fields in spring, weeded the cabbage fields all summer, harvested the cabbage in fall, and helped my mother make pickled cabbage for winter. There was no chance to have an adventure." He lifted his chin. "My father was very sad to see me go, because he was so proud of me. Maybe someday I'll return as a wealthy and famous adventurer."

"Maybe." Nathan detected something odd in the young man's words.

Bannon brought out his own sword as he sat on deck next to Nathan. Its steel wasn't perfect, but the edge was sharp enough. "I still think Sturdy will serve me well."

Since the young man seemed to expect sage advice, Nathan decided to give it. "A blade can only serve its wielder if he knows how to use it. You serve the sword just as the sword serves you." He withdrew his own blade from its scabbard to admire the fine workings on the grip, the inlaid gold, the gleam of the expensive steel. He had always felt that it made him look bold and gallant, a man to be reckoned with, a warrior as well as a wizard. Standing, he held the blade in front of him, watching the play of sunlight along its edge. He gave the young man a hard look. "Do you know how to use your sword, my boy?"

"I know how to swing a blade," Bannon said.

"We're not cutting cabbages. What if you were fighting against a bloodthirsty warrior from the Imperial Order? Or worse, one of the flesh-eating half men from the Dark Lands?"

Bannon paled. "I'm sure I could take down at least five of them before they killed me."

"Only five? So I would have to deal with the thousands that remained?" Nathan flexed his arms and bent his knees in his supple new travel pants. "Why don't we practice? I could use a good training partner. I'll teach you a few moves, so that if you ever find yourself facing a savage enemy horde, you could maybe kill fifteen of them before they took you down."

Bannon grinned. "I'd like that." A troubled expression crossed his face. "Well, I don't mean I'd like being killed, but I would like to make a brave accounting of myself if I were ever in a great battle."

"Those fighting at your side would like you to make a brave accounting as well, my boy." Nathan stroked his chin with his left hand. "I may be a thousand years old, but I'm relatively new at being an adventurer. A sword looks so . . . dashing, don't you think?" He held up the point.

"Your sword is fine, sir," Bannon admitted. "But will a fine sword and a dashing appearance frighten away a horde of monsters?"

"I suppose not," Nathan said. "Maybe we both could use the practice." He wrapped his hands around the hilt and tried different stances. "Shall we learn together, Bannon Farmer?"

Grinning, the young man lifted his sword and stepped back to crouch into a fighting stance, or at least the best imitation of a fighting stance he could manage.

When Nathan swung, Bannon slashed sideways to meet the blade, but Nathan had to adjust the sweep of his arc to insure that their swords met with a clang. Then he struck backward, hitting the young man's blade as it came up in defense. In a flurry of attack, Bannon swung and chopped, flailing from side to side.

The wizard scolded, "Are you a woodsman trying to clear a forest?"

"I'm trying to slay a thousand enemy soldiers!"

"An admirable goal. Now let's try a combination of strokes and jabs and deflections."

Bannon responded with another wild combination of slashes and counterslashes, which the wizard easily met, although he was by no means a master swordsman himself. In any confrontation, Nathan would always rely on magic as his first line of attack rather than a sword, but to teach the cocky young man a lesson, he worked his way through Bannon's defenses and smacked him on the bottom with the flat of his blade.

Stung, Bannon yelped, his face flushing so crimson that even his freckles vanished. "You'll pay for that, Wizard!"

"Take my payment on credit," Nathan said with a proud smirk. "It may be quite some time before you can make me fulfill the debt."

Some of the other sailors observed, amused by the swordplay. They howled with laughter. "Look at the cabbage farmer!" snorted Karl, a muscular veteran of many voyages, who considered it his duty to make sure Bannon was well initiated.

"Indeed, look at him," Nathan called back. "Soon enough you'll be afraid of him."

Attacking again, Bannon released a bottled-up anger that startled Nathan, even frightened him. Ducking and defending himself, the wizard chided, "Show *control* as well as enthusiasm, my boy. Now then, let's do it slowly. Watch me. Match my strokes."

The two practiced for an hour in the hot sun, sweating with exertion. After Nathan had led him through several fluid but basic exercises, Bannon began to grow more confident with his weapon. He was bright-eyed and grinning as they picked up speed. The ring of blades brought out most of the crew to watch.

Finally panting with exhaustion, Nathan raised his hand to signal a halt. "Dear spirits, you've had as much instruction as you can handle for one day. I'd better give you time to absorb what you've learned." He tried to control his heavy breathing so Bannon would not notice how winded he was.

The young man's hair was damp with perspiration, but the sea breezes blew it in all directions. He showed no sign of being ready to give up.

Nathan continued, "Maybe it's time for me to tell stories and teach you a bit about history. A good swordsman is also an *intelligent* swordsman."

Bannon kept his sword up. "But how will a story from history teach me to be better with my blade?"

Nathan smiled back at him. "I could tell you the tale of a poorly skilled swordsman who had his head chopped off. Would that be a good enough object lesson?"

Bannon wiped his brow and sat on a mound of coiled rope. "Very well then, let's hear the tale."

Nicci spent the day at the ship's stern in Captain Eli's large chart room on the piloting deck. The captain had opened up twin windows at the rear to let in fresh breezes. The view of the ocean behind them showed a curl of foamy wake as the *Wavewalker* sailed along. The line of stirred water reminded Nicci of the broad imperial roads that Jagang had built across the Old World, but while Jagang's roads would endure for a long time, this watery path faded as soon as the ship passed.

"I would like to study your charts and maps," she told the captain. "As an emissary for Lord Rahl, I must see the far reaches of the Old World, where the Imperial Order conquered. That is all part of D'Hara now."

Captain Eli toyed with his long-stemmed pipe, tapping its bowl on the hard wood of a map table. "Many captains keep their routes confidential, since the swiftest passage means money for a trader. I once knew the currents and the reefs and the shoreline so very well." He sucked on the end of his pipe, musing to himself, but he didn't light it inside the chart room, lest a stray ash catch the maps on fire. "But I suppose it doesn't matter anymore."

"I am not your competition, Captain," Nicci said. "I have no interest in a map of the ocean. I want to know the coastline and the landscape inland. My companion and I are searching for a place called Kol Adair."

"Never heard of it. Must be far inland, and any place away from shore doesn't have much meaning for my life." He scratched the side of his face. "But I did not mean you were my competition. I meant that the current maps don't matter because all is changed, you see. Everything's different now.

"In the last two months the currents have shifted. The wind patterns that I knew so well have now changed direction, as if the seasons are all mixed up." He let out a long groan. "And the stars at night are in the wrong places. How am I supposed to navigate? My astrolabes and sextants are useless. My constellation maps don't show the same stars. Sweet Sea Mother, I don't even know if the compass points true north anymore. I am making my way by instinct."

Nicci knew full well what had happened. "It is a new world, Captain. Prophecy is entirely gone. Magic has changed in ways that we haven't begun to fathom." Then she turned her bright blue gaze toward his, and drew a breath of the damp air as a breeze rippled the papers on the chart table. "But someone has to be the first to make new star charts, the first to map out the changed currents, and the first to discover the best places to drop anchor. You can be one of those firsts, Captain."

"That would be a wonderful thing . . . if I fancied myself an explorer." The captain scratched his trim of a beard around his jaw. "But my ambition has always been to serve as a successful cargo captain going from port to port. I have families to support, many children. I see little enough of them as it is, and I want to be able to arrive on time."

"Families?" she asked. "More than one?"

"Of course." Captain Eli ran his fingers over his dark hair, tucking a silver-shot lock behind his ear. "I have a wife and two daughters in Tanimura, a younger wife and three sons at Larrikan Shores, and a very beautiful one in Serrimundi, the daughter of the harborlord."

"Do they know about your other families?" Nicci asked. "Is this an unusual arrangement among sea captains?"

"I take care of each one in turn, wherever I go. Every wife has a fine house. Each of my sons or daughters is comfortable, with food, shelter, and an education. Most sailors and captains would simply visit the brothels at every port city, and I know of many a captain who caught a loathsome disease and gave it to his wife when he came home." Captain Eli stared out at the endless sea behind the stern. "No, that's not for me. I have chosen my wives, and I am faithful to them. I am an honorable man."

Considering the countless women Emperor Jagang had taken, including her, and how he had thrown Nicci and others into the tents to be raped again and again by his soldiers, she did not judge Captain Eli Corwin. She had never felt any inclination to be a man's wife, or one of his wives, except for the time she had forced Richard Rahl to pretend to be her husband. Nicci had imagined a perfect domestic existence, sure that she could convince him to adopt the philosophy of the Imperial Order. That had been not only a lie, but a bitter lie, and Richard had hated her for it.

Unconsciously, Nicci rubbed her lower lip, still imagining the long-healed scar there from Jagang's gold ring. Nicci had never realized that her sick dream of forcing Richard to be her husband was a delusion as foolish as Bannon Farmer's imagined perfect world.

Fortunately, she was a different person now. After living secretly as a Sister of the Dark for so many years, then being enslaved by Jagang, broken, then rebuilt—but rebuilt *wrong*, until she was finally fixed by Richard—she understood everything better now. Nicci owed Richard more than she could ever repay. And he had given her a mission.

"Let me see your charts nevertheless," she said, driving away the memories. "The more I know about the Old World, the more I know for Lord Rahl's sake."

Captain Eli spread the maps out before her on the table, sorting the broad papers until he found one that showed the coastline far south of Tanimura. "These are our major stops. Lefton Harbor, Kherimus,

Andaliyo, Larrikan Shores, even Serrimundi—we have a special agreement with the harborlord there, thanks to my wife." He smiled wistfully at the thought of her.

Nicci ran her fingers to the edge of the map, seeing no sign of Kol Adair. "And what is farther south? These charts are incomplete."

"No one goes farther south, no reason to go there. That's the Phantom Coast. Barely settled, even though the imperial roads stretch far into that land." Captain Eli sucked on his unlit pipe again, set it aside, and wiped his lips. "Who knows what the old emperors had in mind when they built those roads?"

Nicci frowned at the cities marked on the maps. "I need to make sure that everyone in the Old World knows about the end of war, the defeat of Emperor Jagang. We'll ask for your help as well, Captain. Even after we depart your ship, I will give you something in writing which you can take to these ports and help spread the message about Lord Rahl. All lands must be brought under one rule, even though each will keep its own culture and separate governance—so long as the people do not break the basic rules as determined by all."

"A fine sentiment," the captain said, rolling up the maps, "if everyone felt the same way. But I doubt you will get them to agree."

"That is the core of our quest. We'll have to make them feel the same way," Nicci said, and added a small, confident smile. "I can be very persuasive. And if I'm not sufficient, then there's a large D'Haran army to help make the point."

She and the captain left the chart room, stepping out onto the high deck from which they could watch the sailors doing their daily chores. The five shirtless men lounged about, disdaining the work and the crew. They turned their arrogant gazes toward Nicci, and one called up to her, "Come to play with us? We've got time."

"You can waste your own time until we reach the reefs," said Captain Eli. "But I don't think the lady wants to play with you."

Nicci said in a hard voice, "I doubt they'd enjoy how I might play with them."

The shirtless layabouts responded with leering laughter, which annoyed Nicci. She turned to the captain. "Why don't they work for their passage? They are worthless men."

"They are wishpearl divers. They've been with me for three voyages—extremely profitable voyages." He nodded to them all. "Sol, Elgin, Rom, Pell, and Buna. They might be lazy louts now, but they will earn ten times their keep in one day, once we reach the reefs."

CHAPTER 10

Seagulls wheeled overhead, following the *Wavewalker* under sunny skies. Fascinated, Nathan joined the sailors crowding the ship's rails, excitedly pointing down at the strange drifting infestation that surrounded them on the open seas.

Hundreds of thousands of jellyfish floated on the surface like soap bubbles, each one as large as an ox's head, throbbing like jellied brain tissue. The mindless translucent creatures posed no threat that Nathan could see as the *Wavewalker* cruised along and nudged them aside. Some of the jellyfish splattered against the hull boards and left a glutinous film, but the rest simply bobbed out of the way.

Captain Eli stood on deck, cautious. "Steady onward. If it was a sea serpent or a kraken, I'd be worried, but those jellyfish are just a nuisance."

Bannon stared in wonder. He turned to his mentor, flushed. "I never saw the likes of these on Chiriya, but other kinds of jellyfish would drift close to shore in the quiet coves . . . where a boy and his friend might go swimming. They sting!" He let out a wistful sigh, dreaming of home. "Ian and I had our own special lagoon where there were tide pools. The water was just right for wading, but we didn't see the jellyfish. We both got terribly stung once. My leg swelled up like a week-old pig carcass, and Ian was even worse. We could barely walk home. My father was angry because I couldn't work in the cabbage fields for days afterward."

The young man's expression darkened, and then, like clouds parting, he smiled again. "We all had a good laugh about it." He blew air between his lips. "And those jellyfish were only the size of my fist." He leaned far out over the side to get a better look. "I'll bet a sting from one of those things would kill you—probably five times over!"

"Being killed once would be sufficient." Nathan liked the young man. Bannon Farmer seemed earnest and determined, perhaps a bit too innocent—but Nathan didn't mind innocence. The wizard had written his own tales for young boys like Bannon, *The Adventures of Bonnie Day* and countless other stories carried far and wide on the mouths and lute strings of minstrels. Right now, Nathan saw no reason not to take the young man under his wing.

Out in the open air, Nicci stood aloof, away from the sailors. Her thick blond hair blew in the breezes, and her blue eyes pierced the distance. The tight-fitting black dress embraced her breasts and accentuated her curves. Cinched tight at the waist, the flowing skirt angled down to her right knee. On board, she'd decided to forgo her black travel leggings and high boots. She looked beautiful in the way a pristine work of art was beautiful, to be admired and appreciated, but definitely not to be touched.

Bannon occasionally looked at her with the wrong kind of sparkle in his eyes. Not lust, but infatuation. Nathan would have to watch that, lest it become a problem later on. The young man had no idea what he would be getting into.

Now, Bannon lowered his voice to an odd whisper as he asked Nathan, "Is it true she was really called Death's Mistress?"

Nathan smiled. "Dear boy, our Nicci was one of the most feared women in Jagang's Imperial Order. She has the blood of thousands on her hands."

"Thousands?" Bannon swallowed.

The wizard waved his hand. "More like tens of thousands, maybe even hundreds of thousands." He nodded. "Yes. I would suppose that's more accurate. Hundreds of thousands."

Although Nicci stood presumably out of earshot, Nathan saw her lips quirk in a thin smile. He continued in a stage whisper, "She was also a Sister of the Dark, served the Keeper for years before she served

Jagang the dream walker." He glanced around, noting that some of the other sailors were listening as well, and they muttered uneasily. While Bannon seemed in awe of Nicci's past, the others were fearful and superstitious.

Nathan didn't mind. Fear generated respect. "But that was before Nicci joined Lord Rahl, saw the light, became one of the staunchest fighters for freedom. Did I tell you she stopped Richard's heart and sent him to the underworld?"

"She—she killed him?"

"Only for a time. She sent him to the Keeper so he could rescue the spirit of his beloved Kahlan. But that's another story." He clapped the young man on the shoulder. "And on a long voyage, we'll have plenty of time for tales. No need to tell them all now."

The young man muttered in disappointment. "I've had a boring life, growing up as a farmboy on a sleepy island. No stories worth telling."

"You got stung by a jellyfish once," Nathan pointed out. "You must have other tales."

The young man leaned back and pondered. Below in the water, the crowded jellyfish bumped against one another with muffled slurping sounds.

"Well, it might just have been my imagination," Bannon said. "A person's thoughts tend to run wild when drifting alone in a small boat in the fog."

Nathan laughed. "Dear spirits, boy! Imagination is a critical part of a story. Tell your tale."

Bannon pursed his lips. "Have you ever heard of the selka? A race that lives beneath the sea and watches the activities of people above? They observe our boats and ships from below, which are like wooden clouds floating high in their sky."

"The selka?" Nathan frowned, drawing thumb and forefinger from his lips to his chin. "Sea people . . . ah yes. If memory serves—and my memory is as sharp as a finely honed dagger—the selka were created to be fighters in the ancient wizard wars. Humans altered by magic into another form, like the mriswith, or even the sliph. The selka were made to be an undersea army that could rise up and attack enemy ships." He narrowed his eyes. "But they're either extinct, or just legends."

"I never heard that part of the story before," Bannon said. "We just told tales about them on Chiriya. Sometimes the selka grant wishes."

Nathan chuckled. "If I had a copper coin for every story about a mythical creature that grants wishes, I'd have so many coins that I could buy whatever I liked and have no need for wishes."

"I . . . I don't know about that either," Bannon muttered. "It was just a story they told in the village. And there are times when you just want something to believe in."

Nathan nodded solemnly, sorry he had teased the young man. "I've felt the same way myself."

Bannon stared out to sea, seeming not to notice the jellyfish anymore. He lowered his voice to a whisper. "Just as there are times when an unhappy person needs to run away. I was foolish and young . . . too young to know that I was foolish."

Perhaps too young for that still, Nathan thought, but kept his words to himself.

"I set off in a little fishing boat all alone, meaning to leave Chiriya forever. I didn't have any friends on the island."

"What about Ian? The one who was also stung by a jellyfish."

"This was later. Ian was gone." Bannon frowned. "I set off at dusk as the tide went out, and I knew the full moon would light my way throughout the night. I hoped to see the selka, but in my heart, I suspected they were just stories. I'd been told so many things that turned out to be untrue." He looked sickened, but with obvious effort he restored his expression to a happy grin. "There's always a chance, though. I rowed into the darkness as the stars came out overhead, and I kept rowing until my arms felt as if they would fall off. After that, I just drifted in the open water. For about an hour I could see the dark line of Chiriya Island, with the lights of hearth fires and lamps from the shoreline villages high above the beaches. Then they vanished into the distance, and I kept on rowing."

"Where did you think you were going?" Nathan asked. "Just heading out into the open sea?"

Bannon shrugged. "I knew the Old World was out there, a continent filled with cities like Tanimura, Kherimus, Andaliyo—a whole continent! I figured if I simply went far enough, I was bound to bump into shore sooner or later." He glanced away in embarrassment. "Growing up on an island did not give me a good grasp of large distances. I drifted all night, and when dawn came I saw only water—water in all directions. Like this." He gestured over the side of *Wavewalker*.

"I didn't have a compass or nearly enough supplies. I drifted on the open sea all day long under the baking sun, and I began to grow deeply worried. The heat of the day burned and blistered my skin, but the next night seemed colder than ever. And by the third day, I ran out of water and most of my food. I felt like such a fool. I saw no sign of land, had no idea which direction the Old World lay, or even how to find Chiriya again.

"I cried like a heartbroken child, and I'm not ashamed to admit it. I stood up in the wobbly fishing boat and shouted into the distance, hoping someone would hear. That made me feel even more foolish than crying.

"That night the moon was still bright, but a thick blanket of fog settled in—although it wasn't a blanket, it was cold and clammy. I shivered, more miserable than ever. I couldn't see anything around me—not that there was anything to see. The moon was just a gauzy glow overhead."

His voice became a whisper. "On a foggy, silent night you can hear sounds from far away, and distances deceive you. I heard splashes that I thought were sharks, then it sounded like swimming . . . an eerie voice. I called out again for help. In my imagination I thought it might be the selka come to rescue me, but common sense told me it was just a distant whale, or even a sea serpent. I shouted and shouted, but I heard no answer. Maybe my voice startled whatever it was, and I listened to the silence, nothing but the lapping waves and another distant splash, something that might have been laughter, a giggle . . . but that couldn't be true.

"I was so distraught, anxious, exhausted—not to mention hungry and thirsty—that I eventually collapsed during the darkest part of the night and fell into a deep sleep."

Nathan smiled to encourage the young man. "You have the makings of a storyteller, my boy. You've got me intrigued. How did you ever get out of it?"

"I don't know," Bannon said. "I honestly don't know."

Nathan frowned. "Then you have to work on a better ending for your story."

"Oh, there's a good ending, sir. I woke up the next morning, and instead of the silence of the endless waves, I heard the rush of water against a shore, surf riding up on the shingle. I realized that my boat wasn't rocking anymore. I stood up and nearly fell out. I had washed up on the shore of an island, a place I recognized! This was Chiriya, the same cove where Ian and I used to swim."

"How did you get back there?"

The young man shrugged. "Sweet Sea Mother, I told you—I don't know. Sometime during the night when I was unconscious from exhaustion, something had taken me back to our island, brought me safely to shore."

"Are you sure the currents didn't just circle you around to your starting point? In the fog, how would you ever know?" Nathan looked down his nose. "You're not saying it was the selka who rescued you?"

Bannon seemed embarrassed. "I'm saying that I found myself safely back on shore, where I had started from, and I don't know how. In all the vast ocean and all the islands in the sea, I had come back to the very place I called my home, the cove where I'd started from." He paused for a long moment, then looked at the wizard and smiled in wonder. "And in the soft dirt of the shore, beside my boat—which had been dragged much farther up out of the water than even a high tide would have left it—I saw a footprint."

"What kind of footprint?"

"It looked human . . . almost. But the toes were webbed, like a sea creature's. I saw the faint impression of what looked like a fin's edge and sharp points like claws, instead of human toenails."

Nathan chuckled. "A fine story that is! And you said nothing had ever happened to you."

"I suppose. . . ." Bannon did not sound convinced.

The jellyfish swarm showed no sign of abating. Egged on by his crewmates, the broad-shouldered Karl picked up a barb-tipped harpoon and tied a rope through the metal eye on the tail end of the shaft. As the others cheered and hooted, the veteran sailor leaned over the side and tossed the harpoon down to pop one of the jellyfish like a large ripe blister. The iron point pierced the membrane, bursting the gelatinous creature into a smoking puddle. As the residue drifted out among the other jellyfish, its companions scooted away from the remains like fleeing robber bugs.

With guffaws of laughter, the other sailors ran to get more harpoons, but when Karl pulled the harpoon back up by the rope, he grunted in amazement. "Look! Look at this." The sharpened iron tip was smoking, and it began to droop as acid pitted and ate away the metal.

The other sailors stopped, poised to throw their harpoons as part of the game to pop the jellyfish. Curious, Karl extended a callused finger, but before he could touch the smoking iron tip, Nathan barked a warning. "Leave that alone, or you might lose a hand as well as a harpoon tip."

Captain Eli scolded them all. "I told you to leave those jellyfish be! The sea has enough dangers for us. We don't need to make any more."

With a clatter, the other sailors lowered their harpoons, then sheepishly stowed them away.

CHAPTER 11

The *Wavewalker* sailed south for a full week. Captain Eli bypassed the larger coastal cities in the Old World, and Nicci was concerned about the changed currents, altered wind patterns, and unreliable stars in the night sky. "Are we lost?" she asked, standing next to the captain at the bow one afternoon.

"Lady Sorceress, I know exactly where I'm sailing." He wiped the thin end of his pipe between thumb and forefinger, then inserted it back into his mouth. "We are heading straight for the reefs."

Overhearing, Nathan stepped up to them. "That sounds ominous."

Pushed along by a steady sea wind, the *Wavewalker* moved at a fast clip. The captain gazed ahead. "Not if you know where you're going."

"And how can you be sure? You claimed the charts and currents were no longer accurate," Nicci said.

"They aren't, but I'm a captain, and the salt water of the sea runs through my veins. I can feel it in my senses. But before I can trade in Serrimundi or Lefton Harbor, I need to take on my most valuable cargo. Tomorrow morning, you'll see what I mean."

Captain Eli was right.

Taking his shift on the lookout platform high on the mainmast, Bannon called out, "A line of foam due south, Captain! Looks like rough water."

The captain leaned closer to the carved figurehead of the Sea Mother, shading his eyes. "That'll be the reefs."

Nicci watched the shirtless wishpearl divers rouse themselves, as if awakening from a long sleep. "Our services are required," said the one named Sol, who seemed to be their leader.

Elgin stretched lazily. "I'll get the ropes and the weights."

The other three, Pell, Buna, and, Rom, began breathing deeply, inhaling, exhaling, stretching their shoulders, loosening their arms. Given the size of their chests, and their commensurate lungs, Nicci guessed these divers might be able to stay underwater for some time.

Buna narrowed his eyes at Nicci. "After a good day's haul of wish-pearls, maybe we'll all get to have our wish with the lady."

With a huff, Nathan took insult at the comment, but Nicci answered calmly, "If I get *my* wish, you won't be physically capable of thinking such thoughts ever again."

E ven without charts, Captain Eli guided the *Wavewalker* through the choppy water, dodging dark barriers of exposed reefs, but the ship had room to maneuver in the deep channels. The crewmen tied up the sails, rolling the canvas against the yardarms and lashing it tight. When the ship slowly drifted into position, they dropped anchor in a calm sheltered area, while the waves continued to break and foam along the outer lines of submerged coral.

Once the ship was safely anchored, the eager sailors watched the five wishpearl divers make their preparations. Sol barked orders to his comrades. "We go down two at a time. I dive first with Elgin, second will be Rom and Pell. After they come up, I'll be rested enough to go down with Buna." He flexed his arms back to display his broad pectorals marked with a chain of tattooed circles.

The divers opened a clay pot of grease, which they smeared over their skin. The grease would keep them warm as they went deep into the intricate coves and crannies of the reef. The grease also made them slide through the water, according to Rom, who smeared an extra layer across his chest.

Although the five divers had similar lines of circular tattoos, some sported more circles than others. Nicci learned that the tattoos were a tally of how many chests of wishpearls each diver had collected. Sol had been down so many times, he had started a second line on the right side of his chest. They each wore a braided belt from which dangled long, curved hooks to hang iron weights on, as well as a mesh sack for harvesting shells while they were underwater.

As the first divers, Sol and Elgin each tied one end of a long hemp rope to the belt around his waist and secured the other end to the foremast. Then they climbed up onto the rail, poised on callused bare feet. They fastened iron weights to the hooks on their belts, which would drag them down to the bottom so they wouldn't waste time or breath stroking down to their destination. Once deep among the reefs, they could easily unhook and discard the weights before swimming back up.

As the two divers stood balanced in the sunlight, they inhaled, exhaled, then sucked in another great breath, expanding their chests and filling their lungs. With unspoken synchronization, the pair dove over the side and vanished with barely a ripple. The rope reeled out as they sank.

Captain Eli scratched the line of beard on his jaw. He seemed very calm and satisfied. "We might stay here at anchor a day or two. Depends on how long it takes to fill up our cargo chest."

"A chest holds a lot of wishpearls," Nathan observed.

"Yes, it does." The captain took off his cap and wiped his hair, then settled it back in place.

After some minutes had passed, Bannon looked over the side, watching for the two divers to return. He glanced at Rom and Pell, who were fixing belts to their waists, attaching iron weights to the hooks, and securing their mesh sacks as they prepared to make their own dive as soon as the first pair surfaced.

Bannon asked the two men, "Do you think I could be a wishpearl diver someday?"

Rom looked at him as if he were an insect. "No."

The young man's expression fell, but he continued to peer over the side. "Here they come!"

The divers burst to the surface. Gasping, they shook their heads, flinging water from their long, clumpy hair. It had been nearly ten minutes, and Nicci was amazed the men were able to stay underwater for that long. Their lung capacity was as great as their arrogance.

Each man grabbed one of the dangling ropes and scampered up the hull boards. After they swung themselves over the rail to stand dripping on the deck, Sol and Elgin emptied their sacks, spilling out dozens of lumpy gray shells, which were eerily shaped like hands folded in prayer.

"Sweet Sea Mother, that's lovely," said Captain Eli as the crew rushed forward. "Absolutely lovely."

The *Wavewalker*'s crew set to work with stubby flat knives to split open the wet shells, tear out the rubbery flesh, and pluck out icy-silver pearls.

Next, Rom and Pell dove overboard while their comrades rested. Sol spread his lips in a grin for Nicci. "If you offer me a proper reward, I'll give you your very own wishpearl."

Nicci simply said, "I already have one. Bannon gave it to me." Sol responded only with an annoyed grunt.

By the time Rom and Pell swam back to the surface with an equally successful harvest, the next two divers were ready. For hours, the bare-chested men went down and came up again, over and over, as the crew shucked the shells and removed the pearls.

Curious, Nathan picked up one of the split-open shells discarded on the deck. "Remarkable. They look like human hands cradling the pearls."

"Hands folded to make a wish," Bannon said.

To Nicci, the crudely formed fingers appeared to be holding tight to the treasure hidden inside.

"These reefs are lush with shells," said Buna after his third dive. "There's enough treasure for a hundred trips."

"And we'll keep coming back," Captain Eli promised.

Because the *Wavewalker*'s crew took some of their pay in wish-pearls, they pressed the divers to descend over and over again. Nicci was just glad to see the arrogant layabouts actually working.

But at the end of the day, with the sun setting in a blaze of orange and golden fire, the five divers were weary. Although Sol, Elgin, and

Rom did not seem inclined to do extra work, Pell and Buna agreed to make one last dive. The two tied ropes around their waists, attached iron weights to the hooks, and jumped overboard.

The sailors sat around on deck, chatting, shucking wishpearl shells, and piling the discards against the side wall. Pell and Buna stayed down for a long period—longer than any other previous dive that day. Nathan paced the deck, wearing an increasingly concerned look. The captain also looked worried.

Finally, Sol frowned, went to the rail, and leaned over to peer into the darkening water. "Pull on the ropes—haul them back up." He clasped one of the wet hemp cables and strained, while an eager Bannon took the other rope tied to the second diver.

Bannon's rope went taut in his hands, then suddenly yanked downward, tightening, burning through his fingers. He cried out and let go as the cable smacked against the *Wavewalker*'s hull. Something dragged it down from below.

"No swimmer could possibly pull that hard!" Sol said, straining against the rope.

The second rope creaked as an unseen force deep below dragged back. Rom and Elgin rushed to help haul on the ropes to bring their comrades back up. The strange grip tugged back with such strength that the whole ship began to tilt.

They all strained together, shouting, heaving. "Pull them up!" Sol yelled again.

Suddenly, both ropes snapped and hung loose in the water, like drifting seaweed. Working hand over hand, the men furiously pulled the ropes until the frayed end of the first one came free. "Why would they cut their own ropes?" Elgin demanded.

Bannon stared at the torn, stubby end. "That's *frayed*, not cut."

Nicci immediately understood the significance. "Something tore the rope apart."

As the would-be rescuers hauled up the second loose rope, Rom climbed on the rail, ready to dive overboard to rescue his comrades, but before he could jump, the end of the second rope came dripping out of the water, still tied to the woven belt that had been ripped free from the wishpearl diver. Tangled in the belt were flaccid, wet loops of torn intestine and three connected vertebrae, as if an attacker had simply ripped the belt entirely through the diver's spine and abdomen.

The sailors howled in fear, backing away.

"But how—?" Rom staggered backward, falling onto the deck. "We didn't see anything down there."

"Something killed Pell and Buna," Sol said. "What could have caused this? What attacked them?"

Elgin glared over at Nicci. "Maybe Death's Mistress summoned a monster."

The three surviving divers stared at the sorceress in horror and fear, which quickly turned to obvious hatred.

Bannon whispered to Nicci in amazement, "Did you really do that? Just like you killed the thieves in the alley?"

She quietly chided him for his foolish statement, but after having seen the potential violence in the wishpearl divers, she was glad that they feared her.

CHAPTER 12

The crew stared from the dissipating bloom of blood in the water to the shreds of flopping intestines that dangled from the loop of woven belt. Captain Eli shouted for the sailors to set the sails and weigh anchor as clouds gathered in the dusk. Although the *Wavewalker* was in warm latitudes, far to the south of Tanimura, the wind seemed to carry a chill of death.

Nimble sailors scrambled out on the yardarms to untie the ropes, while others pulled on the halyards and stretched the canvas. The ship moved away from the reefs, slinking like a whipped dog, while the navigator pushed hard on the rudder and the lookouts guided the course to keep from scraping the dangerous rocks.

The captain called in a hoarse voice, "We've already lost two men today. I do not wish to lose more."

Catching the wind, the ship retreated from the angry line of reefs and reached open water again. As full night fell, clouds obscured the stars, which mattered little since the captain could not navigate by the unfamiliar night sky anyway. He simply wanted to put distance between their ship and the reefs.

Although the crew was superstitious about deadly sea monsters, Nicci simply assumed that some shark or other aquatic predator had attacked Pell and Buna in the reefs. Nevertheless, she remained alert for danger. An ominous mood surrounded the crew like a cold and suffocating mist. After several hours, the blame the three surly wishpearl divers cast on Nicci took hold like an infection among the jittery sailors, and they all looked at her with fear. She did nothing to dispel their concerns. At least they left her alone.

The *Wavewalker* sailed for three more days, and the weather worsened, like an overripe fruit slowly spoiling. Troubled, the captain emerged from his chart room to stare at the clotted gray skies and the uneasy froth-capped waves. He spoke to Nicci as if she were his confidante. "With a full chest of wishpearls harvested, this voyage has been very profitable, despite the cost in blood. Every captain knows he might lose a crewman or two, though I doubt those divers will ever sail with me again."

Nicci gave the man a pragmatic look. "You'll find others. Where are they trained? One of the coastal cities? An island?"

"Serrimundi. Wishpearl divers are revered among their people."

"I noticed the arrogance."

"It won't be easy to replace them." The captain sighed. "Those three will talk once we get back to a port city."

"Then invest your new fortune wisely," Nicci said. "Those pearls in your hold may be the last you ever harvest." The single pearl Bannon had given her was tucked away in a fold pocket of her black dress.

When the watch changed, a lookout climbed down from the high platform, and another scrambled up the ratlines to take his place. Nathan joined Nicci and the captain on the deck as the windblown, deeply tanned lookout approached. "The clouds look angry, Captain. You can smell a storm on the wind."

Captain Eli nodded. "We may have to batten down for a rough night."

"Are there more reefs to worry about ahead?" Nathan asked. "Will we run aground? It would be much harder to find Kol Adair if we're stranded out on a reef somewhere."

"Yes, I'm sure it would be quite inconvenient all around." The captain sucked on his unlit pipe and pressed a hand on his cap to keep the wind from snatching it away. "We are in open water. No reefs that I know of." The sailor nodded and went back to his duties.

When the other man was gone, Nicci lowered her voice. "You said that your charts were no longer accurate and you weren't exactly sure where we were."

Captain Eli's expression was distant. "True, but I don't think reefs appear out of nowhere."

As the blustery wind increased, the anxious crew performed only the most important chores. The potbellied cook came up with a bucket of frothy milk, fresh from the cow kept tied below. "She doesn't like the rocking of the waves," he said. "Next time the milk may be curdled when it comes out of her teats."

"Then we'll have fresh cheese." Captain Eli took a ladle of the proffered milk.

Nicci declined, but the wizard was happy to taste it. He smacked his lips after he drank. The cook offered milk to the surly wishpearl divers, but they scowled at the bucket, focusing their glares on Nicci.

"She might have poisoned it," said Rom.

Hearing this, Nicci decided to drink from the ladle after all.

As the wind whistled through the rigging and the hours dragged on, Nathan suggested that he and Bannon practice their swordplay on deck. The clang of steel rang out in a flurry as the two pranced back and forth, dodging coiled ropes and open rain barrels that had been set out to collect fresh water in anticipation of the imminent storm.

Bannon had gotten noticeably better as a swordsman. He had a reckless energy that served to counteract his gracelessness, and Sturdy lived up to its name, receiving and deflecting blow after blow from Nathan's much finer blade. For a while, the performance distracted the uneasy crewmen from their gloom.

By the time the young man and the wizard were both exhausted, the afternoon clouds were so thick with the oncoming storm that Nicci couldn't even see the sunset on the open water. Instead, she merely watched the daylight die.

"Will you show me some magic?" Bannon suggested to Nathan, climbing up on a crate that was too high to serve as a comfortable chair.

"Why would I show you magic?" Nathan asked.

"Because you're a wizard, aren't you? Wizards do magic tricks."

"Wizards *use* magic. Performing monkeys do tricks." Nathan raised his thick eyebrows. "Ask the sorceress. Maybe she'll perform a trick for you."

Bannon glanced over at Nicci, swallowed hard, then turned back. "I've already seen her magic. I know what she can do."

"You know *some* of what I can do," said Nicci.

The carrack rocked back and forth in the rough seas, rising on the swells, then dropping into the troughs. Though most of the *Wavewalker*'s crew had iron stomachs, some sailors bent over the rail and retched into the open ocean. The masts creaked and groaned; the sails rippled and flapped.

Captain Eli stood with hands on hips and his woolen jacket secured with silver buttons across his chest. "Trim the sails! The wind is getting stronger, and we don't need any torn canvas."

Above, the lookout had strapped himself to the mast to keep from being flung overboard when the ship lurched.

With an exaggerated sigh, Nathan acceded to Bannon's request for a demonstration of magic, even though the young man had not continued to pester him. "All right, watch this, my boy." The wizard knelt down, smoothed the ruffles of his fine travel shirt, and briskly rubbed his palms together as if to warm them up. "This is just a small hand light, a flame we could use to ignite a fire or illuminate our way."

"I use sulfur matches, or flint and steel," Bannon said.

"Then you have magic of your own. You don't need to see mine."

"No, I want to see it!" He leaned closer, his eyes bright. "Make fire. Show me."

Nathan cupped his hands to form a bowl. His brow wrinkled, and he stared into the air, concentrating until a glimmer of light appeared. The wisp of flame curled up and wavered, but when a gust of wind whipped across the deck, the hand fire flickered, then went out. Nathan could not sustain it.

The wizard looked completely baffled. Nicci had seen him create blazing balls of fire before with barely a glance, not to mention far more horrific wizard's fire that caused great destruction. As if incensed, he concentrated again, then scowled when only a tiny thread of fire appeared, which was again extinguished by the breezes.

"Is it supposed to be that difficult?" Bannon asked.

"I'm not feeling at all well, my boy," he said, in an obvious, awkward excuse. "Magic requires concentration, and my mind is troubled. Besides, there's too much wind for a proper demonstration."

Bannon looked disappointed. "I wasn't aware that wizards could use magic only under ideal conditions. You told me I had to be ready to fight with my sword, no matter my mood."

"What do you know of wizards?" Nathan snapped. "Your sulfur matches couldn't light a fire in a situation like this either."

Stung, Bannon conceded.

In a more apologetic voice, Nathan said, "It isn't you, my boy. My Han seems to be . . . troubled. I'm not entirely sure what to do about it."

"Your Han?"

"It is what we call the force of magic, the force of life within us, particularly within a wizard. The Han manifests differently in different people. My Han was intertwined with prophecy as well as the ability to use magic, but now that's all untangled. I'm certain I'll get it sorted out."

"Are you sure you're not just seasick?" Bannon asked, with a teasing lilt in his voice.

"Maybe that's exactly it," Nathan said.

Disturbed by what she had seen, Nicci wondered what might be bothering the wizard. Nathan had lost his gift of prophecy with the shift in the world, but his core magic should have remained unaffected. Still, a fire spell was supposed to be quite simple.

"I'm retiring to my cabin." Nathan turned away, trying to keep his dignity and balance on the rocking deck. "If I am hungry, I may go to the galley for supper when it's ready."

Nicci decided to take shelter in her own cabin as well. She didn't want to distract the superstitious sailors by staying out in the worsening weather.

Despite the sorceress's cold beauty, Sol had known that she was evil and dangerous from the moment he first saw her. His companions noticed only Nicci's shapely figure, her long blond hair, and a face even more attractive than carvings of the Sea Mother.

When stuck alone on a ship, long at sea, sailors tended to lower their standards of beauty, but there was no denying that this Death's Mistress was more beautiful than the most expensive whore in the cleanest brothel in Serrimundi. And Nicci was right here for the taking. Whenever the woman flaunted herself on deck, her black dress clung to her curves and rippled around her in the breezes, tightening against her full breasts. Sol imagined the breasts would be soft and pliable, just waiting to be squeezed. He tried to picture her nipples, wondering whether they were dark or pale pink, whether she would gasp if he pinched them.

The other two divers wanted to lay claim to her, but Sol was their leader, and he would have to be first. Their two comrades were dead, and the survivors deserved something. The sorceress owed them all a few rounds of gasping, squirming pleasure. In fact, she owed them the lives of their murdered friends, Pell and Buna. She had somehow used her magic to summon underwater monsters to kill them. Nicci had taunted the divers for days, rebuffed their attentions, insulted them— and now two of his comrades were dead. It was her fault.

Back home in Serrimundi, Sol and his fellow wishpearl divers were treated as heroes. From the time he was a young boy, his parents had taught him to dive deep, and then they had sold him to a mentor for a portion of Sol's pearl harvest over the next five years. The mentor had trained him—and such training consisted of him trying to drown young Sol over and over, tying heavy weights to his ankles, sinking him to the bottom of a deep lagoon and counting out minutes. The mentor did not pull any of the apprentice divers back into blessed air until he decided they had been down there long enough. Over a third of the trainees came up dead, their lungs filled with water, their eyes bulging, their mouths open and slack.

Sol himself had drowned once, but he had coughed up the water and come back to life. That was when he knew he *would* be a wishpearl diver. He could have any Serrimundi woman he wanted, and he usually did. His lovers all expected wishpearls as gifts, which he freely gave. Sol could always find more.

Out in the southern reefs, the supply of folded-hand shells seemed inexhaustible, but Captain Corwin paid him in more than wishpearls. It was a lucrative arrangement, giving Sol and his companions power and status whenever they returned to port.

But Pell and Buna would not be coming back home. Because of Nicci. The aloof sorceress thought that she was untouchable, that she would not be held to account for killing his friends, but the Sea Mother demanded justice, and Sol knew how to deliver it.

After he whispered his plan to Elgin and Rom, the three met on deck where the sailors had piled discarded wishpearl shells. Most had already been thrown overboard, but these last few remained, unnoticed after the disaster and the rapid escape from the reefs.

Now, the divers used their knives to pry loose the inedible and worthless meat inside, but Sol knew more about these particular shells. A gland inside the flesh of the shellfish contained a toxin—a poison potent enough to incapacitate even a sorceress.

The three men worked quickly to gather the extract, because the cook would soon be preparing supper.

Bannon had first watch in the thickening night, and he was nervous. On Chiriya he had seen many terrible storms roar across the ocean, hurricane-force winds that whipped the flat island and tore the roofs off of houses. Fishing boats in the coves had to be tied securely or dragged to safety up on the shore.

He had never been through a storm at sea, but he could smell danger in the air. Sharp bursts of breezes tried to rip the breath from his lungs. He didn't like the look of the clouds or the feel of the winds.

The off-duty sailors had gone belowdecks to play games in the lantern-lit gloom. Some men swung in their hammocks, trying to sleep as the *Wavewalker* lurched from side to side; others puked into buckets, which they emptied out the open ports.

Bannon was startled when three shapes loomed up beside him on the deck, lean men who stood shirtless even in the blowing wind and pelting droplets of cold rain. Sol, the leader of the wishpearl divers, held a pot covered with a wooden lid. "The cook is finished serving supper."

Though he was queasy from the rocking deck, Bannon's mouth watered. He hadn't eaten all day. "Is that for me?"

Rom scowled at him. "No, you'll get your own meal when your watch is over. But the cook wanted to make sure the sorceress ate."

Bannon frowned. "He's never done that before."

"We've never had a storm like this before," Elgin said. "Best for the two passengers to stay in their cabins. If the fools walk around in the rain and wind, they might fall overboard, and the captain wants to be sure they pay him a bonus when we get into port."

Bannon nodded. That made sense.

"We already delivered a meal to the wizard, but the sorceress . . ." Sol looked away, as if in shame. "She knows we've been unkind to her, insulted her." He thrust the pot into Bannon's hands. "Better if you deliver dinner personally."

Rom nodded. "Yes, it would be awkward if the three of us did it."

"Awkward," Elgin agreed.

Bannon was skeptical. He'd never seen the wishpearl divers run errands for the cook before. But most of the sailors were belowdecks, after all. And the divers rarely did any work, so he was glad to see them cooperate. Maybe the deaths of their comrades had given them a change of heart.

Besides, Bannon was glad for the opportunity to bring Nicci her dinner. "I'll take it," he said.

CHAPTER 13

As the ship rocked in the sway of the increasing storm, Nicci looked at the pot Bannon had delivered to her cabin. She lifted the wooden lid and sniffed.

"It's fish chowder," Bannon said, happy to be of service. He caught himself against the door of her cabin as the ship lurched, but his smile didn't fade. "The cook wanted to make sure you ate."

"I will eat." Nicci had not intended to venture out into the wind-lashed night to make her way to the galley. The young man was so eager, so solicitous; if she did not accept the food, she knew he would only continue to pester her. "Thank you."

"I'm on watch. I have to get back to my duties." Bannon obviously wanted to chat with her, hoping she would ask him to stay for a few more moments.

"Yes, you have to get back to your duties." Nicci took the pot in a swirl of savory, fishy aromas, and when the young man awkwardly retreated, she closed the flimsy cabin door.

Her room had plank bulkheads, a washbasin, a narrow shuttered porthole, and a tiny shelf. A hard narrow bunk with a woolen blanket served as her bed, and a small oil lamp illuminated her quarters with a flickering flame.

Sitting on the bunk, Nicci lifted the pot's lid and used a splintered wooden spoon to stir the milky broth. Chunks of fish floated amid wilted herbs, gnarled tubers, and pieces of onion. She ate. The taste was sour, flavored with unfamiliar spices.

When serving Emperor Jagang, Nicci had traveled the Old World, eaten many strange cuisines, and sampled flavors that only a starving woman could enjoy. This stew was one of those, possibly because the milk had curdled in the broth. But she needed the nourishment. This was food, nothing more.

The hull creaked and shifted as the ship felt the pressure of the waves and the building wind. Finished with her meal, she turned the key in her oil lamp to retract the wick and extinguish the flame. In her cramped cabin she had only the darkness and the sounds of a struggling ship for company.

She lay back on her narrow bunk, trying to sleep, feeling her insides churn much like the waves outside. Before long, she wrapped the blanket around herself, shivering. The shivers became more violent. Her muscles clenched, her head began to pound.

Within an hour she knew that the chowder was poisoned. Not just spoiled, but containing some deadly substance. She should have known. She should have been more wary. Others had tried to kill her before, many others.

But she found it incomprehensible that *Bannon* would poison her. No, she couldn't believe it. The simple, eager young man was not a schemer, not a traitor. She had trusted the food because *he* had delivered it.

But he could have been duped himself.

Nicci curled up, panting hard, trying to squeeze out the fire in her gut. Sweat blossomed on her skin, and her shivers became so severe they were like convulsions. Her insides roiled as if someone had plunged a barbed spear into her stomach and twirled it, twisting her intestines until she feared they might be torn out, like what remained of the wishpearl diver.

Barely able to see or think, she slid off her bunk and swayed on weak legs. Her knees nearly buckled, but she clutched the joined planks of the bulkhead. Her head spun. She retched, as if some invisible hand had reached down her throat and was trying to pull out her insides.

Slumping against the wall of her cabin, Nicci was so unsteady that she barely noticed the *Wavewalker* shuddering in the heavy seas. Her vision blurred, but the cabin was so dark she couldn't see anyway. Her muscles felt like wet rags.

Nicci needed to find help—needed to get to Nathan. She could think of no one else. Maybe the wizard would be able to purge the poison, heal any damage. But she couldn't find the door. Her entire cabin was spinning.

She retched again—this time vomiting all over the floor—but the poison had already set in. She tried to call upon enough of her own magic to strengthen herself, at least to get out of this trap, but she was too dizzy. Her thoughts spun like a wheel edged with jagged razors.

She had to get out, had to find her way onto the deck, where she hoped the fresh, cold air would revive her.

She felt along the walls of her cabin, forced herself to focus, knowing she would find the door if she just kept moving. How could she be lost in such a cramped space? She encountered the small shelf and held on to it, placing so much weight on it that the nails ripped loose from the planks and came crashing down. She collapsed, and crawled across the deck, her hand slipping in the wet pool of her vomit. When she found her bunk again, Nicci was able to pull herself to her feet. Finding the wall, she worked her way around the cabin, one agonizing step at a time.

The deck kept heaving, but she needed to find the way out. She knew it was here . . . somewhere close.

Her cabin door burst open as someone pushed it inward. Nicci reeled back and barely caught her balance as she saw three men crowded in the doorway. She knew that Bannon was on watch, Nathan was in his cabin, and the rest of the *Wavewalker*'s crew were huddled belowdecks, hiding from the storm.

Nicci was here all alone.

The three wishpearl divers faced her. Rom carried a small lamp turned down low, so they could make their way along the corridor. They were still shirtless, and the unsteady lamplight cast dark shadows that chiseled their muscles. Their loose trousers had been cinched tight around their waists—and in her distorted vision, Nicci saw that Sol was aroused, his manhood poking against the fabric like a short, hard harpoon.

She retreated a step deeper into her cabin. Her knees wobbled, and her weak helplessness made Sol burst out in laughter. The other two divers joined him in their husky chuckles. "The sorceress appears to be under the weather," said Elgin, then snickered at his own joke.

"She'll be under *me* in a minute," said Sol. He pushed his way into the cabin with the other two close behind him. "You'll be too sick to fight or use your evil magic, bitch, and after we're done with you, you'll be too sore and exhausted to move."

"Go," Nicci managed, and forced herself to add, "last chance."

"I get the first chance," said Sol. "These two can take their turns afterward."

With a careless gesture, he knocked Nicci backward onto her bunk. The muscular man stood over her, slammed her shoulders down against the wadded blanket, and fumbled with her breasts. She pushed at his hands, tried to claw them. Even though she was sick and unable to find her magic, Nicci's nails were sufficient weapons, and she ripped deep gouges in his forearm. Sol slapped her hard across the face, and her head slammed against the pallet. Nicci reeled, but the physical blow was no worse than what the poison was doing inside her.

Sol managed to yank down the front of her dress to expose her breasts. "Bring the lamp, Rom. I want to see these."

The three men leered down, laughing. Sol said, "Pink nipples, just like I thought! It's good to see for myself after dreaming about them for days." He put a paw over her left breast, crushing down, squeezing hard.

Nicci fought against the poison, delved deep into her mind, and struggled to find her strength. She had been raped before, not just by Jagang, but countless times by his soldiers when he had forced her to serve in their tents, to be a toy as punishment . . . as training. The powerful emperor had been able to force her—but these worthless men were not dream walkers. They were not emperors. They were disgusting.

Anger made Nicci's blood burn. Whatever it was, the poison was just a chemical, and her magic was more potent than that. She was a

Sister of the Dark. She possessed the abilities she had stolen from wizards she had killed. She could summon a ball of wizard's fire and incinerate all three of these men, but that might also engulf the *Wavewalker* in fire.

No, she had to fight them in a different way, a direct way. A more personal way.

Grunting, Sol fumbled with the string on his trousers, loosening the fabric at his waist. He pulled his pants loose to expose his meaty shaft.

"For all your bluster," Nicci managed to say, "I expected something larger."

Elgin and Rom cackled. Sol slapped her again, then grabbed her thighs, pushing her legs apart.

It had happened so many times before. She had been powerless. She had been forced to endure.

But Nicci didn't have to endure now. Even weak, even poisoned, she was stronger than these scum. She was better than they were. She felt flickers of fire within her hands, not much more than the little flame Nathan had summoned on the windy deck. But it was enough.

She clapped her burning hands against Sol's naked shoulders, searing his skin. He howled and lurched back. Nicci released more magic into the fire in her palms, but it flickered and weakened.

The wishpearl divers backed away in fear. "She still has her magic."

"Not enough of it," Sol growled and came back at her.

Normally, calling fire was not difficult, but she had seen Nathan struggle with his powers, too. Still, she knew even more straightforward spells. She could move the air, stir currents, create breezes. Now, she summoned air in the confined cabin, not just as wind, but as a *fist*.

The invisible blow shoved Sol away from her, and he was so startled that his erection drooped. The other two men were still stiff, bulges poking prominently against the fabric of their pants, though the arousal probably stemmed as much from the promise of violence as from the anticipation of physical pleasure.

Sol recovered himself. "Bitch, you'll lie back and—"

Nicci ignored the poison, ignored the dizziness, ignored the sickness raging through her. She called on the air again, focused it, pushed it, forming a weapon.

The storm outside blew with greater fury, and winds lashed against the *Wavewalker*. Sizzling, splattering rain came down so loud outside that no one could hear her struggles inside the cabin. But if she made these men scream loudly enough, someone would hear.

Nicci manipulated the air, shaping it like a hand . . . and then a fist. She used it to clutch the testicles between Sol's legs.

He cried out in sudden alarm.

Nicci created two more hands of air that seized the sacs of the other two wishpearl divers. They cried out, flailing their hands against the invisible grip.

"I warned you." She rose up from the pallet, not caring that her breasts were still exposed, and she glared at the three with her blue eyes. "I warned you—now choose. Do you want them torn off, or just crushed?"

His face a mask of red fury, Sol lunged toward her. Nicci manipulated the air to tighten her hold around his scrotum, and then twisted as if she were wrenching off the lid of a jar. She contracted her air fist with sudden force—but not so swiftly that she couldn't feel each of his testicles squeeze until it popped like a rotten grape. Sol let out a high wail that could not begin to express his pain.

Giving the men no chance to beg, because she had no interest in mercy, Nicci crushed the testicles of the other two, leaving them moaning, whimpering, and unable to manage much of a scream as they fell to the floor of her cabin.

"I think you would rather I killed you." Nicci pulled the front of her dress back up to cover herself. "I can always change my mind and come back." Standing straight on her wobbly legs, she glared down at the writhing men. "Even poisoned, I'm better than you."

She didn't have time to clean up the garbage, though, before the main attack struck the ship.

CHAPTER 14

The air-breathing thieves drifted overhead in their great ship, vulnerable at the boundary between the water-home and the sky. The dark hulk cut across the waves high above, aloof but not unreachable. The interface was choppy and stirred, indicating a turbulent storm on the surface. The fragile creatures up there would be fighting for their lives against the wind and rain, but down here, the water was calm and warm—peaceful. A true home.

The selka were not the ones who had declared war.

The stirring currents carried the faintest echoes from the raging storm. The selka queen could taste the difference in the delicate flavors of salt as water flowed through the fine gill slits at her neck. Though the selka were far from the reef labyrinth where they kept their precious treasure, the queen could still taste the bitter, alien taint of humans in the water.

She swam faster than a shark, stroking along with webbed hands, her beautiful smooth skin sliding through the water. Behind the queen, like a school of predator fish swimming in formation, came her selka army. Enraged, they swooped through the currents with their fin-sharp bodies and claws that could mangle a kraken. The selka queen had proven herself in undersea battle many times, gutting a hammerhead with her hands, spilling its entrails in clouds of murky blood. As a people, the selka remembered the days of great human wars from thousands of years ago . . . when their race had been created. Those were times of legend, times of enslavement.

Selka history told of how human wizards had tortured and modified unwilling subjects, turning vulnerable swimmers into lethal aquatic weapons to fight in their wars. Back then, the selka had been terrors of the sea, sinking entire enemy navies.

But that had been long ago, and the air-breathing wizard masters had forgotten about the selka. Their discarded warriors—former humans, now changed and improved—had withdrawn into the deep cold waters, building homes in the reefs and on the seabeds. The selka were a free people now, frolicking, mating, exploring. They had their own civilization, unknown to the air breathers, undisturbed and at peace.

Until the humans intruded, until the thieves wrecked the reef labyrinths, took away those things most precious to the selka, losses that could never be recovered. All those dreams . . .

The selka had killed and devoured two of the thieves that swam down to take the wishpearls. They had seized those divers, holding them down. The queen knew that the weak air breathers would drown soon enough, expended air boiling out of their exhausted lungs, but such a quiet death was not a sufficient price for them to pay. With her long claws the queen had torn open the throat of the first diver, watching red blood gush out in an explosion of bubbles.

The second diver had struggled to escape from the selka soldiers, but he was weak, unable to squirm away. As her people closed in to drink the flowing blood from the first victim's gaping neck wound, the selka queen saw the wide-eyed terror of the second victim, watched his last breath of air gasp out in terrified astonishment. Before the light could dim from his eyes, she tore open his throat as well and let her people feed.

It was a beginning—and it was not enough.

From the shape of the ship's hull overhead and the lingering taste that its barnacled wood left in the water, the selka queen knew this was the same vessel that had robbed the reef labyrinth several times. She knew it would come back, and therefore they must stop it. Perhaps if they killed the entire crew and sank the wooden ship, this one battle would be enough. The humans might be wise enough to stay away.

Perhaps . . . perhaps not. And then it would be all-out war.

Her people were hungry for blood. Human blood had a sharper, brighter taste than fish, and tonight the selka would feed well.

She arced upward, stroking toward the vessel that hung overhead. All told, more than a hundred of her people swarmed up to the hull and grasped the slimy wood with their clawed hands. Kicking and stroking, they emerged into the hostile air and scaled the side of the ship.

A s she stepped over them, Nicci ignored the three moaning, emas-culated men on the floorboards wallowing in her vomit just inside her cabin. She still felt weak from the poison, but she took satisfaction from the fact that she had permanently disarmed the would-be rapists. She left them entirely behind.

The *Wavewalker* shuddered in the throes of the storm, and Nicci stumbled against the wall of the narrow corridor as she tried to make her way to Nathan's cabin. She wondered if the old wizard had heard the men's screams, but the howling storm and the lashing wind were so loud she could barely think. Her skull pounded. Suddenly, Nicci doubled over, retching onto the deck. She hoped the wizard could help her, draw out the poison and spill it into the open air.

When she reached his cabin, though, Nicci found the door ajar. He had gone out on deck into the whipping wind and the spray of waves. When she emerged outside, cold raindrops slapped her face, but the frigid shock braced her. The wind flung her hair in all directions. She sucked in a breath and shouted Nathan's name.

She saw him clinging to a ratline at the base of the mizzenmast. His long white hair hung like wet ropes down past his shoulders. He had wrapped himself in an oilskin cloak, but the storm blew so hard that he was surely drenched. His face was drawn, his expression queasy, and Nicci wondered if the wizard had been poisoned as well. More likely, Nathan was just seasick. He wore his sword at his side, as if to battle the rain.

Nicci stepped onto the wave-washed deck, as if drawing energy from the storm to drive away the lingering effects of the poison. Her black dress was soaked, but she kept her balance. She made her way along by grabbing a ratline to hold herself steady as the ship plunged into the trough of a wave and then rose up again in a sickening lurch.

When Nathan saw her, his face split in a broad grin. "You look ill, Sorceress. The storm is not to your liking?"

"Poison is not to my liking," she shouted back into the howling noise. "But I'll recover. Unfortunately, Captain Eli will have to find new wishpearl divers." She said nothing more.

Nathan gave a small nod as he drew his own conclusions. "I'm sure you took care of them as was necessary."

Whitecaps foamed over the bow, spilling like a slop bucket across the deck. Several supply barrels broke loose from their ropes, rolled down the deck, smashed into the side wall, and bounced up and overboard to be lost in the waves.

Nathan caught himself on a rope and held on, then let out a disconcerting laugh as he straightened. "A good storm and a surly crew make for a fine adventure, don't you think?"

Nicci tried to quell the pain that echoed through her skull, the knotting in her stomach. "I'm not doing this for adventure, but for Lord Rahl and his empire."

"I thought you were supposed to save the world."

"That is what the witch woman thinks." She hunched as another spasm twisted her gut. "I will let Richard save the world in his own way."

The watch lookout had lashed himself to the platform for safety, but he maintained his post to scan for rocks, reefs, or an unexpected coastline. The swaying of the ship made his high perch like the end of an inverted pendulum, and he held on for dear life.

The storm clouds knotted tighter over the night sky, like a strangler's garrote. Flashes of lightning illuminated the sea and the rigging with jagged slices of liquid silver.

When Nicci heard a familiar shout, she shielded her eyes from the rain to see a drenched Bannon descending from the yardarm on the mainmast. He carried his sword, as if he might find enemies in the sky. It was an impractical choice, but the young man took the blade wherever he went. Nathan watched his young protégé with a measure of pride and incredulity.

Halfway down the mast, Bannon stared out at the roiling sea and yelled something unintelligible. He pointed frantically.

When another large wave crashed against the ship, the *Wavewalker* tilted at an extreme angle. Water rolled across the deck, sweeping away ropes, crates, and broken debris. One young sailor was caught unawares and slipped from his anchor point on the rail. He tumbled and rolled, scrabbling with his hands until he caught a precarious perch, holding on.

Nicci tried to gather her control of the air and wind, just enough to catch the hapless sailor, to save him. Then she spotted what had struck such a look of terror on Bannon's face from his high perch.

Just as the clinging sailor lost his grip and was about to fly over the edge in the curling wash of water, a *creature* climbed over the rail and caught him, a humanlike figure with clawed, webbed hands. The panicked young sailor grabbed for anything, any hope of rescue, and the thing snagged him. The pale-skinned creature grabbed the sailor's striped shirt and seized his wet brown hair with the other hand.

For a moment it seemed as if the slimy thing had saved him—but then it opened a mouth full of sharp, triangular teeth and bit down on the side of the seaman's head, taking away half of his face and the top of his skull. As the sailor screamed and struggled, the monster tore open his throat, then cast the body onto the deck, discarding its victim in a wash of blood and seawater.

Nicci knew instinctively what they were. "Selka," she whispered. "They must be selka."

Sailors on deck shouted an alarm as a dozen more slick figures scrambled from the depths, climbing the *Wavewalker*'s hull to swarm the decks.

CHAPTER 15

The invading creatures were sleek and smooth, with muscles rippling beneath their gray-green skin. Nicci remembered Nathan's story that the selka had been human once, tortured and reshaped into a race of aquatic warriors. These things, though, looked as if they had forgotten their humanity long ago.

They opened their slit mouths wide, gasping in the rain-lashed air, to reveal rows of triangular fangs. A filmy membrane covered their large eyes, and pupil slits widened to encompass the few hardy sailors on duty. A serrated fin ran from the hairless head down the spine, and frills of swimming fins adorned their forearms and legs.

The *Wavewalker* was vulnerable, caught in the fierce storm. The sailors could barely survive the weather's fury, and now deadly sea people swarmed aboard. Shouting for help, crewmen scrambled across the deck to find harpoons and boat hooks for weapons.

Three selka skittered forward like the flash of fish in a brook. The veteran sailor Karl grabbed a harpoon and swung the wooden shaft with a grunt to defend himself, but he had inadvertently seized the harpoon whose point was eaten away by jellyfish acid, rendering the weapon little more than a club. Karl fought nevertheless. He smashed the face of one selka, flattening its smooth head. Its gill slits flapped, oozing blood.

The other two creatures were upon Karl. The big seaman punched and struggled, but one selka held him down while the second ripped open his chest, splitting the sternum and peeling his ribs apart. Together, the selka dug into the gaping wound and yanked out his slippery organs as Karl shrieked into the raging winds.

Nicci stood her ground by the door to the stern deck, still trying to drive back her disorientation as she searched for magic inside her, any kind of spell that would let her fight. The poison had debilitated her, and she had just exerted herself to defeat Sol and his vile companions. She was in no shape to attack.

Nevertheless, she clutched at shreds of power inside her, trying to summon a fireball, but the winds tore around her. A cold, wet backwash dashed into her face, disrupting her concentration. Flinging salt water out of her eyes, she used her anger to bring focus, and fire blossomed in her right hand. Finally. She felt a rush of relief.

A male selka prowled toward her, its slitted eyes focused on her. The creature lunged just as Nicci hurled the fireball, which splattered against its slimy chest. The flames burned and bubbled its skin, and the selka hooted a strange resonant cry that echoed through flapping gill slits in its neck. Mortally wounded, the selka staggered away and collapsed on the deck.

Bannon managed to swing himself down from the ratlines, holding his sword. He looked terrified, but ready to fight. When he tried to make his way over to the wizard and the sorceress, Nathan spotted him. His voice was hard, grim. "Remember what I taught you, my boy!"

Dozens more selka swarmed over the side of the ship and fell upon the sailors. Two burly men stood side by side, jabbing and slashing with the serrated iron spear points of harpoons. They sliced open slime-covered hides, wounding three attackers—but fifteen more fell upon them. The men kept stabbing with their harpoons until clawed hands tore the weapons out of their grasp; then the selka turned the weapons upon the sailors in a feeding and killing frenzy.

Bannon tottered forward on the rocking deck, trying to keep his balance while he swung his lackluster sword against the monsters. Sturdy's edge was sharp, and he took off the arm of one attacker, then swung backward to chop the neck of another, nearly cutting off its head.

A selka rushed toward Bannon from behind, webbed hands outstretched, but Nicci summoned another fireball and hurled it at the creature's head. The flames struck home, and its flesh steamed and exploded. Shrieking, the thing dove overboard, ignoring its victim.

Bannon whirled, blinking in astonishment, and shouted an unintelligible thanks to Nicci.

As the sailors kept yelling for reinforcements, some of the off-duty crew threw open a deck hatch and emerged from below. Seeing the swarming creatures, the crew shouted to rouse the sailors in the lower decks. Rallied at last, the men grabbed whatever weapons they could find and boiled up out of the hatch to defend the ship.

But when the disoriented seamen climbed into the open storm, hissing selka converged on the hatch. The next sailor up was a tall, thin man who had been adept at patching sails. As soon as he popped his head up into the air, a selka slipped claws beneath his chin, hooked into his jawbone, and lifted him like a fish on a line. The man dangled by his head, and his arms and legs jittered spasmodically as the monsters gutted him, letting his blood spill down onto the other sailors trying to climb up. The selka discarded the body and then poured down the ladder, invading the lower decks where the crew members were trapped—and slaughtered.

Four attackers stalked forward as rain slashed down and salt water scoured the deck. Nicci stood firm, defiant, despite the roiling dizziness inside her. She felt the rage within, and reminded herself that she had been a Sister of the Dark, that she had stolen magic from many wizards. Even weakened by the poison, she was more powerful than any foe these creatures had ever seen.

The wind howled, and she pulled energy from it, reshaped it, brought the storm closer. As the selka attacked her and Nathan, she pushed back, throwing a battering ram of air. The blow knocked six creatures up over the ship's rail, high into the air, and flung them far out to sea.

Striding forward, Nathan raised both hands, trying to summon a blast of his own magic. She could tell by his stance and his intent expression that he must be calling on a powerful spell. As ten more aquatic attackers climbed aboard the *Wavewalker,* Nathan gestured to fling a magical bombardment at them—and his face filled with a perplexed expression when nothing happened. He waved his hands again to no effect, and the selka surged toward him, undeterred.

"Nathan!" Nicci shouted.

The old wizard kept trying to summon magic, but failed. He seemed too confused to be afraid.

Just in time, Bannon leaped next to him, swinging his sword to hack into the nearest selka. As that one collapsed, he stabbed a second one, offering a dark grin to the wizard. "I'll save you if you need it."

Nathan looked at his empty hand in confusion. "I'm not supposed to need it."

Nicci wondered if the wizard had also been poisoned. She trembled dizzily. Her last spell had left her spent, but Nicci could not afford to be spent—there were still too many attackers.

A blond sailor picked up an empty barrel and threw it at a selka. The creature grappled with him just as a large wave smashed into the deck, sweeping both overboard. The sailor went under, and Nicci never saw him resurface in the churning cauldron of waves.

Captain Eli burst out of his stateroom, screaming commands to his men. "Selka!" he cried, as if he had encountered them before. "Damn you, leave my ship alone!" He had brought his cutlass and a long rod that he used for clouting unruly sailors. With a weapon in each hand, he marched forward to meet the attackers.

Identifying the captain, the selka closed in on him, but he stood his ground on the wet deck. As the creatures came forward, the captain struck sideways with his long rod and slashed wildly with his sword in the other hand.

The cutlass lopped off a webbed hand at the wrist, and he hacked and clubbed, driving the selka back, but more closed in around him. His rod flattened slimy faces, broke sharp teeth, but selka hands snatched at him. Finally, one seized the club and tore it from his grasp.

Outnumbered, the captain kept fighting with his cutlass, slicing and chopping the attackers, but one of the selka took up the club he had lost and used the hard rod to strike Captain Eli's wrist, shattering his forearm. He gasped in pain, no longer able to hold his sword, and the curved blade clattered to the deck.

Unable to fight, the captain retreated into the chart room, nursing his broken arm. He barricaded the door, but the selka made short work of it, splintering the wood before flooding into the chamber. Captain Eli's screams were quickly followed by the sounds of shattered glass from the stern windows. Hurled out into the night, the man's body floundered into the roiling wake of the ship. The sea creatures dove after him to have their feast before he could drown.

As the storm surged and Nathan struggled unsuccessfully to call on his gift, Nicci used every trick she knew, summoning a tangled combination of Additive and Subtractive Magic to draw bolts of black lightning. The first blast lashed one selka through the heart, leaving a smoking crater.

Beside her, Nathan looked bleak. "The magic . . . I can't find my magic! It's gone." He raised his hand again to work a spell, curling his fingers. His azure eyes filled with fury, but with no result. "It's gone!"

Nicci had no time to understand what was wrong with him. Desperate, she managed to call up a deadly gout of wizard's fire. When the crackling ball boiled in her hand, she released it. The wizard's fire swelled like a comet in the air and engulfed four selka that had cornered a lone sailor. The sailor's screams changed, then ended abruptly along with their hissing, writhing shrieks as the deadly incineration erased them all.

But the uncontrolled wizard's fire kept sizzling across the deck, charring a stack of barrels, and setting the deck and hull boards on fire. The magical incendiary kept burning, but the pounding rain and waves eventually doused the relentless fire.

Nicci sagged, not sure how much more energy she possessed, though she needed to keep fighting, because the selka kept coming.

Three weak and wretched men staggered out of the doorway from the cabins in the stern deck. The shirtless wishpearl divers walked with agonized scissorlike steps, blinded and disoriented. Sol, Elgin, and Rom could barely move, and they certainly couldn't fight.

But the men were not entirely useless. At least they provided a moment's diversion for the attacking selka.

When two sea creatures closed around the divers, Sol's eyes were filled with pain and blood. He reached out, as if he didn't realize that the selka was not one of his shipmates. The aquatic creature wrapped a webbed hand around his throat, slamming him against the wall as it grabbed his lower abdomen with its other hand. A hooked claw dug deep into Sol's pubic bone and slowly curled upward to slice through the man's groin all the way up to the base of his throat, like the knife of a fisherman gutting his catch. Sol's entrails spilled out like wet, tangled ropes. As he collapsed, the selka passed him into the arms of another creature, who pulled him open wider, then dug pointed teeth into Sol's chest cavity and began to eat his heart.

More creatures grabbed a gibbering Elgin, who slapped uselessly with his bare hands as the monsters ripped him open as well and tossed him aside for the other creatures to devour.

The third diver, Rom, turned and tried to flee, but the selka grabbed him from behind and sliced open his back, prying loose his entire spine with a few ribs still attached. After uprooting the vertebrae from his body, the creatures dropped the jellylike bag of skin and meat to the deck.

Giving up on trying to fight with magic, Nathan tore his ornate sword from its scabbard and held it up, defying the sea people. Standing shoulder-to-shoulder with Bannon, the two men attacked the monstrous creatures. With a fixed and brutal expression, Bannon swung Sturdy like a woodcutter hacking his way through a thicket.

For his own part, the wizard embraced his new role of swordsman. He threw off his rain slicker for freedom of movement and swung his blade in a graceful arc, catching one of the monsters under the chin and cutting its throat all the way back to the neck bone. He spun with a downsweep that cleaved through the shoulder and the chest of another.

While Nicci recovered from unleashing her wizard's fire, two selka closed in on her. She summoned enough energy to shove them aside with a barricade of air, but she couldn't call sufficient force to knock them overboard. Within moments, the selka came back, angrier now, and she faced them, ready to do whatever she had to do.

A panicked sailor scrambled up the ratlines, trying to climb to escape. He reached the yardarm on the mainmast, then pulled himself to the dubious safety of the lookout platform. When the attacking selka saw him unprotected up there, they swarmed up the ropes, closing in, and the man had nowhere to run.

With a loud and startling crack, a natural bolt of lightning struck the topyard, shivering the entire mast into splinters, and throwing the sailor from the platform. His smoking body was already limp as it crashed into the water out of sight.

The blast also scattered the climbing selka. Falling, one grabbed on to the furled mainsail, pulling on the unrolled canvas and slicing the fabric with its claws. With a groan, the smoking, splintered mast toppled forward, crashing into the rigging and snapping the *Wavewalker*'s foremast as well.

When Nathan gaped in dismay at the disaster, one of the creatures sprang on him from behind, grabbing his back and tearing his fine new shirt. Bannon ran his sword sideways through the selka's ribs, skewering it. He used all of his strength to tear the dying creature from the wizard, stomped on its slimy chest, and yanked his sword back out.

"Thank you, my boy," Nathan said in disbelief.

"You taught me well," Bannon said.

Nicci dredged deep for another scrap of energy to create a second ball of wizard's fire, but she knew it wouldn't be enough.

Bannon's expression fell as he looked toward the bow. "Sweet Sea Mother, they keep coming!"

CHAPTER 16

Storm waves slid across the deck, but even that wasn't enough to wash away the blood of the slaughtered sailors. The attacking selka devoured their victims, fighting over hearts and livers, gnawing through arms and legs.

Nicci summoned another branch of blue-black lightning that lashed the selka like a cat-o'-nine tails. The stench of roasting meat and coppery blood was mixed with a powerful odor of burnt, salty slime.

After releasing her lightning, though, Nicci reeled, barely able to keep her balance as she continued to fight off nausea and the hammering pain in her head. When she staggered back to recover her strength, Nathan defended her against more oncoming creatures. Although the wizard's magic had been rendered impotent, his sword remained deadly.

Wild and reckless, Bannon stabbed and slashed, but forgot to protect his flank. A selka dove in and raked a long cut down Bannon's left thigh, although before the creature could do more damage, Nathan leaped in and decapitated the thing. The selka's face stared up as it rolled, the thick-lipped mouth reflexively opening and closing to show its pointed teeth. Nathan kicked the severed head over the side of the boat as if it were a ball in a game of Ja'La.

When Nicci sensed a change come over the attackers, she looked toward the bow as one creature more magnificent than the others climbed over the rail. The selka was obviously female, and a flush of leopardlike spots swirled along her slick greenish body. The other selka turned to regard their queen with reverence.

Even with the howling wind, crashing waves, and creaking timbers, a hush settled over the *Wavewalker*. The selka queen stood at the bow, her back turned to the carved wooden figurehead of the beautiful Sea Mother. The queen spoke in an eerie, warbling voice, as if she had not spoken words in the air—or words in the normal language of humankind—in her entire life. "Thieves must die. Your blood cannot pay for the damage you've caused."

Nathan shouted, "We have stolen nothing."

Bannon's eyes went wide, as if he suddenly understood the answer. And then Nicci knew as well. "The wishpearls," she said.

The selka queen said, "Wishpearls are the seeds of our dreams. Teardrops of our essence, our greatest treasure. The selka are no longer part of your race, no longer part of your world. We have come to take our dreams back. Our pearls."

The dead bodies of sailors on deck far outnumbered sailors who remained alive. The ship itself was nearly destroyed, its mainmast toppled, the foremast smashed, and fires smoldered in the wreckage of sails and snapped yardarms. Vicious selka swarmed below, ransacking the lower decks and the cargo hold. More screams accompanied a clash of swords and clubs, until the last sailors defending the lower decks were also killed.

Through the large open hatch, Nicci could hear the desperate lowing of the milk cow rise to a crescendo then fall silent. Before long, three selka returned to the deck, carrying large hunks of raw, bloody meat to offer their queen.

As the female creature glared at Nicci, Bannon, and Nathan crowded together in mutual defense, two burly selka climbed back to the open deck. They hefted a wooden chest that they had found behind locked doors in the cargo hold, and now they dropped it with a crash in front of the regal creature. The queen's eye slits widened as her followers tore off the lid with such force that they ripped the hinges entirely off and splintered the wooden sides.

The chest was full of wishpearls harvested only days before.

Staring down at the treasure, the inhuman queen scooped the pearls in her webbed hands and held them up as if they were the raindrops of miracles. She raised her alien face to let out a hissing cry. "The seeds of our dreams!"

The queen cast the pearls back into the water, returning them to the sea. She picked up more wishpearls and gently, lovingly, scattered them into the raging ocean, as if she were planting a crop. She continued until she had emptied the entire chest.

As if hearing an unspoken command, the selka redoubled their attack and threw themselves upon the last desperate sailors aboard the *Wavewalker*.

Bannon and Nathan crouched on either side of Nicci, holding their swords and ready to fight to the death. As the attackers came toward them, Nicci opened herself to her magic, called upon everything she had learned, and stolen, from other wizards. Even though she had little left within her, she nevertheless managed to summon more wizard's fire, a desperate act. A small blazing sphere appeared in her hands, which she augmented with normal fire, then an even brighter halo of illusion. To the selka, it appeared as if she held a sun in her hands.

The crackling globe of wizard's fire hung ready, but Nicci kept it as her last defense. Once she used it, she doubted she would have any flicker of magic left with which to attack. But Nicci didn't need magic. She had taken a knife from one of the fallen sailors, and she would keep fighting.

The selka queen strode forward to face them. The rest of her warriors snarled and gurgled. Nicci lifted her wizard's fire into the standoff. "With this, I can kill most of you, including the queen. Would you like to taste my fire?"

The female creature was terrifying and magnificent. As the sea people pressed closer, several seemed curious about Bannon, their gill slits flickering. The queen fixed her slitted eyes on the young man. "We know you," she finally said. "We saved you. Once. Why did you come back?"

"We didn't mean any harm." He blinked at her, covered with blood. Claw marks and gashes marked his skin and face, and his sword dripped with blood and slime from the selka he had killed. He said in a whisper of dismay, "I thought the selka were magical. I called on you to save me when I was younger. But now I see you're just monsters."

A flush suffused the leopard spots on the female creature, and the frills of her bodily fins extended. "*We* are the monsters?"

From below, a loud cracking sound rumbled through the deck, a sickening, destructive blow to the hull. The selka were breaking the ship. Storm lightning shattered the sky again.

The queen turned to Nicci, who refused to flinch. Her crackling ball of fire reflected off of the slick greenish skin of the creatures. Even with all the selka they had killed, more than sixty remained to face them.

All the other sailors aboard had been murdered, and even if she used her ball of wizard's fire, Nicci knew she would kill some, but not enough, of the creatures. Then she remembered.

Nicci fished in the fabric of her dress, found the hidden pocket, and withdrew the wishpearl Bannon had given her just after their departure from Tanimura. It felt cold in her fingertips. One last wishpearl, probably the last aboard the ship. *The seeds of our dreams.*

She held it up in the fingers of her free hand, and the selka queen hissed. The other creatures reacted, simmering, ready to lunge forward even with the threatening ball of magical fire Nicci held.

While the selka watched her intently, Nicci threw the wishpearl as far out to sea as she could, and the storm-churned waves quickly swallowed it. "Let the fish have my wishes," she said. "I make my own life."

The selka queen watched her with respect and finally announced, "Maybe *you* are not thieves." She turned to the remaining creatures in her army. "We are finished."

The blood-spattered selka grabbed some of the remaining human corpses and dragged them overboard into the raging sea. Others took the bodies of the slain selka with them.

At the splintered side wall of the ship, the selka queen faced Nicci for a long moment, staring at the threat of the wizard's fire, before she turned and dove overboard in a perfectly graceful arc. The rest of her people joined her, abandoning the *Wavewalker.*

They left Nicci, Bannon, and Nathan alone as the storm finished the destruction that the selka had begun.

CHAPTER 17

The *Wavewalker* had been mortally wounded. Two of her masts were broken, and the torn sails whipped about like spectral streamers. The battle with the selka had smashed the vessel's bow, torn the ropes and the rigging. The deck boards were splintered, and an even greater slaughter had taken place in the lower decks. The smell of blood and offal wafted up from the open hatches.

Nicci and her companions stood together, the only survivors on the ship, tense and waiting for some renewed attack from the undersea creatures. Unable to maintain the flow of magic, she finally let the manifested sphere of wizard's fire dissipate in her hand. She hoped they were safe from further attack, even though the selka queen had made no promises. As the fireball faded, she heaved a deep breath and clung to the tattered remnant of a ratline to keep her balance.

As the *Wavewalker* rode up on the high crest of a wave and crashed down again, they were all thrown to their knees.

"Sorry I couldn't help you during the battle, Sorceress." Nathan sounded both baffled and afraid. He looked at his hands. "I could not find the magic inside me. I tried to summon spells I've used all my life, even simple ones. I couldn't do them."

"It was the heat of the battle. You couldn't concentrate," Bannon said. "But your sword proved deadly enough. You saved me."

"Oh, more than once, I expect." Nathan forced an unlikely smile. "But you saved me as well. We made a decent accounting of ourselves." His shoulders rose and fell, and he turned to Nicci again. "Try as I might, I couldn't touch my Han." He reached up, ran his fingers gingerly along his neck. "Is there an iron collar I can't see? An invisible Rada'Han placed on me to prevent me from using my powers?"

Nicci knew full well how the Sisters in the Palace of the Prophets had controlled their gifted male students through the use of an iron collar, which blocked them from using the force of life. Nathan had worn such a collar for much of his life as a captive prophet, and Richard had been forced to wear one when he was taken for training by the Sisters.

"I'm not aware of any outside force neutralizing your gift, Wizard," Nicci said as they stood back up. "But you were losing your magic earlier, even before the selka arrived. You couldn't even summon a flame as a trick to show Bannon."

Nathan hung his head. "Dear spirits, I knew I'd lost my gift of prophecy, but now I have lost my magic as well? I don't even feel whole anymore."

Rain continued to pelt them, and the wind was so heavy the droplets felt like thick pellets of ice. Another broken yardarm splintered, cracked, and crashed to the deck after a loud gust of wind wrenched it loose. The waves smashed the prow, sending a violent shudder through the entire ship, and Nicci barely kept her feet by clinging tighter to the ropes.

"If we make it through this night, I will be happy to consider further explanations," she said.

Bannon struggled to make his way closer to them. Water ran down his face, and Nicci couldn't tell whether he was crying. "What do we do now?"

Nicci found a grim strength in her answer. "We survive. That is up to us."

The deck had begun to tilt alarmingly, and the *Wavewalker* rode much lower in the water. "We should search belowdecks," Bannon said. "There might be other survivors."

"Yes, my boy, we'd better check." Nathan gave Nicci a knowing glance. They both understood there would be no survivors.

Nicci remembered hearing the sea creatures smashing about,

battering the hull boards. "We also need to see what damage the selka did. I think they intended to wreck the ship even after they killed us all."

They climbed down through the open hatches. The confined spaces reeked of blood and entrails, a gagging stench like a butcher shop filled with chamber pots. They found the cow's head and scraps of its hide that the selka had peeled away and left like discarded drapes against the bulkheads.

The selka had left the ravaged bodies of dead sailors down in the crew decks, hammocks torn loose from the bulkheads and support beams. One young sailor hung by the back of his skull from a hammock hook.

A thundering sound of rushing water down in the cargo hold was even more ominous. When they lifted the hatches and stared down into the lower hold, Nicci managed to create a small hand light to illuminate the inky shadows. Part of the hull had been smashed and splintered from the outside, the cracked boards pressed inward. Swimming beneath the vessel, the selka must have attacked the wooden planks until they opened a jagged hole. Water roared in now, unstoppable, filling the hold.

"The *Wavewalker* is going to sink," Nathan said. "It's only a matter of hours."

"We can seal the hatches," Nicci said. "Confine the flooding to the bottom hold. That might buy us half a day."

"Can't we patch the hull?" Bannon asked. "I could hold my breath, swim down there, and do some work."

Seawater gushed in, already half filling the lower hold. Nicci understood that the force of the flow would shatter any repairs as quickly as they were put in place.

"If I had my magic," Nathan said, "I could restore the planks, grow more wood in place."

"Let me try," Nicci said. It was Additive Magic, using the wood itself, building upon what already existed. She reached into herself, but her every fiber trembled, wrung dry. She had already used so much magic in the battle, and the insidious poison still hadn't worn off.

Nevertheless, the ship was sinking, and she had no time to lose.

Nicci squeezed her eyes shut, focused her thoughts, summoned all the magic she could find. With her gift, she sensed the shattered hull planks, found the ragged edges, and used magic to draw more wood, making it grow. She pulled the smashed hole together like a scab over a wound, but the ocean continued to push its way in, and her newly formed wood broke apart, leaving her to start all over again.

Nathan grasped her shoulder as if to force strength into her, but she could draw nothing from him. Instead, she thought of her anger, thought of the murderous selka, thought of Sol, Elgin, and Rom and what they had done to her—what they had done to the entire crew of the *Wavewalker*. The repercussions went far beyond their attempted rape, because if those fools hadn't poisoned her, Nicci would have been at her peak strength as a sorceress, and the selka would never have defeated them.

In the flash of her disgust and fury she found another tiny spark, pulled more magic, and made the planks grow again, closing up, until she forcibly sealed the hole that the selka had smashed through the hull. When the water finally stopped pouring in, she shuddered. "It's fixed, but still fragile."

Bannon sighed with delight. "Now that we're not sinking anymore, we have time to find scraps of wood! I'll dive down and shore up the patch. We can make it solid."

For the next hour the young man threw himself into the task, holding his breath like a wishpearl diver and plunging down into the flooded hold. Remnants of cargo and crew floated all around: crates, heavy casks, bolts of sailcloth, and several bodies. But Bannon eventually succeeded in reinforcing the patch of magically repaired wood.

Outside, the storm continued with full force, and when they finally climbed back to the open, tilted deck, they looked in dismay at the torn rigging, the broken masts, the charred spots where wizard's fire had burned the prow.

At the stern, the chart room was a shambles. The navigator's wheel had been knocked off its pedestal. The currents and winds pushed the wreck onward, unguided. They had no captain, no charts, no way to steer. Though the night had already seemed endless, the darkness remained thick, strangled with clouds.

Standing at the bow, shielding his eyes, Bannon pointed ahead. "Look at the water there. That foamy line?" Then he yelled in alarm. "It's reefs! More reefs!"

With added fury, the storm shoved the helpless ship forward, and Nicci saw that they were being inevitably pushed toward the fanged rocks and the churning spray.

"Brace yourselves!" Nathan shouted.

Nicci tried to manipulate the wind, the waves, but the ship was an ungainly, doomed hulk. The sea had an implacable grip. The winds were ugly and capricious.

With a terrible grinding roar the ship drove up on the reefs. Dark rocks broke the keel and gouged open the lower hull. The deck boards splintered and scattered apart. The mizzenmast toppled into the water.

As the night thickened through flickers of lightning, Nicci thought she saw the dark silhouette of a distant coastline. Impossible and unreachable, the land provided only the mocking hope of safety. But only for a moment.

Angry seawater rushed aboard as the great ship broke apart and sank.

CHAPTER 18

Having wrought sufficient havoc, the storm dissipated and fled. The scattered clouds moved on like camp followers after a victorious army. Waves rolled and washed up on the rock-studded sand.

Nicci awoke to the shrieks of gulls fighting over some prized piece of carrion. Her entire body felt battered. Her muscles and bones ached from within, and her stomach still roiled, mostly from seawater she had swallowed in her struggle to swim ashore in the wind-blasted night. She brushed gritty sand from her face and bent over to retch repeatedly, but produced no more than a thimbleful of sour-tasting bile. She rolled onto her back and looked up into the searing sky, trying to get her bearings in her spinning mind and memories.

She heard the waves rumbling and booming as they crashed against the shore, slamming into the headlands, but here on the long crescent of a sandy beach, she seemed safe. She propped herself up on an elbow to reassess her situation, one step at a time. First, her own body. She felt no broken bones, only some bruises and abrasions from being thrown overboard and hurled by waves onto the shore.

Nicci inhaled again, exhaled, forced a calm on the queasiness inside her. Her heart was beating, her blood pumping. Air filled her lungs. She was restored now and could once again touch the tapestry of magic that was a familiar part of her entire life. She had been so weak after the wishpearl divers poisoned her, and Nicci did not like to feel weak.

The flood of memories crashed in like a riptide—the storm, the selka attack, the shipwreck. . . .

She climbed to her feet and stood swaying, but steadied herself. She was alive, and she was alone.

The gulls shrieked and cawed, challenging one another. A flurry of black-and-white wings settled around several corpses washed up on the shore, broken sailors from the *Wavewalker*. Birds fought over the bodies, pecking at the flesh, squabbling over choice morsels, although there was feast enough to gorge a hundred gulls. One seized a loose eyeball and plucked it out, held it by the optic nerve, and flew away while four other birds stormed after it with accusing screams.

At first Nicci thought one of the bodies might be Bannon's, but she saw that the dead man had long blond hair. Just one of the sailors she did not know. Since these dead men were beyond her help or her interest, she turned to scan down the strand for any survivors.

The beach was strewn with wreckage deposited by the storm: splintered hull planks, smashed kegs, a spar that had been strangled by ropes and tattered sailcloth. Larger barrels lay tossed along the sand, some halfway buried by the outgoing tide, like dice tossed by giants in a capricious game of chance.

She waited motionless, like a statue, just trying to regain her mental balance. So much for their quest to find Kol Adair. She was cast on this desolate shore, with no idea where she was. She had never believed the witch woman had any secret knowledge. Nicci stood there bedraggled and bruised, lost, and she did not feel ready to save the world in any fashion, not for Richard Rahl, not for herself.

Even with the crashing waves, the whistling wind, and the shrieking gulls, Nicci felt overcome by oppressive silence. She was alone.

Then a voice called to her. "Sorceress! Nicci!"

She spun to see Bannon Farmer coming toward her. He looked waterlogged, his ginger hair clumpy and tangled, his face bruised. His left cheek had been smashed and discolored, and a long cut ran across his forehead, but his grin overshadowed those details. He bounded around a large curved section of broken hull that had piled up against a rock outcropping.

"Sweet Sea Mother! I didn't think I'd find anyone else alive." His homespun shirt was drying in the hot sun, leaving a sparkle of crusted salt on the fabric. "I woke up with sand in my mouth and no one around. I'd been caught in some tide pools about fifty feet from shore. I called out, but no one answered." The young man lifted his arm to display his lackluster sword. "I somehow kept my grip on Sturdy, though."

Nicci ran her eyes over his body, checking to make sure he hadn't been wounded more severely than he realized. On the battlefield, she had often witnessed how shock and fear could deceive a man about how hurt he really was. Bannon seemed intact and resilient.

She asked, "Have you found Nathan?"

A look of alarm crossed his face. "No, you're the first person I've seen." He squared his shoulders. "But I just started looking. I'm sure Nathan's alive, though. He is a great wizard, after all."

Nicci frowned, knowing that Nathan had been unable to use magic during the selka attack. With concern for the old wizard, she made her way down the beach, shaking off any lingering aches and dizziness. "Where did you search? Have you gone this way?"

"I came from back there." Bannon pointed. "That's where I washed up. But most of the *Wavewalker* wreckage is scattered down here. Maybe the currents brought Nathan in this direction."

The sunlight was so bright on the sand that it hurt Nicci's eyes. She squinted, shaded her brow so she could look down the coastline, which curved out into an elbow of headlands that drew fierce waves like a magnet. Whitecaps battered the rocks, and the explosive boom could be heard even a mile away. If Nathan's body had been thrown into that cauldron, he would have been smashed into a pulp.

With surprising energy Bannon ranged ahead, calling the wizard's name. Nicci half expected that they would find his smashed corpse sprawled on the sand under another busy cluster of seagulls.

Halfway to the loudest crashing waves, they saw yards of sailcloth draped like a burial shroud on the beach, amid the remnants of splintered crates. Bannon spotted a tumbled pile of barrels, rope, and more wadded canvas. Nicci caught up with the young man just as he lifted a ragged swatch of sailcloth and cried out, "Here he is!"

Bannon grasped the shoulders of Nathan's ruffled shirt. The old man lay facedown, draped over a broken barrel. His long white hair hung in tangles around his face. When she saw him there unmoving, Nicci's immediate impression was that he was dead, drowned and cast aside.

Bannon rolled him off the barrel and laid the man flat on his back on the sand. Nathan's skin was a pale gray; his eyelids didn't even flicker. Bannon bent over him, listened for a breath, touched the older man's cheeks, peeled open his eyes. With an urgent, determined look, he rolled the wizard over, wrapped his forearms around Nathan's waist from behind, and put his fists right up against the abdomen. He pulled hard with a short, sharp jerk, forcing Nathan to convulse. Bannon clenched his arms again with enough power that Nicci thought he might snap the wizard's spine. Instead, a fountain of seawater spewed from Nathan's mouth. He convulsed again and then coughed.

His hands feebly swatted at Bannon, but the young man showed surprising strength. He laid him on his back in the sand again and began pumping his long legs, pushing Nathan's knees up against his chest as hard as he could. Nathan coughed and expelled more water from the side of his mouth before finally gaining enough strength to push Bannon away.

"Enough, my boy! I've survived as much as I'm going to." He looked miserable and shook his head, then ran his fingers through his hair.

Nicci looked curiously at the young man. "He was drowned. Where did you learn that?"

"On Chiriya we knew how to rescue drowned fishermen. Often it doesn't work, but if there is still a spark of life and we can get the water out of his lungs, the Sea Mother sometimes lets a man breathe again."

"I'm not just a man," Nathan said in a rattling voice. "I'm a wizard." He bent over and vomited copious amounts of seawater.

"Clearly the Sea Mother showed you mercy," Nicci said.

As he sat up, still wobbly, Nathan put a hand to his right temple, where a long deep gash in his forehead still bled. "I'm pleased to find myself alive again. A good way to start the day." He touched the gash again and winced. He closed his eyes, obviously concentrating, and his expression fell. When he looked up at Nicci, his face was forlorn. "Alas, the gift still eludes me. Might I humbly request that you heal me, Sorceress? Remove at least one inconvenience." He gave her a sudden worried look. "Or is your power gone as well? You were having difficulty during the battle—"

"I am fine," she said. "Those were aftereffects of the wishpearl divers' poison. Fortunately, I am recovering better than those men are."

Bannon turned to her with a strange expression. "The divers poisoned you?" He wiped sand out of his reddened eye.

Nicci gauged his expression carefully. "Yes, in the pot of chowder you delivered." She could tell by the look on his face that he hadn't known, which gave her a sense of relief. "That was why I felt so weak I could barely fight the selka. I was racked by poison."

His expression turned to dismay. "In the food I brought? *I* poisoned you? I didn't know! I didn't mean to! Sweet Sea Mother, I am so sorry, I—"

In a similar circumstance, Nicci knew that Jagang would have murdered the young man, slowly and painfully, for such an error. There were times when Death's Mistress would have killed him as well, but she was different now. Richard had changed her. Seeing Bannon's abject misery, his open honesty, she was reminded again of why she had not suspected the meal he'd brought.

Nodding slowly to herself, she said, "That is why they used you, Bannon Farmer. I would never think you capable of treachery or of trying to harm me in any way."

"I'm not! I would never poison you."

"You see, your very innocence was a weapon that others turned against me. They duped you." She hardened her voice. "Don't let it happen again." As he stammered and offered far too many apologies, Nicci flexed her fingers, felt the magic, felt *strong* again. "It no longer matters. I have recovered." She laid her hand on Nathan's temple and easily summoned what she needed to knit the torn flesh of his wound.

He let out a sigh of relief. "Thank you. It was not dire, but it was an annoyance."

She turned to Bannon, looked at his battered form. "And now you."

The young man took a step away, uneasy about her magic, or maybe not convinced that she had actually forgiven him. "There's no need, Sorceress. They are but minor injuries. I will recover by myself in time." He touched the slash on his thigh.

But Nicci, needing to reassure herself that she had full control over her powers again, reached out to grasp his arm. "I insist." She let the power flow, and his bruises vanished, his cuts healed. The flicker of fear vanished from his face. "That's wonderful! I feel like I could fight the selka all over again." He gripped his sword.

"Let's hope we don't have to do that, my boy," said Nathan.

Nicci brushed sand off her black dress and tied her hair back out of her eyes. "I want you both intact. We have work to do." She looked up and down the coast. "We need to learn where we are."

CHAPTER 19

After he accepted his disheveled appearance, Nathan insisted on searching the wreckage to locate his sword, as well as any other items they might find useful for their survival. After all the misfortunes they had suffered, he had little hope of retrieving his precious weapon, but by a stroke of good luck he did find his ornate blade. The sword was wedged between a splintered wine cask and a crate that had held brightly dyed fabrics for market, which were now waterlogged and ruined.

The wizard pulled the blade free and raised it into the sunlight with a sigh of satisfaction. "That's much better!" He winked at Bannon. "Now you and I, my boy, can defend our sorceress against any attackers."

"The gulls and crabs are surely trembling in fear." Nicci rolled her eyes and got down to serious business. "Before we set off, we should salvage any supplies we can find. There's no telling how far we are from civilization, or how long it will take us to get back to the D'Haran Empire." Even after their ordeals, she continued to think of what she needed to do for Richard and his vision for the future.

Along with several other mangled corpses of *Wavewalker* sailors, they found an intact keg of drinking water, from which they drank their fill, then a crate of salted meat. Nathan was discouraged to have lost all the new shirts, vests, and cloaks he had purchased in Tanimura, but he did discover a sailor's trunk that contained a fresh shirt that fit Bannon, a tortoiseshell comb, and a packet of waterlogged letters, the ink now running and smeared. The few decipherable words indicated they were notes from a lost sweetheart who would now never get a response from her beloved.

"Take only what we can use." Nicci pulled out a long fighting knife the nameless sailor had kept in the bottom of his trunk. She fastened the sheath to her waist. The bout with the insidious poison had left her weak and incapacitated, but it had taught her a lesson. Even if she couldn't use her magic, Nicci would not let herself be unarmed. Never again.

Using scraps of sailcloth, they fashioned makeshift packs to carry the salvaged supplies. Just after the sun reached its zenith, the three set off down the expansive beach.

Around them, the headlands rose up in sheer sandy ledges dotted with tufts of pampas grass and fleshy saltweed. They worked their way up to the point, from which they paused to look out into the sparkling sea. Nicci saw no other sails, no approaching ships, not even the line of angry water that marked the reefs that had destroyed the *Wavewalker*.

"We must have been blown far south," Nicci said, scanning back the way they had come. From Captain Eli's maps, she thought they might be somewhere down on the Phantom Coast.

In such an empty land devoid of any human markings, an artificial structure stood out like a shout. Bannon spotted it first with his sharp eyesight, pointing ahead across the windswept uplands to a promontory half a mile away on which stood a monolith of rocks, obviously built by people and just as obviously placed there so it could be seen from afar.

Squinting, Nathan said, "Without any frame of reference, it's difficult to tell how large the structure is."

Nicci set off. "We have to go see. It might give us our bearings, or point the way to some nearby town or military outpost."

Above the beach, the bleak, grassy emptiness played tricks on them, and the promontory with its stone tower was much closer than it had seemed. As they approached, Bannon sounded disappointed. "It's just a pile of rocks."

"A marker. A cairn—it's to signal a waypoint," Nathan said.

The marker was a tower of neatly piled rocks, with the largest boulders around the base stacked and wedged to form a solid foundation on which a thin, tall pyramid had been erected. The apex of the cairn was only a head taller than Nathan. Thick scrub grasses grew around its base, and orange and green lichen mottled the rough black surfaces of the mounded rocks. The rocks did not look like any others in the vicinity.

"Someone went to great difficulty to build this," Nicci said. "It has obviously been here a long time."

The wizard shaded his eyes and stared out into the sparkling ocean. "It might be for passing sailors. A point to mark on their maps. Or a signal tower . . . not that we could signal them anyway." He sighed. "There isn't enough brush to build a decent bonfire."

Nicci turned to him with a thin smile. "A ball of wizard's fire hurled into the air might draw some attention."

Bannon circled the cairn, looking for any clues. He squatted down, brushing aside the lichen and moss. "Oh! Words are carved on these bottom stones," he said, revealing chiseled letters. "It's a message."

Nicci and Nathan came around to see the first stone, and Nicci froze. The incised letters read, *To Kol Adair.*

"Well." Nathan rocked back, sounding pleased. "I suppose that is the waypoint we were looking for."

Nicci's chill deepened as she saw the rough, weathered words carved into the next stone. *From there, the Wizard will behold what he needs to make himself whole again.*

The words on the third stone made her throat go dry. *And the Sorceress must save the world.*

Nathan looked at her in astonishment. He lifted his hand, flexing his fingers. "Made whole again? Do you think it means I will be able to touch my Han again? Use magic? Red knew! She *knew.*"

Nicci frowned, feeling a knot in her stomach. "Much as I hate to admit it, this lends credence to what the witch woman wrote."

Bannon was confused. "What? What is it? A prophecy?" He looked from one to the other.

"Prophecy no longer exists," Nicci said, but her insistence did not sound convincing. Maybe if this prediction was old enough, burned into the fabric of the world before all the rules themselves changed . . .

"I thought we were shipwrecked and lost," Nathan said with a tone of wonder in his voice. "Ironically, this debacle may have put us exactly where we were supposed to go."

"I prefer to choose my own direction," Nicci said, but she could not argue with the evidence of her own eyes. She did not need a prophecy to help save the world or to aid Richard Rahl in any way possible. And if she had to journey toward a mysterious place called Kol Adair, then she would do it, as would Nathan.

The wizard pursed his lips as he regarded the stones. "Only a fool tries to resist a clear prophecy. In doing so, the person usually brings about the same fate, but in a far worse fashion."

Nicci set off, leaving the cairn behind. "We go to Kol Adair, wherever it is," she said.

After the tall stone cairn dwindled in the distance, Nicci heard a loud crack and rumbling clatter in the windblown silence behind them. They all spun in time to watch the spire of piled stones shifting and collapsing. The tallest rocks crumbled from the pinnacle, the center buckled, and the whole structure collapsed into a mound of rocks. The cairn had served its purpose.

Leaving the high point, they descended the headlands, and came upon the bones of a monster. A long skeleton sprawled among the rocks and weeds just above the high-tide line. Its head was the size of a wagon, a triangular skull with daggerlike fangs and cavernous eye sockets. Its vertebrae draped along the rocks and down into the sand like a rope of bones as long as ten horses in a row. Innumerable curved ribs formed a long and broken tunnel that tapered to a point at the creature's tail.

"It's not a dragon," Nathan observed.

"Dragons are mostly extinct," Nicci said.

Bannon crossed his arms over his chest. "Sea serpent, but just a small one. We often saw them swimming past the Chiriya shore during mating season, when the kelp blooms."

Looking at the long skeleton, Nicci surmised that the creature had died out at sea, and the tides had cast its body up on shore, where gulls and other scavengers picked it clean. Only a few iron-hard scraps of meat remained on the curved bones. "If that is a small sea serpent, I'm glad the *Wavewalker* did not encounter one."

They walked along the beach until the tide came in with late afternoon. The sun lowered in a ruddy ball toward the expanse of water. The three trudged on, finding no path, no villages, no docks, nor even old campfire circles that would indicate a human presence. This land seemed wild, unsettled, unexplored.

Bannon bounded off ahead, heading toward another large cliff that blocked their way, pushing out into the sea. "Hurry, the tide is coming in, and it'll block our way. I'd rather walk along the beach than climb those cliffs."

They were sloshing in ankle-deep water by the time they rounded the point, climbing over seaweed-covered rocks. "This way," Bannon said. "Be careful of your footing."

But when they came around the corner into a cove, the young man froze in place. He reached out to catch his balance on a tall rock.

Nicci saw what had caught his attention. Another wrecked ship had been smashed like a toy high up on the rocks. Little was left beyond a few ribs, some hull planks, and the long keel. Time and weather had reduced it to skeletal remains.

Nathan paused to catch his breath. "Now, that is interesting. What sort of ship is it?"

The wreck's curved prow was adorned by a ferocious carved serpent head—a sea serpent like the bones they had seen, Nicci realized. The hull planks were rough-hewn and lapped one over the top of the other, rather than being sealed edge-to-edge as those of the more sophisticated *Wavewalker* had been. Several of the ship's intact ribs curved up, draped with moss and seaweed. The rest of the hull had fallen apart.

Nicci turned to Bannon, who looked as if he had seen an evil spirit. "Is the design familiar to you?"

Too quickly, he shook his head. Nathan pressed, "Why are you shuddering, my boy?"

"I'm just cold and tired." He cleared his throat and trudged up on the rocks. "It'll be dark soon. We should keep going and find a place to make camp."

Nicci looked around, made her decision. "This is a good enough spot. The cove is sheltered, and that wreck is above the high-tide line. It'll provide shelter."

"And ready firewood," Nathan said.

Bannon sounded uncertain. "But maybe if we kept going, we could find a village."

"Nonsense. This is much better than sleeping out in the windy headlands." Nathan picked his way closer to the ominous serpent ship. "It'll all look better with a nice roaring fire." He began to gather shattered fragments of the planks for kindling.

Nicci found a sheltered area in the curve of the ruined hull. "The sand is soft here. We can build a fire ring out of rocks."

Bannon sounded defeated. "I'll go find us dinner. There'll be crabs, shellfish, maybe some mussels in the tide pools."

He trotted off into the deepening twilight, while Nathan gathered scraps of wood and prepared a fire, but he had to rely on Nicci's magic to ignite it. Soon, they had a large crackling blaze.

After smoothing the sand for a decent cushion, the wizard situated himself on the ground. Nicci dragged up a wave-polished log to use as a makeshift seat. Nathan propped his elbows on his knees and gazed into the cheerful bonfire, looking miserable. "I do not believe I've ever felt so weary and lost, even if I know we're on our way to Kol Adair."

"We've endured a lot of hardship, Wizard. This is just more of it." She poked a stick into the flames.

"I'm lost because my magic failed us when I needed it most. I've had the gift all my life. I wasted so many centuries locked in that dreadful palace, receiving prophecies and forced to write them down so that everyone could misinterpret them." He snorted. "The Sisters had the best of intentions, but their results left much to be desired."

He shifted his position, but could not seem to find a comfortable spot to sit. "They considered me dangerous! Prophecy was integral to me, woven through my flesh and bone and blood, and when Richard sent the omen machine back to the underworld, he unraveled that part of me."

"Richard did what was necessary," Nicci said.

"No doubt about that, Sorceress, and I'm not complaining." He fumbled around in his makeshift pack to withdraw the tortoiseshell comb he had claimed from the unnamed sailor's trunk. He began to wrestle with the tangles, grimacing as his unkempt hair fought against his efforts. "The world is a better place without that damnable prophecy."

He held up his hand, concentrated, even squeezed his eyes shut, but nothing happened. "But now I'm losing the rest of my magic. I haven't been able to use my gift properly since before the storm, before the selka. I have tried, but . . . nothing. How can that be, Sorceress?"

"Are you asking if magic itself is going away, as did prophecy? I don't see the correlation. My gift functions properly." Then, as an afterthought, she added, "So long as I haven't been poisoned."

"But I was a prophet *and* a wizard." He looked at her with a flare in his azure eyes. "If the gift of prophecy unraveled within me, what if it was connected to the rest of my gift? You can't pluck one loose strand from a complex tapestry without unraveling other parts. Could it have disrupted my entire Han? Maybe by yanking out prophecy, Richard loosened other strands of interconnected magic." He pushed his hands out toward the blaze, visibly straining. "What if I can't create a light web ever again? Or manipulate water? Or make fire? Will I have to resort to doing card tricks, like a traveling charlatan? How can I be made whole again?"

"I don't have answers for you, Wizard," Nicci said.

He looked stung. "Maybe you won't be able to call me that anymore."

Interrupting them, Bannon returned with an armload of misshapen oysters and mussels, which he dumped in the sand at the edge of the fire. "There were crabs too, about the size of my hands," the young man said. "I couldn't carry them all, and the crabs tried to run away. I can go catch some later."

Nathan used a stick to push the shells into the coals, and the moisture hissed and spat as it steamed away. The mussels yawned open, gasping as they died. Bannon used a stick to fish them back out of the flames, rolling them onto the sand. "They cook quickly."

Nicci and Nathan each picked up one of the hot shellfish, juggling them in their fingertips until they could pry the shells wide enough to get at the meat inside. After they devoured the entire haul, Bannon took a flaming brand from the fire and ventured into the darkness again. Before long, he returned with crabs, which they also roasted.

Squatting down on the smooth log near Nicci, Bannon laid his sword on his lap and ran his finger gently along the blade's edge. He kept glancing around, deeply uneasy.

At last having the chance to think and plan, Nicci gazed at the skeletal remnants of the wrecked serpent ship, then looked up into the sky to view the altered constellations. "Tomorrow, we decide where to go."

Paying little attention to their discussion, Bannon tossed the empty shells against the wooden ribs of the derelict ship.

Nathan opened the leather satchel at his side, glad he still had his life book. It had mostly dried, and the blank pages suffered little enough damage. Using a lead stylus he had procured in Tanimura, he began to sketch the coastline on one of the blank pages.

"I have no cartographic instruments, but I do have a good eye." He added the rocky points, the crescent-shaped beach, the site of the tall stone cairn, and now the sheltered cove that held the wreck of the serpent ship. "It's difficult to make an accurate map if you don't know where you're starting, but I'll do my best. After all, I am the roving ambassador, and Richard will want a map when we come home again." He worked his hands, concentrated, looked down at the pages, then sighed in disappointment. "A map-making spell could do a much better job, but this will serve."

Nicci said, "At least that book provides blank paper. It is not entirely useless."

Nathan sat up straight as a thought occurred to him. He looked at Nicci and extended a finger. "The witch woman wasn't useless. She knew we had to be here. *You* had to be here."

"Yes, to save the world, to save Richard's empire. I'm sure it will all become clear enough . . . once we find someone to ask."

Bannon looked up at them. "So if we find a place called Kol Adair, you'll get your magic back? And the sorceress will save the world."

"Yes!" Nathan said, then frowned. "Possibly. Or maybe it's just a foolish, vague prediction that has no merit at all."

Nicci added, "No one can be certain of anything a witch woman says. And prophecy no longer exists."

"Do we have another choice? We're here anyway. You and I came to explore the Old World. That quest seemed pointless before, but it is more important now."

"Then we will go to Kol Adair," Nicci said as she went to stand at the edge of their firelight, "as soon as we have any idea where to find it."

CHAPTER 20

Bannon did not sleep well, despite the shelter of the cove and the familiar lullaby of the surf. Restless, he fought against swirling thoughts of all that had happened in the past few days, and fears of what might lie ahead.

Since he was awake, he volunteered to keep watch, brooding through the darkest hours of the night. He jumped at every sound in the darkness, fearing that burly, ruthless men would stride up the beach to seize him, to gag and bind him. But it was just his imagination . . . his memories.

While the beautiful sorceress slept on the sand not far from Nathan, Bannon called upon peace, reshaped the world the way he *wanted* it to be, and fashioned a contented smile for himself. The wizard looked unsettling as he lay near the waning fire, sound asleep but with his eyes open. Near dawn, though, his eyelids fluttered closed.

The young man roused his companions as morning light edged the high headlands. He was amazed at how instantly Nicci came awake without yawning or stretching. She rose to her feet, her blue eyes bright and alert, her expression clear as she absorbed her surroundings in a flash. She brushed sand off her black dress, and despite all the ordeals, didn't look at all rumpled; that in itself seemed like sorcery to Bannon.

He'd been infatuated with pretty girls on Chiriya, but Nicci was unlike any woman he had ever met. She was more beautiful and intelligent than the young island women, but it was more than that. She seemed fascinating, but also dangerous. Bannon flushed with embarrassment when she caught him staring at her—and she stared right back, but with an expression that carried little warmth.

They set off into the wilderness together. After leaving the small cove behind, Bannon let out a silent sigh of relief to be away from the wreck of the ominous Norukai ship. . . .

"The beach gets rockier farther on," Nicci said, scanning south along the shore. "We'd better travel inland."

The wizard agreed. "That is where we'd likely encounter some settlement, since we haven't seen any docks or boats on this section of the coast."

"I'll find a way for us to climb up," Bannon volunteered. Scouting ahead at his own pace, he picked a feasible route, zigzagging up the crumbling sandstone cliffs. The other two followed him, hand over foot, and together they reached the open, windy flats above the surf.

The breeze was sharp and chilly, and thin clouds scudded across the sky. The tall pampas grass and low vegetation rippled as if some invisible stampede charged across the flatland. Dark green cypress trees hunched against the constant gale, their tufted branches pointed in the direction of the prevailing winds.

Nathan and Nicci discussed their plans, but the rustling breezes snatched their words from Bannon's hearing as he scouted ahead. He was reluctant—or perhaps not brave enough—to make small talk with the beautiful sorceress. He wanted to hear where Nicci had grown up, if she'd had a perfect life, a peaceful upbringing, loving parents. Bannon didn't need to know—didn't want to know, actually. He just *made it so* in his own mind.

When Nathan startled a black-winged tern from a matted clump of grass, the old wizard bent down. "Ah, look, a nest—and better yet, three eggs." He cradled them in his palms. "This can supplement our breakfast."

Bannon came back, feeling his stomach growl. "Eggs? Are we going to make a new cook fire?" They had only been traveling for an hour.

Nicci took the eggs from Nathan's hands. "No need to stop. Let me." She wrapped her fingers around them, and Bannon saw tendrils of steam rise up. Within moments she handed him one of the eggs, and the shell was so hot that he had to juggle it in his hands. "We can eat as we walk," Nicci said. "We have a long distance to cover—even if we don't know where we're going."

Nathan finished his breakfast and tossed the crumbled eggshell to the ground. He dry-washed his hands and rubbed them on his pants.

From the outstretched headlands they could see the coastline snaking southward for miles. The hills inland were covered with dark pines and silver-leaved eucalyptus with peeling bark.

The three maintained a steady pace, and the wizard called to Bannon, "If you see any more signposts pointing the way to Kol Adair, my boy, be sure you let us know."

Bannon cheerfully agreed, then realized Nathan was just teasing him. But was it such an unlikely possibility?

He ranged ahead, foraging, and wound his way through the bent cypress trees, then explored the stands of pine and the spicy-smelling eucalyptus. Seeing no sign of human habitation, the young man wondered if they were the first human beings to set foot on this untamed land. It felt wonderful, and it felt terrifying at the same time.

Chiriya Island had been settled for countless generations. The people grew their cabbages and set out in their fishing boats, and the only excitement was the occasional trading ship that tied up in the small harbor. He had long pretended that his younger years were perfect, with every neighbor waving a hearty hello, everyone chipping in to help one another, the weather always sunny, food on the table, a fire in the hearth on even the coldest winter nights.

He had left that place . . . a place that never really existed.

He was robbed in the dark alleys of Tanimura. He fought bloodthirsty selka and saw his shipmates slaughtered, certain that he, too, would die that night. But he had survived the *Wavewalker* being shipwrecked on an unknown shore. He had left Chiriya for this, had left his father's hard fists and drunken shouts, had left the blood. And the kittens . . .

Bannon winced at the memories. He brushed aside tall, brittle blades of pampas grass, walked around a hummock, and ducked into a rustling tangle of cypress that offered shelter from the wind. Even with the fearful ordeals, this was better than Chiriya. Far better.

Exploring by himself, he entered the forest. He heard the chuckle of a creek flowing through the pines to a beautiful round pool with a smooth sandy bottom. He saw the silvery flashes of small fish darting around, evading his shadow. Bannon knelt in the weeds and flowers on the edge of the pond and scooped handfuls of the cold, clear water, drinking his fill. Fresh water!

He studied the darting fish, but they were much too small to bother with. A handful would barely make a meal, even if he could catch them. The water, though, was pure and delicious. He filled his waterskin and ducked out of the pines and eucalyptus into the brisk wind again.

Now that he had shaken his darker memories, Bannon felt light-footed as he continued to explore. Yes, he had suffered terrible hardships, but he would make the best of his situation. He reminded himself that he had left Chiriya intending to seek adventure—and he had found exactly that. A small, shadowed part of him acknowledged that he had fled his island in shock and denial at what had happened . . . but he drove those thoughts away again, blinking his eyes and looking at the bright world. He drew another clean breath.

"I am not running away—I am exploring!" he said aloud with enough force to convince himself. He was in an unknown land with a great wizard as his mentor, a man who taught him history and swordplay. And there was the mysterious and beautiful sorceress Nicci, who intruded more and more into his thoughts. He could not help but be attracted to her.

As he roamed the grassy headlands, he headed back toward the cliff edge to watch the white waves roll in. He wondered who Nicci was, what drove her. Did she think about him, too? Bannon pondered what he could do to make her notice him, to consider him a worthwhile traveling companion, instead of just a coincidental one.

Bannon peered over the verge and watched rooster tails of spray leap into the air. A flash of color caught his attention, wedged into the mossy sandstone just down the cliff, and he knelt to see a clump of unusual flowers growing within arm's reach. The blossoms were vibrant, the deepest and most intense violet he had ever seen, shot through with veins of crimson and a central splash of yellow stamens. They had thick fleshy stems and swordlike green leaves.

The beautiful flowers gave him an idea, a perfect idea. Beautiful flowers for a beautiful woman!

Bannon stretched out, extending his arm over the edge to reach the blossoms. He picked four of them—a bouquet. It was a small gesture, but perhaps Nicci would be grateful. Perhaps she would notice him.

He bounded back through the grasses, searching for his companions, and he was panting hard by the time he caught up with them. The breezes blew his ginger hair wildly around his head as he hurried up to Nicci.

When he extended the flowers, all his suave words were snatched from his mouth as if the wind had stolen them. He could only manage to blurt, "I found these for you."

She frowned with a glimmer of annoyance, but when she looked at the flowers, her expression filled with interest. She narrowed her blue eyes and reached out to take one of the flowers from his bouquet, leaving him with the other three. She showed extreme care as she touched the stem with just her fingertips.

Bannon waited for her to smile with delight or nod in warm appreciation. He couldn't remember whether he had ever seen her respond with a genuine smile.

"Where did you find these?" she demanded.

"Over by the cliff." He pointed. "Growing in a cranny in the rock."

"Such flowers are rare. I could have made use of them many times." She looked over at Nathan.

The wizard's eyes were wide with recognition. "Do you know what those are, Bannon Farmer?"

"Pretty flowers?"

"*Deathrise* flowers," Nicci said, studying the one in her hand.

Bannon looked at the rest of his bouquet, confused.

"Deathrise flowers," she repeated. "One of the most dangerous plants in existence. They are extremely hard to find, and valuable. Assassins would pay a king's ransom for these four. But this is far more than we could ever use." She held up the stem in her hand. "One will be more than sufficient."

"What—what do you mean?" Looking down at the violet-and-crimson flowers, he felt his skin crawl.

"Do you expect to kill an entire city, my boy?" Nathan asked. "Or maybe just a village?"

Bannon blinked, still trying to grasp what they were telling him. "You mean they're . . . poison?"

Nicci's face smoothed in a fascinated smile as she rolled the thick stem in her fingers, careful not to touch the broken end. "The deathrise flower has many uses. From the petals one can concoct an ink so lethal that any victim who reads a message written with such ink will die a painful, lingering death. Consuming even one seed causes a horrible agony that has been described as swallowing mouthfuls of glass shards, then regurgitating them, and swallowing them all over again."

Bannon's stomach twisted into a knot. "I—I didn't mean . . ."

Nicci continued, "Tinctures, extracts, and potions can be made from all parts of the deathrise flower. Emperor Jagang had his alchemists and apothecaries test the various mixtures on his prisoners of war." She raised her eyebrows. "About five thousand died in those preliminary experiments. The camps for the test subjects became known as the Places of Screaming. Emperor Jagang pitched his tent nearby so he could drift off to sleep listening to that music."

Bannon felt sick. He stood trembling, looked down at the other three deathrise flowers in his hand, afraid to move his fingers.

"Even touching the juice to your skin will cause rashes and boils to break out." Nicci looked at the single flower she had kept, obviously impressed although not in the way Bannon had wanted. "I thank you very much. One never knows when such measures might be required." She wrapped the flower carefully in a scrap of cloth and tucked it into her pack. "I am pleased with how you think."

Embarrassment—and the fear that his hands and arms were about to burst into leper's sores or swollen boils—rendered him speechless. He turned and bolted headlong into the wind, running toward the pine trees, intent on reaching the pond and the stream again. When he reached the weeds of the shore he flung the deathrise flowers as far as he could out into the water, then dropped to his knees, plunged his hands into the pond, and dug his fingers into the sand. He scrubbed and scrubbed his palms, his fingers, the backs of his hands, his wrists, all the way up his arms. He frantically tried to remember any place he had touched with the deathrise flower. He filled his cupped palms, and was about to splash water in his face, but he didn't dare go near his mouth or eyes.

Even when his hands looked clean, he plunged them into the sand again, scrubbing and scrubbing. He scoured his skin a third time and a fourth, until even his fingertips were raw, his palms pink, his knuckles sore. Finally, he stepped away, breathing hard, still afraid that the poison had gotten inside him.

He swallowed. What more could he do? He would find no antidote here . . . if an antidote even existed.

Heart pounding, pulse racing, he struggled to regain his composure. Finally, he left the pond and ran to catch up with Nicci and Nathan.

At dusk, four dwarf deer crept out of the eucalyptus forest where they had rested in the tangled shadows throughout the day. They ventured forth, their delicate hooves stepping on twigs while they worked their way along a faint game trail.

Though there were few large predators here on the coastal headlands, the deer possessed natural caution on their journey to the freshwater pond where they drank each night at sunset. The deer approached the shore, uncertain and skittish. They took several steps, then paused, their ears flickering to detect any threat, then moved forward again. One hung back as a sentinel while the other three stepped to the pond's edge.

The deer sensed something amiss. The water was smooth and clear as always, but they noticed, without comprehension, the glimmering silver shapes that drifted on the surface of the pond. Hundreds of the small fish that had darted like small mirror flashes in the last sunlight now floated belly-up like a stain on the water.

The deer struggled to understand what had changed. Frozen like statues in the forest, they waited for long minutes, but nothing approached, nothing attacked. Finally, one of the deer dipped into the water and drank. The next two joined her, drinking their fill. When it was his turn, the sentinel buck also drank, and the twilight shadows deepened around them. . . .

By the next morning numerous fish still drifted on the surface, though some of the bodies had begun to sink. On the shore, four dwarf deer also lay dead.

CHAPTER 21

They camped in the shelter of thick cypress. During the night, the maddening, mournful breezes died down, which allowed a thick fog to settle in. The cold wet swaths made the three miserable while they huddled near a small fire, adding more moist twigs in an attempt to keep the blaze going. Nicci used her magic to maintain the fire, but the flames gave out too little heat.

Nicci had never been overly concerned with her personal comfort, so long as she could function. Now that they'd been shipwrecked on the unknown coast, despite the unexpected rock cairn reaffirming their destination of Kol Adair, she could not guess how many miles they might need to walk before they found a settlement in this wild coastal wasteland.

Despite the solitude, Nicci reminded herself that this land, bleak and untamed as it was, was now part of the D'Haran Empire. Nicci was doing what she had promised Lord Rahl, and she would, in fact, walk from one end of the world to the other for him, if that proved necessary. But neither she nor Nathan could continue their quest until they actually found a village or city.

Finally, morning brightened the murk, and Nicci stopped wasting effort to keep the useless fire going. "We should get moving. That will generate heat."

Nathan used the tortoiseshell comb to untangle his long white hair. "I don't know if even running will keep us warm enough." He looked in disappointment at his moist and rumpled shirt. "I never realized how many ways I relied on my gift. A little internal magic could always keep me warm on a blustery, miserable day like this."

Nicci shouldered her makeshift pack. "We won't be any colder than we are now, and at least we'll cover distance."

Bannon squinted into the fog. "But can we see where we're going?"

"We'll see when we get there," Nicci said.

Nathan tucked away his life book in the leather pouch and fastened the flap. "I doubt I can add much detail to my map today."

They headed out. Guided by the rush and boom of the ocean off to their right, they walked far enough from the edge to stay safe. "I'm not so much worried about falling off a cliff, as I am of reaching the edge of the world," Bannon said, panting. "Then we would just fall forever."

Nathan lifted his bushy eyebrows. "You believe we'll find the actual edge of the world, my boy?"

"I've seen maps that cut off. . . ."

"If we find the edge of the world, then we will know that we've come to the boundaries of Lord Rahl's empire." Nicci did not waste time or effort worrying about such things. "Then we will turn and explore in a different direction."

"I hope we find Kol Adair before then," Nathan said.

Ever since offering her the deathrise flowers, the young man had seemed subdued. Before she rebuffed him, Nicci had noted the bright gleam in his eyes, recognizing that he was probably smitten with her—and those feelings were woefully misplaced. His imagination was already too active.

Nathan had a certain fondness for the young man. Despite the thousand-year difference in their ages, the two had much in common, since even the old wizard had a flash of naiveté about him.

The fog thinned for an hour as they continued, but the chill deepened. Bannon shivered. "Maybe we should go inland to the thicker forest, where at least the trees will shelter us."

Nicci shook her head and kept going. She walked in a straight, determined line, defeating the distance as if it were an enemy. "If we follow the coastline, we'll be more likely to discover a river outlet or a port. And we can see farther ahead, once the fog clears."

Nathan kept his eyes to the ground, preoccupied with finding berry bushes, wild onions, or bird's nests and breakfast eggs. Bannon ranged ahead like a dutiful scout.

The wind went quiet again and the fog closed in, so that Nicci didn't see the young man until he was right beside her. He looked sheepish, smiling for the first time since the debacle of offering her deathrise flowers. This time, Bannon held a handful of orange lilies on long stalks. "I found these for you, Sorceress. I hope you like them better than those poison blossoms."

Nicci regarded him coolly. "But I valued the deathrise flower. I told you in great detail about all its uses."

"These are pretty flowers, though," Bannon said, extending them toward her. "Grass lilies. They used to grow all over Chiriya. They won't last long after they've been picked, but I wanted you to have them." When Nicci did not reach out to accept them, his expression faltered. "Are they not to your liking?"

She recognized that Bannon Farmer was competent enough, and he had proven his mettle in fighting the selka. She would let him accompany her for as long as she considered him useful, or at least not a hindrance. She could imagine far worse company, but she had to nip his infatuation in the bud.

She realized that her response to his clumsy offering yesterday had not been a sufficient rebuff. She had to set him straight, or she would have to kill him sooner or later.

Nicci recalled all the times she'd been abused, forced to spend weeks with Jagang's soldiers as a plaything for their sadistic enjoyment, as well as the times when Jagang had taken her himself, sometimes beating her bloody. With her twisted experience of so-called love, she had convinced herself she was in love with Richard Rahl. Back then, she had been a Sister of the Dark, corrupted by her service to the Keeper as well as her brutal enslavement by the emperor. Her attempt to express that misguided love for Richard—forcing him to live a false life with her as man and wife—had only made Richard resent her more.

Nicci had eventually learned her lesson. She herself had killed Jagang, and now she served Richard wholeheartedly, in her own way.

She knew that she did love Richard, that he was the only man she *could* love . . . but it was a different kind of love now. He had Kahlan, and he would never be satisfied with Nicci, not in that way, no matter how much he respected and valued her. Because of her iron-hard devotion, Nicci had made up her mind to conquer the Old World for Richard Rahl—single-handedly if necessary.

She had no time or patience for a young mooncalf who thought she was pretty.

Bannon beamed when Nicci reached toward the flowers, but instead of accepting them, she wrapped her grip around his wrist. Clenching tight, she released a warning flow of magic that sent a sharp tingle into his flesh like a hailstorm of steel needles.

His hazel eyes widened, and his mouth gaped open in shock. Before the young man could say anything, Nicci spoke through gritted teeth. "I am only letting you stay with us because Nathan likes you, and because you may be useful in helping us get where we need to go. But know this"—she lowered her voice to a growl—"I am not some fawning village girl looking for a stolen kiss."

His fingers spasmed and he let the lilies fall to the ground. Nicci didn't even glance at them. She maintained her tight grip on his arm.

"I'm—I'm sorry, Sorceress!"

She had to drive the point home, so that the problem did not occur again. She didn't soften her voice at all. "We face serious problems. We are lost, and we must find out where we are in order to continue our mission. If you ever get in my way, I will skin you alive without a second thought."

He gawked at her with just the proper amount of terror and dismay, which would resolve itself into appropriate respect soon enough. She would not need to worry about this nonsense from him again.

She let go of his wrist, and Bannon flexed his hand, flapping it as if to fling away the pain. He stammered, "But—but . . . I only—"

She had no wish to be part of his starry-eyed view of the world or his nostalgia for a peaceful island home. "I've heard the stories you tell yourself. I am not part of your perfect boyhood. Do you understand me, child?" She used the last word intentionally.

His fearful expression suddenly darkened, as if she had torn the scab off a still-festering wound. "It wasn't perfect. It was never perfect." Looking ashamed, he turned away to find Nathan standing there with a concerned and compassionate look on his face.

Nicci didn't interfere as the wizard put a comforting hand on Bannon's shoulder. "Best you understand the way of things, my boy. Remember, she was called Death's Mistress."

Bannon walked away, his expression downcast. Heading off into the thickening mist, he said, "No. I will never forget that."

The fog melted around him.

CHAPTER 22

After they traveled for three more days, the headlands shifted to forested hills and fertile grasslands. Bannon nervously kept his distance from Nicci and spent even more time with the wizard. Though she spoke no more of the incident, Nicci was inwardly relieved that he had learned his lesson.

She heard Nathan telling the young man tidbits of history or ruminating about his time locked in the Palace of the Prophets. Some of the legends sounded absurd to Nicci, as did events in the wizard's own life, but Bannon had no filter to determine what might or might not be true. He lapped up each of Nathan's tales like a cat facing a bowl of cream. At least it kept the two occupied as they trudged along, which Nathan did his best to document on the rudimentary map in his life book.

On the fifth day, they came upon a path that was too wide and well traveled to be a game trail. Ahead, they saw stumps where trees had been cut down.

Bannon cried out, "That means people have been here!"

The trail soon widened into a footpath, then an actual road. Coming over a rise, they could see the hills spilling down to a neat, rounded bay into which a narrow river drained. A large village of wooden homes, shops, and warehouses had sprung up on both sides of the river. A high wooden bridge joined the two banks. Piers thrust into the water, providing docks for small boats in the bay. A point of rocky land swooped around the far end of the harbor, punctuated with a lookout tower.

The hills held terraced gardens and pastures where sheep and cattle grazed. Down by the docks, people were unloading a catch from the fishing boats. Stretched nets hung on frameworks drying in the sun. High on the beach, five overturned boats were being repaired by ship-wrights.

"I was beginning to think we'd have to walk around the entire world," Nathan said.

Nicci nodded. "We'll find out where we are, and choose our next course. We can inform them of Lord Rahl's rule, and maybe someone here can tell us where to find Kol Adair."

"I assume you are anxious to save the world, Sorceress," Nathan said. "As anxious as I am to be made whole again."

Nicci's mouth formed a hard, straight line. "I will reserve judgment on just how seriously to take the witch woman's words."

Nathan frowned down at his shirt, disappointed by the now limp and ruined ruffles of the garment he had purchased in Tanimura less than two weeks earlier. "At the very least, a town that size should have a tailor who can replace my clothes. I hate to feel so . . . scruffy."

Considering how barren the lands had been in their journey from the north, Nicci wondered how often these people saw strangers. When she noticed other roads leading upriver, as well as the fishing boats and the substantial harbor, she realized that they must have contact with other settled areas—just not from the wilderness up the Phantom Coast.

On the outskirts of town, the road took them past a cemetery on the hillside, where grave markers covered the slopes. Names had been chis-eled into the low stone markers, while other graves were marked only by wooden posts with names carved into the wood. These flimsier posts were arranged much too closely to mark individual burial sites. Seeing the wooden posts and stone markers, Bannon seemed very disturbed.

Nathan ran his fingers down the weathered wood, where the name was all but unreadable. "I assume the two types of markers indicate a class system? The wealthy can afford fine stone markers and a spacious grave, while those less fortunate are simply marked with a post?"

"Maybe there are no bodies at all because there were no bodies to bury," Nicci said. "Fishermen lost at sea, for instance."

Bannon looked gray. "I think they are memorials for people who are not dead, but are gone."

Nathan's brow furrowed. "Gone? What do you mean by that, my boy?"

"Maybe they were . . . taken." The young man swallowed hard.

Nicci turned to give him a hard look. "Taken by whom?"

His voice came out in a whisper. "Slavers, possibly."

The idea troubled Nicci, and she led the way at a faster, more determined pace. Slavers had no place in Lord Rahl's new rule, and Nicci looked forward to putting the matter to rest. One way or another.

When they reached the outskirts of the town, children playing in the dirt streets noticed the three travelers coming from the unexpected direction and called excitedly for their parents. Stout women worked at their washing, while two older couples sat together mending fishing nets that were stretched across wooden benches. Men and women working in the vegetable patches and farm fields looked up to see the strangers.

Nathan shook trail dust and sand from his pants and shirt, frowning at himself. "I don't make a very formidable presence as the roving ambassador for D'Hara." He tapped the sword in its scabbard at his hip. "But at least my fine blade shows me to be a man of some note."

Bannon put his hand on the leather-wrapped hilt of his own sword, but couldn't seem to think of what to say.

Nicci cautioned them both. "We won't be drawing our swords unless there's a need. We come bearing word that the Old World is now at peace. They will be glad to hear it."

A middle-aged woman with brown hair tied in a thick braid raised a hand in welcome. A ten-year-old boy at her side stared at the newcomers as if they were monsters from the sea. "They came from the north!" he said, pointing vigorously. "There's nothing up to the north."

"Welcome to Renda Bay," said the woman. "You look as if you've had a long journey."

"We were shipwrecked," Nicci said.

"We've been walking for days," Bannon interjected. "We're glad we found your village."

"Renda Bay?" Nathan said. "I'll mark it on my map."

As more people gathered, Nicci assessed the modest homes, wooden common buildings, gardens and flowerbeds. The children did not look shabby, gaunt, or desperate. Much of the activity in the town had to do with cleaning fish in large troughs at wooden tables down by the docks. Iron racks loaded with fish filets hung over smoky kelp fires. Rows of broad basins were lined along the beach under the sun, filled with sea-water that would slowly evaporate to leave a residue of valuable salt.

The villagers peppered them with questions. Nathan and Bannon told disjointed parts of their story, and the noise of conversation swelled around them. Nicci interrupted, "Call a gathering, and we will address everyone at once, so we don't have to repeat ourselves."

They met the town leader, a man named Holden, who was in his late thirties, with rich brown hair marked by a distinctive frosting of white at the temples. They learned that until recently he had owned his own fishing boat before he devoted his days to local administration.

Holden led them to the town square, where many eager people had already gathered to hear the strangers' tale. Nicci let Nathan speak, because the wizard was quite comfortable with the sound of his own voice. "I am Nathan Rahl, currently the representative of Lord Richard Rahl of the D'Haran Empire, the man who defeated Emperor Jagang." He looked at them, as if expecting cheers. "You may have been wondering why you are no longer under the crushing boot heel of the Imperial Order?"

The villagers' expressions did not show terror or even awareness. Holden said, "We've heard of Jagang, but it's been three decades or more since we saw troops or any representative from the Imperial Order."

Bannon interjected, "We were on a ship that sailed south from Tanimura—the *Wavewalker* under Captain Eli Corwin—but we were attacked by selka. Hundreds of them, maybe thousands! They killed our crew, and our ship ran aground on the reefs. Only the three of us survived. You're the first people we've seen since."

Many listeners stared at them in horror and fascination, while others frowned with clear skepticism, as if they expected castaways to embellish their stories.

Nicci interrupted, "The important news we bring you is that Lord Rahl has overthrown the evil tyrants, and that you are all free. You need not fear oppression, slavery, or tyranny. As he consolidates his empire, Lord Rahl is gathering emissaries so that all may decide a common set of laws to which everyone must agree. This will be a golden age for human history." She crossed her arms over her chest. "And you are part of it."

Nathan brightened as he looked out at the villagers. "You must have maps. You must know the area. Choose several of your best people to travel north, make your way up to the New World, the heart of D'Hara and the People's Palace, so you can join Lord Rahl. He'll provide the protection and support your village needs. Now is a very important time for the building of the new empire."

Holden had a habit of nodding sincerely, demonstrating that he listened to people when they expressed their concerns, but he didn't appear convinced. "That is heartening news, and I am proud to hear what your Lord Rahl has accomplished." He gestured to the gathered audience. "Our people here trade with villages upriver and larger cities to the south, but we have barely heard of D'Hara or Tanimura. It's grand for you to say that we are free of tyranny and slavery . . . but has everyone who would threaten us also heard this news?"

"They will," Nicci said.

He spread his hands, sounding perfectly reasonable. "Your Lord Rahl is too far away to have any real effect in our lives. How could any D'Haran help us from the other side of the world? We are on our own here . . . against whatever might prey on us."

"He will be able to protect you," Nicci said. She knew well enough not to underestimate Richard.

Holden gave them a conciliatory smile and did not argue further. "Still, it is good to know, and you are welcome in Renda Bay. We will help you as we can, since you seem to have lost everything."

"We could use a good meal," Nathan said. "And new clothes." He pulled up his frayed sleeve. "Do you have a tailor? I require several new outfits."

"We would also appreciate supplies and provisions," Nicci said, "before we continue our journey. We are looking for a place called Kol Adair."

The people didn't immediately show any sign of recognition, but they offered to help in any way possible. As conversation buzzed in the square, Holden declared, "We'll have a welcoming dinner tonight. Because of the season, our boats just brought in a fine catch of redfins. We can roast enough for a banquet."

Nathan smiled. "We appreciate your hospitality, and we would dearly enjoy a good meal. Now, from whom might I request a new shirt?"

That night, the villagers set up long plank tables in an open festival area just above the docks in the harbor. A warm, cheery glow came from the windows of the village dwellings, and tall torches surrounded the gathering. Candle pots flickered along the wooden bridge that crossed the narrow river.

As dusk descended, people came for the welcome feast. Fat redfin fish, seasoned with sea salt and pungent herbs, roasted over coals in fire pits. The meal was accompanied with tubers boiled in large cauldrons, and a salad made of bitter flowers.

Nicci found the redfin to be a dark, meaty fish with a strong flavor. Bannon had a second helping as he talked with his companions at the long table. To their great fascination, he described the many dishes that could be made with cabbage.

Nathan had obtained a new shirt, a gray homespun tunic that laced up the front. The old wizard found the color unflattering, but he agreed that it was far superior to the remnants of his once fine clothes. "Thank you so much, my dear Jann," he said to a short, dark-haired woman with plain features but pretty eyes. She was one of the town's seamstresses who spun her own cloth and made garments for her family and others.

"My last tailors in Tanimura had numerous patterns and styles to choose from, countless grades of fabric, endless cuts." Nathan heaved a sigh. "But they weren't nearly as pretty or as kind as you."

Jann giggled. "You should thank my husband. That shirt was supposed to be for Phillip." A broad-shouldered older man sat next to her. Nearly as tall as Nathan, he had tightly curled dark hair and a rugged face. When Nathan asked him about the scar across his nose, he explained that a fishhook had once cut him down to the cartilage when a line had snapped.

"I have plenty of shirts, and you obviously need that one more than I," said Phillip. "And now I can boast that the ambassador for Lord Rahl wears clothes made by my wife." His big callused hand clasped Jann's much more delicate hand. He savored another bite of redfin. "It's good to feast on fish I didn't have to bring in myself. Those days are over for me."

Jann explained, "Phillip is a successful fisherman, but he prefers to be a boat builder. We've just set up a new dry dock, and he'll be repairing fishing vessels and building a new one to sell."

Phillip smiled proudly. "A new one that I plan to name the *Lady Jann*."

"That is sure to increase the asking price," said Nathan.

Town leader Holden stood up in the middle of the meal, and the dinner chatter died down. "We welcome our visitors from far-off lands. We give what we can and hope that the Sea Mother remembers our kindness to strangers."

While the villagers cheered and toasted, Nicci heard some of the villagers muttering, as if they thought the Sea Mother had let them down many times in the past. She realized that Renda Bay had no armed guards, no strong military presence, no defenses whatsoever. Nicci knew that if one relied on ethereal deities to solve problems, then those problems usually remained unsolved.

Suddenly, several villagers stood up from the plank tables, gesturing toward the dark harbor. A bright warning fire sprang from the watchtower on the southern point of the breakwater. Someone threw a torch into a pile of dry wood, which swelled into a blazing beacon. When Holden saw the fire, his face fell into an expression of dread.

Looking out into the harbor, Nicci could see the ominous silhouettes of four large, dark ships that closed in on the bay with unnatural speed.

Holden looked at Nicci with a sick expression. "Where is your Lord Rahl's protection now?"

Nicci straightened. "I'm here."

CHAPTER 23

Villagers bolted in panic from the outside festival area. Some ran to their homes to seize knives, clubs, bows, and anything else they could use as a weapon. Nathan and Bannon both drew their swords and stood together next to the plank feasting tables, although the young man's expression was far different from what Nicci had seen on his face when he fought the selka. This time, he looked disgusted as well as terrified.

The massive dark ships slid forward swiftly even though the night was without breezes. Each vessel had one mast with a single broad sail dyed a deep blue, so as to be invisible at night.

Nicci heard splashing sounds and the gruff shouts of men. Peering intensely into the night, she enhanced her vision with an obscure distance spell, which let her see that the four invading ships were propelled by long lines of oars. The oars cut into the water like axe blades and swept back to push the vessel forward, then lifted into the air dripping moonlight, and stabbed the water again.

Bannon's voice cracked. "Norukai slavers!"

"Norukai slavers," Holden echoed, then added his own shout. "Prepare to defend yourselves! It's another raid."

"What is it, my boy?" Nathan asked. "Who are they?"

"Nightmares."

The slaver ships came in fast, crushing a small fishing boat as they ground up against the Renda Bay piers. A chorus of guttural, challenging shouts came from the longboats. With a chill, Nicci saw that each of the four curved prows sported the monstrous carving of a sea serpent, and she recognized the design from the crumbling wreck they had found in the sheltered cove on their first night ashore.

The four raider ships careened like rampaging bulls into the harbor. Bright orange streaks soared into the sky from the longboat decks, arced downward, and scattered upon the village, striking streets, rooftops, and unfortunate townspeople. Several fire arrows stuck into the lapped roofs of the houses and set the buildings on fire.

Water crews raced with buckets to stop the conflagration from spreading, while the rest of the defenders converged toward the docks, carrying whatever weapons they had. But even at a glance, Nicci could see that the villagers could never drive off such an aggressive raid. By her guess, the four Norukai ships held nearly three hundred warriors. She turned to Nathan. "It is up to us to fight them."

He raised his sword. "My thoughts exactly, Sorceress."

Releasing magic, Nicci ignited a bright fireball in her hand and tossed it into the air, where it expanded, growing more diffuse until it exploded high overhead like a wash of chain lightning. The glow illuminated the big serpent ships and the raiders boiling off the decks. The nearest two vessels crashed against the piers and fastened with iron hooks and heavy planks, while the raiders from the outer two vessels dropped smaller boats into the water and rowed toward the shore.

Jann and her husband Phillip accompanied Nathan as they braced themselves for the attack. Jann cried, "Spirits save us!"

"*I* will save you," Nicci said.

The wizard turned to the retired fisherman. "Are your people at war with the Norukai? Why do they attack Renda Bay?"

"We are prey to them," said Phillip, his face haggard. "Normally, they dart in with a single boat, snatch five to ten victims, and flee into the night. But this . . . this is a full invasion."

"Then we arrived just in time," Nicci said.

Norukai warriors thundered across the docks, rushing to the village, while others jumped out of landing boats and sloshed up from the shallow water to shore, carrying clubs, ropes, and nets.

The sorcerous illumination dissipated overhead, but Nicci's magic swelled. She stretched her mind in one direction, tapping into Additive Magic and the energy there, while she also drew upon Subtractive Magic. Combining both, she conjured jagged lashes of black lightning, which she whipped against the first three invaders who reached the end of the docks. Her lightning ripped their broad chests into smoking wreckage, and the burly men collapsed into a heap of bones.

Despite this unexpected attack, the slavers showed no hint of fear or even caution. They charged forward, sneering at her lightning, arrogant in their invincibility. A team of four left their landing boats and waded to the beach.

Nicci killed the next wave of them as well.

The Norukai were squat men with disproportionately broad shoulders, shaved heads, and bare arms, and they wore vests of scaled armor made of some reptile skin. Most horrific, their cheeks had been slit from the corners of their lips back to the hinge of the jaw, then sewn up again, as if to widen their mouths like a snake's. Now, as they roared their fearsome battle call, their jaws opened wide, as if they were vipers about to strike. Only a few Norukai carried swords or spears, while the rest obviously expected to subdue and capture their victims, not to kill. They meant to harvest the people of Renda Bay.

A second rain of flaming arrows launched from the deck of a Norukai ship, pelting the village. By now several healthy fires were spreading among the wooden buildings, and when Nicci saw a blaze jump from one rooftop to the next, she flung out her hand and summoned her control of air and wind. Her directed blast swept the flames away, and as she pulled it back, she sucked away all the oxygen and extinguished the fire.

Nathan looked at her and groaned. "I can no longer help you in that way," he said, gripping his sword. "But I will do my part, even without magic." He ran beside Bannon, both of them holding their blades high as the muscular slavers charged ashore. As he prepared to fight, the young man had a strange look in his eyes—though not of fear. He seemed obsessed.

The villagers of Renda Bay had their own swords and spears, but did not seem skilled in their use. Holden shouted orders and ran bravely to meet the surge of attackers, although he had no tactical plan.

Nicci watched the fourth raider ship grind up against another dock, splintering wood as the invaders shouted. She did not intend to let them make it to shore. No longer crippled by poison, her command of magic was at its peak strength, and she could do more than summon wind or lightning.

She called forth a large roiling ball of wizard's fire, a molten sphere that she hurled at the prow of the ship just as the Norukai lashed up against the damaged pier. The magical blaze incinerated the carved serpent figurehead and billowed back over the bow. Flames spilled across the deck and ignited fifteen of the armored slavers. They shrieked as the skin boiled off their bones, and their ugly, slitted mouths yawned open in a scream so wide their jaws cracked.

Wizard's fire could not be easily extinguished, and it burned the ship's deck boards, set the tall mast on fire, and ignited the midnight-blue sail, which roared up in flickering orange curtains. When she had used weaker balls of wizard's fire during the selka attack on the *Wavewalker*, the storm and the washing waves had mitigated the fire, but here at the Renda Bay docks, the magical flames burrowed through the raider deck and ate through the hull.

Many Norukai leaped overboard, some with skin on fire. The ship went up like a blazing beacon. The death wails of the burning enemy satisfied Nicci. Although she had changed since then, those screams reminded her of when she had burned Commander Kardeef alive, roasting him on a spit in front of the people of a newly conquered village, just to prove how ruthless she could be.

By now, hundreds of Norukai had made their way into town. Raising their clubs and nets, they met the villagers who fought back with any weapon at hand. The hideous warriors showed no fear, and they were far more skilled with their cudgels and nets than the villagers were with their seldom-used weapons.

The slavers threw weighted nets on a group of three men who harried them with pikes and swords. Entangled, the men stumbled and thrashed, trying to throw off the strands, but the Norukai swarmed over them and clubbed them until they were stunned. It seemed to be a well-coordinated operation. Once the three men were beaten senseless, the Norukai bound and trussed them like wild animals. They picked up the fresh captives, one at each man's feet, one at each man's arms, and hauled them back aboard the nearest raiding ship.

Flaming arrows continued to soar through the air like shooting stars. Nicci tried to extinguish them one by one before they could fall upon new fuel, and she struggled to take care of other fires as well, but she could not keep up. There were hundreds of flashpoints. The Norukai seemed intent on destroying the whole town, strictly to cause chaos so they could snatch more victims. The slavers moved like professional hunters rather than a well-ordered army, ranging free and looking for targets. They swarmed into the town.

N athan told himself that a blade could be as deadly as an attack of magic, so long as it was wielded by a skilled swordsman. His new shirt was loose, comfortable, and clean . . . for the moment. He charged into the front ranks of the burly Norukai, sweeping his sword sideways.

Beside him, Jann and Phillip recklessly joined the fray. Phillip carried a long hooked pike that he had used as a fisherman. He threw it like a harpoon and skewered one of the slavers through the sternum. Even though the hideously scarred man was dead with his heart punctured, he clawed at the shaft before he fell still.

Though she was small, Phillip's wife was nimble. Jann darted among the attackers with a long butcher knife, hacking at the arms of one slaver, slicing open the side of another. Blood ran down his exposed ribs.

Nathan swung his sword with both hands, using all his strength, and his blade went right across the wide-open mouth of one of the grotesque Norukai, slicing off the top of his head. Next to him, Bannon became a whirlwind, not even watching where he hacked and cleaved. Even the slavers backed away from the young man's mad, uncontrolled attack.

But the Norukai were not deterred for long. They let out a hissing growl as if it were a strange war cry, and a new group of invaders pushed forward, carrying long spears. Each weapon was tipped with the ivory tusk of some unknown animal, carved into serrated edges. As the front ranks of slavers swept in, holding thick clubs, the spear throwers took their stances and identified the centers of resistance.

Town leader Holden stood on top of one of the plank tables in the festival square and shouted to rally his people. "Stand up to them! Do not let them take our wives and children! Don't let—"

One of the spear throwers cocked back his arm and flung the shaft with a mighty heave. The weapon whistled through the air and buried itself in Holden's abdomen. The blood-smeared tusk sprouted from his back.

At the front lines, Nathan slashed with his sword, first to the left and then to the right, chopping off arms and stabbing through rib cages. He looked up just in time to see a spear hurtling toward him. He felt a ripple inside, a twinge that he thought might be a spark of magic. He reached into himself, trying to grasp it to deflect the spear. A simple, instinctive spell. Time seemed to move so slowly . . . but the flicker of magic vanished, snuffed out. The magic abandoned him again, and he was helpless.

Bannon grabbed his arm and yanked him sideways, and the spear whistled past. "Watch yourself, Nathan. I need you alive to help me kill more of these animals."

The vitriol in his voice shocked Nathan. Something seemed to have been triggered inside him. The young man's eyes were wild, his lips drawn back, and his normally cheerful smile had now become a death's-head grimace. Blood flecks were more prominent than the freckles on his face.

Bannon leaped forward, paying no attention to the clubs and nets and blades of the slavers. His ginger hair flew wild, and he howled wordlessly as he hacked through the neck of one squat man, then cleaved the shoulder of another. "Animals!" he shrieked.

A vicious slash from Sturdy opened the guts of another attacker, who sneered down at his snakelike entrails and reached out to grab Bannon's sword hand. But the young man tore himself away and spun to chop off the slaver's arm, and in an unthinking malicious retaliation, he cut off the other arm, so that both stumps spouted blood onto the man's exposed entrails.

"You'll get yourself killed, my boy," Nathan cautioned. He ran after Bannon, trying to keep up as the Norukai closed in on this unexpectedly wild attacker.

One of the enemy spear throwers hurled his weapon at the young man, but Nathan swept his sword just in time to strike the wooden shaft with a loud clack, knocking it aside. The ivory-tipped spear flew at an angle, ricocheted, and buried itself between the shoulder blades of another advancing Norukai.

Closing around the seamstress Jann, the slavers threw a net over her. She tugged at the strands, driven to the ground. She used her bloody knife to cut herself free, peeling the net away, but two muscular Norukai stooped over her and raised their clubs to beat her senseless.

Nathan came up behind them and stabbed one slaver in the back. When his partner turned to glare at Nathan, Jann freed her arm and plunged the butcher knife deep into the slaver's calf. Roaring, he reached down to grab at the knife, and Nathan sliced off his head with one clean blow. The old wizard quickly pulled away the remaining strands of the net, freeing Jann. The small woman crawled out, exhausted and shaking.

Her husband strode up, covered with blood and filled with gratitude. "You saved her. Thank you, Wizard," Phillip said. He reached out for his wife—just as one of the falling fire arrows struck him in the back of the neck. The steel arrow point, still covered with gobs of flaming pitch, sprouted from the hollow of his throat. Phillip reached up and grasped the arrow as if annoyed that it had distracted him from his reunion. Jann screamed, and Phillip turned to her, his eyes wet and longing, then collapsed, dead.

Bannon howled at the sky, slashing with his sword at the falling rain of fire arrows. He threw himself upon two more Norukai with such fury that they staggered back, and Nathan was forced to help him, leaving Jann to sob over her fallen husband.

* * *

Blazes had begun to spread through the town. Nicci extinguished as many fires as she could, but that was a losing battle for now. She realized that if she could not drive away these attackers, it wouldn't matter if Renda Bay burned.

The villagers made a good accounting of themselves, though by now at least thirty had been beaten into unconsciousness, trussed, and dragged to the first raider ship. Dozens of Norukai swarmed back aboard, stomping on the decks. Loud drumbeats rumbled through the hold, and the oars lifted and lowered as the galley slaves were forced to back the ship away from the dock.

Nicci summoned more black lightning and brought it down, killing six Norukai who thought themselves safe aboard the retreating ship. She didn't think she could stop the vessel from escaping, so instead she devoted her efforts to the remaining raiders on the shore.

Well over a hundred slavers still attacked. They had seen Nicci and her powers, and a few seemed to have decided that the beautiful, powerful sorceress would be a worthy slave. They were fools.

One monster-jawed slaver swung a mace tipped with a ball and chain, while two others held up their nets, closing in on Nicci from either side. They must have thought she would be an easy target.

She didn't have time for this. She stretched out her hand, pointing from one slaver to the next, and the third, in quick succession, stopping their hearts cold. They fell dead in a tangle of their own nets.

She panted, catching her breath, flexing her fingers. She had enough strength to summon another blast of wizard's fire. She could ignite the retreating slaver ship, but that would kill everyone aboard, including the new captives. Would they prefer that fate? That was not for her to decide. No, she would fight the Norukai here.

Nicci called up wizard's fire and, instead of concentrating it in a ball, flung a fan of deadly magical flames at the line of advancing slavers, spattering at least thirty of them. The relentless inferno did not sputter out. Even a glob of wizard's fire no larger than her thumbnail would burn and keep burning until it burrowed its way through its victim.

Writhing and screaming, the Norukai fell like trees in a forest blaze. Even though she felt depleted from expending so much magic, Nicci called normal fire and sent it through the air until it struck the sails and masts of two more ships, setting the dyed fabric on fire. Soon, the raider vessels were engulfed in flame.

Nathan and Bannon had each killed fifteen or twenty slavers themselves. They continued to attack with their swords, as did hundreds of shouting, angry villagers. The Norukai spear throwers hurled the last of their shafts into the crowd, indiscriminately choosing targets.

With the last of her strength, Nicci sent out a wall of wind, a solid battering ram of air that knocked the burly Norukai backward. With the angry armed villagers storming toward them, the slavers at last retreated.

As the Norukai frantically tried to extinguish the burning sails on their ruined ships, the attackers piled onto the last vessel with shouts and curses. Accompanied by threatening drumbeats, the slaves at the oars began to push the serpent craft back, tearing the ships free of the piers, leaving wreckage behind.

Nicci took out her knife and saw she had more work to do. She didn't need magic to kill the stragglers left behind when their raiding ships retreated. She and the villagers still had a long night ahead of them.

CHAPTER 24

Even as the Norukai ships limped away into the night, the pain and terror of their raid lingered in Renda Bay. The villagers pulled together to put out the fires, tend to the wounded, and count the dead—and missing.

Nathan looked down at his gore-spattered sword. His new homespun shirt—which Jann had made for her husband—was now torn and soaked with blood. The wizard found himself staring at the fabric, picking at the sticky, crusty mess. Magic was so much *cleaner* than this! When he realized he was focusing on such a trivial thing, he knew he was feeling the effects of shock.

He checked over his hands and arms, ran fingers across his scalp to see if he had been injured without realizing it. In the heat of battle a fighter could suffer grievous wounds and never notice until he dropped dead from blood loss. Thankfully, Nathan found only minor cuts, scratches, and a bump behind his right ear. He didn't even remember being struck there.

"I appear to be intact enough," he muttered to himself. He looked around at the flurry of people, some standing stunned and helpless while others ran about frantically trying to help. He realized with an ache in his heart that, even though he had briefly felt a twinge of his gift during the heat of the battle, he had no magic now and was unable to heal even his small wounds.

Bannon Farmer looked lost and drained, like a rag wrung out and left to dry. He was covered with blood, clumps of uprooted hair, gray smears of brain tissue, even bone fragments caught in the material of his shirt. During the battle, he had fought as if possessed by a war spirit; Nathan had never seen anything like it. Now, though, Bannon just looked like a broken boy.

But Nathan had to worry more about the injured and the dying. Without powerfully gifted healers, the people of Renda Bay needed to tend their wounded by traditional means. They had only a few trained doctors to care for maladies or injuries, such as when the fishhook had cut poor Phillip's nose and left a long scar.

Nathan swallowed hard, remembering the man. Jann knelt next to her husband's body sprawled on the ground in the festival square, the extinguished fire arrow still protruding through his throat. He had died with a look of surprise on his face; at least the man had suffered no pain. Jann wept, her head bowed, her shoulders hitching up and down.

Moving from person to person, Nathan helped the healers bandage knife wounds and wrap cloth around cracked skulls. The victims moaned or cried out in pain as doctors used needle and thread to bind the worst gashes. When the night breeze blew in his face, the smell of blood and smoke overpowered the salty iodine smell of the bay. So much damage . . .

Fortunately, Nicci had unleashed her full powers, and Nathan knew how formidable the sorceress was. But he was a formidable wizard himself—or at least he had been. If he had possessed his gift tonight, if he could have woven spells just as destructive as Nicci's, most of these casualties wouldn't exist. The raiders would have been driven back before they could set foot ashore. These villagers who lay wounded and dead would still be alive, tending crops, fixing nets, or setting sail into the bay for the next day's catch.

He had failed. Magic had failed him—and in his own turn, he had failed the people of Renda Bay. Nathan Rahl had failed *himself.*

If only he could have thrown wizard's fire at the Norukai vessels, incinerated the sails, kept the raiders from disembarking! He could have used a binding spell to stop them from advancing, or even unleashed a sleep web to fell them all like stalks of harvested wheat, and then the people of Renda Bay could have tied up the slavers, seized their ships, freed the captives chained to the oars below like animals in pens. . . .

Nathan clenched his fists, gritted his teeth, and shouted, "I am a wizard!" Even if prophecy was gone from the world, he could not lose everything. He refused to believe that with the unraveling of prophecy, his other skills had disappeared as well, no matter what the witch woman had cryptically predicted. No, he did still have magic. He knew it. It was part of him. He was gifted!

As anger swirled within him, Nathan felt an unexpected sizzle along his forearms, tracking back into his chest, as if some arcane lightning had shot through his bloodstream. Yes, he knew that spark!

The magic might have gone dormant inside him, but Nathan dredged it out, pulled it kicking and struggling like one of these captives being hauled to a slaver ship. "I am a wizard, and I am in control of my magic!" he said to himself. He could use it to help these people now.

He saw two matronly healers beside a man who made low gurgling sounds. Still feeling the rejuvenating tingle inside his fingers, inside his body, Nathan hurried over to them. He could help.

The victim lay on his back with a broken Norukai spear shaft through his chest. Although the jagged ivory point had missed his heart, it had ripped through his lung. Blood streamed out of his blue lips, and he kept coughing. He spasmed, and the two distraught tenders could do nothing for him.

When Nathan approached, the women shook their heads. The victim's face contorted with silent pain. His eyes were round and glassy. He coughed again, and a pink foam of blood covered his lips.

"We can only wait for the Sea Mother to take him," said one of the women. Her face was streaked with blood and tears.

Nathan looked down at the broken shaft of wood, which kept the dying man propped upright. "We must remove the spear," he said.

The other woman shook her head. "If you do that, he will die. Let the man have peace and dignity."

"And if you leave the spear *in,* he will die." His azure eyes became steely. "There might be a chance. He is beyond your skills, but I have magic—let me try." The two women stared at Nathan, and he encouraged them to leave. "You go tend to someone you might save."

They nodded, gently touched the dying man, and hurried off to the other injured townspeople.

When the pair of healers had gone, Nathan grasped the slick, bloody spear. As gently as he could, though there was no gentle way to deal with such an insult to the man's body, he pulled the wooden shaft out. The man let out a gasping scream. Fresh blood gushed from his mouth, and a bright flow ran out of the ragged hole in his chest. As the man writhed, the wound in his lung made a loud sucking, gasping sound. He would be dead in minutes.

Nathan summoned the magic within him, grasped for the tingle, the touch of his Han, and increased it to a surge, a flow of energy. Additive Magic. He had done this many times before—so many times. It was child's play for one with the gift, and he knew he could control it.

He pressed his hands against the open wound, pushed his palms down on the streaming blood. He could feel the healing force, and he let the magic flow through him. With his restored gift, he sought out the ripped blood vessels, the torn tissue inside the lung, the brutal hole the spear shaft had tunneled through his chest and back. He could re-attach strands of muscle fibers, cement the splintered fragments of bone. He would fix this! He would knit it all together, make this man whole again . . . *whole*, as the witch woman Red had said Nathan needed to be. Whole again! The gift wasn't gone from him. The magic was still his to control, even if he hadn't yet found Kol Adair.

Nathan gritted his teeth and concentrated harder, *forced* this man to heal. The magic writhed like a serpent trying to escape, but Nathan made his demands. He could heal. He was in control. He was strong again!

But in a malicious twist, the healing magic fought back, recoiled, and did exactly the opposite of what he wanted. Instead of sealing the bleeding wound, the magic ricocheted and rebounded, becoming a monster that destroyed rather than repaired.

Magic flowed out of Nathan as he pressed down with his hands to stop the blood. The vengeful backlash erupted—ripping the spear wound into a huge gash, splintering the man's ribs, and turning him inside out. His heart and lungs spilled out in a horrific explosion of blood and tissue. The man didn't even have time to scream, but lay back arching his neck, then collapsed.

Nathan stared in revulsion and disbelief down at his blood-drenched hands. He had felt the magic. He had tried to heal the poor victim . . . but instead of just dying peacefully, the man had been split open like an overripe fruit. Nathan had done that! The victim would have died anyway, but not like this!

Nathan staggered back, opening and closing his mouth, but he had no words. He thought he had lost his magic, but this was worse than merely being impotent. The gift had turned against him. If his ability did come back to him, what if he couldn't control it?

He stared in dismay at the appalling, mangled corpse, sure that a crowd would gather to accuse him of a terrible crime. He wondered if even on her worst days as Death's Mistress, Nicci had done such an awful thing.

When he looked up, he met Bannon's glassy gaze. The young man seemed so filled with horror at the events of the night that this new instance had very little effect on him.

Bile rose in the wizard's throat, and he turned away, his shoulders slumped. He didn't want Nicci to see this either, though perhaps she could help him understand what had happened. How could his gift have turned so violently against him? For now, even if he sensed magic returning to him, he didn't dare use it. He might cause an even worse disaster.

Another astonishing realization came to him. What if he had decided to hurl a ball of wizard's fire at one of the Norukai ships during the battle, and it recoiled on him instead? If the furious white-hot flames had struck back, they could have wiped out half the town of Renda Bay.

Nathan groaned deep in his throat and lurched away from the people who were busy bandaging and tending the injured, splinting broken bones, propping up wounded heads on rolled cloths. He felt ashamed and afraid.

He was dangerous.

Instead, he picked up a bucket and joined the firefighting crews to help extinguish the last blazes that still spread through the town. In that, at least, he could cause little damage.

CHAPTER 25

The fires in Renda Bay burned until morning, and afterward smoke continued to curl into the gray sky, staining the dawn. Houses and boat sheds still smoldered, some charred all the way to blackened mismatched skeletons. A group of fishermen had salvaged six boats from the ruined docks, while throughout the town numb-looking people assessed the damage, talking in subdued voices.

Nicci reflected on the previous day's easy activity, the relaxed conversations among neighbors, the quaint town activities, the small but busy market square—a way of life now struck down by swords, fire, and blood from the raid.

Seemingly in a stupor, Bannon sat recovering on a splintered wooden bench next to an overturned gutting trough. Silver fish scales spangled the wood of the trough like miniature coins in the morning light. He gripped Sturdy's leather-wrapped hilt with both hands, as if drawing on its strength. His shirt was torn and stained with soot and blood.

As she stepped up to him, Nicci noted at least five deep cuts on his arms, across his back, on his shoulder. The young cabbage farmer looked engrossed in thought, refighting his battles. He had aged greatly.

Though Nicci was exhausted from expending so much magic during the battle and treating the grievously wounded afterward, she found enough strength to heal Bannon's cuts and wounds. He didn't even seem aware of them.

Nathan came up to them with haunted eyes, his long white hair and his borrowed shirt matted with clumps of gore. Dried blood caked his hands.

When Bannon looked up at his mentor, his face showed little recognition. The wizard said in a soft voice, "You fought like an unbelievable warrior last night, as if someone worked a rampaging spell on you—but I know that was no spell."

The young man's face was drawn and pale. "Slavers were attacking the village. I had to fight. What else could I do?"

"You did well enough," Nicci acknowledged. "You fought even harder than you did against the selka."

"These were *slavers*," he said, as if that were explanation enough. With an obvious effort, Bannon struggled to compose himself and even managed a false, horrid-looking smile. "It's what I was supposed to do. I hated the thought of all of these people being hurt . . . and enslaved. They . . . they had a very nice life here in Renda Bay, and I didn't want it ruined."

Nicci glanced at Nathan, who wore a skeptical frown. Neither of them believed Bannon's explanation. Nicci said, "That is an acceptable answer, but it's not the complete one. Tell me the truth."

His expression filled with alarm. "I—I can't. It's a secret."

She knew it was time to be stern, to push him in a way that would make him respond. His wounds were far deeper than the obvious ones, and they might become either tough scars or dangerously unstable fractures. Her assessment of him had changed in the past week, and she suspected there was more than the naive, careless country boy. She needed to find out.

Grasping Bannon's shirt, she pulled him to his feet and pressed her face close to his so she could capture his attention with her searing blue eyes. "I don't want your secrets for the sake of titillation, Bannon Farmer. I ask because I need to know the answer. You travel as my companion, and therefore your actions might affect my own mission. Are you unreliable? Are you a hazard to me and what I must accomplish for Lord Rahl?" She softened her voice. "Or are you just a brave, but reckless fighter?"

Swaying, Bannon looked at the sorceress and then at Nathan with a beseeching expression. He tore his gaze away to stare out at the burned wreck of the nearest Norukai vessel, which was half sunk in the calm bay. Nicci suddenly remembered how oddly the young man had also behaved when they camped near the much older hulk of a wrecked serpent ship.

"You've seen those ships before," she whispered. "You know about the Norukai."

Finally, he said, "It's because of *Ian* . . . my friend Ian. The slavers . . ." He sucked in a long, deep breath. His hazel eyes were bloodshot from the fires and smoke, as well as his own convulsive weeping. His eyes held much deeper secrets, a clear and colorful childhood memory being stripped away to reveal the raw bones of truth.

Hauling out his words like a man surrendering precious keepsakes to a moneylender, Bannon told his tale. "Ian and I were boyhood friends on Chiriya Island. We would run down to the shore or race each other across the windswept grasses. One time, we walked all the way around the island—it took us a full day. That was our whole world.

"As boys, we pulled weeds in the fields and helped harvest the cabbage heads, but we also had time to ourselves. Ian and I had a special cove on the far side of the island, where we would explore the tide pools. Most of the time we just played. We were best friends, both the same age, thirteen summers old that year . . . the last year."

His voice grew raspy and hard. "One morning, Ian and I got up early because we knew it was a low tide. We went to our special cove, climbing down the sandstone cliffs, finding footholds like only boys can. We had empty sacks stuffed in our belts because we knew we would bring home a good haul of shellfish and crabs for the dinner pot. Mostly we enjoyed the peace of each other's company, instead of being back in our own homes . . . which weren't very peaceful." His voice turned sour.

Nicci said, "You always described your island home as idyllic and perfect, but dull."

He turned his bleak, empty eyes toward her. "Nothing is perfect, Sorceress. Shouldn't you be telling *me* that?" He shook his head and stared out at the still-smoldering Norukai ship.

"That day Ian and I were preoccupied with the tide pools, watching hermit crabs scuttle among the sea anemones, the little fish that had been trapped there until the next high tide. We didn't see the slavers' boat coming around the point. The six Norukai spotted us, rowed in, then splashed onto shore. Before Ian and I knew it, we were surrounded.

"They were burly, muscular men with shaved heads and those awful scarred and sewed mouths. They had nets, and ropes, and clubs. They were hunters . . . and we were just prey." He blinked. "I remembered when hunting parties from my village would march across the grassy pastures in the headlands with nets, banging pots to chase down goats and round them up for the winter slaughter. The Norukai were just like that. They came after me and Ian.

"We both screamed and ran. Ian was ahead of me. I made it to the base of the cliffs and started to climb before the first two slavers caught up to me. I was just out of their reach, but my foot slipped, and I fell. The men grabbed me, swung me around, and dropped me to the rocky beach. It knocked the wind out of me, and I couldn't make a sound. But Ian was yelling from halfway up the beach. He had almost gotten away." Bannon sniffled. "He could have gotten away.

"I fought back, but there were two of them, and the Norukai were strong. They tried to pull my arms together so they could lash my wrists. Another slaver grabbed my feet. I couldn't get away, couldn't even scream. Even when I caught my breath, my voice was hoarse. I thrashed and kicked.

"Just when they were wrapping a rope around my wrists, I heard an even louder shout. Ian had turned and come back, yelling at the slavers. They threw a net at him, but it missed. He just shrugged them off and came running toward me. In the struggle he snatched up one of the Norukai cudgels and bounded across the rocky beach, leaping over tide pools. He came to save me.

"Ian swung the club. I heard a skull crack—it was one of the men trying to tie me. Blood gushed from his eye and nose. Grunting, the other man grabbed at Ian, but my friend smashed him in the teeth, turning his lips to pulp. Ian yelled for me to run, and I tore my wrist away, sprang to my feet, and raced toward the sandstone cliff. I ran as I never had before. Tugging the ropes from my wrists, I made it there and began scrambling up, climbing for my very life.

"Ian shouted again, but I didn't turn back. I couldn't! I found the first foothold and pulled myself higher. My fingers were bloody, my nails torn." Bannon was breathing hard as he told his story. Perspiration sparkled on his forehead. "I pulled myself up, found a foothold, climbed, and then turned back to see the slavers closing in on my friend. Two of them threw a net again. The men he had clubbed now pounded him with their fists. They crowded around him and he couldn't get away. He screamed."

Bannon's voice hitched with a sob. "Ian had come back to save me. He risked his life to stop those men from tying me up. He made it so I could get away! But when they captured him, I froze. I could only watch as they wrapped the net around Ian and beat him again, kicking him over and over. When he cried out in pain, they laughed. I could see blood running from a gash in his face—and I didn't do a thing. They bound his wrists and ankles with rope—and I just watched.

"It should have been me under that net. He had helped me—*and I just watched!*"

Bannon released his grip and let Sturdy fall with a clatter to the ground. He pressed his palms against his eyes, as if to hide. "I was halfway up the cliff when the slavers came for me again, and I panicked. When I reached the higher ground, I looked back down at the beach. The Norukai were dragging my friend toward the longboat. He still struggled, but I knew he was lost. *Lost!* I caught a last glimpse of Ian's face, full of despair. He knew he would never get away . . . and he knew I wasn't coming back to rescue him. Even at that great distance, his eyes met mine. I had abandoned him.

"I wanted to shout that I was sorry. I wanted to promise that I would come for him, but I had no voice. I was out of breath." He turned away. "It would have been a lie anyway.

"Ian stared at me with a look of shock and confusion, as if he couldn't believe I would betray him. I saw hatred behind those eyes just before the slavers threw him into the longboat.

"And I just ran." Bannon shook his head, sniffling. "I left my friend behind. I didn't help him. He came back to save me, and I . . . I just saved myself. I ran away." His voice hitched and he sobbed again. "Sweet Sea Mother, he fought to save me, and I abandoned him."

The young man looked down at the blood on his shirt, at the cuts on his arms. He touched a deep wound on his neck and winced in surprise, but he clearly didn't remember how he had gotten it. The tears in his eyes had not washed away the stinging, painful memory.

"That's why I fought so hard against the slavers here in Renda Bay, why I hate them so much. I was a coward when the Norukai took Ian. I didn't fight then, but I have a sword now, and I will fight to my last breath." He snatched up Sturdy from where it had fallen on the ground and inspected it, satisfied that the edge still looked sharp. "I can't rescue Ian. I'll never see him again . . . but I can kill slavers whenever I see them."

CHAPTER 26

After a full day of picking up the pieces, the grieving survivors of Renda Bay were exhausted. With Holden dead, a man named Thaddeus accepted the position of town leader. Thaddeus was a beefy, square-faced fisherman with a long, frizzy beard. He was well liked among the villagers, but he looked completely out of his element.

Nicci had been watching the people throughout the day. She had always hated slavery, and it was her mission to stop tyranny and oppression in the name of Lord Rahl, as well as for her own soul. In a way, this was how she could help save the world for Richard, but she doubted this was what the witch woman's prophecy had meant.

Nathan and Bannon had washed the grime from their hands and faces, but their hair was still tangled, and their clothes were still covered with blood that had long since dried.

Together, the villagers made a solemn procession out to the hillside graveyard, with mules and shaggy oxen drawing a line of carts to carry the dead. The people, already weary, sore, and heartsick, spread out to mark burial sites for the thirty-nine villagers who had died in the battle. The townspeople carried spades and shovels but seemed daunted by the task of digging all those graves.

"We must also erect twenty-two wooden posts," Thaddeus said in a wobbly voice, "to remember the good people taken by the raiders."

"Carve the names into the stone and make your wooden markers," Nicci said. "I can use my gift to assist with the other work." She released a flow of magic to scoop aside the grasses and dirt on the hillside to fashion a perfect grave. It was easy enough once she went through the process. She made an identical grave adjacent to the first, and then a third. She had many more to go.

The villagers watched, too tired to be amazed, too frightened to express their gratitude. When she finished the thirty-ninth grave, Nicci stepped back, feeling weary. "I sincerely hope you will not need more anytime soon."

With little ceremony and acknowledging that they would all grieve later, in their own time, the people of Renda Bay buried their dead. The men and women spoke the names aloud as they took each body from the cart and interred the victims, a mixed range of farmers, a carpenter, a jovial brewer, two young boys killed in a fire after the house in which they had taken refuge burned to the ground, and town leader Holden, who had given up his life on the sea to lead Renda Bay.

The seamstress Jann spoke her husband's name and wept, bowing her head over the grave as Phillip's body was laid to rest and covered with dirt. "He just wanted to build boats," she said. "After the accident with the fishhook, he prefered to stay on land. He thought it would be safer." Her shoulders shuddered. "Safer."

Nathan stood next to the small woman, his gaze somber, his head lowered. Awkwardly, the seamstress held out a folded gray garment for him. "This is another of Phillip's shirts, Nathan. You fought with us, you saved me, and—" Her voice broke with a quick choking sound. She sniffled, and her lips trembled. "And your first new shirt was ruined. Phillip would want you to have this."

"I would be honored." The wizard pressed the clean linen against his chest.

Although they had fought alongside the people of Renda Bay, Nicci did not feel she had finished her mission here. After they had filled in the graves and woodcarvers had cut names into the fresh-cut posts, Nicci addressed the villagers before they left the graveyard.

"This is why you need Lord Rahl," she said. "His goal is to stop such violence and bloodshed, to crush slavers so that all people can live their lives in freedom. Yes, he is far away, but the D'Haran army will not tolerate such lawlessness and oppression. It may take time, but the world will change—the world has already changed. You must have noticed the stars."

The villagers muttered, listening to her with a different attitude after their ordeal.

She continued in a stronger voice. "But you have to be responsible for yourselves as well. When you've picked up the pieces here, send an envoy on the long journey north to the People's Palace. In D'Hara, swear your loyalty to Lord Rahl and tell him what happened here. Tell him about all the lands of the old empire that need him. He will not let you down."

Nathan said, "Before you send envoys, we will write a message for him, as well as a summary of what we have seen. If someone could deliver that, we would be most grateful."

Thaddeus swallowed hard. "Even though they were defeated last night, the Norukai will return. How soon can your Lord Rahl send his army?"

Nicci wasn't finished. "You cannot simply wait for help. All people are responsible for their own lives, their own destinies. You must improve your own defenses, and you will need more than a bonfire and a lookout tower. The slavers believe you are weak, and that is why they prey on you. The best way to insure your peace is through *strength*. Maybe last night was a lesson for them. We were here to help this time, but you would not need to be rescued if you weren't victims in the first place."

"You can learn how to defend yourselves," Bannon said, looking away. "I did."

"But how?" Thaddeus said. "Erect walls along the shore? String a barrier chain across the harbor? How are we to raise an army? Where do we get weapons? We are just a fishing village."

Nathan suggested, "In addition to your bonfire and lookout platform, build guard towers on either side of the harbor, and be ready to launch a rain of fire arrows down on any raiders who come. Keep several longboats at the ready to go out and sink them before they enter the harbor. The raider vessels will be flaming wrecks before they ever get to shore."

Nicci said in a hard voice, "The Norukai are slavers, not conquerors. You have an advantage, because they want to capture you alive, otherwise you are no good to them. Other attackers may just slaughter you all."

"I would be happy to kill them," Jann growled.

Nicci approved. "Let nothing hold you back. Arm your people so they can fight better."

"Keep boat hooks and pikes ready on the docks," Bannon said. "Even if the slavers get through, your people could fight them off as they try to disembark."

"Make them think twice before they come back here again," Nicci said. As she watched determination grow like a slow-burning fire among them, she felt gratified. "When your wounds become scars and you've rebuilt your homes, do not forget what happened here, or it will happen again."

The next day, Nicci, Nathan, and Bannon went to the small building that served as Renda Bay's town hall. The interior smelled of smoke. Three of the glass windows were shattered, and the roof was partially charred, but teams of villagers had extinguished the fire before it caused severe damage.

The beefy town leader's posture seemed hunched with duty. "I'll need workers to help rebuild this hall, but it may take time. Our first priority is to strengthen our defenses, as you said." Thaddeus looked at them with a hopeful expression. "Would you stay with us, defend us? We've seen how powerful your magic is, Sorceress. And the wizard could try to use his magic, too."

Nathan looked as if he might be sick. "No . . . that could be dangerous."

Nicci bit her lower lip. "I have a larger purpose to serve for Lord

Rahl, and now we must move on. The storm blew the *Wavewalker* far off course, and we need to look at maps and determine where we are."

"We need to find a place called Kol Adair," Nathan said. He patted the life book in his leather pouch. "We were told that something important awaits us there."

"We do have some maps," said Thaddeus, distracted and troubled. "They're in here somewhere." He rummaged in Holden's cabinets, shifting aside old documents that listed the names of registered fishing boats, a ledger for taxes, charts of land ownership. Finally, he found an old and sketchy map that showed the Phantom Coast, the southern part of the Old World marked with a spiderweb of clear, straight lines that joined the open lands.

"These are imperial roads that Emperor Jagang constructed to move his armies, but he spent little time this far south. All I know is that the port cities of Serrimundi and Kherimus are up here somewhere." He gestured vaguely off the top of the map. "And Tanimura is farther north. I've heard rumors of the New World, but I know nothing about it."

While Nicci studied the map, Nathan took out his life book and quickly sketched in some details on his own map, correcting some of his crude estimates of the terrain they had seen.

"Kol Adair . . ." Thaddeus sat heavily in the chair behind Holden's old desk. His brow furrowed as he looked at the charts, but they seemed unfamiliar to him. He scratched his frizzy beard. "I've barely been beyond Renda Bay, myself. Even in my fishing boat, I never sailed out of sight of the coast.

"I've heard stories of distant lands, though. I believe Kol Adair is well inland, beyond the foothills and over a mountain range, across a vast fertile valley, and then more mountains. The place you seek lies somewhere in those mountains . . . according to the stories."

He ran his hand along the easternmost part of the map as if he could draw topography on the scarred desk. "No distant travelers have come through here in such a long time." He pointed to the middle of the map. "But we know of other settlements upriver, ports, mining towns, farming villages." He shuddered visibly. "And in the other direction there are islands out at sea, rugged windswept rocks where the Norukai live." He bit off his words, then said with hollow calmness, "I would not suggest you go there."

"We won't," Nathan said. "We are looking for Kol Adair."

Nicci asked, "Can you supply us with provisions, packs, garments, tools for our journey? We lost almost everything in the shipwreck."

"Renda Bay owes you far more than we can ever repay," said Thaddeus.

"If you send your emissaries up to D'Hara bearing our message to Lord Rahl, that will be all the payment I require."

After resting one more day and helping the villagers collect the ragged debris of their lives, the three set out again. They all wore clean clothes. Bannon's sword, now sharpened and oiled, hung at his side in its plain scabbard. Nathan's ornate sword had also been cleaned, polished, and sharpened.

Bannon seemed troubled as they set off on the road. "Can we make a slight detour to the graveyard? There's something I want to do."

"We already paid our respects to the fallen, my boy," Nathan said.

"It's more than that," Bannon said.

Nicci saw how the young man had changed after his experience here. He no longer seemed so cheerful and naive . . . or maybe his cheeriness had always been an act. She said, "I do not wish to delay for long."

"Thank you," the young man said.

They followed the curve of the hill until they reached the line of new graves, the fresh-packed earth that held thirty-nine resting bodies. Bannon went straight to the part of the burial ground crowded with wooden posts. Twenty-two new ones had been pounded into the ground, each etched with the name of a villager taken by the slavers.

Bannon clenched his fists as he walked among the posts until he chose one—a clean, bright post of freshly sanded wood. On one side, a villager had carved the name *MERRIAM*.

Bannon dropped to his knees on the opposite side of the post. He pulled out his sword and held it awkwardly, using the point to gouge three letters into the fresh wood. Tears sparkled in his eyes as he looked at the name.

IAN.

Nathan gave him a solemn nod.

Bannon stood again, and placed the sword back in its sheath. "Now I'm ready to go."

CHAPTER 27

They followed the river inland from the town of Renda Bay, looking forward to "Lands Unknown"—the farms, logging towns, and mining settlements that Thaddeus had described for them. Someone along the way would know more about Kol Adair and give them guidance.

Occasional flatboats drifted by on the river as farmers or merchants brought goods down to Renda Bay. The flatboat pilots used poles to guide the loaded vessels downstream. Some of them would wave in greeting, while others just stared at the strangers walking the river path.

After the ordeal with the shipwreck, Nicci felt as if they had been given a fresh start. Her long black traveling dress was cleaned and mended; Nathan wore the homespun shirt from Phillip, and Bannon also had a new set of clothes.

As they went farther up the river valley, Bannon seemed to recover his pleasant fantasy of life again, but now Nicci realized that his smile and his optimism were just a veneer. She saw through it now. At least he no longer tried to flirt with her; she had frightened that foolish attraction out of him.

But the young man wasn't entirely daunted. He approached her, striking up a conversation. "Sorceress, it occurred to me that like prophecy, wishes sometimes come about in unexpected ways. And your wish did come true."

She narrowed her blue eyes. "What wish?"

"The wishpearl I gave you on the *Wavewalker*. Remember?"

"I threw it overboard to appease the selka queen," Nicci said.

"Think of the chain of events. After you made the wish, we sailed south, the selka attacked, and that storm wrecked the ship, but we found the stone marker, which confirmed the witch woman's prophecy. Then we made our way to Renda Bay, where we fought the slavers, and the town leader told us what he knew about Kol Adair. See, that was your wish—that it would help us get to Kol Adair." He spread his hands. "It's obvious."

"Your logic is as straightforward as a drunkard walking down an icy hill in a windstorm," she said. "I make my own wishes come true, and I make my own luck. No selka magic bent the events of the world around my desires just to put us here at this exact place. We would have found our way in any case."

"Wishes are dangerous, like prophecy," Nathan interjected, walking close beside them. "They often lead to unexpected results."

"Then I will be careful not to make any more frivolous wishes," Nicci said. "I am the one who determines my own life."

They continued inland for days and found several settlements, large and small. While Nathan and Nicci gathered any information they could, they explained about the D'Haran Empire and about Richard's new rule. The isolated villagers listened to the news, but such obscure and distant politics had little bearing on their daily lives. Nathan marked the names of the villages on his hand-drawn map, and they moved on.

Once, when he introduced himself as the wizard Nathan Rahl, the villagers asked for a demonstration of his powers, and he faltered in embarrassment. "Well, magic is a special thing, my friends, not to be used for mere games and showmanship."

When Nicci heard this, she flashed him a skeptical expression. When Nathan had possessed his powers, he did indeed use them for just that, whenever he considered it useful. Now, however, he had to pretend that such demonstrations were beneath him. When the village children learned that Nicci was a sorceress, they pestered her instead, although one glance from her made them quickly reconsider their requests.

Bannon offered to do tricks with his sword, but they were not interested.

As they left that village, Nathan quietly vowed, "I won't mention my magic again . . . not until I am made whole again after Kol Adair. For now I don't even dare make the attempt."

"You should still try," Nicci said as they continued along the forested road. "Can you feel your Han at all? You may have lost your gift, but you could regain it."

"Or I might cause a terrible disaster." Nathan's expression turned grayish. "I didn't tell you what happened in Renda Bay when I . . . I tried to heal a man."

They walked along a good path up into foothills, as the main river branched and they took the north fork. "I saw you helping some of the injured," Nicci said.

"You didn't see everything." Nathan waved at a fly in front of his face. "Bannon saw me . . . but we have not discussed it since."

The young man blinked. "I saw so much that night, I think my eyes were filled with blood and I couldn't absorb it all. I don't remember . . . I don't remember much at all."

"One of the Norukai spears had pierced the man's chest, and he was dying," Nathan said. "Even the healer women knew he couldn't be saved. But I felt a hint of my magic. I was desperate, and I wanted to prove myself. I had seen you save the town with your gift, Sorceress, and I knew how much I could have helped. I was furious and I grasped at any small spark of magic. I felt something and tried to use it."

He paused on the path, seemingly out of breath, although the route was quite level. He wiped sweat from the side of his neck. The weight of his tale seemed so great a burden that he couldn't walk and speak at the same time. "I wanted to heal him . . . but much has changed inside me. Dear spirits, I don't understand my gift anymore. I thought I touched my Han, and I released what small amount of power I could find. It should have been Additive Magic. I should have been able to knit the man's tissues together, repair his lungs, stop the bleeding." Nathan's azure eyes glistened with tears.

Nicci and Bannon both paused beside him.

"I tried to heal him . . ." Nathan's voice cracked. "But my magic did the opposite. It ricocheted, and instead of sealing his wounds and stopping the bleeding, my spell . . . *tore him apart.* It ripped that poor man asunder, when I was only trying to save him."

Bannon looked at the wizard, aghast. "I think I remember now. I was staring right at it, but . . . I didn't see, or I didn't trust what I was seeing."

Nicci tried to understand what he was saying. "You felt the magic come back to you, but it did the opposite of what you intended?"

"I don't know if it was exactly the opposite . . . it was uncontrolled. A wild thing. My Han seemed almost vengeful, fighting against whatever I wanted. That poor man . . ." He looked up at her. "Consider, Sorceress—if I had unleashed that kind of magic in a fight against the Norukai, I might well have annihilated all of Renda Bay. I could have killed you and Bannon."

"Can you feel the gift inside you now?" Nicci asked.

Nathan hesitated. "Maybe . . . I'm not certain. As I'm sure you understand, I'm afraid to try. How can I take the risk? I don't even want to practice. What if I try to create a simple hand light—and instead I unleash a huge forest fire? Those village children who asked to see a little trick . . . I could have killed them all. Magic that I can't control is worse than no magic at all."

Nicci said, "That depends upon the circumstances. If we are being pursued by an army of monster warriors, even an uncontrolled forest fire might prove useful."

As usual, Bannon tried to inspire them with his cheer. "Obviously, our best solution is to find Kol Adair as soon as we can. Then we will have our wizard back."

"Yes, my boy," Nathan said. "A perfectly simple solution." He set off down the road at a brisk pace.

Three days later, while passing through wooded hills with few signs of habitation, they came upon a wide imperial road that cut straight through the uneven terrain, then down into a broad valley. The road headed northward like a straight spear that Jagang had hurled toward the New World.

From the crest of the hill they looked down at the abandoned thoroughfare, which had been carved by great armies, but not in recent years. The road looked weathered and overgrown.

Nathan turned to Nicci. "When you were Death's Mistress, did any of your expeditions come this far south?"

She shook her head. "Jagang did not consider this wilderness to be worth the effort, although from his ancient maps, we knew there were once great cities and trading centers beyond the Phantom Coast."

"This road may have been a built by another emperor." Nathan smiled. "The history of the Old World is full of them. Have you heard of Emperor Kurgan? The warlord they called Iron Fang?"

They descended to the wide, empty road. Nicci raised an eyebrow. "I remember some of the history I learned in the Palace of the Prophets, but I'm not familiar with his name. Was this Iron Fang a ruler of any significance?"

"I spent a thousand years reading history, dear Sorceress, and countless rulers have laid claim to historical significance, but Emperor Kurgan might well have been the most infamous ruler since the time of the wizard wars. At least according to his chroniclers. I'm surprised you didn't know of him."

"Jagang preferred that I help him make history, not ruminate about it," Nicci said. She had certainly made history when she killed Jagang herself, without fanfare, without spectacle, exactly as Richard had asked.

"We have a long walk ahead of us, so plenty of time for the tale." Nathan strolled ahead, following the great empty road, which took them in the general direction they wished to go. "Fifteen centuries ago, Emperor Kurgan conquered much of the Old World and the vast lands to the south." He quirked a smile at Bannon as the young man walked on the weed-overgrown paving stones. "Not long ago at all, only five hundred years before I was born."

"Only five hundred years?" Bannon seemed unable to grasp that span of time.

"Kurgan was brutal and ruthless, but he earned the name Iron Fang mostly because of his affectation. He had his left canine tooth replaced." Nathan opened his mouth and tapped the corresponding tooth with a fingertip. "Replaced it with a long iron point. I have no doubt that it made him look fearsome, although I can't imagine how it was possible for him to eat with the thing in his mouth." He snorted. "And he had to replace it regularly, due to rust."

"Doesn't sound very terrifying to me," Nicci said.

"Oh, he was fearsome and powerful enough. Iron Fang's relentless armies overwhelmed land after land, conscripting all available young fighters, which increased his army . . . and thereby helped him conquer more lands and conscript more fighters. It was an unstoppable flood.

"But, as I'm afraid dear Richard is now beginning to realize, *conquering* territory is one thing, while *administering* it is quite another. Kurgan's downfall was that he actually believed the praise heaped upon him by the minstrels and criers, when as far as I can tell, Iron Fang's true genius was his main military commander, General Utros."

"Even an emperor needs excellent military commanders to conquer and hold so many lands," Nicci said.

Nathan waxed poetic. "General Utros was the strategist who led Kurgan's armies to victory after victory. Utros seized all the territory of the Old World in the name of Emperor Kurgan." Walking along the easy path of the ancient imperial road, he kept glancing to the foothills in the east, in the supposed direction of Kol Adair. "And once Utros was gone, Iron Fang simply could not function without his general."

"What happened to Utros?" Bannon asked. "Was he defeated or killed?"

"Oddly enough, that is not entirely certain, but I have my ideas. The story is far more complicated than a list of military campaigns. You see, Emperor Kurgan had married a beautiful queen from one of the largest lands he seized. Her name was Majel. Some say she was a sorceress, because her beauty was indeed bewitching." He gave Nicci a wry smile. "Perhaps like our own sorceress."

She frowned at him.

He continued his story. "Majel's beauty was so entrancing that General Utros was put under its spell. She found him to be a handsome man, not to mention brave and powerful—certainly he was a mate superior to Iron Fang himself, who might not have been as awe-inspiring as his propaganda would suggest." He gave a dismissive wave of his hand. "Or maybe there was nothing magic about it at all. It could just be that Empress Majel and General Utros fell in love. It's clear to me, and to many historical scholars, that Utros intended to conquer the world, then overthrow Kurgan and take Majel for his own."

"What happened then?" Bannon asked.

Nathan stopped at a shoulder-high pinnacle of weathered rock that had been erected at the side of the road, as a mile marker, although the carved letters had long since worn away. He removed his life book, opened to his map, and glanced at the foothills, trying to orient himself. None of the foundation rocks gave any hint about the chilling prophecy or Kol Adair, though. Nicci was almost relieved. . . .

"Utros took the bulk of the imperial army, nine hundred thousand of Kurgan's best soldiers, on a campaign to conquer the powerful city of Ildakar. And he simply vanished—along with the entire army.

"It's generally believed that they deserted, all nine hundred thousand of them. Maybe they even joined the forces of Ildakar. Suddenly finding himself without his army, Emperor Kurgan was weak and utterly lost. Then he discovered evidence of Empress Majel's affair with Utros, and in his rage at this betrayal, Kurgan stripped her naked and chained her spread-eagled in the center of the city square. He forced his people to watch as he used an obsidian dagger to peel away her beautiful face in narrow ribbons of flesh, leaving her eyeballs intact so she could watch as he skinned the rest of her body, strip by strip. He finally gouged out her eyes and made sure she was still alive before upending urns of ravenous, flesh-eating beetles onto the raw, bloody meat that remained of her body."

Bannon looked queasy. Nicci gave a grim nod, imagining that Jagang could well have done something similar. "Emperors tend to be . . . excessive," she said.

The wizard continued, "Iron Fang did that to strike terror into the hearts of his people, but he only appalled them, for they had loved Empress Majel. His people were so disgusted and outraged that they rose up and overthrew Emperor Kurgan. He had no army to defend him and only a handful of imperial guards, many of whom were just as outraged at the crime they had witnessed. The people killed Kurgan and dragged his body through the streets until all the flesh was ripped off his bones. They hung his corpse by the ankles from a high tower of the palace until jackdaws picked the skeleton clean."

"That is what should happen to tyrants," Nicci said. "Jagang himself was buried unmarked in a mass grave."

Nathan strolled onward, smiling. "And, of course, the citizens chose another emperor, who was just as ruthless, just as oppressive. Some people simply don't learn."

CHAPTER 28

The foothills rose up from the river valley to form a mountain range, and according to the information they had been told, beyond those mountains would be a broad, fertile valley with another line of even higher mountains beyond. And then they would find Kol Adair.

Nathan thought the journey would be quite a challenge. He corrected himself: quite an *adventure*. During his sedentary centuries in the Palace of the Prophets, he had waited for exactly this, although he had not foreseen losing his gift along the way.

Leaving the rigidly straight imperial road, which headed north, the three travelers wound their way into hills covered with aspens. The forest was eerily beautiful, with tall, smooth trunks of green-gray bark and rippling leaves that whispered and rustled in the breeze. They walked on a carpet of mellow, sweet-smelling fallen leaves.

By late afternoon, Nathan found an open spot near a creek and suggested they set up camp. Bannon went off to hunt rabbits for their supper, but came back with only some swollen crabapples and an armful of cattails, whose pulp, he said, could be cooked up into a filling, if bland, mash. They added smoked fish from their packs, given to them by the people of Renda Bay. Later, Nicci drifted off to sleep while Nathan recounted more obscure and barbaric tales from history. At least Bannon was interested.

The next day they continued into the rolling hills, following a path that was wide enough for a horse, although they had not seen a village in days. Nathan consulted his notes. "There should be another town up ahead. Lockridge, according to the map." He frowned as he looked from side to side, still trying to get his bearings. "At least, as best I can tell. We should easily reach it by nightfall."

"I'm happy just to travel with you as my companions," Bannon said, "for as long as you'll let me."

Nathan wondered how many days, months, or even years it would take them to find Kol Adair, but once they reached that mysterious place—whether it was a mountain, or a city, or some magical wellspring—he would become whole again. In the meantime, he felt empty and unsettled. Although he was perfectly competent without his gift, a decent swordsman and a true adventurer, the magic was part of him, and he did not like the idea that his own Han was a restless, rebellious force.

Alas, the farther they got from Renda Bay, the less reliable Thaddeus's sketchy map proved to be. "I'm sure the townspeople ahead will be able to help us out," Nathan said aloud.

When they reached an elbow in the ridge and walked out onto a cleared outcropping that sported only a single gnarled bristlecone among the rocks, Nathan paused to take a look around him, taking advantage of the exposed view to get his bearings.

Bannon pointed to a higher ridge several miles away, a large granite peak that stood above the other hills like a citadel. "There's a kind of tower over there. What do you suppose that is?"

"Another cairn?" Nicci asked.

"No, no. This is much larger. A great tower, I think."

Nathan shaded his brow. The midmorning sun was in his eyes, blocking details, but he could make out a stone watchtower topped with partially crumbled crenellations. "Yes, yes, you're right, my boy. But I see no movement, no people." He squinted harder. "It looks empty."

"That would be a good place to erect a watchtower," Nicci said. "A sentinel outpost."

Nathan turned in a slow circle, looking at the ridges, the trees, the unfolding landscape. "Yes, that's the highest point all around. From there, a person could see for quite some distance." He began to grow excited as an idea occurred to him. "I could get over there and come back to the main road in a few hours. Getting a perspective on the land ahead would definitely be worth the detour."

Nicci shrugged. "If you feel it is necessary, Wizard, I will accompany you."

Nathan felt strangely defensive as he turned to her. Since he had lost his gift, she clearly felt she needed to be his protector, his minder. "It is not necessary for us all to go on such a side trip. With or without magic, Nathan Rahl is not a child who needs a nanny." He sniffed. "Leave it to me. I'll make my way over there, get the lay of the land, and update my map while you two keep following the path. Once you reach that town ahead, I trust you to find lodgings and make arrangements for a meal. I'll certainly be hungry by the time I rejoin you."

Bannon beamed as he stepped up. "I'll come along with you, Nathan. You might need Sturdy and me to protect against any dangers. Besides, I'll keep you company. You can tell me more stories."

Nathan knew that the young man was earnest—in fact, Bannon was probably intimidated by the thought of being left alone with Nicci—but Nathan wanted to do this by himself. Ever since losing his grasp on magic, and now afraid even to try lest he trigger some unknown disaster, he had felt a need to prove his own worth.

"As tempting as that is, my boy, I don't need your help." He realized his voice was unintentionally sharp, and he softened his tone. "I'll be fine, I tell you. Let me go alone. I'll follow that ridge—see, it looks easy enough." He let out a disarming chuckle. "Dear spirits, if I can't find the highest point all around, then I'm useless! There's no need for you both to go so many miles out of your way."

Nicci saw his determination and accepted it. "That is your decision, Wizard."

"Just make sure you two don't need *my* help while I'm gone," Nathan added with a hint of sarcasm, and he nudged Bannon's shoulder. "Go with the sorceress. What if she needs the protection of your sword? Don't abandon her."

Nicci grimaced at the suggestion, while Bannon nodded with grave dedication to his new assignment.

Without further farewell, the wizard strode off into the slatted lines of aspens, following the crest of the ridge and marking the distance to the sentinel tower. He hurried out of sight because he didn't want Nicci or Bannon to change their minds and insist on joining him. "I am still a wizard, damn the spirits!" he muttered. The Han was still within him, even though it now felt less like a loyal pet and more like a rabid dog chained to a post. But at least he had his sword and his fighting skills, and he had a thousand years of knowledge to draw upon. He could handle a simple scouting expedition by himself.

The line of the undulating hills guided him down a slope following a drainage, then up around to another high point. He caught a glimpse of the tower, which still seemed miles away, but he didn't let himself grow discouraged. He would achieve his goal, find the tower, and learn what he could. This was all unexplored territory, and he was the first roving D'Haran ambassador to behold it, in the name of Lord Richard Rahl.

His legs ached as he bushwhacked over the rough terrain. He paused to marvel at a series of arcane symbols he found carved into the bark of a large fallen aspen—ancient and unreadable letter scars that had swelled and blurred with age as the tree grew. The symbols were not in any language he knew, not High D'Haran, not any of the old spell languages from the scrolls and books he had studied in Tanimura. The markings reminded him that he was indeed in a place far from his knowledge. . . .

When he was miles away from his companions, all alone in the wilderness and supposedly safe, Nathan let himself fully consider how his circumstances had changed since he and Nicci had left their lives back in D'Hara. Yes, he was certainly in fine shape for a man his age: well muscled, physically fit, active, nimble. And very good with his sword, even if he did say so himself. But his magic had gone astray, and that bothered him in ways he could not articulate—and Nathan Rahl considered himself a very articulate man.

He could never forget the horror of the backlash when he had tried to heal the wounded man in Renda Bay, how the magic had dodged and twisted when he tried to use it. He was afraid of what other consequences he might endure. Whenever he had tried to reach for it, struggling for some touch, some grasp, he had felt only a hint, an echo . . . then a *sting*. He didn't want to be around his friends in case some monstrous backlash might occur. But he needed to learn more about his condition.

Now, he decided to take his chance. Out here in the forest, walking along the wooded ridges, far from anyone else, Nathan decided to experiment.

Considering his options, he decided not to dabble with any fire spell, because it could so easily erupt into a great conflagration that he wouldn't be able to extinguish. Like Nicci, though, he had easily been able to manipulate air, nudge breezes, and twist the wind. Maybe he could try that.

Nathan looked around himself at the forest of dizzyingly similar aspen trunks, all the rounded leaves knit together in a crown. Winds rippled through the branches overhead.

What did he have to lose? He reached inside himself, searched for his Han, tried to pull just enough that he could create a puff of air, a bit of wind, to stir the twigs and leaves. A gentle little twirl . . .

At first nothing happened, but he strained harder, reached deeper, released his Han, *pushed* it, to create just an outflowing breeze, a gentle gust.

The leaves did stir, and suddenly the air sucked toward him. The wind swirled and twisted, wound up as a cyclone. Nathan had intended only to nudge, but the air whooshed around him in a roar and rushed upward, like a hurricane blow.

He struggled, grabbed at nothing with his hands, tried to pull it in, reining back his power—but the wind only increased as the magic fought against him. Branches overhead snapped. A thick aspen bough broke in half and came crashing to the forest floor not far from him. Leaves were torn asunder, thrown apart like green confetti in the air. The storm kept building, pushing branches, thrashing like a furious seizure.

"Stop! Dear spirits, stop!" Nathan tried to center his Han, reaching for some inner valve to turn it off, to calm himself, and finally the wind died down, the storm abated, and he was left standing there, panting hard.

His white hair was tangled, whipped around his head. Nathan steadied himself against a sturdy aspen trunk. That was not at all what he had intended! And it was an even more ominous hint of the dangerous consequences he might face if he tried to use his magic. Most of the time he couldn't find the gift at all, but when he did try to work a spell, he had no idea what might actually happen.

Certainly not what he wanted to happen.

He was glad that Nicci and Bannon hadn't seen this. He couldn't be responsible for what might occur if he blundered again. His throat was dry, and he gradually caught his breath. "Quite extraordinary," he said, "but not something I would like to do again. Not until I understand this more."

An hour later, another high clearing showed him that he had covered half the distance to the watchtower, and he picked up his pace. It was already past noon, and he wanted to see the view, take his notes, and make his way back to the main trail—and a comfortable village, he hoped—before nightfall.

And, no, he would not dabble with magic again.

The sentinel tower sat on top of a rocky bluff dotted with stubby bristlecones that grew among large talus boulders. The nearer side of the outcropping was a sheer, impassable cliff, so Nathan worked his way around to the bluff's more accommodating side, where he discovered a worn path wide enough for three men to walk abreast . . . or for warhorses to gallop up the slope.

The breezes increased as Nathan broke out of the forest and climbed into the open area around the base of the watchtower. The stone structure was far more imposing than he had first thought, rising high into the open sky. The looming tower was octagonal, its flat sides constructed of enormous quarried blocks. Such a mammoth project would have required either an inexhaustible supply of labor or powerful magic to cut and assemble the blocks like this.

He stopped to catch his breath as he looked across the open terrain. From this high citadel, sentinels would have been able to keep watch for miles in all directions. He wondered if this place had perhaps been built by Emperor Kurgan during the Midwar, and he imagined General Utros himself climbing to this summit from which he could survey the lands he had just conquered.

Nathan heard only an oppressive silence that pressed down around him. He craned his neck to get a view of the top of the single structure, he saw large lookout windows, some of them with the glass intact, while others were shattered. Several of the crenellations had fallen, and large blocks lay strewn around the base like enormous toys.

Nathan called, "Hello, is anyone there?" Any watchers would have seen him approach for the last hour, and a lone man would have been completely vulnerable as he ascended the wide path to the summit. If someone meant to attack him, they had certainly had ample opportunity. He wanted at least to begin the conversation under the auspices of friendship. "Hello?" he called again, but heard only the muttering whispers of wind in and out of the broken windows. Not even birds had taken up residence there.

Despite his uneasiness, Nathan felt the reassuring presence of his sword. He would not try to use magic again, but he reminded himself that he wasn't helpless if he encountered some threat. He stepped up to the broken tower entrance, where a massive wooden door had fallen off its hinges and lay collapsed just inside the main entry. He braced himself, inhaling deeply. He had promised his companions that he could do this, and he could hardly walk all this way and then be afraid to climb up to see the view.

"I come in peace!" he shouted at the top of his voice, then muttered to himself, "At least until you make me change my mind."

He stepped over the fallen door and passed under the archway to see another set of doors, iron bars, a portcullis—all of which had been torn asunder and *destroyed*. The iron bars were uprooted from where they had been seated in the blocks, twisted as if by some supreme force.

Inside the main chamber, wide stone stairs ascended the side wall, running in an octagonal spiral up the interior faces. Five ancient skeletons in long-rotted armor lay broken on the central floor, as if they had fallen off the stairs from a great height.

Though he couldn't find his Han, didn't dare try to summon it, he could sense a power inside this watchtower, a throbbing energy as if this structure had been bombarded by the magic of an attacking sorcerer . . . or maybe it had been saturated with magic by the defenders who tried to save it.

Nathan climbed the stairs and found himself out of breath. Though he was a fit man with travel-conditioned muscles, he was still a thousand years old.

The whistling breezes grew louder as he reached the pinnacle of the watchtower, a wide, empty lookout chamber with an iron-reinforced wooden floor. The ancient planks were petrified. Although parts of the outer walls had broken, the damage did not seem to be due to age. In fact, instead of merely crumbling and falling downward, as would have been caused by gravity, the missing stone blocks had been *flung* far from the base of the tower . . . as if blasted outward.

Every wall of the octagonal lookout chamber had an expansive window, which would allow sentinels to watch in all directions. Each such window had been filled with a broad pane of deep red glass. Three of the eight windows had been shattered by time or brute force, and now shards of broken glass protruded from the window frames like crimson daggers. The other five windows were miraculously intact despite their obvious age, which led Nathan to guess that the glass had been enhanced by magic somehow. The wind whispered more loudly, whisking through the broken windows.

Standing in the middle of the open platform, he turned slowly as he tried to determine what had happened here. Sprawled on the iron-hard floor were more skeletons, all clad in ancient armor. Dark stains on the stone wall blocks marked a varnish of blackened blood, and long white grooves seemed to be scratches, as if desperate fingernails had gouged the quarried stone itself.

Nathan walked across the wooden boards, and one plank gave an alarming crack, as if it was about to give way. He instinctively lurched back, and his boot came down on the femur of one of the fallen warriors. Stumbling, he lost his balance, fell into the wall, and reached out to grab for balance.

His hand caught on the open sill of a lookout window where broken red glass protruded. He hissed in pain and pulled back, looking at the deep gash in his palm. Blood oozed out, and he grimaced.

Looking at the blood, he muttered, "It would be such a simple task to heal myself if I had magic." He was embarrassed by his clumsiness even though he was alone. Now he would have to bind the gash and wait until Nicci could take care of the wound.

Just then he realized that the sound of the wind had taken on an odd character. The tower itself thrummed with a deep vibration. A bright, scarlet light increased inside the observation room, throbbing from the splash of blood Nathan had left behind.

The five intact red panes began to glow.

CHAPTER 29

Continuing down the path, Nicci moved through the forest, and Bannon hurried after her. "Don't worry, Sorceress, I can keep up. A woman traveling alone on an empty trail might attract trouble, but if any dangerous men see me and my sword, they will think twice before they harass you."

She turned her cool gaze on him. "You've seen what I can do. Do you doubt my ability to take care of any problem that might arise?"

"Oh, I know about your powers, Sorceress—but others may not. Just having me here with a sharp blade"—he patted his sword—"is sure to prevent problems. The best way out of a difficult situation is to make sure it doesn't arise in the first place." He lowered his voice. "You taught me that yourself, after you rescued me from the robbers in Tanimura."

"Yes, I did." Nicci gave him a small nod of acknowledgment. "Don't make me rescue you again."

"I won't, I promise."

"Don't make promises, because circumstances have a way of making you regret them. Did you promise your friend Ian that you would always stay by his side? That you wouldn't abandon him in times of danger?"

Bannon swallowed hard, but he kept walking beside her. "I had no choice. I couldn't do anything about that."

"I did not accuse you, nor did I say you had a choice. I just point out that if you had made such a promise, it was one you could not have kept."

He pondered in silence for a dozen steps. "You know that my child-hood wasn't as perfect as I wish it had been. That doesn't mean I can't hope for better." He moved aside an aspen branch that dangled across the path. Nicci ducked and kept moving. "And what about you, Sorceress? Did you have a terrible childhood? Someone must have hurt you badly to give you such a hard edge. Your father?"

Nicci stopped in the track. Bannon took several more steps before he realized she had paused behind him. He turned.

"No, my father didn't hurt me. In fact, he was rather kind. His business was making armor, and he was quite well known. He taught me the constellations. I grew up in a village that was nice enough, I suppose, before the Imperial Order came." Nicci looked up, finally admitting aloud what she had known for a long time. "It was my mother who made my childhood a nightmare. She scarred me with lessons that she called the truth, made me think that my hardworking father was the evil one, that his beliefs were oppressive to all people. And the Imperial Order reinforced those beliefs."

She strode ahead at a faster pace, not caring whether Bannon kept up with her. "She made me live in terrible, dirty places. Again and again I was infested with lice, but it was all for my own good, she said. It was to build my character, to make me understand." Nicci sneered. "I loathe my mother for it now, but it took me a century and a half to realize it."

"A century and a half?" Bannon asked. "But that's not possible. You, you're—"

She turned to look at him. "I am over one hundred and eighty years old."

"You're immortal, then?" he asked, wide-eyed.

"I age normally now, but I still have a long life ahead of me, and I intend to accomplish much."

"As do I," Bannon said. "I'll accompany you and do my best to help you and Wizard Nathan achieve your purpose. I can prove myself."

She barely gave him a glance. "You may stay with us, so long as you don't become a nuisance."

"I won't become a nuisance. I promise." He realized what he had said and bit back his words. "I mean, I don't *promise*, but I will do my best not to be a nuisance anymore."

"And will you know when you become a nuisance?"

He nodded. "Absolutely. There is no doubt."

Nicci was surprised at his confidence. "How will you know?"

"Because you will tell me in no uncertain terms." His face was so serious she couldn't help but believe him.

Though the wide path implied that it had once been well traveled, the downed aspens and oaks hadn't been cleared after several winters, and she and Bannon frequently had to climb over or step around. If there was a village ahead, its people did not often come this way. She had seen no footprints, no sign of other travelers, and she decided they would probably end up camping again in the forest.

The young man broke the silence again. "Do you think anyone has the perfect life I imagine? Do you believe there is an idyllic place like that?"

"We would have to make it for ourselves," Nicci said. "If the people create an oppressive culture, if they allow tyrannical rulers, then they get what they deserve."

"But shouldn't there be a peaceful land where people can just be happy?"

"It is naive to entertain a fantasy like that." Nicci pursed her lips. "But Lord Rahl is trying to build a world where people live in freedom. If they wish to make an idyllic place, they will have the chance to do so. That is what I hope for."

The path widened into a road, and the forest thinned into an open park, an expansive area where they could see homesteads with a patchwork of crops across the cleared land. The farmhouses were built from logs and capped with shake-shingle roofs.

Bannon said, "Those must be outlying farms for the village we're looking for. See how the trees have been cut down, the land cleared? All those fences made from fieldstones?"

"I see no one about, though," Nicci said.

Although the road remained a prominent track, it was overgrown with grass, showing no recent hoofprints or wheel marks. They passed stone walls that had fallen into disrepair; weeds and grass protruded from the cracks. Even the fields were wild and overgrown. The area seemed entirely abandoned.

Nicci grew more wary as the silence deepened. On one farm, a field of tall sunflowers drooped, their large heads sunbursts of yellow petals around a central brown circle. Bannon pointed out, "Those fields went to seed over several growing seasons. Notice how disorganized they are." He shook his head. "No cabbage farmer would be so unruly." He stepped up to the nearest sunflower, ran his hands along its hairy stalk. "These were planted in rows several years ago, but they grew up and went unharvested. The new ones are scattered everywhere. Birds spread them out, and next year after those go to seed, the pattern disappears even further." He glanced around. "And look at the vegetable garden. It's entirely untended."

Nicci felt uneasy. "This homestead has been abandoned. They're all abandoned."

"But why? The land looks fertile. See these crops? The soil is dark and rich."

Hearing an odd sound, she spun, ready to release her magic in case she had to attack, but it was only the bleat of a goat. Two gray and white animals came forward, attracted by their conversation.

Bannon grinned. "Look at you!" The goats came forward, and each one let him pat it on the side of the neck. "You look like you're eating well." He frowned at Nicci in puzzlement. "If goats run loose, they'll ransack the vegetable garden. My mother would never let goats come close to our house."

They walked up to a log cottage, where the shake roof had fallen into disrepair. An overturned cart with a sprung wheel was covered with weeds. "No one lives here," Nicci said. "That much is apparent."

They went around to the side of the farmhouse, where they came upon two unexpected ornamental statues, a life-size man and woman dressed as farmers. The expressions on their stone faces showed abject misery. The man's lips were drawn back in anguish, his face turned to the sky, his marble eyes staring. His mouth was wide open in a word-less wail of grief. The woman was hunched, her hands to her face as if weeping, or maybe clawing out her eyes in despair.

Bannon looked deeply unsettled, and Nicci could not help but re-call the stone carvings Emperor Jagang and Brother Narev had com-missioned in Altur'Rang, making sculptors depict the corruption and pain of humanity, rather than its majesty. Jagang and Narev had wanted all statues to reflect the most horrific expressions, just like what Nicci saw now. Was this some other follower of Narev's teachings?

When she had lived with Richard in Altur'Rang, he worked as a stone carver and ultimately sculpted a breathtaking representation of the human spirit, a statue he called Truth. That was when Nicci had experienced a fundamental epiphany. She had *changed*.

That had been the end of her life as Death's Mistress, as a Sister of the Dark.

But whoever had carved these statues had apparently not received the same epiphany.

"We should find another farmhouse," said Bannon. "I don't like those statues. Who would want something like at their home?"

Nicci glanced at him. "Obviously someone who does not share your vision of an idyllic world."

CHAPTER 30

T he wind whistling around the sentinel tower took on a deeper tone, like a lost moan. The intact panes of crimson glass in the observation windows shimmered, pulsed, *awakened*.

Nathan held up his sliced hand, cupping the drops of blood in his palm. "Dear spirits," he muttered. As the upper observation platform of the watchtower throbbed with a deep angry light, he stared at the glowing red-glass panes with more fascination than fear. Though he couldn't use his gift, he still felt the restless magic inside him, twitching, uncontrollable. His innate, uncertain Han felt attuned to what was happening.

A memory tickled the back of his mind, and he smiled with recognition. "Bloodglass! Yes, I have heard of bloodglass."

The temperature around him increased, as if the glass reflected some distant volcanic fire, but this magic was heated by blood. Curious, the wizard went to one of the intact panes as the thrumming grew louder, more powerful.

Bloodglass was a wizard's tool in war. Glass bound with blood, tempered and shaped with the spilled blood of sacrifices, so that the panes themselves were connected to bloodshed. In the most violent wars, the seers of military commanders could gaze through panes of bloodglass to monitor the progress of their armies—the battles, victories, massacres. Bloodglass did not reveal an actual landscape, but rather the patterns of pain and death, which allowed warlords to map the topography of their slaughter.

Nathan stood close to the nearest window and peered through the glowing crimson glass. From the top of this watchtower, he had expected to see for great distances—the old imperial roads, the mountain ranges, maybe even the vast fertile valley that lay between here and Kol Adair.

Instead, he viewed the inexorable march of memory armies, hundreds of thousands of fighters who wielded swords and shields, sweeping like locusts across the land. The bloodglass was so perfectly transparent that he could look through time as well as distance at a panorama magnified by the impurity of blood in the crystal.

The Old World was vast and ancient, allowing him to gaze across the sweep of invasions and pitched battles, a succession of armies, of emperors, of countless generations of bloodshed. Barbarians struck villages, killing men who tried to defend their homes and families, raping the women, beheading the children. After the wild and undisciplined warriors came another type of predator: organized machinelike armies that moved in perfect formation and killed without passion but with relentless precision.

Nathan followed the octagonal wall of the tower and peered through a second bloodglass window. This one blazed even brighter, and the armies in the image seemed closer. The glass vibrated, and the whole massive tower structure thrummed as if awakened . . . as if afraid.

Nathan spun upon hearing a sound—a rattle of hollow bones. He looked at the dismembered skeletons scattered on the iron-hard wood of the platform. Had they moved? The light filling the watchtower seemed uncertain, a thicker crimson. Outside, the afternoon sun dipped lower, but this murderous magical light was entirely independent of it. Nervously, he rested his hand on the hilt of his sword—his slick bloody hand. He lifted his palm to look at the scarlet drops that ran down his wrist.

He whirled again at a louder clatter of bones, but saw nothing. Surely, the skeletons had moved. He hurried to look through two more of the intact crimson panes, and saw another army approaching. This one seemed more ominous than the others, more real.

The warriors had pointed steel helmets, scaled armor, and shields emblazoned with a stylized flame. Nathan remembered that flame . . . the symbol of Emperor Kurgan's army. Through the sorcerous magnification, he discerned a fearsome warlord at the vanguard, and Nathan realized that he might be seeing General Utros himself, suffused through blood and time.

The wind howled louder around the broken walls, as if an invisible storm swept across the top of the bluff. Carried along with the breezes came the shouts of soldiers, the clatter of steel, and the pounding thud of marching boots. The red light grew more intense, as if it shone through a fine mist of blood.

Nathan drew his sword now, clamping his fingers hard around the ornate hilt, but his blood made the grip slippery. He turned slowly, but saw no movement from the scattered bones. He hurried over to look through another of the windows and saw the army of General Utros marching toward the high citadel, an inexorable flood of armed men converging on the watchtower. Somehow, the magic had brought them back: these ruthless soldiers seemed absolutely real. They stormed up the wide stone paths, approaching the tower from three sides. He stared at the bristling, relentless force closing in.

Another clatter tore Nathan's attention away from the bloodglass. Whirling, he did see the bones of the long-forgotten defenders twitching, shuddering, reassembling. Bathed in red light from the eerie windows, the skeletons rose up as if they were marionettes.

The wizard raised his sword to fight them, but these were only a few clumsy threats. He was much more worried about the hordes of ghost soldiers pressing toward the tower. He could hear them below, a surging crowd of swords, armor, and muscles. A gruff voice—Utros?—shouted in an accented language that Nathan somehow understood, "Take the tower. Kill them all!"

Surrounded by suffocating red light, Nathan braced himself to fight the skeletons. A thunder of pounding feet came up the tower stairs. He struggled to find the magic within him, ready to release his recalcitrant gift, whether or not it caused a disaster. He was all alone here. Even if a backlash from using magic caused terrible damage and leveled this entire watchtower, at least he wouldn't hurt Nicci or young Bannon. He might, however, destroy these spectral soldiers.

One of the reanimated soldiers clattered toward him, bony hands outstretched as if the skeleton thought Nathan himself was an invader. The wizard swung his sword and sliced through the neck vertebrae. The skull toppled off and rolled across the wooden floor, its jaws still clacking. The fleshless hands and arms flailed, clawing at him. He smashed them, splintering the wickerwork of bones. Then he spun to dismember another skeleton, this one wearing tatters of armor. He kicked out with a boot to knock apart the loose bones of a third rattling opponent.

Then the greater threat arrived. Armored spectral warriors with flame-emblazoned shields and wide swords pushed through the door to the tower chamber, two abreast. They shimmered in the deep red light.

Nathan backed toward a wall, hoping to find some protection with his back to the stone blocks. He had no place to hide.

A flood of long-dead soldiers flowed through the door, as if they meant to take over the sentinel tower and simply drown anyone there with their sheer numbers.

The wizard faced them, mustering all his strength. "Come at me, then!" He slashed his blade across the air, surrendering the hope that he could find the ragged thread of magic within him again. The flow of Han wouldn't come to him now. He would have to make do with his sword.

Oddly, he wished Bannon were here. He and the young man could have slain dozens before they fell. "I'll just have to do it myself!" His straight white hair flew as he hurled himself at the ancient attackers.

Crimson light from the bloodglass throbbed around him, and he felt as if he were in a trance. He swung his sword at one of the ancient warriors, bracing himself for the hard impact against scaled armor, flesh, bone. But his sword passed through, and the enemy collapsed. Nathan didn't slow, but slashed at another, cleaving through misty armor.

He felt a sharp pain in his ankle. One of the clawed skeleton hands had grasped his boot like a vise. With a vicious kick, he flung it aside, then ducked as another ancient warrior charged at him. He realized he was yelling. He could barely see through the thick, almost palpable light around him.

Nathan lost track of his movements. He was in a wild fighting fury. Something about the magic of the bloodglass, the violence and the slaughter that permeated the history of this place, possessed him. He had no choice but to fight, to kill as many of these enemies as possible before his own blood stained the floorboards, before his own body lay here among the ancient dead, until he slowly became a skeleton just like them.

He charged across the platform, seeing enemies that were no more than crimson shadows, and he heard a shattering of glass like a crystalline scream. He whirled and attacked and slashed, but he couldn't see the result. He struck and shattered, struck and shattered. His blood and his sword seemed to know what to do.

The hard clang and sharp shock of his steel against stone jarred him enough to dissipate the red glare around his vision. His trance was broken. The enemy was gone.

Exhausted, Nathan heaved great breaths. His arms trembled. The blood from his cut hand ran down the hilt and onto the blade—but that was the only blood he saw. When he blinked, the air cleared to reveal bright yellow sunlight again and open air. The bloodglass was gone.

In his fury, Nathan had shattered the remaining panes. The red windows no longer looked out onto visions of slaughter and murder, only onto an open landscape in the slanted afternoon light. The spectral army and the remnants from centuries-old wars had faded, and the spell from the bloodglass was destroyed.

He had been fighting against illusions. The skeletons lay broken and strewn about, and he couldn't say if they had actually been reanimated, or if he had just been doing battle with his own nightmares.

He stood for a long time, catching his breath, shaking with weariness. Then he forced a smile. "That was an adventure. Quite exciting."

With his wounded hand he wiped sweat from his forehead, not caring that it left a smear of blood across his face.

He was alone in the tower, and the wind whispering through the broken glass sounded like the distant scream of ghosts.

CHAPTER 31

Leaving the abandoned and disturbing farmstead, Nicci and Bannon continued down the weed-overgrown road past houses and farms. The lonely goats followed them for a time, but eventually gave up and wandered off into a wild cornfield that was more tempting than the prospect of Bannon scratching their ears.

Most of the dwellings they found were empty, and some also displayed more unsettling, anguished statues in the yards. Why would the people feel a need to own such decorations of misery? Nicci led the way toward the main town, growing more tense, fearing what she would find ahead. Though the land seemed fertile and the weather hospitable, these homes had clearly been vacant for years. "It makes no sense. Where did everyone go?"

Nicci paused in front of a large home with unruly flowerbeds, a scraggly garden patch, and drooping apple trees with half-rotted fruit ravaged by birds. Two more statues stood there: a boy and girl no more than nine years old, both on their knees, expressions full of despair, weeping stone tears.

While Bannon stared at the unsettling figures, Nicci was angry that some mad sculptor would revel in displaying such pain, and that these villagers had willingly displayed them. Nicci had felt no deep emotions when Emperor Jagang commissioned such sculptures, because she knew what a ruthless, twisted man he was. Only Nicci, with her heart of black ice, had been his match.

But this isolated village, far from the reach of the Imperial Order, had for some reason decided to depict a very similar misery. Nicci found it deeply disturbing.

They came upon a stream flowing down the wooded hillside, where a miller's waterwheel caught the current and turned. Water sluiced over the paddles to rotate a grinding stone, but after years without maintenance, the wheel wobbled off center and made a loud scraping sound. Some of the wooden planks in the walls of the mill had fallen in.

She and Bannon reached the town itself, a hundred homes around a main square and marketplace. Most dwellings had been built for single families, but others were two stories tall, constructed with wood from the hillsides and stones from a nearby quarry. The entire town was simply deserted.

The open square held a stone fountain, now dry; a smithy fallen into disrepair, its forge long cold; a silent and empty inn and tavern. There were also a warehouse, several merchant offices, an eating establishment, a livery, and barns filled with old hay, but no horses. Around the square, wooden tables and kiosks showed the remnants of what must have been a thriving market. Shriveled husks and rotted cores showed what remained of the produce at farmers' stalls. Feral chickens scuttled through the town square.

Although peripheral details sank into Nicci's consciousness, her attention was fixated on the numerous statues in the square. Countless stone figures stood in the market, in the doorways, by the vegetable stalls, by the water well.

Bannon looked sick. Each of the sculptures wore the same look of horror and anguish, smooth marble eyes open wide in appalled disbelief, or clenched shut in furious denial, stone lips drawn back in sobs.

Bannon shook his head. "Sweet Sea Mother, why would someone do that? I always try to imagine a nice world. Who would want to imagine this? Why would someone do this to a town?"

A deep voice rang out. "Because they were guilty."

They whirled to see a bald man emerging from a dark wooden building that looked like the home of an important person. Tall and thin, with an unnaturally elongated skull, he strode down the street. A gold circlet rested on his head just above the brow. The stranger's long black robes flowed as he walked. The sleeves belled out at the cuffs, and a thick gold chain served as a belt around his waist. His piercing eyes were the palest blue Nicci had ever seen, as clear as water in a mountain stream. His face was so grim, he made even the Keeper look cheerful.

Bannon instinctively drew his sword to defend them, but Nicci took a step forward. "Guilty of what? And who are you?"

The gaunt man stopped before them, drawing himself even taller. He seemed satisfied to be surrounded by numerous statues of misery. "Each was guilty of his own crimes, her own indiscretions. It would take far too long for me to name them all."

Nicci faced the man's implacable, pale stare. "I asked your name. Are you the only one left here? Where did the others go?"

"I am the Adjudicator," he said in a deep baritone voice. "I have brought justice to this town of Lockridge and to many towns."

"We're just travelers," Bannon said. "We're looking for food and a place to sleep, maybe to get some supplies."

Nicci focused her concentration on the strange man. "You are a wizard." She could sense the gift within him, the magic he contained.

"I am the Adjudicator," he repeated. "I bear the gift and the responsibility. I have the tools and the power to bring justice." He looked at them sternly, his water-pale eyes raking over Nicci's form and then Bannon's, as if he were dissecting them and looking for corruption within.

"Who appointed you?" Nicci asked.

"*Justice* appointed me," he said, as if Nicci were the most foolish person he had ever met. "Many years ago I was just a magistrate, and I roved the districts by common consent, for the people required an impartial law. I would go from town to town, where they presented the accused to me, and I served as judge. I would hear the laws they had broken, I would look at the accused, and I would determine the truth of what they had done, as well as the punishment for their crimes."

He pressed a long-fingered hand to the center of his chest, which was covered by the black robes. "That was my gift. I could know the truth of what someone said. Through magic I determined whether they were innocent or guilty, and then I decreed the appropriate sentence, which the town leaders imposed. That was our common agreement. That was our law."

"Like a Confessor," Nicci said. "A male Confessor."

The strange man gave her a blank stare. "I know nothing of Confessors. I am the Adjudicator."

"But where are all the people?" Bannon asked. "If you passed sentence and the villagers agreed to it, where are they? Why did they all leave this town?"

"They did not leave," said the grim wizard. "But my calling changed, became stronger. *I* became stronger. The amulet, by which I determined truth and innocence, became a part of me, and I grew much more powerful."

The Adjudicator pulled open the folds of the black robe to expose his bare chest and an amulet: a golden triangular plate carved with ornate loops, arcane symbols, and spell-forms surrounding a deep red garnet. The amulet hung by a thin golden chain around his neck.

But the amulet was no longer just an ornament—the golden triangle had *fused* to his flesh. The skin of his chest had bubbled and scarred around it, as if someone had pressed hot metal hard into skin like pliable candle wax and let the flesh harden around it. Parts of the chain had cut into the Adjudicator's collarbone and the tendons of his neck, becoming permanently bonded there. The central garnet glowed with a deep simmering fire of magic.

Bannon gasped. "What happened to you?"

"I became the Adjudicator." His stony, accusing stare turned toward the young man. "For years, the crimes I judged were mostly small—assaults, thievery, arson, adultery. Sometimes there were murders or rapes, but it was here in Lockridge . . ." He looked up, and his water-blue gaze skated past them, over their heads, as if he was calling upon the spirits. "It was here that I changed.

"There was a mother, Reva, who had three fine daughters, the oldest eight years old, the youngest only three. The mother was lovely in her own way, as were the little girls, but her husband desired another woman. Ellis was his name. He cheated on his wife, and when Reva learned of the affair, she became convinced that it was her fault—that she paid too much attention to their three daughters and not enough to her husband. Reva was desperate to regain his love." He made a disgusted sound. "She was mad.

"So, Reva smothered her three daughters in their sleep, to make sure that they would no longer come between her and Ellis. She thought he would love her more. When he came home that night, after his furtive passions with his mistress, Reva proudly showed him what she had done. She opened her arms and told him that her time and her heart now belonged only to him again.

"When Ellis saw their three dead daughters, he took a hatchet from the firewood pile and killed his wife, chopping her sixteen times."

The Adjudicator's expression didn't change as he told his story. "And when I came to judge Ellis, I touched the center of his forehead. We all thought we knew what had happened. I called upon the power in my amulet, and I learned the full story. I learned his thoughts and his black, poisoned heart. I already knew the horrors of his wife's crimes, but then I discovered what this man had done. Yes, he had killed his wife after she had killed his daughters. There was no question as to the murder Ellis had committed, but some even sympathized with him.

"Not I. I found within Ellis a most poisonous guilt, because he had not truly killed Reva out of horror that she had murdered their girls, as we all expected. No, I saw in Ellis's heart that he was actually pleased to have the nuisance of his family gone, and he used it as an excuse to be rid of his unwanted wife as well as his children. He thought he would get away with it.

"As that guilt flooded into me, those crimes charged the amulet. The magic grew stronger, and I unleashed it with wild abandon. I was angry and sickened. I made Ellis *feel* the guilt. I made him experience that moment of the greatest, most intense, horror. It rose to the front of his mind, and I froze it there. I turned him to stone in that instant as he experienced the most intense, most painful guilt of his life, reliving that appalling moment."

The Adjudicator let out a long sigh. "And releasing that magic freed me." The wizard touched the scar where the amulet had fused to the flesh of his chest. "I became not just a magistrate, not merely one who uncovered the truth of the accused. I became the Adjudicator." His voice grew deeper and much more ominous. "I have to protect these lands. That is my charge. I am to find anyone who is guilty. I cannot allow travelers to pass over the mountains into the fertile valley beyond. I must stop the spread of guilt."

Bannon swallowed audibly and took a step backward, holding up his sword.

Nicci didn't move, though she remained poised to fight. "And you judged all of these people as well?"

"All of them." The Adjudicator turned his chilling, watery gaze on her. "Only those without guilt can be allowed to proceed." He narrowed his eyes. "And what is your guilt, Sorceress?"

Nicci was defiant. "My guilt is none of your business."

For the first time she saw the Adjudicator's thin, pale lips twitch, in what might have been the distant shadow of a smile. "Ah, but it is." The garnet in his amulet glowed.

She reacted by reaching inside herself, ready to release the coiling magic, but she suddenly found that she couldn't. Her feet were frozen in place. Her legs were locked. Her arms refused to bend.

Bannon gasped. "What's . . . happening?"

"I am the Adjudicator." He took a step closer. The fused amulet throbbed in his chest. "The punishment I have decreed for all criminals is that they must experience their moment of greatest guilt. Continually. I will petrify you at that exquisite point, so that you face that worst moment for as long as time shall last."

Nicci's legs felt cold, leaden. She couldn't turn her head, but from the corner of her eye she saw her arm, her black dress, everything becoming white. Becoming stone.

"You have nothing to fear, if you are blameless," said the man. "You will be judged, and I am fair. I am the Adjudicator."

He stepped toward them, and Nicci tried to find a way to fight, to summon her magic, but her vision dimmed. A buzzing roar built in her mind, as if her head were filled with thousands of swarming bees.

Though she could barely see him, she heard the grim wizard's words. "Alas, in all these lands, I have yet to find someone without guilt."

CHAPTER 32

As the Adjudicator's magic closed around her like a clenching fist, Nicci struggled, but her body wouldn't move and her brain felt as if it had fossilized from the core outward. She could hardly think. She was trapped.

The dark wizard must have sensed her own powerful gift, because he struck in a way that she could not resist, with a spell she had never previously encountered. Her flesh tightened, hardened, and crystallized her body. Time itself seemed to stop. The warm tones of her skin turned to cold gray-white marble. She felt her lungs crush, her bones grow impossibly heavy.

Vision dimmed as her eyes petrified. Her blue irises crackled, hardened . . . and with the last hint of vision she saw young Bannon with his long red hair and his pale, freckled face. His expression had often been so innocent, so cheerful and unscarred by reality, that it set Nicci on edge. Now, though, his face filled with despair and misery. His mouth dropped open, his lips curled back, and even though her own ears roared with the sound of encroaching silence, she thought she heard him say ". . . kittens . . ." before he became completely fossilized, the sculpture of a man buried under an avalanche of unbearable grief and guilt.

When Nicci's vision faded, all she was able to see were the nightmarish remnants of her own past actions. Her memories rose up, as if they, too, were preserved in perfectly carved stone. Horrific, tense memories.

* * *

Shaken from his encounter with the spectral army that manifested through the bloodglass, Nathan left the watchtower. Alone and wary, he made his way through the darkening, sinister forest as the sun fell below the line of hills.

He hadn't expected his side trip to take so long, but the experience had been valuable for what he had seen and learned, in a historical sense if nothing else. These lands of the Old World were soaked with the blood of centuries of warfare, petty warlords turning against one another after the great barrier was erected to seal off the New World during the ancient wizard wars. Reading history was one thing; experiencing it was quite another.

He picked his way through the increasing shadows, heading back in the direction of the faint road they had been following, but Nathan feared he would walk right past the trail in the deepening twilight.

Much as he would have liked to join Nicci and Bannon in a town, hoping for a fine inn and hot food, he decided to make camp where he was. He was eager to tell his companions about the sentinel tower, and just as eager to sample the local ale. Instead, he would have to spend the night alone in the forest. "Not all parts of an adventure have to be charming and enjoyable," he said aloud.

He found a quiet clearing under a large elm tree, where he could use his pack as a pillow. As he sat under the branches and the night grew darker and colder, he pondered his lack of magic and what had happened when he had tried to practice en route to the tower. Right now, looking at the pile of dry sticks he had assembled, he could not help but think how it would have been so simple to make a cheery campfire, if he had magic to light the spark. He had never been good at using flint and steel. He didn't have the patience or the skill; when had Nathan Rahl ever needed it, if he could simply twitch a finger and light a fire?

Resigned, he ate cold pack food and wrapped himself in his brown cape from Renda Bay for warmth, then bedded down to a restless, uncomfortable sleep. The homespun linen shirt that had belonged to Phillip also kept him warm.

He set off at first light, bushwhacking through low saplings and shrubbery, heading instinctively in the right direction, and when he finally encountered the main path, he felt a sudden flush of satisfaction. Now that he was back on the road again, he could catch up with Nicci and Bannon. According to the map, a sizable town—Lockridge—should be only a few miles ahead.

It was late morning before he saw the first abandoned farmstead. He drank from the well, sure no one would complain, and chased off two pesky goats who were hungry for attention. The hideous ornamental statues seemed bizarre and out of place, but Nathan had seen many odd and inexplicable things before. People often had questionable tastes in art, and these sculptures were indeed questionable.

The road took him past other farms and dwellings, all of them just as silent, all populated with anguished statues. Maybe some petty local prince fancied himself a sculptor and required each of his subjects to own his hideous work.

By noon, Nathan reached the town, a typical mountain village with all the expected shops and houses, a marketplace, a square, a livery, an inn, a blacksmith, a potter, a woodworker—but it was populated with hundreds more statues, stone people depicted at a moment of horrific nightmares.

Nathan cautiously walked ahead, scratching the side of his face, stepping carefully in his high leather boots, afraid he might awaken the eerie sculptures. He felt like an intruder here. Under normal circumstances, he should have been able to sense sorcery or danger, and he dug deep within himself, found the writhing, sleeping magic there, the frayed tangles that remained after his gift of prophecy had been uprooted. But his Han was restless and uncooperative, and he didn't dare use it. He knew better.

At another time, he might have raised his voice and shouted out, but the hush was too ominous, even more so than at the ancient watchtower. The palpable horror and despair in the faces of these sculptures made his skin crawl. He saw people of all sorts: tradesmen, farmers, washerwomen, children.

In the Lockridge town square two fresh statues looked whiter and cleaner than the others, new creations made by the mad sculptor. The appalled expression made the young man's face unrecognizable at first, but then Nathan knew. Bannon!

Next to him stood the beautiful sorceress, whose curves and fine dress would have been a work of art for any imaginative sculptor. Nicci's face showed less misery than the faces of the other statues, but her expression still carried clear pain, as if her guilt and regrets had been smashed into numerous sharp shards, then imperfectly reassembled again.

A deep chill shuddered through Nathan, as he slowly turned around. Some terrible magic was at work here, and even though he could think of no spell that would have caused this, he was certain these were not mere sculptures of his friends, but Nicci and Bannon themselves, transformed somehow.

A powerful baritone voice cut through the crystalline silence of the town. "Are you an innocent man? Or have you come to be judged like the others?"

A tall black-robed man came striding toward him, his elongated bald head crowned with a gold circlet. The robes were open at his chest to display bubbling scars and waxy skin fused around a golden amulet.

On guard, Nathan replied, "I have lived a thousand years. It's hard to hold on to innocence and purity for all that time."

"A righteous man could do it."

"I haven't been overburdened with guilt, either." Nathan was certain this grim wizard had created the statue spell, trapping or petrifying these victims—including Nicci and Bannon. "I am a traveler, an emissary from the D'Haran Empire. The roving ambassador, in fact."

"And I am the Adjudicator." The man stepped forward, and the deep red garnet on his fused amulet began to glow.

At another time, Nathan would have released his magic to attack, but he had no gift that would help him. His hand darted down to grab the hilt of his sword, but his arm moved slowly, lethargically. He realized his feet were rooted in place. Nathan guessed what was happening.

The Adjudicator closed in, his water-blue eyes fixed on him. "Only the innocent shall pass onward, and I will find your guilt, old man. I will find all of it."

N icci was frozen inside a petrified gallery of her life, the accusatory moments of her actions. She had no choice but to face the terrible things she had done, the darkness of her life . . . Death's Mistress . . . servant of the Keeper. That psychological weight was far greater than tons of rock.

She had tortured and killed many as a necessary part of her service to Jagang. She had aided the Imperial Order, falsely believing that she served all humanity by enforcing equality, helping the poor and the infirm, redistributing the wealth of greedy manipulators. She felt no guilt for that.

From a long time ago, she regretted that she had missed her father's funeral, but the Sisters had not allowed her to leave the Palace of the Prophets. Her father, an ambitious armorer, a good manager (she realized now), a man whose work had been appreciated by his customers until the Order ruined him. Nicci had been part of that downfall, as a dedicated young girl, brainwashed by her mother. She had become a believer, a wholehearted follower.

When one believed and followed something that was wrong, must there be guilt?

Kept inside the Palace of the Prophets for so many years, Nicci had also missed the death of her overbearing mother. She had attended that funeral, however, although she felt no guilt over the loss of the abusive woman. In order to obtain a fine black dress for the ceremony, Nicci had surrendered her body to the groping, lecherous embraces of a loathsome tailor, but it was the price she had agreed to pay. She had done what was necessary. That held no guilt. And she had preferred to wear a black dress ever since.

As those preserved dark memories rose inside her mind, she felt a need to atone for abducting Richard from his beloved Kahlan, forcing him to go away with her in a sham partnership to Altur'Rang. That had been a terrible thing, even if Nicci had been doing it to convince Richard of the correctness of her beliefs. During that time, she had fallen in love with him, but it was a twisted and broken emotion that even Nicci didn't understand.

The worst thing she had done, perhaps, was when Richard had rebuffed her advances, refused to make love to her, and so she had thrown herself upon another man in the city, letting him treat her roughly, slap her and rape her—though it hadn't been rape, because she herself had insisted on it. And all the while she knew that because of the maternity spell that linked them, *Kahlan* would experience every physical sensation that Nicci felt . . . and Kahlan would believe in her heart that Richard had been unfaithful to her, that *he* was the one taking his pleasure on Nicci's body, wild with lust.

How that must have hurt Kahlan . . . and Nicci had taken great joy in it.

Yes, for that she felt guilt.

But Nicci had already made her peace with it. Kahlan and Richard had forgiven her. That embittered, evil person might have been who she was a long time ago—Death's Mistress—but Nicci was different now. She did not wallow in her past and was not haunted by the ghosts of her deeds. She had served Richard, had fought for him, had helped overthrow the Imperial Order. She had commanded Jagang to *die*. She had served Richard with relentless dedication and killed countless numbers of bloodthirsty half people from the Dark Lands. She had done whatever Richard asked, had even stopped his heart to send him into the underworld so he could save Kahlan.

She had given him everything except for her guilt. Nicci did not hold on to guilt. Even when she had committed those crimes, she had felt nothing.

And now in this new journey of her life, she served an even greater purpose—not just the man Richard Rahl, whom she loved, but the *dream* of Richard Rahl—and in that service there could be no guilt.

Nicci was a sorceress. She had the power of the wizards she had killed. She had all the spells the Sisters had taught her. She had a strength in her soul that went beyond any imagined calling of this deluded Adjudicator.

The magic was hers to control, and the punishment was not his to mete out.

Her body might have turned to stone, trapping her thoughts in a suffocating purgatory, but Nicci's emotions had been like stone before, and she had a heart of black ice. It was her protection. She called upon that now, releasing any spark of magic she could summon, finding her flicker of determination and her refusal to accept the sentence this grim wizard imposed upon her.

As her fury grew, the magic kindled within her. She was not some clumsy, murderous villager, she was not a petty thief. She was a sorceress. She was *Death's Mistress.*

Inside and around her Nicci felt the stone begin to crack. . . .

The Adjudicator's long face was sallow and dour, as if all humor had been leached away. He showed no pleasure as he explained Nathan's punishment and worked the spell to trap him. "They are all guilty," he said, "every person. I have so much work to do . . ."

Nathan strained, struggling to move his petrified arm. "No, you won't." His hand had nearly reached the sword, but even if he touched the hilt, it would do no good. The stone spell surrounded him and was rapidly fossilizing his tissues, stopping time inside his body. Nathan could not fight, could not flee, could barely even move. His only recourse would have been to use magic, to lash out with a retaliatory spell. But if he couldn't light so much as a campfire, he certainly couldn't fight such a powerful wizard.

Even if he summoned his wayward magic, though, Nathan knew he couldn't control it. He could not forget trying to heal the wounded man in Renda Bay, ripping him asunder with what should have been healing magic. Nathan had only tried to help him. . . .

Maybe *that* was the moment of great guilt the Adjudicator would force him to endure for as long as stone lasted.

He heard the grinding crackle as the spell petrified even his leather pouch, along with his travel garments, and the life book. He could not breathe.

Nathan felt the magic squirming within him, ducking away like a snake slithering into a thicket. What did it matter if he unleashed it now and the spell backfired? What greater harm could it cause than the harm he was already facing? Even Nicci had been trapped in stone, and Bannon, poor Bannon, was already paralyzed in endless anguish.

Nathan had nothing to lose. No matter what unexpected backlash his magic might trigger, if he could release it and strike back, even in some awkward way, at least that would be something.

His lungs crushed down as the stone weight of guilt squeezed him, suffocated him, but he managed to gasp out some words. "I am Nathan . . . Nathan the prophet." He caught one more fractional breath, one more gasp of words. "Nathan the *wizard!*"

The magic crawled out of him like a fanged eel startled from a dark underwater alcove. Nathan released it, not knowing what it would do . . . not caring. It lashed out, uncontrolled.

He heard and felt a white-hot sizzle building within his body. For a moment he was sure that his own form would explode, that his skull would erupt with uncontained power.

In front of him, the statue of Nicci seemed to be changing, softening, with countless eggshell cracks all over the white stone that had captured her perfection. Nathan didn't think he was doing it. His own magic was here . . . boiling out—and spraying like scalding oil on the Adjudicator.

The grim wizard recoiled, staggering backward. "What are you doing?" He raised a hand and clapped the other to his amulet. "No!"

The petrification spell that the Adjudicator had wrapped around Nathan like a smothering cloak now slipped off of him, ricocheted and combined with Nathan's wild magic. Reacting, backfiring.

The dour man straightened, then convulsed in horror. His lantern jaw dropped open, and his expression fell into abject despair. His water-blue eyes began to turn white, and his robe stiffened, changing to stone. "I am the Adjudicator!" he cried. "I am the judge. I see the guilt . . ."

With a crackling, shattering sound, Nicci fought her way out of her own fossilization, somehow using her powers. Nathan's vision became sharper as he felt the intrusive stone drain out of his body like sand through an hourglass. His flesh softened, his blood pumped again.

Nathan's unchecked magic likewise thrashed and curled and whipped. The Adjudicator writhed and screamed as he gradually froze in place, even his robe turning to marble.

"You. Are. *Guilty!*" Nathan said to the transforming Adjudicator when he could breathe again. "Your crime is that you judged all these people."

Stone engulfed the Adjudicator, crackling up through his skin, stiffening the lids around his wide-open eyes. "No!" It wasn't a denial, but a horror, a realization. "What have I done?" His voice became scratchier, rougher as his throat hardened and his chest solidified so that he couldn't breathe. "All those people!" The stone locked his face in an expression of immeasurable regret and shame, his mouth open as he uttered one last, incomplete "No!" He became the newest statue in the town of Lockridge.

Staring at the stone figure, Nathan felt his rampant magic dissipate. Just like that, it was no longer available to his touch. He sucked in a deep breath and felt life flow through him again.

CHAPTER 33

When the Adjudicator himself turned to stone, his spell shattered and dissipated throughout the town.

No longer petrified, Nicci slowly straightened and let out a long breath, half expecting to see an exhalation of dust from her lungs. Her blond hair and the skin of her neck became supple again, the fabric of her black dress flowed. She lifted her arms, looked at her hands.

Through her own determination, she had broken the fossilization spell that ran throughout herself, but Nathan had defeated the farther-reaching stranglehold of the twisted Adjudicator. Now, the old wizard flexed his arms and stamped his legs to restore his circulation. He shook his head, bewildered.

Nearby, the statue of Bannon, his expression locked in guilty despair, slowly suffused with color. His pink skin, rusty freckles, and ginger hair were restored. Instead of being amazed to find himself alive again, though, Bannon dropped to his knees in the town square and let out a keening wail. His shoulders shook, and he bowed his head, sobbing.

Nathan tried to comfort the distraught young man, patting him on the shoulder, although he did not speak. Stepping close to Bannon, Nicci softened her voice. "We are safe now. Whatever you experienced was your past. It is who you *were*, not who you are. You need have no guilt about who you are." She guessed that he continued to suffer over losing his friend Ian to the slavers.

But, why had he uttered the word "kittens" as he turned to stone?

In the streets and square around them, a low crackle slowly grew to a rumble accompanied by a stirring of breezes that sounded like astonished whispers. Nicci turned around and saw the villagers trapped in stone by the Adjudicator's brutal justice: one by one, they began to move.

As the gathered, tortured sculptures were restored to flesh, they remained overwhelmed by the nightmarish memories they had endured for so long. Then the sobbing and wailing began, rising to a cacophony of the damned. These people were too caught up in their own ordeal to look around and realize they had been released from the terrible spell.

Bannon finally climbed back to his feet, his eyes red and puffy, his face streaked with tears. "We're safe now," he said, as if he could comfort the villagers. "It'll be all right."

Some of the people of Lockridge heard him, but most were too stunned to understand. Husbands and wives found each other and embraced, clinging in desperate hugs. Wailing children ran to their parents to be swept into the warm comfort of a stable family again.

The disoriented villagers finally became aware of the three strangers among them. One man introduced himself as Lockridge mayor Raymond Barre. "I speak for the people of this town." He looked from Nicci, to Nathan, to Bannon. "Are you the ones who saved us?"

"We are," Nathan said. "We were just travelers looking for directions and a warm meal."

With growing anger, the townspeople noticed the grotesque, horror-struck statue of the Adjudicator. Nicci indicated the stone figure of the corrupted man. "A civilization must have laws, but there cannot be justice when a man with no conscience metes out sentences without compassion or mercy."

Bannon said, "If each one of us carries that guilt, then we are living our sentences every day. How can I ever forget . . . ?"

"None of us will forget," said Mayor Barre. "And none of us will forget you, strangers. You saved us."

Other townspeople came forward. An innkeeper wore an apron

stained from a meal he had served an unknown number of years before. Farmers and grocers stared at the ramshackle appearance of the village, at their broken-down vendor stalls, the remnants of rotted fruits and vegetables, the dilapidated shutters around the windows of the inn, the collapsed roof on the livery, the hay in the barn turned gray with age.

"How long has it been?" asked a woman whose dark brown hair had fallen out of its unruly bun. She wiped her hands on her skirts. "Last I remember, it was spring. Now it seems to be summer."

"But summer of which year?" asked the blacksmith. He gestured toward the hinges on the nearby door of a dilapidated barn. "Look at the rust."

Nathan told them the year, by D'Haran reckoning, but these villagers so far south in the wilderness of the Old World still followed the calendar of an ancient emperor, so the date meant nothing to them. They didn't even remember Jagang or the march of the Imperial Order.

Although he was as overwhelmed as the rest of his people, Mayor Barre called everyone into the town square, where Nicci and Nathan helped explain what had happened. Each victim remembered his or her own experience with the Adjudicator, and most recalled earlier times when the traveling magistrate had come to judge their petty criminals and impose reasonable sentences—before the magic had engulfed him, before the amulet and his gift had turned him into a monster.

One mother holding the hands of a small son and daughter walked up to the petrified statue of the evil man. She stood silent for a moment, her expression roiling with hate, before she spat on the white marble. Others came up and did the same.

Then the innkeeper suggested they use the blacksmith's steel hammers and chisels to smash the Adjudicator's statue into fragments of stone. Nicci gave them a solemn nod. "I will not stop you from doing so."

It was like a grim, furious mob as the Lockridge villagers battered and smashed the hated statue until the Adjudicator was nothing but rock shards and crumbling dust. When all that remained was a pile of rubble, the people were drained, though not satisfied.

Mayor Barre said, "We must go back to our homes and rebuild our lives. Clean up our houses, tend our gardens. Find all of that man's other victims and explain what happened."

Nathan said, "Magic has changed, and the world has changed. Even the night sky is shifted. After night falls, you will discover that the constellations are different from those you remember. We don't yet know all the ways the world has been altered."

Nicci also spoke up. "In the D'Haran Empire, Lord Rahl has defeated the emperors who oppressed both the Old World and the New. We came here to see his new territory and to tell you all that the world can be free and at peace. We found this town, we freed you, we destroyed the Adjudicator." She looked down at the unrecognizable rubble, saw a smooth curved chunk that might have been an ear. "This man is exactly the sort of monster that Lord Rahl stands against." She squared her shoulders. "And we did stand against him."

As the people muttered, absorbing the knowledge, Nathan kept shaking his head, troubled. He said to Nicci, "I studied magic for many centuries, and I recall stories of how the ancient wizards of Ildakar had a way of turning human beings into stone. Some of them even called themselves *sculptors*. They did not merely use convicted criminals, but also warriors defeated in their great game arena. Such statues were used for decoration."

He drew his thumb and forefinger down his smooth chin. "This kind of magic did more than transmute flesh into marble, like an alchemical reaction. No, this spell was another form of magic that allowed the slowing and stopping of time, petrifying flesh as if thousands of centuries had passed. I need to consider this further."

For the rest of that day, Nicci and her companions learned that there were many other towns in the mountains connected by a network of roads, and many of those villages had been served by the same traveling magistrate. Nicci feared that the Adjudicator had petrified other people as well, but with the spell now broken those populations would also be reviving.

Perhaps this entire part of the Old World had just reawakened. . . .

"Saving the world, just as the witch woman predicted, Sorceress," Nathan mused.

"You had as much to do with that as I did," she said.

He merely shrugged. "A good deed is still a good deed, wherever the credit lies. I left the People's Palace to go help people, and I am happy to do so."

Nicci could not disagree.

The unsettled townspeople drifted apart to explore their abandoned homes and find their lives again. Nicci, Nathan, and Bannon joined the innkeeper and his wife for a meal of thin oat porridge made from a small sack of grain that had remarkably not gone bad.

Bannon remained extremely distraught, though, and he struggled in vain to find his contentment and peace again. He was short-tempered, skittish, brooding, and finally when they were alone in one of the inn's dusty side rooms, Nicci asked him, "I can tell you are still suffering from the ordeal. What did you see when you were trapped in stone? The spell is broken now."

"I'll be fine," Bannon said in a husky voice.

She pressed him, though. "The expression of guilt on your face looked worse than when you told us about Ian and the slavers."

"Yes, it was worse."

Nicci waited for him, encouraging him with her silence until he blurted out, "It was the kittens! I remember a man from my island. He drowned a sack of kittens." Bannon looked away from her before continuing. "I tried to stop him, but he threw the kittens into a stream, and they drowned. I wanted to save them but I couldn't. They mewed and cried out."

Nicci thought of all the terrible things she'd endured, the guilt that she had lifted and cast away, the blood she had shed, the lives she had destroyed. "That is the greatest guilt you feel?" She didn't believe him. A greater halo of pain than what had happened with Ian?

His hazel eyes flashed with anger as he spun to her. "Who are you now, the Adjudicator? It's not up to *you* to measure my guilt! You don't know how much it broke my heart, how bad I felt." He stalked away to find one of the unoccupied rooms where he could bed down for the night. "Leave me alone. I never want to think about it again." He closed the door against her continuing questions.

Nicci looked at his retreating form, trying to measure the truth of what he had said, but there was something wrong about Bannon's eyes, about his expression. He was hiding the real answer, but she decided not to press him for now, although she would need to know sooner or later.

Everyone here in Lockridge had been through their own ordeal. Weary, she went to find her own bed. She hoped that they would all have a quiet sleep, untroubled by nightmares.

CHAPTER 34

After leaving the Lockridge villagers to pick up the pieces of their lives, Nicci, Nathan, and Bannon followed the dwindling old road deeper into the mountains. Though preoccupied with helping his people, Mayor Barre had confirmed for them that Kol Adair did indeed lie over the mountains and beyond a great valley. The ordeal with the Adjudicator had made Nathan even more determined to restore himself by any means necessary.

What had once been a wide thoroughfare traveled by commercial caravans was overgrown from disuse. Dark pines and thick oaks encroached with the slow intent of erasing the blemishes left by mankind.

Bannon was remarkably withdrawn, showing little interest in their journey. His usual eager conversation and positive outlook had vanished, still festering from what the Adjudicator had made him see and suffer. Nicci had faced the consequences of her dark past, and she had overcome that guilt long ago, but the young man had far less experience in turning raw, bleeding wounds into hard scars.

Nathan tried to cheer the young man up. "We're making good time. Would you like to stop for a while, my boy? Spar a little with our swords?"

Bannon gave an unusually unenthusiastic reply. "No thank you. I've had enough real swordplay with the selka and the Norukai slavers."

"That's true, my boy," he said with forced cheer, "but in a practice sparring session you can let yourself have fun."

Nicci stepped around a moss-covered boulder in the trail, then looked over her shoulder. "Maybe he thinks the actual killing is fun, Wizard."

Bannon looked stung. "I did what I had to do. People need to be protected. You might not get there in time, but when you do, you have to do your best."

They reached a fast-flowing stream that bubbled over slick rocks. Nicci gathered her skirts and splashed across the shallow water, not worried about getting her boots wet. Nathan, though, picked his way downstream, where he found a fallen log to use as a bridge. He carefully balanced his way across and arrived on the other side, then turned to face Bannon, who crossed the log with barely a glance at his feet.

Nicci kept watching the young man, growing more troubled at his worsening inner pain. A companion so haunted, so preoccupied and listless, might be a liability if they encountered some threat, and she could not allow that.

She faced Bannon as he stepped off the log onto the soft mosses of the bank. "We need to address this, Bannon Farmer. A boil must be lanced before it festers. I know you're not telling the truth—at least not the whole truth."

Bannon was immediately wary, and a flash of fear crossed his face as he drew back. "The truth about what?"

"What did the Adjudicator show you? What guilt has been eating away inside you?"

"I already told you." Bannon stepped away, looking as if he wanted to run. He turned pale. "I couldn't stop a man from drowning a sack of kittens. Sweet Sea Mother, I know that may sound childish to you, but it's not your place to judge how my guilt affects me!"

"I am not your judge," Nicci said, "nor do I want to be. But I need to understand."

Stepping up to them on the stream bank, Nathan interrupted. "You would not have us believe that the Adjudicator considers the loss of kittens to be more damning than losing your friend to slavers?" He gave a wistful smile, trying to be compassionate. "Although, truth be told, I do like kittens. The Sisters in the Palace of the Prophets let me have a kitten once—oh, four hundred years ago. I raised it and loved it, but the cat wandered away, happily hunting mice and rats in the palace, I suppose. It's an enormous place. That was centuries ago. . . ." His voice degenerated into a wistful sigh. "The cat must be dead by now. I haven't thought about it in a long time."

Nicci tried to soften her stern voice, with only marginal success. "You are our companion, Bannon. Are you a criminal? I do not intend to punish you, but I need to know. You are a handicap to our mission and safety in the state you are in."

He lashed out. "I'm not a criminal!" He strode away, following the stream and trying to avoid them. Nicci went after him, but Nathan put a hand on her shoulder and shook his head slightly.

She called after the young man. "Whatever it is, I would not judge you. I could spend months describing the people I've hurt. I once roasted one of my own generals alive in the middle of a village, just to show the villagers how ruthless I could be."

Bannon turned to stare at her, looking both surprised and sickened.

She crossed her arms over her chest. "You failed to prevent someone else from killing a sack of kittens. That may be true. But I don't believe the Adjudicator would condemn you forever because of that."

Bannon splashed cool water on his face, then left the stream and began climbing uphill through a patch of meadow lilies. "It's a long story," he sighed, without looking at her.

From behind, Nathan said, "Maybe it can wait until camp tonight, after we find some food."

As Bannon moved through the brush, he startled a pair of grouse. The two plump birds clucked and waddled quickly for a few steps before they exploded into flight.

Nicci made an offhand gesture with her hand and released her magic. With barely a thought, she stopped the hearts of the two grouse, which dropped to the ground, dead. "There, now we have dinner, and this is as good a place to camp as any. Fresh water from the stream, wood for our fire—and time for a story."

Bannon looked defeated. Without a word he began to gather dead branches, while Nathan dressed the birds and Nicci used her magic to ignite the fire. While the meal cooked, Nicci watched Bannon's expression as he dredged through his memories like a miner shoveling loads of rock, sifting through the rubble and trying to decide what to keep.

At last, after he had picked part of the grouse carcass clean and wandered back to the stream to wash himself, Bannon returned. He lifted his chin and swallowed hard. Nicci could see he was ready.

"On Chiriya Island," he began, and his voice cracked. He drew a deep breath, "Back home . . . I didn't just run away because my life was too quiet and dull. It wasn't a perfect life."

"It rarely ever is, my boy," Nathan said.

Nicci was more definitive. "It *never* is."

"My parents weren't as I've described them. Well, my mother was. I loved her, and she loved me, but my father . . . my father was—" His eyes darted back and forth as if searching for the right word and then daring to use it. "He was *vile*. He was reprehensible." Bannon caught himself as if he feared the spirits might strike him down as he paced back and forth. Then that odd look came to his face again, as if he were trying to paint over the memories in his mind.

"My mother had a cat, a female tabby she loved very much. The cat would sleep on the hearth near a warm fire, but she preferred to curl up on my mother's lap." Bannon's eyes narrowed. "My father was a drunken lout, a brutal man. If he had a miserable life, it was his own fault, and he made our lives miserable because he wanted us to bear the blame. He would beat me, sometimes with a stick, but usually with just his hands. I think he enjoyed the idea of hitting.

"I was always his second choice, though. I could outrun him, and my father never wanted to make much effort, so he hit my mother instead. He would corner her in our house. He would strike her whenever he lost a gambling game down at the tavern, or he would strike her when he ran out of money and couldn't buy enough drink, or he would strike her because he didn't like the food she cooked, or because she didn't cook enough of it.

"He made my mother scream and then he punished her for screaming and for screaming so loudly that the neighbors might hear—although they had all known how he abused her for many years. But he liked it when she screamed too, and if she didn't make enough sounds of pain, he would beat her some more. So she had to walk that narrow path of terror and hurt, just so she could survive—so we could both survive."

Bannon lowered his head. "When I was young, I was too small to stand up to him. And when I grew older, when I might have defended myself against him, I simply couldn't because that man had trained me to be terrified of him." He sat so heavily on a fallen tree trunk that he seemed to collapse.

"The cat was my mother's special treasure, her refuge. She would stroke the cat on her lap as she wept quietly when my father was gone. The cat seemed to absorb her pain and her sorrow. Somehow that restored her in a way that no one else could. It wasn't magic," Bannon said, "but it was its own kind of healing."

Nathan finished eating his grouse and tossed the bones aside, then leaned forward, listening intently. Nicci hadn't moved. She watched the young man's expressions, his fidgeting movements, and she absorbed every word.

"The cat had a litter of five kittens, all mewling and helpless, all so cute. But the mama cat died giving birth. My mother and I found the kittens in a corner the next morning, trying to suckle on the cat's cold, stiff carcass, trying to get warmth from their mama's fur. They were so plaintive when they mewed." He squeezed his fists together, and his gaze was directed deep into his memories. "When my mother picked up the dead tabby, she looked as if something had broken inside her."

"How old were you then, my boy?"

Bannon looked up at the old wizard, as if trying to formulate an answer to the question. "That was less than a year ago."

Nicci was surprised.

"I wanted to save the kittens, for my mother's sake. They were all so tiny, with the softest fur—and needle-sharp claws. They squirmed when I held them. We had to give them milk from a thimble to take care of them. My mother and I both drew comfort from those kittens . . . but we didn't have a chance to name them—not a single one—before my father found them.

"One night, he came home in a rage. I have no idea what had angered him. The reasons never really mattered anyway—my mother and I didn't need to know, but in some dark corner of his alcohol-soured mind we were to blame. He knew how to hurt us—oh, he knew how to hurt us.

"My father stormed into the house, grabbed a sack full of onions hanging on the wall. He dumped the onions across the floor. Even though we tried to keep him away from the kittens, my father grabbed them and stuffed them into the empty sack one at a time. They mewed and mewed, crying out for help, but we couldn't help. He wouldn't let us." Bannon's face darkened, but he didn't look at his listeners.

"I tried to hit my father, but he backhanded me. My mother begged him, but he just wanted the kittens. He knew that would be a far more painful blow to her than his fist. 'Their mother's dead,' he growled, 'and I won't have you wasting any more milk.'" As he spoke, Bannon made a disgusted sound. "The idea of 'wasting' a few thimbles of milk was such an absurd comment that I could find no answer for it. And then he slammed open the door and stormed out into the night.

"My mother wailed and sobbed. I wanted to run after him and fight him, but I stayed to comfort her instead. She wrapped her arms around me and we rocked back and forth. She sobbed into my shoulder. My father had taken away the last thing my mother loved, the last memory of her beloved cat." He swallowed hard.

"But I decided to do something, right away. I knew where he was going. There was a deep stream nearby, and he would throw the sack there. The kittens would drown, wet and cold and helpless—unless I saved them.

"No matter what I did, I knew I'd get a beating, but I had suffered beatings before, and I had never had a chance to save something I loved, to save something my mother loved. So I ran out into the night, following my father. I wanted to chase after him, shouting and cursing, to call him a lout and a monster. But I was smart enough to remain silent. I didn't dare let him know I was coming.

"The cloudy night was dark, but he was drunk enough that he didn't notice anything else around him. He wouldn't dream that I might stand up to him. I had never done it before.

"He reached the streamside, and I saw the sack squirm and sway in his grip. He didn't gloat, didn't even seem to think about what he was doing. Without any apparent remorse, he simply tossed the knotted onion sack into the swift water. He had weighted it with rocks, and after bobbing a few times as it flowed along in the current, the sack dunked beneath the water. I thought sure I could hear the kittens crying. Sweet Sea Mother . . ." His voice hitched.

"I did not have much time. The kittens would drown in a minute or two. I didn't dare let my father catch me, and if I went too close he would reach out and grab me with those awful hands. He would seize my shirt or my arm, and he would slap me until I collapsed. He might even break a bone or two—and worse, he would prevent me from saving the kittens! I hid in the dark for an agonized minute. My heart was pounding.

"He didn't even pause to savor his murderous handiwork. He stood at the streamside for a dozen breaths, then lurched away into the night, back in the direction he had come.

"I bounded as fast as I could run along the stream, stumbling and tripping on the rocks and low willows. I followed the cold current and tried to see in the dim moonlight, searching for any sign of the bobbing sack. I scrabbled along the banks of the stream, splashing and stumbling, but I had to hurry.

"After the spring rains, the water ran high, and the current was swifter than I remembered it. I couldn't see how far the kittens had drifted, but up ahead around a curve in the stream, I spotted just a flash of the onion sack bobbing up before it sank down again. I tripped on the mossy rocks and slick mud, and I fell into the water, but I didn't care. I splashed deeper, wading along, sweeping my hands back and forth ahead of me as I tried to grab the sack. I caught weeds, cut myself on a tangled branch, but the sack had drifted along, still under the water. I couldn't hear the kittens anymore, and I knew it was too long, but I kept trying. I sloshed forward and dove ahead until finally I caught the sack, wrapped my fingers around the folds of rough cloth. I had it!

"Laughing and crying, I yanked it out of the water and held it up, dripping. It was waterlogged and heavy. Rivulets of stream water ran out of it, but I stumbled to the shore and sprawled up on the bank. With my numb, bleeding fingers I couldn't pull open the wet knot closing the sack. I tore at it with my fingernails, and finally I ripped the fabric. More water gushed out, and I dumped the kittens out onto the streamside.

"I remember saying 'No, no, no!' over and over again. Those poor, fragile kittens flopped out, slick and wet, like fish from a net. And they weren't moving. Not a one of them.

"I picked them up, pressed gently on them, blew on their tiny faces, trying to get them to respond. Their perfect little tongues lolled out. I couldn't stop imagining them mewing for help, trying to breathe, dragged under the cold water. They were so young and hadn't even known their own mama, so I knew they had been crying out for me and my mother. And we hadn't saved them—we hadn't saved them!"

Bannon hunched his shoulders and sobbed. "I ran as fast as I could. I tried to get the sack from the water—I really tried! But all the kittens were dead, all five of them."

Nathan listened with a compassionate frown. He stroked his chin as he sat on his rock next to the campfire. "You tried your best. There was nothing else you could have done. You can't carry that guilt around with you forever. It'll kill you."

As Bannon wept, Nicci watched him intently. In a low voice, she said, "That's not what he feels guilty about."

The old wizard was surprised, but Bannon looked up at Nicci with remarkably *old* eyes. "No," he said in a hoarse voice. "Not that at all."

He laced his fingers together, then unraveled them again as he found the courage to go on. "I found a soft spot under a willow near the stream, and I dug out a hole with my bare hands. I buried the kittens and placed the wet sack on top of them, like a blanket that might keep them warm in the cold night. I piled rocks on top of the grave, so that I could show my mother where I had buried them, but I never wanted my father to find out where they were or what I had done.

"I stayed there for a long time, just crying, and then I made my way home. I knew I could never hide my tears or my wet clothes from my father. He would probably beat me for it, or maybe just look at me with smug satisfaction. At the time, with the kittens all dead, I didn't think he could hurt me any more and I was tired of running." The young man gulped. "But I came home to find something far worse."

Nicci felt her shoulder muscles tense, and she braced herself. Bannon spoke in a bleak voice, as if he no longer had any emotion in the memory. "After he drowned the kittens and came back to our cottage, my mother was ready for him. She'd had *enough*. After all the pain and suffering and fear he had inflicted on her, the murder of those poor innocent kittens was the last straw for her. When he staggered through the door, my mother was waiting.

"I saw the scene afterward, and I guessed what happened. As soon as he entered the house, she held a loose oak axe handle like a warrior's mace. She attacked my father, struck him in the head, screaming at him. She nearly succeeded, but it was only a glancing blow, enough to draw blood, perhaps crack his skull—and certainly enough to make his anger erupt.

"In a futile effort, she tried to hurt him, maybe even kill him. But my father snatched the oak handle from her hands, tore it right out of her grip, whirled around—" Bannon swallowed. "And he beat her to death with it." He squeezed his eyes shut.

"By the time I came home from burying the kittens, she was already dead. He had smashed her face so that I couldn't recognize her, couldn't even see the usual parts of a face at all. Her left eye had been pulped, and broken shards of skull protruded upward, exposing brain. Her mouth was just a ragged hole, and teeth lay scattered around, some of them pounded into the soft meat of her face, like decorations. . . ."

His voice grew softer, shakier. "My father came for me with the bloody, splintered axe handle, but I had nothing to defend myself with, not even a sword. I threw myself on him nevertheless, howling.

I . . . I don't even remember it. I hit him, clawed at him, pounded at his chest.

"This time the neighbors had heard my mother's screams, worse than ever before, and they rushed in only moments after I arrived. They saved me, or else my father would have killed me, too. I was screaming, trying to fight, trying to hurt him. But they pulled me away and subdued him. By that time, most of the fight had gone out of my father. Blood covered his face, his clothes, and his hands. Some from the gash on his scalp where my mother had struck him, but most of the blood belonged to her.

"Someone had raised the alarm, and one goodwife sent her little boy running to town to get the magistrate." Bannon sucked in a succession of breaths and kneaded his fingers as he stared like a lost soul into the small campfire before he could continue. Overhead, a night bird cried out and took flight from one of the pine trees.

"I couldn't save the sack of kittens. I couldn't prevent my father from drowning them, but I ran after him, nevertheless. I waded into the stream and tried to catch them before it was too late. But I always knew it would be too late, and when they were dead I wasted precious time burying them and crying over them . . . when I could have been there to save my mother."

He looked up at his listeners, and the empty pain in his hazel eyes struck a deep chill even in Nicci's heart.

"If I had stayed with my mother, maybe I could have protected her. If I hadn't gone chasing after the kittens, I would have been there. I would have stood up to him. I would have saved her. She and I would have faced him together. The two of us could have driven him off somehow. After that night, my father never would have hurt me again. Or her.

"But I went to save the kittens instead. I left my mother behind to face that monster all by herself."

Bannon stood up again, brushed off his pants. He spoke as if he were merely delivering a scout's report. "I stayed at Chiriya long enough to see my father hanged for murder. By then, I had a few coins, and out of sympathy other villagers gave me money to live on. I could have had a little cottage, started a family, worked the cabbage fields. But the house smelled too much like blood and nightmares, and Chiriya held nothing for me.

"So I signed aboard the next ship that came into our little harbor—the *Wavewalker*. I left my home, never intending to go back. What I wanted was to find a better place. I wanted a life the way I imagined it."

Nathan said, "So you've been changing your memories, covering up the darkness with fantasies of how you thought your life should be."

"With lies," Nicci said.

"Yes, they're lies," Bannon said. "The real truth is . . . poison. I was just trying to make everything better. Was that wrong?"

Nicci was sure now that Bannon Farmer had a good heart. In his mind, and in the way he described his old lie to others, the young man was struggling to make the world into a place it would never be.

When the wizard placed a reassuring hand on his shoulder, Bannon flinched as if in a sudden flashback of his father striking him. Nathan didn't remove his hand, but tightened his grip, like an anchor. "You're with us now, my boy."

Nodding, Bannon smeared the back of his hand across his face, wiping away the tears. He straightened his shoulders and responded with a weak smile. "I agree. That's good enough."

Even Nicci rewarded him with an appreciative nod. "You may have more steel in you than I thought."

CHAPTER 35

Rain and gloom set in for the next four days as they traveled higher into the mountains. The mornings were filled with fog, the days saturated with drizzle, and the nights accompanied by a full downpour. Low-hanging clouds and dense dripping trees kept them from seeing far into the distance, and they could not gauge the high and rugged mountains ahead of them. Eventually, Nicci knew they would find the high point and look down into the lush valley that lay between them and Kol Adair.

Nicci walked along wrapped in a gray woolen cloak the Lockridge innkeeper had given her, which was drenched and heavy. Bannon and Nathan were just as miserable, and the sodden gloom weighed on them as heavily as the young man's reticence.

On the fifth night out of Lockridge, the downpour increased and the temperature dropped to a bone-penetrating wet cold. Nicci was pleased to find a thick wayward pine, a pyramid-shaped tree with dense, drooping boughs. For those travelers who knew how to identify them, wayward pines formed a solid, reliable shelter in the forest. Richard had shown her how to find and use them.

Nicci shook the long-needled branches to disperse the collected beads of rainwater, then lifted the bough aside to reveal a dark and cozy hollow within. "We'll sleep here."

The wizard found a comfortable spot inside under the low overhanging branches. "Now, if you could just find some roasted mutton and a tankard of ale, Sorceress, we'd have a fine night."

Bannon sat with his knees pulled up against his chest, still withdrawn.

"Be satisfied with what I've already provided," Nicci said. She did use her magic to light a small fire inside the shelter, and the crisp greenwood smoke curled up into the slanted boughs and away from them. Because they were soaked and cold, Nicci also released more magic to dry the moisture in their clothes, so that for the first time in days they actually felt warm and comfortable.

"I can tolerate unpleasant conditions," she explained, "but not when I don't have to. We need our strength and a good rest. There's no telling how far we have yet to go."

"The journey itself is part of our goal," Nathan said. "After we find Kol Adair and I am whole again with my magic, we have the rest of the Old World to explore."

"Let us get a good rest for tonight," she said, "and explore the whole world tomorrow."

They warmed water over the fire and made a fortifying soup with barley, dried meat, and spices. Afterward, they collected enough rainwater in a pot outside the wayward pine that they could make hot tea.

Bannon rolled up in his now-dry cloak and pretended to go to sleep, and Nathan looked at him with concern. "Adventures rarely turn out the way one expects," he said in a low voice to Nicci, but Bannon surely heard as well—as the wizard no doubt intended.

The next day as they continued through the drizzle, splashing in puddles and slipping in the trail mud, Nathan exuberantly drew his sword and rounded on Bannon. "You walk like a sluggard, my boy. And with your eyes so downcast, a dragon could be upon you before you even noticed." He held up his sword and stepped in front of the young man, blocking his way. "Defend yourself, or you're useless to us."

Though Bannon was startled, the wizard swung his sword, but without malice, and he did so slowly enough that the confused young man had a chance to duck. "Stop, Nathan! What are you doing?"

"Waking you up." The wizard swung again, more earnestly this time.

Bannon leaped out of the way. He fumbled Sturdy from its scabbard. "I don't want to fight you."

"Such a pity," Nathan said, coming after him. "When bloodthirsty enemies come for me, I always let them know whether I'm in the mood for fighting. It makes all the difference." He swung again, and Bannon lifted his sword to meet the blow with a loud clang. Sparrows in the branches overhead were startled into flight, swooping away to find a drier, more peaceful bough.

Nicci knew exactly what Nathan was doing, although she also understood the young man's lethargy. After Bannon had been forced to face the fact that his nostalgic life was nothing more than a foolish fantasy, he was like a ship cast adrift with no rudder or sails. Nicci had spent years building shields around her mind and heart, but Bannon was still so young.

Nathan cried out in happy surprise as his opponent counterattacked, whistling his blade through the air. The solid ringing of steel against steel echoed through the waterlogged forest. "That's better, my boy! I want to know that you can handle yourself if we're set upon by monsters again."

They crashed through the underbrush as Nathan chased him. Bannon wheeled to defend himself and press an attack, sending the wizard into full retreat; then, in a furious volley of blows, they brought each other to a standstill. His face animated now, Bannon pressed forward, pushing Nathan, who slipped in the slimy mud of the trail. The wizard tumbled flat on his back, and then Bannon also lost his balance and sprawled beside his mentor. The two men picked themselves up, panting, and laughing. Both were covered in mud.

Nicci watched them, her arms crossed, the woolen traveling cloak pulled around her. Meeting Nathan's eyes, she gave him a nod of acknowledgment.

The wizard reached out to take the young man's hand, and pulled him up beside him. "Dear spirits, that didn't stop the rain, but it may have lifted your gloom."

"I'm sorry," Bannon muttered. "When I wanted to leave Chiriya Island, I think . . . I may have been running away. But now, I realize that isn't the point at all." He lifted his chin, which was smeared with mud. The rain kept coming down, fat droplets falling from the dense branches above in a constant cold shower. "I want to go with you. This is the journey I've always dreamed about."

"Good," Nathan said. "Then, let's keep exploring."

Nicci set off in the lead. "If we go far enough, we may even walk out of this rain."

The higher they climbed, the colder the nights got, but finally the rain ceased. The downpour had lasted long enough to wash the mud from their clothes.

Two days later, the skies cleared of clouds, opening to a fresh blue, and Nicci picked up the pace, rejuvenated by the sunshine. By now, the path had become all but indistinguishable from a game trail, and they had seen no one since leaving Lockridge. Nicci could understand why Emperor Jagang had not bothered to send his armies down to these isolated lands, where there were few people to conquer.

Occasionally, they came upon ruins of large stone buildings that had fallen into disrepair, overgrown by the forest and reclaimed by time.

"This land must have thrived thousands of years ago," Nathan said. "After the great barrier was erected at the end of the wizard wars, Sulachan and his successors were forced to push south instead, since they could no longer reach the New World. There were cities and roads, trading posts, mining towns, great leaders and internal wars. In fact, Emperor Kurgan devoted most of his conquest to the southern part of the Old World."

"That is why we've heard little of him in our history," Nicci said. "He was unimportant."

"He was important enough to these people," the wizard said.

"I don't see any people," Bannon said.

"Use your imagination. They were here."

They stopped at a mossy, overgrown building foundation. Squares laid out on the ground marked what must have been a large fortress, but now only crumbling remnants outlined the rubble. "The world tends to pass you by when you live your life in a tower." He kept talking while Nicci and Bannon followed him away from the ruins. "Did I tell you about the time I foolishly tried to escape from the palace? I was young, with little concept of how impregnable my prison was."

Nicci frowned. "The Sisters never mentioned to me that you had tried to escape."

"I was only a century old, just a boy, really. I was brash and willing to take chances . . . and I was also impossibly bored. Yes, I had the freedom to roam through the high tower rooms, to look at the wonderful books in the library, but such diversions can only distract a young man for so long before he begins to dream. I didn't want to be their pet prophet, so I laid my plans for months. Yes, they had placed an iron collar around my neck, and with the Rada'Han they could control me and my magic." His lips quirked in a smile, and he tossed his straight white hair behind him. "So I had to be resourceful and not just use a spell or two to get away.

"When I kept telling the Sisters I was cold, they brought me more blankets, and I used just a tiny bit of the gift to unravel the fibers, which I reassembled into a rope, a long rope, thread after thread. It was strong enough to hold my weight.

"I spent a week being cheerful and attentive to my studies so as to lull the Sisters into a sense of complacency, and then one moonless night I made my way to one of the highest rooms. I barricaded the door after claiming that I meant to study spell books throughout the night. I was a curious young man and wanted to build my powers as a wizard, even though I knew they would never free me." He unconsciously rubbed at his neck, as if he still felt the iron collar there. "Because a prophet is too dangerous, you see."

He looked at Bannon to make sure the young man was listening. "I opened the high window and fastened my rope securely to an anchor. I was precluded from using a levitation spell, so I had to resort to more traditional means. When I lowered myself over the sill and looked down, I felt as if the drop went all the way to the underworld." He regarded Bannon, cocking an eyebrow. "When one lives inside stone-walled rooms, it's difficult to get a sense of the vastness of the sky or the long drop to the ground below. But I was resolved. I wrapped the rope around my waist and began to lower myself down the wall."

Nicci was skeptical of the story. "The Palace of the Prophets is guarded by wards and shields. No one could just climb through a window and escape."

He lifted a finger. "And why do you think the Sisters added all those protective spells? Back then, the women assumed the shields blocking the lower doors would be sufficient. They never thought I would be foolish enough to climb out the highest tower." He cleared his throat. "The important part is that I was dangling by a rope from the tower wall—very brave, I might add. But I had miscalculated. When I was still nearly a hundred feet from the base of the tower, the rope ran out. I was just hanging there!"

He paused for suspense, and looked at Bannon. "I did know how to use Additive Magic, so I made the strands of the rope grow. I should have guessed that the Sisters would detect this through the Rada'Han, but what could I do? I certainly couldn't climb all the way back up. I extended the rope one foot at a time and eased myself down, but it took a great deal of energy. I was so exhausted I could barely hold on to the rope by the time I reached the ground."

He let out a long, wistful sigh. "By then, the Sisters had discovered what I was doing, and they captured me as soon as my feet touched the paving tiles."

"Even if you did make it away from the Palace of the Prophets and over the bridge into Tanimura, your Rada'Han would have prevented you from escaping. The Sisters could have rounded you up at any time," Nicci said. "I find your story questionable."

"My story is entertaining, and it also has a point." He turned to face Bannon. "Sometimes you must be daring to accomplish a great thing, but no matter how daring you are, your deeds will be diminished if you forget to plan properly."

They toiled higher along a steep switchbacked path. The trees thinned, leading up to a high point ahead.

Nathan stretched his arms. "After that, the Sisters kept me bottled up so tightly that I could never again plan a serious escape. Therefore, I amused myself by writing other adventures and secretly distributing them throughout the land. They became quite popular, enjoyed by many."

They were out of breath as they finally reached the summit of the ridge and crossed over to take in a sprawling, breathtaking view.

When asking about the way to Kol Adair, they had repeatedly been told about a vast fertile valley filled with green forests, croplands, and villages. But this sight was not at all what they expected.

As the three surveyed the landscape, Nicci saw only brown desolation to the horizon. This was no verdant valley, but a dry and cracked crater, bounded to the north by a high plateau. The heavily forested foothills spilled down to a pale, fuzzy boundary of death. Dust devils skirled across the dry basin. White expanses of sparkling salt indicated where lakes had dried up, leaving only poisoned soil. The terrible desolation spread outward from a central point, countless miles away.

And the dead zone was clearly growing.

Nathan drew a deep disappointed breath. "I will have to update my map."

CHAPTER 36

With all the vegetation dead, the old road ahead became more plain, and they walked down the rocky trail toward the wide desolate valley. When Nicci inhaled, the air carried a burnt, powdery smell with a hint of rot, as if vapors stirred up by thermal currents wafted into the foothills.

They paused at a rocky switchback to look across the great basin. Nicci could discern straight lines etched across the barren lands, man-made paths that were now covered with blown dust. She could also see what had been small villages, larger towns, possibly even the ruins of a city.

Nicci said, "This was a well-traveled and inhabited area, but something sucked it all dry."

"There are still habitable areas on the fringe of the desolation," Nathan said, pointing to the transition zone where the green of vegetation faded into the cracked brown of death. He shaded his eyes and looked into the hazy distance, beyond the valley. "That blowing dust impairs visibility, but you can see the towering mountains off in the distance far to the east." He pointed. "Kol Adair may be somewhere up on one of those mountain passes."

"But how can we cross that desolation?" Bannon asked.

Nicci scanned the landscape. "We should go around, skirt the valley to the north, stick to the greener areas in the foothills."

"In fact, I suggest we visit one of those villages," Nathan suggested. "I'd like to learn what happened down there, if that was once a great fertile valley." He screwed up his face in a distasteful expression. "It does not appear natural."

Nicci bit her lower lip. "Agreed. Lord Rahl will need to know."

"And the world may need saving, Sorceress," Nathan said, without any obvious hint of humor. She did not respond.

As the path descended, they worked their way into the badlands, where rocks towered like monoliths, reddish sandstone eroded by wind and water. The vegetation transitioned from tall pines to gnarled scrub oak, mesquite, and spiky yucca that had survived as the terrain grew less hospitable.

In the heat of the day, Nicci packed away her traveling cloak. Her black dress was comfortable, but the rocks underfoot were hard through the soles of her boots. Bannon's face quickly became sunburned.

Their road took the path of least resistance, following the curves of the slickrock bluffs and winding into rocky arroyos. Pebbles pattered down from above, and they saw skittering movement—lizards darting from sunny rocks into shadowy crevices.

Nicci listened to the silence punctuated by stray breezes and the rustle of twigs. She narrowed her eyes, sensing movement from something larger than a lizard. She and Nathan were instantly alert, while Bannon kept plodding, distracted by the scenery. Then he also stopped. "What is it? Are we being stalked?" He drew his sword.

"I don't know," Nicci said. "I heard something." She remained motionless, extending her senses, trying to pick up on some unseen threat.

They waited in tense silence. Nathan frowned. "Actually, I don't hear anything."

Suddenly, they heard a burst of bright and refreshing laughter, the high voice of a child. All three looked at the rocks overhead, the smooth bluffs marred with occasional blind ledges. A young girl stood up from a hiding place above. Small-statured and elfin, she looked about eleven years old.

"Been watching you for a long time." She placed her hands on her hips and giggled again. "I wondered how long it would take for you to notice. I was going to surprise you!"

She looked like a waif dressed in rags. She had an unruly mop of dusty brown hair that was styled more in tangles than curls. Her honey-brown eyes twinkled as she regarded them. She had caramel-colored skin and a triangular face with a narrow chin and high cheekbones. Her arms were wiry, her legs spindly beneath an uneven skirt made of patchwork cloth. Four large lizards dangled by their tails from a rope tied around her waist; the lizard heads were smashed and bloody.

"Wait for me," she called. "I'm coming down."

"Who are you?" Nicci said.

"And why have you been spying on us?" Nathan demanded.

Like a lizard herself, the girl scrambled down the rock wall, finding hand- and footholds that were all but invisible, but she displayed no fear of falling. Her feet were covered with moccasins made of rope, fabric, and scraps of leather. She dropped the last five feet, landing in a resilient crouch on the rocks in front of them. The lizard carcasses at her hip flopped back and forth.

"I am spying on you because you're strangers—and because you're interesting." She looked up. "My name is Thistle."

"Thistle?" Bannon asked. "That's an odd name. Is it because you're prickly?"

"Or maybe I'm just hard to get rid of—like a weed. I'm from the village of Verdun Springs. Is that where you're going? I can take you there."

"We're not sure where we're going," Nicci said. "Are you all alone here?"

"Me and the lizards," said Thistle. "And there aren't as many lizards now because I've had a good hunt today." She squatted next to them and opened a pouch on her other hip. "I don't often see people. I'm usually the only one who goes out exploring. Everyone else in Verdun Springs works all day just to survive."

She tugged open the pouch's drawstring and pulled out strips of dried, grayish meat. "These are yesterday's lizards. Do you want some? They dried all afternoon, so the meat will be just right." She put a strip into her mouth, seized it with her front teeth, and tore it into shreds. As she chewed and swallowed, she kept holding out her other hand to extend the offering of meat.

Bannon, Nicci, and Nathan each took a small portion of dried lizard. Bannon looked at it skeptically, but the wizard munched away without hesitation. "My uncle Marcus and aunt Luna taught me about hospitality," said Thistle. "They say we should be kind to strangers because maybe they can help us."

"We might be able to help," Nicci said, thinking about her broader quest. "First we need to learn what happened here. How far is your village?"

"Not far. I've only been out two days, and I have enough supplies for a week. Marcus and Luna won't be expecting me back home yet." Thistle's grin widened. "They'll be surprised when I bring visitors. You sure you can help us? Can you stop the Scar from growing?" She gave them a frank assessment, then sniffed. "I don't think you're strong enough."

"The Scar?" Bannon asked.

"She must mean the desolation," Nathan said. "The whole valley ahead."

"We call it the Scar, because that's what it looks like," Thistle said. "I've heard stories of how beautiful the valley used to be when I was just a baby. Farmlands and orchards and forests—they even had flower gardens. Can you imagine?" She snorted. "Flower gardens! Wasting water, fertilizer, and good soil just to grow flowers!"

Nicci felt sad for the girl, and her innocent comment was a poignant indication of what sort of life the people in her village must be enduring as the devastation expanded.

She continued to chatter. "If you can save us, if you can break the Lifedrinker's spell and bring the fertile lands back, how I would love to see it! All my life I've dreamed of making the land beautiful again." She sprang to her feet, ready to go. She trotted off, calling over her shoulder, "Do you really think you can destroy the Lifedrinker?"

"Who is the Lifedrinker?" Nathan asked.

Nicci cautioned, "We did not promise we could do anything."

When the girl shook her head, the tangled brown curls bobbed about like weeds. "Everyone knows about the Lifedrinker! The evil wizard at the heart of the Scar who sucks the life out of the world to feed his own emptiness." She lowered her voice. "That's what my uncle Marcus says. I don't really know anything more."

"Won't your uncle be worried about you alone in the wilderness for days?" Nicci asked.

"I can take care of myself." Thistle set off with a pert stride, skipping over the stones. Without slowing, she bent to snatch rocks in her right hand and kept moving down the wash, knowing that they would follow. "I've raised myself since my parents died when I was just a little girl. Uncle Marcus and Aunt Luna took care of me, but they didn't have any extra food or water, so I have to feed myself most of the time, and I try to bring in enough to help them."

Thistle jerked her head to the left, focused on a flash of movement she had spotted. Quicker than even Nicci could see, the girl hurled the rocks. They clacked, clattered, and struck their target, and she bounded ahead and squatted down to retrieve a small lizard she had just killed. Thistle held it up, pursing her lips. "Almost too tiny to be worth the effort." Nevertheless, she tucked it among the other carcasses at her waist. "Aunt Luna says never to waste food. Food is hard enough to come by these days."

The energetic girl led them along at a pace that Nicci had trouble matching. Nathan and Bannon started to slow down as they trudged over the rough rocks. Thistle scampered along, overjoyed to have company. "You're very pretty," she said to Nicci. "What is your home like? Where do you come from?"

"I am from far to the north," Nicci said. "In the New World."

"This is the only world I know. Are there trees where you live? And water? Flowers?"

"Yes. And cities . . . and even flower gardens."

Thistle frowned. "Flower gardens? Why would you leave such a nice place to come here?"

"We didn't know we were coming here. We're on a long journey."

"I'm glad you came," Thistle said. "You can fight the Lifedrinker. You'll find a way to restore the valley and the whole world."

Nicci felt a chill as she recalled Red's words. "Maybe that's why we're here."

"We will do exactly that, child," Nathan said, "if it's within our power."

They worked their way along the widening arroyo and around the bluffs to where the last line of trees had died and the creeks had long since dried up. Thistle gestured proudly ahead. "This is my village."

Nicci, Nathan, and Bannon stopped to look. They were not impressed.

Verdun Springs had obviously been a much larger town once, thriving at the intersection of imperial roads, forest paths, and commercial routes that led into the fertile farmland and trading villages deep in the valley. But the cluster of low mud-brick buildings had retracted into a squalid settlement, as if the population had dried up as well as the landscape.

Dust skirled along the streets. Rocks had been dumped in piles next to a building. A cart with a broken wheel—and no horse to draw it—leaned against the rubble mound. Countless empty buildings were covered with dust, some of them falling apart.

Nicci counted no more than twenty people toiling under the harsh sunlight. They wore frayed clothes and floppy hats woven from dry grass. Several men were working around the town's well. One man lowered himself by a rope down into the stone-walled shaft. "Keep digging! If we go deep enough, we're sure to find clear water again." Others tugged on a second rope attached to a pulley, drawing up a bucket that held only mud and dirt.

To announce their arrival, Thistle let out a loud, shrill whistle. The man at the well looked up, and the other haggard people stopped to stare. Thistle called out, "This is my uncle Marcus—I told you about him. Uncle, this woman is a sorceress, and the old man is a wizard, but he doesn't have any magic."

"I still have my magic," Nathan corrected. "It's just not accessible at the moment."

"The other one is named Bannon," Thistle continued. "I don't know what he can do." The young man frowned in annoyance.

Marcus was a skinny man with dark brown hair going to gray and a bristly beard. His shirt was splattered with mud from helping at the well; he wore a faded, scuffed leather vest. "I welcome you to Verdun Springs, strangers, but I have little hospitality to offer. None of us does."

"I brought lizards!" Thistle said.

"Why, then we can have a feast." Marcus smiled. "You always bring more than your share, Thistle. Our family will eat well tonight—and so will our guests."

Aunt Luna also introduced herself, a dark-skinned woman in a drab skirt with a scarf of rags tied around her head. Though faded now, the scarf had once been bright red. In front of her home Luna had been tending large clay planters, turning rich, dark dirt fertilized with human night soil. Each planter held a splash of green vegetables. Luna wiped her hands on her skirts and tousled the girl's mop of hair. "We may even find some vegetables that are ready. Better to eat them as soon as they're ripe than let the Lifedrinker have them."

Thistle sniffed. "As long as the vegetables are in the pots, the Lifedrinker can't touch them. He can't reach through the planters."

"Maybe he just doesn't try hard enough," said her aunt, adjusting the drab red head scarf.

The villagers muttered. The Lifedrinker's name seemed to fill them with dread.

"We're glad you could come," said Marcus, leading them down the main street. "If you visited any of the other towns nearby, you'd find them all empty. Verdun Springs is all that remains. The rest of the people went away, or just . . . disappeared. We don't know." He wiped dust from his forehead.

"Why didn't you pack up and leave?" Nathan asked, gesturing around at the desolation of the village, the drying well, the dusty streets. "Surely you could find a better place to live than this."

"Someday this will be a lush valley again, as it was a decade ago. We know how beautiful it can be," Luna said, and the few villagers next to her nodded.

Thistle beamed. "I can only imagine it."

Luna said, "I've urged my husband to pack up and go into the mountains. We hear there may be other towns up and over the ridge, even an ocean if you walk far enough west." She heaved a great sigh. "An ocean! I can't remember so much water. At the time when Thistle was born, there was a lake in the valley, before the Scar spread that far."

"We won't leave." Marcus brushed dried mud from his leather vest. "We will eke out our existence day by day." He squared his shoulders and added with great pride, "We are hardy people."

"Hardy?" Nicci raised her eyebrows, thinking that "foolhardy" was a better description.

CHAPTER 37

When night fell, Nicci and her companions sat around a fire pit outside of Marcus and Luna's home, which was built from mud bricks. The house was spacious and cool, with a large central room, wooden beams across the open, airy ceiling, and small high windows below a clay tile roof. The large home reflected a more prosperous time.

Sitting outside in the warm dusk as they prepared for the evening meal, Nathan and Bannon told the adults the story of their journeys, and Nicci explained about Lord Rahl's new golden age, though it was clear that neither Marcus nor Luna took hope.

"We can barely find enough water to survive," said Marcus, "and our food is rapidly dwindling. As I told you, the other towns that once filled this valley twenty years ago are silent and dead." He pressed his hands together, hunched his shoulders, and looked at Nicci. "I am glad to hear of the overthrow of tyrants, but can your Lord Rahl come to our aid? The Scar keeps growing."

Nicci narrowed her eyes. "We are here. Now. But we need to know more about the Lifedrinker."

Worry lines seamed Nathan's face. "I am not convinced how much assistance I can offer, Sorceress—at least until we get to Kol Adair."

Thistle sat cross-legged in the dust next to Nicci as she cleaned the fresh lizards for dinner. "Kol Adair? That's far away." The girl used her little bloody knife to skin another of the lizards, inserted a stick through the body cavity, and handed it to Bannon, so he could roast it over the low cook fire in the pit. Somewhat queasy, the young man lowered the carcass over the coals, and soon the flesh began to bubble and sizzle.

Bannon wiped a hand across his mouth while turning the stick over the cook fire so the lizard didn't burn. "How fast is the Scar growing?"

"In twenty years, the entire valley died away, and the devastation continues to spread," Luna said. "We are one of the last villages on the outskirts."

"The Scar grows faster as the Lifedrinker becomes more powerful . . . and his appetite is insatiable," Marcus added. "I remember when the heart of the valley started dying, just before Luna and I were married. But we'll stay here. We've lasted this long."

The night was silent, but the breezes carried an ashy breath with bitter chemical taint. At the scattered mud-brick houses or larger quarried-stone structures around the town, quiet villagers ate their own meals outside, keeping apart from one another. Verdun Springs had fallen into a sullen hush, as if caused by the mention of the Lifedrinker's name.

Luna looked sad. "Verdun Springs used to have a population of a thousand, and now fewer than a dozen families remain."

"We are the strongest twenty," Marcus insisted. It was clear they had had this argument before.

Bannon said, "There are forests and farmlands on the other side of the mountains, plenty of places for you to settle and be happy."

"It would only delay our fate," said Marcus, with a stubborn frown. "The Scar is spreading, and sooner or later the Lifedrinker will swallow the world."

Nicci hardened her voice. "Unless someone stops him."

Thistle retained a thread of optimism. "I want to stay until the land grows fertile and beautiful again—the way it was before my parents died. I remember it . . . just a little."

"You were too young," said Marcus.

The spunky girl finished cleaning the smallest lizard, which she cooked for herself. She licked the blood off her fingers and left a smear of red on the side of her mouth. Nicci reached forward to wipe off the stain. "Your face is covered with dust."

"We don't have much opportunity to wash," Marcus explained.

Giggling, Thistle licked her fingers and smeared saliva over some of the dust, which did little to clean her face.

The travelers had supplemented the meal by offering dried fruits and leftover smoked fish from their pack. The smoked redfin from Renda Bay was quite a novelty to the young girl, who frowned at the taste and announced that she preferred her fresh lizards.

Nicci got back to business. "Who is the Lifedrinker? And how can he be defeated? Does he have weaknesses?" Maybe this was indeed the reason why they had been driven here. She remembered the witch woman's words: *And the Sorceress must save the world.*

Marcus ground his heel in the dust. "We don't know the full story. We're just simple villagers affected by that ever-growing stain. But we know he was a wizard from Cliffwall, and something went terribly wrong." He nibbled on the last shreds of meat on the roast lizard, picking specks of flesh from the bones, and then he crunched the bones, appreciating every morsel. "That's where you'll find the means to destroy him—if it can even be done."

"And what is Cliffwall?" Nathan asked.

"A great archive of magical lore. We thought it was a place of legend for centuries," Luna said.

Thistle piped up. "It's real—I've seen it!"

"You haven't wandered that far, child," chided Marcus.

"I have! It was four days' walk up into the plateau, but I made it."

"It was hidden since the time of the ancient wizard wars," Luna said, "but it reappeared fifty years ago."

The wizard raised his eyebrows and looked over at Nicci. "A great archive? It sounds like a place we should investigate, regardless. We may find something to help my . . . condition, even before we reach Kol Adair." He stroked his chin. "As well as the background on the Lifedrinker, of course."

Thistle's honey-brown eyes sparkled. "I can take you there. I've seen it with my own eyes!"

"Now, girl . . ." Marcus gave her a scolding look.

"It is said that someone broke Cliffwall's camouflage spell decades ago," Luna said. "The location is still secret, but the hidden people who guarded the place invited a few outside scholars from the towns in the valley. That hasn't happened in a long time, not since the Scar started to spread and consume all the towns and farms."

The lonely breeze picked up, carrying more dust in the wind. Nicci heard the cry of a hunting night bird and something stirring in the empty houses. Unexpectedly, she saw shadows moving in the dark alleys between the abandoned stone structures. She sat up straighter, suddenly alert, trying to penetrate the darkness with her gaze.

She also sensed magic in the air—not the usual pervasive vibration that she could always touch. Since arriving in Verdun Springs, she had felt an odd and unsettling note that seeped out of the Scar, but now it suddenly swelled, like the flush of heat just after an oven door was opened. Tense, she rose to her feet and tossed the cooking stick and the last scraps of her roast lizard aside. She stepped away from the fire pit and out into the wide, dry street.

Before Marcus or Luna could ask her what was wrong, the night filled with screams.

CHAPTER 38

Things moved in the night beyond the quiet rustling dust. The terrified cries came from one of the few inhabited houses on the outskirts of the village, where an old man and his wife had been brooding outside by their small fire.

Nicci was already running, her black dress just a deeper shadow in the darkness. Another scream. She bounded toward the old couple's cook fire, saw many silhouettes as the gray-haired man and woman struggled against figures that closed around them.

The attackers looked gaunt and skeletal, lit by the orange flickers of the small fire. Without thinking, Bannon sprinted along beside her, drawing Sturdy from its scabbard. Ahead, Nicci saw that the attackers were the desiccated remnants of humans, their skin sucked dry of all moisture and baked brown like dried meat.

Running hard, Thistle caught up with Bannon and Nicci. "Dust people! They've never come into town before."

Three shriveled reanimated corpses closed around the old couple, who fought back with helpless terror. They had no weapons, but Nicci did. The sorceress swept out a hand and released her magic. A hammer blow of wind knocked one of the dust people into the air as if he were no more than chaff. When he struck the brick side of the house, his body broke apart, crumbling like twigs and straw.

The old woman battered at her attacker, raking the dried flesh with her nails, but the mummified figure wrapped its arms around her. Immediately, the dry ground beneath their feet *changed*, becoming no more substantial than foamy water. The desiccated thing pulled the old woman down, dragging her into the pit of dust until they vanished underground.

Seeing his wife disappear, the old man fought even more frantically. A strong blow from his hand knocked the mummified creature's skull loose, but even headless, the thing grappled with him. The ground turned to soup beneath the old man's feet, and he sank in up to his knees. He gave a despairing wail, reaching out for something to hold on to.

Nicci struck out with her magic again, the blow of concentrated air so sharp and forceful that it shattered the old man's undead attacker.

But four more hideous dust people boiled up out of the ground, emerging from the soft dirt like striking vipers, and together they grabbed the old man and dragged him under. His screams were drowned in sand and dust.

Nicci and Bannon arrived too late. The ground had smoothed over, the attackers gone and leaving only ripples of dry dust.

Bannon crouched with his sword upraised, alert for a continued attack as he turned from side to side in search of other enemies. Nicci grabbed his shirt and pulled him back from where the ground had become dry quicksand.

Then, from additional houses around the dying town, shouts echoed through the night—more people being attacked.

Nathan finally reached them, holding his sword as well. "What are the attackers? Have you seen them?"

"Dust people," Thistle said. "The Lifedrinker swallows up people wherever he can, and then makes them into his puppets."

Nicci stood close to the girl. "Stay safe."

"Where is safe?" she asked, and Nicci had no answer for her.

Darkness filled the streets of Verdun Springs, and the cook fires and lamps in the stone houses shed far too little light for certainty, but the ground stirred. The wind picked up, carrying a choking fog of dust into the town.

Nicci cautiously led her group back toward the center of town. "Stay with me."

The normally placid dirt streets squirmed, stirred, and gave birth to more horrors. Skeletal hands rose up from the dirt, showing long clawed nails and gray-brown skin that had hardened around the knuckles. The dry ground became as fluid as water, and dust people swam to the surface to hunt the last hardy survivors.

Grasping mummified hands surged around Nathan's feet, reaching for his dark boots. One latched on, but he swept down with his sword to sever the arm bones before kicking the clutching hand loose.

Bannon ran forward, using Sturdy to chop one of the reanimated corpses through the rib cage, scattering vertebrae, but the cadaverous creatures came on like an army of horrific puppets, boiling up from the ground.

Nicci blasted them with magic, knocking two creatures away from Thistle before she grabbed the girl's arm.

Bannon slashed apart another reanimated attacker, then cleaved one more down the middle with his backstroke. As he lunged toward a third, though, the dirt street turned into powdery soup beneath his feet, and he stumbled. He let out a terrified yelp as he started to sink, but the wizard was there to catch his wrist and wrench him back out of the dust trap.

In the center of town, a raised dais of bricks and tile stood empty, a stage on which minstrels might have performed at one time, or where town leaders gave speeches. "Go to the stone platform!" Nicci cried.

Still holding Bannon's arm, Nathan staggered and lost his balance as the ground shifted again. They both stumbled, but struggled ahead in the direction of the stone platform. Nicci used her magic to push them, lifting them up enough that they could escape the slurry of dust. Once on stable ground again, the men scrambled toward the raised dais, a safe island.

From the terrified screams that rang out around the town, Nicci realized that dust people were attacking other families, destroying other homes. She had to get her companions to safety before she could try to protect anyone else.

Bounding ahead on skinny legs, Thistle gasped as the dirt street collapsed beneath her feet. She plunged in up to her waist, flailing, but

Nicci grabbed her. With a great heave, she pulled the girl out and away from the grasping hands of more dust people. Nicci tossed Thistle closer to the stone platform, and the scrawny girl rolled, sprang to her feet, and ran the rest of the way there.

Extending her hand, palm out, Nicci turned in a half circle, using magic to knock the desiccated attackers back, and finally joined her companions on the dais. The tiles were stable beneath their feet, but mummified corpses kept coming for them.

Bannon and Nathan stationed themselves on opposite corners of the platform, their swords held high, and they hacked apart any of the dust people who approached. When the dry, shambling monsters closed in, Nicci thought of the brittle dead wood the villagers had collected for their cook fires. Everything here in the Scar was dry as a tinderbox, hard, dense . . . flammable.

She released a flow of magic to increase the temperature inside the attackers, igniting a spark. Gouts of hot orange fire burned from their chests, but even on fire, the scarecrowish cadavers lurched forward. The smell of burning sinew and bone filled the air, and greasy black smoke rose up from each staggering form.

Nathan and Bannon kept hacking with their swords. A defiant Thistle had pulled out her skinning knife.

Most of the screams in the outlying buildings had fallen ominously silent, but nearby shouts sounded like familiar voices. Thistle cried out, "That's Uncle Marcus and Aunt Luna. I have to get home!"

From a distance, Nicci could see the girl's protectors trying to fight off a combined onslaught from the dust people. Thistle tried to bolt toward them, but Nicci grabbed her shoulder. "You can't run. The streets will swallow you up."

"I have to. We've got to save them!"

Nicci did indeed have to save Thistle's aunt and uncle—or at least try.

"We can fight our way through," Bannon said, lopping off the head of a dried attacker with his sword. It bounced on the ground and rolled like a hollow gourd.

"We'll never make it," Nathan said. "In three steps, the ground would suck us down."

From their questionable sanctuary, they watched Marcus smash one of the dust people with a rock from the fire pit. Luna's red scarf drooped as she thrashed at the attackers, one wooden cooking skewer in each hand. The woman jabbed a hardened stick straight through the empty eye socket of the closest monster, but even with the shaft through its skull, the thing kept coming.

In a flash of planning, Nicci envisioned how best to run from the stone platform all the way to Thistle's home. "I need to make a safe path." The open dirt streets were deadly, unless she could change the substance of the ground itself, prevent the dust from becoming a possible conduit. She directed a flow of magic into the dirt and sand, using Additive Magic to coalesce and create, to fuse the grains together. The loose dust cemented into a narrow walkway, as if she had just frozen part of a stream. "Run! They might still break through, but it should stop them for now and give us the time we need. *Run!*"

The others did not question her. Together, they leaped from the safety of the raised platform. Nicci sprinted ahead, feeling the vitrified sand crunch beneath her boots. She could feel the vibrations as frustrated dust people moved under the ground, trying to break through the barrier with bony claws. The hard surface needed to last for only a few seconds, just long enough for them to run.

They finally reached Thistle's home. Her aunt and uncle were scratched and bloody, wounded by the claws of the dust people they had fended off. Luna's faded red head scarf had been knocked askew, and she pushed it back out of her eyes. Nicci loosed another flow of power to ignite the two nearest attackers as she shouted to the other woman, "Take Thistle and get inside!"

Marcus and Luna staggered to the doorway. The floor of their home was made of clay tile; Nicci hoped it would grant enough safety against an attack from below.

The house offered very few defenses, but this was their last shelter. Freed from the grasping hands of the undead creatures, Marcus and Luna retreated deeper inside.

Bannon and Nathan hacked apart two more dust people at the threshold, before they all crowded through the door. Behind them, the pathway of fused sand cracked, then shattered apart, and the dust people emerged from underground, pushing aside the hard slabs.

Marcus and Luna huddled in a corner of the home, holding each other. Luna sobbed, while Marcus opened and closed his mouth as if trying to think of something defiant to say. When the two saw that Thistle was all right, they cried out with relief and gestured for her to come over.

Nathan slammed the wooden door and threw the crossbar into place, but it was a flimsy barricade. Soon enough, the mummified creatures were pounding on it, scratching with their claws. The joined planks began to crack and splinter.

Nicci surveyed the home, studying its possible defenses. Bannon and the old wizard stood back-to-back with their swords ready as the thudding continued against the door. It would only be moments before the dust people surged inside.

Thistle's eyes were wild, but determined as she stood next to Nicci. "Are we safe?"

Luna reached out her arms. "Come here, girl. We'll be safe together."

Before Thistle could start to where her aunt and uncle huddled, the hard clay tiles in the corner dissolved into a soup, and the floor opened up like a trapdoor into a hunter's pit. Luna and Marcus screamed as skeletal hands grabbed them by the legs and hauled them under.

Nicci rushed to help them, but at that moment, the barricaded door shattered, and an army of dust people boiled inside. Nathan and Bannon stood to block them, sweeping their swords from side to side. Both were grimly silent as they fought with all their strength.

Nicci felt tiles shift beneath her boots as the foundation gave way. Glancing up, looking for any way out, she spotted the iron-hard wooden crossbeams that extended across the ceiling of the mud-brick structure. The beams led to an upper window that was open to the night and the roof. It was their only way out.

"Thistle, I'm going to throw you up there. Grab the beam and work your way over to the window." She snatched up the scrawny girl. Without arguing, Thistle reached out her hands, and Nicci tossed her high enough that she could grab the crossbeam and nimbly swing her thin legs over it. Once she caught her balance, Thistle scooted along the beam toward the high open window.

Nicci turned to the two men. "Bannon, Nathan, we've got to get up there."

"You're going to throw me up there too, Sorceress?" Nathan asked, then swung back to cleave the dried skull of another attacker. "Do you think I can fly?"

"Not flying, but with magic, I will control the air and change your weight. I can move you."

Without further ado, she released her power and yanked Nathan up high enough to grasp the crossbeam; then she did the same for Bannon. Not expecting it, the young man flailed and nearly dropped his sword, but managed to grab on to the beam without losing Sturdy.

Thistle had scooted her way to the window. The two men, balanced on the crossbeams overhead, reached down, and Nicci jumped, stretching out her hands as ten of the staggering monsters lurched into the dwelling. Bannon and Nathan deftly caught her and swung her up.

Dust people filled the confined home, reaching up toward the open ceiling, but they could not get to their four potential victims overhead.

At the open window, Thistle looked back and stared at the empty corner that had just swallowed her aunt and uncle. Tears streamed down her narrow face, carving tracks through the dust there.

"Climb out onto the roof," Nicci said. "We should be safe up there." Just then, the base of the home's mud-brick walls shifted and started to crumble, as if the hardened structure were beginning to dissolve back into dust. "Quickly!"

Thistle scampered through the window and swung herself onto the tiled roof, while Bannon and Nathan followed with as much urgency. Sliding along the wooden crossbeam behind them, Nicci looked down to see more dust people rising from the broken floor. The walls shivered with rapidly spreading cracks.

She realized that even the rooftop would not be a place of safety.

The group sat gasping for breath out in the open night air and heard the hollow hiss of an army of dust people plodding through the streets of Verdun Springs.

Thistle's entire home began to collapse beneath them. One wall sank down, destabilizing the roof, and loose clay tiles clattered like broken teeth to the ground. Bannon tried to keep his balance, but slipped and scrabbled as tiles broke under him. He was able to snag a wooden anchor beam, and Nathan grabbed the back of his shirt and hauled him back up to temporary safety.

Nicci stood at the roof's apex, searching for any possible escape. The orphan girl ran to the other end of the roof and pointed to an adjacent stone structure, a square, flat-roofed shop building made of quarried blocks rather than mud bricks. "Over here! This looks safer!"

The gap between the buildings was six feet wide. But with desperation, and a possible nudge of magic, the four ran across the crumbling tile roof, jumped, and all landed on the flat, open roof of the stone building.

Behind them, Thistle's home collapsed, the brick walls crumbling, the roof sagging inward. The girl watched in dismay.

Standing on the roof of the much sturdier building, Bannon stomped with his boot. "At least this roof is solid beneath our feet, made of old wood, reinforced. And these stone-block walls won't collapse so easily."

Nathan pointed out an opening in the roof, which led down into the main shop below. "But those creatures could follow us, climb onto the roof."

Pursuing them, the dust people tore open the unlocked door below and burst into the abandoned shop. They made their inexorable way upward, climbing the stairs to the open roof.

"We are still trapped." Nicci scanned toward the edge of town, the rocky bluffs and canyons on the outskirts of Verdun Springs. "If we can get out there away from town, in among the bluffs, the dust people won't be able to attack from underground. Maybe we can defend ourselves in the stone outcroppings."

"It's much too far," Bannon said from the edge of the rooftop, swallowing hard.

"And those things are much too close," Nathan added.

"They are slow-moving . . . unless they ambush us," Nicci said.

With gasping, scratching sounds, two dust people clambered to the top of the stairs and emerged onto the shop roof, climbing through the trapdoor. With a swift kick, Nicci knocked both stick figures back down the steps, but more cadavers surged up the interior stairs.

Nicci looked around into the night and realized that the rest of the town had fallen silent. There were no more screams.

"Are we the only ones left?" Thistle whispered.

Nicci did not give any excuses. "Yes. But we will get out of here."

They watched in dismay as two recently inhabited brick buildings also sagged and collapsed as the Lifedrinker's magic turned the brick structures into dust.

Angry, Nicci focused on the rugged bluffs outside of town—a place of sanctuary where the solid ground would protect them. Better than here.

"Be ready," she said. "I'm going to fuse the dust like I did before. I'll make another path for us to run on, and it won't last long. And the other dust people will come after us as swiftly as they can. We just have to be faster." She turned to the young girl. "Can you do it?"

"Of course I can," Thistle said. "Say when."

Nicci gauged the most direct path to the bluffs outside of town. She gestured. "That way. Don't look back. Don't stop for anything—just run. I'll make the ground hard, but we still have to jump off the roof."

"I would make a comment about my old bones," Nathan said, "but now isn't the time."

Bannon pointed down. "I'm more worried about *those* old bones."

Nicci unleashed her magic and marked a path. With Additive Magic she created a solid structure, melding the sand and dust into flat, hard islands. Stepping-stones, since she did not have enough strength left to solidify the whole area. This would be enough. She made one appear, then another.

"Go!" she shouted. "I'll make the rest along the way."

Without hesitation, Thistle leaped off the roof and landed in the soft dirt. Before the dust people could respond, she sprang onto the nearest hardened stepping-stone, then jumped to the next, running ahead. Nicci dropped after her, following close behind so she could reach out and keep creating the path as fast as the girl could run.

Nathan and Bannon tumbled down after them. By now, some of the dust people realized what their intended victims were doing, and the sticklike mummies streamed around the remaining town structures. Two dry cadavers rose up to the left of Thistle, dodging the hardened sand. Seeing this, Nicci reacted with an angry snarl and thrust with a blast of air, which smashed the dust people to splinters of bone and dried flesh.

But more came.

Nicci and the girl ran toward the rock outcroppings, with Bannon and Nathan close behind. They fled the abandoned town. When they finally reached the hard rocks, Thistle scrambled up the outcropping, finding hand- and footholds as she climbed higher away from the dust people. The other three followed her, crawling up the pocked bluff walls until they reached the relative safety of a solid outcropping.

Thistle didn't want to stop. "I know a way, follow me. If we go deeper into the canyons, they'll never find us."

Together, they fled into the night. Climbing higher into the rocks, Nicci glanced over her shoulder in time to see the last of the brick buildings collapse into dust. Then even the stone buildings began to shift as the ground underneath melted away and swallowed them. Soon enough, all sign of Verdun Springs had vanished forever.

CHAPTER 39

Even terrified and in shock, Thistle knew her way through the dark wilderness. Moving solely on adrenaline, she guided them by starlight along smooth slickrock ledges farther into the canyons, far from the reach of the dust people. They were all too exhausted and shaken to engage in conversation. The girl was obviously struggling to absorb what she had just been through, but she survived with a furious lightning-bolt determination that Nicci admired.

Finally, the companions reached the top of the bluffs, high above any threat from the Lifedrinker's minions, and Thistle squatted on a flat rock under the stars. Her thin legs and knobby knees stuck up in the air; her shoulders slumped. She rested her hands on her patchwork skirt and just stared into the empty distance.

Nicci stood beside her. "I believe we are safe now. Thank you."

Thistle began trembling, and Nicci didn't know how to comfort her.

Fortunately, the wizard came up and bent down next to her. "I am terribly sorry, child. That was your home, your aunt and uncle. . . ."

"They took care of me," Thistle said in a quavering voice. "But I spent most of my time alone. I was fine—and I will be fine." She looked up with fiery determination, but when her honey-brown eyes met Nicci's, they filled with tears. Her lips quivered and her shoulders began to shake. "Uncle Marcus and Aunt Luna always said I was too much responsibility for them to handle. Too prickly." She sniffled, and Nicci could see her iron-hard strength. "I will be fine."

"I know you will," Nicci said. "Truly I do."

A moment later, the girl broke down into sobs, rubbing her eyes. Bannon awkwardly put an arm around her shoulders, like a big brother. She turned, embraced him, and cried into his chest. The young man blinked, not sure what to do in the storm of grief. Reflexively, he held her in return.

"We will rest here," Nicci announced, looking around at their high ground. "This place is defensible. We can move on in the morning."

"Nowhere is safe," Thistle said in a harder voice. She shook herself. "Except with you. We'll all be safe together."

Nicci took first watch while the others tried to sleep. They had lost their packs and traveling supplies during their frantic flight, but they made do. Nicci had her magic to assist them, but she suspected that Thistle's survival abilities would be essential to their mission, even if they headed away from the spreading desolation.

Bannon and Nathan stretched out on the open rock, trying to rest. Exhausted, the old wizard slept soundly, and his eyes fell half closed, so Nicci could see only the whites between his lids. She was used to the fact that wizards slept with their eyes open, an eerie habit that unsettled those unaccustomed to seeing it. Now, though, she was more disturbed to realize that Nathan Rahl's eyes were mostly *closed*. Perhaps it was another indication of how much of his magic he had lost since the world had changed. He was no longer whole. How had Red known what lay in store for them?

Nicci sat in silence, staring up at the stars, still trying to understand the new patterns, but she could find no message there. She listened with suspicion to every rustle of underbrush and clatter of loose pebbles in the night, but the sounds were merely caused by scurrying rodents.

At last she had time to think. She pondered the D'Haran Empire, the sprawling Old World, this mostly unknown continent that Lord Rahl needed her to explore. How was she to save the world? The very idea seemed laughable. Right now, her most immediate concern was the Lifedrinker, whatever he was. His Scar was spreading, encompassing a greater and greater swath of land. And he had already attacked them with his dust people.

That was the Lifedrinker's first mistake, Nicci thought. It was personal now.

She needed to know more about the evil wizard, what his goal was, how and why he had sucked dry those other townspeople from the valley and turned them into his reanimated servants. Was it just his appetite? Stealing more souls, absorbing their energy? The Lifedrinker's dark magic, whatever it was, had spread like a potent poison more deadly than thousands of deathrise flowers, like the one she still kept with her, wrapped in her dress pocket.

She knew they needed to find the place called Cliffwall.

Having seen the people of Verdun Springs dragged beneath the dusty ground, including Thistle's aunt and uncle, Nicci felt a powerful resolve. She had a deep hatred for oppression, for the destruction or enslavement of good people. The Lifedrinker was the epitome of tyranny, and Nicci considered it part of her mission for Richard to put an end to the threat. Prophecy or not, that was what she knew she had to do.

The orphan girl woke before dawn, instantly alert. Thistle looked around, saw Nicci, and scuttled over to be next to her. The two sat in silence for a long moment before the girl spoke. "I can lead us to Cliffwall—I know I can. There, you'll meet the scholars and learn the information you need to destroy the Lifedrinker. I hate him! And I will take you there."

"I believe you," Nicci said. "And you will prove it to us soon enough. Nathan and I are both scholars of magic. If the answer is there, we will find it." She narrowed her blue eyes and looked down at the lost little girl. "Regardless of what is in the library, I swear to you, we will find a way to rid the world of the man who did this."

Thistle gave a solemn nod. Unshed tears welled in her large eyes. "And after that, can I stay with you? I . . . don't have anyone else." When her voice cracked at the end, the girl covered it with a loud clearing of her throat. She looked away, as if ashamed of her desperation.

Nicci could not imagine bringing this child, however talented she might be, along on their difficult journey to Kol Adair. But Thistle had already been broken so badly in one night that the sorceress simply answered with, "We shall see," rather than dashing her hopes.

They were ready to move as soon as dawn broke. Thistle shook Bannon and Nathan by the shoulders to wake them. "It might take several days to get to Cliffwall, and the canyonlands up in the plateau can be a maze, but if you follow me"—she gave them a forced smile— "I'll keep you safe and on track."

Bannon tied back his loose hair. "But we don't have any water or food. We don't have our packs."

The girl placed her fists on her raggedy skirt and lifted her chin. "I'll find what we need." She sprang off and led them along the top of the bluff, then into even higher canyonlands away from the once-fertile valley that was now the Scar. The seemingly endless expanse of slickrock rippled with upthrust fins of red rock formations, like the backbones of some mythical monster.

The landscape was scored with a dizzyingly complex labyrinth of cracks and canyons, deep gorges that spilled into oblivion with no exits that Nicci could see. The muted reds and tans were interspersed with dark green splashes of piñon pines, mesquite scrub, even tall cacti. Down in the sheltered canyons, a fuzz of pale green mixed with spiky black branches showed where thick tamarisks clogged the channels. This was a healthy desert with natural vegetation; the spreading stain of the Lifedrinker had not extended this far . . . but Nicci suspected that would change before long.

Nathan shaded his eyes and looked out across the desert highlands. "It is beautiful, I'll grant you that." He placed a hand on the leather pouch that still held his life book, one of the few things he had managed to keep with him. "But I despair at the thought of mapping it. How can we not get lost?"

Thistle said, "I already told you, I'll be your guide. I can show you where Cliffwall has been hidden for thousands of years. I've explored it all. I know where I'm going."

"You explored all of this?" Bannon sounded skeptical.

She huffed. "I *am* eleven summers old."

"I see no reason to doubt her." Nicci followed as the girl set off, prancing from rock to rock, scrambling up steep slopes while Bannon and Nathan worked hard to keep up.

Thistle guided them along the fingers of canyon rims, then back around again to a deeper cut. As they rested, the orphan girl stayed near Nicci, and gazed back at the barren emptiness of the Scar, many miles behind them. Thistle gave a long wistful sigh, her face a mask of sadness. "I heard people talk about how beautiful this land was once, with forests, rivers, crops. Like a paradise, the perfect place to live. When my aunt and uncle talked about it, they would begin to cry, saying how much it had changed in just my lifetime. It sounded so wonderful." She sniffled. "That's why Uncle Marcus and Aunt Luna insisted on staying here. They said our valley would come back . . . someday." She looked at Nicci. "You're going to bring it back, Nicci, and I'll help you. I will! Together we'll fight. We'll bring all the life back to this valley."

The girl showed such adamant hope that Nicci did not wish to disappoint her. "Perhaps we will."

Toward the end of a long day of traveling, Thistle led them to the lip of a wide canyon and found an impossible trail that took them painstakingly down toward the bottom. "There'll be water here and a place to camp."

Indeed, Thistle knew exactly where to find an excellent shelter under an overhang, where they built a campfire of brittle tamarisk and mesquite wood that burned hot with fragrant smoke. A seep of water provided all they needed to drink and to wash.

As twilight closed in, the girl darted off into the winding canyon and returned a short while later with four lizards for them to eat. They roasted the reptiles whole, and Nicci crunched the crispy scaled skin, bones and all.

Thistle led them onward for three days, climbing higher into the plateau through desert scrub, mesquite, sagebrush, creosote bush, and spiky yucca. They entered the uplands well above Verdun Springs, circling around the foothills that enclosed the vast valley and up into the high plateau.

Eventually, as if the ground swelled as it gained altitude, the land split into more deep canyons. Confident in where she was going, the girl wound them through the maze until Nicci, Nathan, and Bannon had no idea where they were or how they could ever retrace their steps. Even so, Nicci placed her faith in the girl.

As they traveled through one bright morning where the canyons widened and the rock walls broke into towering hoodoos that stood like eerie and misshapen sentinels, Nicci asked, "How old were you when your parents died?"

"I was very little," Thistle said. "Back then, there were still many people in Verdun Springs. The Scar hadn't spread to our town yet, but the Lifedrinker was dangerous even if he was far away. I remember my mother's face . . . she was very beautiful. When I think of her, I think of green trees, wide fields, running water, and pretty flowers . . . a flower garden." She laughed at the absurd idea of wasting garden space on mere flowers.

"As the Scar absorbed the valley, my parents would try to scavenge any crops they could still harvest. One time, they made an expedition to an almond orchard, because even if the trees were dead, there were still dried nuts to gather. My mother and father never came back. . . ." Thistle walked in silence for a long moment, leading the group around looming hoodoos. "The Scar might look dead, but some creatures are connected to the Lifedrinker, and he doesn't just kill them. He changes them, uses them."

"Like the dust people?" Nicci asked.

Thistle nodded. "But not just people. Also spiders, centipedes—and lice, terrible monstrous lice."

Nicci felt a twist inside of her. "I hate lice."

"Lice drink life as well," Bannon said. "No wonder the wizard likes them."

"What killed your mother and father?" Nathan asked.

"Scorpions—big scorpions had infested the almond trees, and when my parents came to harvest the nuts, the scorpions fell upon them, stung them. When Uncle Marcus and two other villagers went to look for them days later, they found my parents' bodies, their faces all swollen from the stings . . . but even though they were dead, the Lifedrinker made them into dust people too. My parents attacked Uncle Marcus."

Her words tapered off, and Thistle didn't need to continue the story of what the villagers must have done to get away. "After that, I stayed with my aunt and uncle. They said they would take care of me, that they would watch over me." Her voice was bleak. "Now they're gone. Verdun Springs is gone." She swallowed hard. "My world is gone."

"And you are with us, child," said Nathan. "We'll make the best of it."

Bannon pushed ahead. "Yes, we will—if we ever get to Cliffwall."

Looking up at Nicci for reassurance, the orphan girl nodded. "We'll be there by tomorrow."

The next morning Thistle led them along the floor of a canyon whose rocky bottom looked as if it had suffered flash floods during storms, but not for some time. The sky closed in as the canyon walls rose higher and drew together, looking sheer and impenetrable.

The wizard frowned, trying to gain his bearings as the shadows lengthened. "Are you certain this isn't a dead end, child?"

"This is the way." Thistle trotted ahead.

The canyon narrowed, and Nicci felt uneasy and vulnerable, realizing this would be a perfect place for an ambush.

"It closes up," Bannon said. "Look ahead—it's a dead end."

"No," the girl insisted. "Follow me."

She led them up to where the rock walls formed the end of a box canyon, leaving only what looked like a narrow crack of two mismatched slickrock cliffs. Thistle turned to the travelers, then rotated sideways and shimmied into the crack.

She vanished.

Nicci stepped forward to see that the crack was a cleverly hidden passageway that led through a narrow elbow in the blind wall. After inching her way along through the claustrophobic passage, Nicci saw light ahead.

The girl squirmed out and stepped into a widening canyon. Nicci joined her, and Bannon and Nathan emerged behind them. Nicci caught her breath.

They all drank in the view of Cliffwall.

CHAPTER 40

Past the bottleneck of the closed-in stone passageway, the hidden network of canyons on the other side of the towering barricade wall was a whole world cut off from the rest of the landscape. Steep-walled finger canyons spread out like outstretched hands cutting through the high plateau. Nicci and her companions absorbed the view. This place was a hidden, locked-away network of secret, sheltered canyons.

The main canyon through the cracked plateau was broad and fertile, cut by the sinuous silver ribbon of a stream that collected drips from numerous overflowing springs. Sheep grazed on the lush green grasses, and fenced fields were bursting with tall stalks of wheat and corn. Vegetable gardens crowded with squash and beans had been laid out in confined ledge niches that pocked the cliffs. Orchards grew along the streamside, many of the trees in blossom. Wooden hutches held beehives that added a faint hum to the air. Hundreds of people worked the fields, tended the flocks, climbed the canyon walls on wooden ladders. It was a thriving, prosperous society.

All along the cliffs that enclosed the canyons, large overhangs and alcoves created natural sheltered caves in which buildings had been constructed, clay brick and adobe buildings. Some of the natural grottoes held only two or three dwellings, while larger overhangs held a veritable city of adobe towers connected with walkways.

The opposite side of the canyon held a singularly enormous cave grotto, a yawning alcove that held imposing stone buildings with blocky façades. The architecture had an air of ancient majesty. Nicci realized this must be the legendary wizards' archive, only recently revealed.

Cliffwall was like a fortress in its huge, defensible alcove, stone-block structures five and ten stories high, massive square walls with defenses. A narrow, winding path chiseled into the cliff was augmented with knotted ropes and short ladders to grant access from the canyon floor to the yawning grotto above.

Once through the bottleneck into the canyon, Nathan tilted his head back and stared in awe, his mouth agape. "It reminds me of the Palace of the Prophets. Ah, I do miss the library there."

Bannon displayed the same wide-eyed wonder Nicci had seen on his face when he was in the city of Tanimura. "Was the Palace of the Prophets really that big?" he asked.

Nathan chuckled. "Size is a relative thing, my boy. The cliffs and the overhang definitely make this look imposing, but the palace was at least ten times the size."

"Ten times?" Bannon said. "Sweet Sea Mother, that can't be possible!"

"No need for comparisons," Nicci said. "Cliffwall is impressive enough, and it has the advantage of being *intact*. Perhaps we'll find what we need to know about the Lifedrinker."

In the bright daylight, some of the local people had spotted the visitors emerging through the hidden entrance to the canyon. Two boys working a vegetable plot halfway up a cliff whistled an alarm. The shrill sound echoed and ricocheted, amplified by the angled canyon walls. Others converged, responding to the alarm.

While Nicci might have preferred to reconnoiter the canyon structures to assess the Cliffwall defenses and any possible threat, Thistle shouted and waved at the people coming closer. "Hello! We are strangers from the outside. We need to look into your archive."

More alarm whistles echoed from the alcove settlements, and in the towering fortress of the Cliffwall archive, dozens of people bustled to the windows and doors. Nicci couldn't hold Thistle back as she boldly strode forward into the canyon, confident they would all be welcome here.

A group of Cliffwall dwellers hurried toward the four travelers. Thistle put her hands on the hips of her ragged dress and raised her voice. "We are here to defeat the Lifedrinker! I brought you a sorceress, a brave swordsman, and an old wizard."

"I don't appear that old," Nathan said, salvaging his pride. "And I am a prophet as well as a wizard . . . although at present I am unable to use either of those faculties." He tapped his head. "Still, the knowledge is here."

"They are here to find out how to stop the Scar," Thistle proclaimed.

Nathan looked up at the people drawing closer. "Hello! We understand you have an archive of knowledge? Ancient records that might prove useful in dealing with this terrible enemy that plagues the land?"

Nicci added in a harder voice, "Information that will give us the tools and weapons to defeat him? We need it."

One middle-aged farmer wore a brown tunic flecked with grass ends and chaff from cutting wheat. "You would have to see Simon for that. He's Cliffwall's senior scholar-archivist." He indicated the towering fortress alcove up the side of the cliff, where more than a dozen people were working their way in single file down the narrow pathway to come meet them.

"And Victoria. They need to see Victoria," added a woman whose tight bun of pale hair was tied in a gray scarf. She had wide hips, stubby callused fingers, and biceps that were larger than Nathan's and Bannon's combined. "She's the one who decides what knowledge the memmers preserve."

The farmer brushed at the fragments of wheat, then placed a stalk between his teeth. "Now, now, it all depends on the type of information they need."

"We haven't seen strangers and outside scholars for years, not since the Scar wiped out the valley," said a red-faced shepherd who came puffing up, catching the end of the conversation.

"The scholars have needed new blood," said the hefty woman. "No one here has found a way to stop the Lifedrinker. We need help."

"Cliffwall was hidden behind a camouflage shroud for thousands of years," said the redhead. "And even though the spell is gone, the spirits

of our ancestors would torment us if we simply handed over that knowledge to any bedraggled visitor who asks! We are very careful about how
many outside scholars we allow here."

"We're here to help," Nicci said.

"And we're not all that bedraggled," Nathan said.

"I'm not a stranger," Thistle insisted. "I watched you a year ago, and
you never noticed. I'm the only survivor from Verdun Springs."

"Never heard of it," said the shepherd.

"That's because you've been locked in these canyons forever," Thistle
said. "The rest of the world has gone on while you stayed hidden here.
Everything is dying, and you don't even know it."

Nicci put a hand on the girl's shoulder to calm her. "We have come
here to help. If I have the right information, maybe I can find a way
to stop your enemy."

"And bring back the green valley," Thistle insisted. "They can do it."

They all turned as the group of robed scholars hurried toward them
from the towering fortress archive. The people began to talk at once.
"Simon, these people came from the outside."

"This girl led them. She says she's from a place called Verdun
Springs."

"One is a sorceress and the other is a wizard."

"And a prophet."

"Victoria, look, that one's a sorceress!"

"They want to study our information, look into our archives . . ."

"We've needed some fresh scholars."

Nicci tried to sort the overlapping chatter as a man stepped forward, obviously in charge. "I am Simon, the senior scholar-archivist of
Cliffwall. I supervise the cataloging of the knowledge preserved here
by the wisdom of the ancients."

Nathan raised his eyebrows. "Senior scholar-archivist? You seem
rather young for the job."

Simon appeared to be in his mid-thirties, with thick brown hair
that stuck out in unruly spikes, since he apparently didn't have the inclination to care for it. His chin and cheeks were covered with a wispy
corn silk of beard. "I'm old enough to do my job. And I started young,

brought here twenty years ago as a prodigy from one of the valley towns."

"The camouflage shroud broke down only fifty years ago," said a matronly woman who took her place next to him—Victoria, Nicci presumed. She was in her sixties, with gray-brown hair tied back into a braid that she wound in a coil around her head. Her face was smooth, showing only the beginnings of crow's-feet around her eyes, and her rounded cheeks were flushed a healthy pink. Her warm voice sounded to Nicci like the voice of a kindly grandmother from a children's tale, but with a hard edge.

"We've been the guardians of Cliffwall since the old wizard wars, but we have only recently opened the archives to outsiders again. Simon's scholars have completed barely half of the cataloging work. But my memmers can perhaps explain what you need to know, directly from our memories—once you convince us of your need."

CHAPTER 41

Simon, Victoria, and the other intense scholars led the visitors to the fortress archive up the sheer cliff. As they toiled up the narrow path that zigzagged along the rock wall, Nicci could see the size of the towering buildings constructed inside the cave alcove, and she grew more impressed with the ancient library. The great stone façades of the Cliffwall buildings towered higher than she had at first guessed.

"This is imposing," she said, trying to imagine how such a mammoth city could have been built in such an isolated place. "Maybe the Palace of the Prophets was only *five times* larger."

Thistle scampered ahead up the precarious path, never missing a step or a handhold. Impatient, she stopped partway and turned. "Come on, Nicci. Don't you want to see the library?"

As Nathan climbed the rock face, he admired the huge buildings, the tower faces, the windows and arches, and the imposing primary doors, twice as high as a man. "Look at the massive stone blocks in those walls. The only way such a fortress could have been erected—especially in this isolated canyon—is through magic."

"Powerful magic," Nicci agreed. "In a time before so much magic was purged from the Old World."

The wizard paused on the steep cliff path, resting a hand against the smooth rock at his left. He nodded. "Indeed, it must have been quite an undertaking."

After clambering to the overhang of the great alcove, Thistle waited for them in front of the imposing stone buildings. "Sweet Sea Mother," Bannon whispered. "I've never seen anything like it."

The matronly Victoria looked at him, a troubled expression crossing her apple-cheeked face. "Your Sea Mother had nothing to do with it, young man. She is far away and did not aid in the effort. This was accomplished through human labor, and it cost the lives and energy of many gifted wizards."

Simon turned to look at the buildings with clear reverence. "The most powerful wizards in the world came here in secret back at the time of the ancient wizard wars. It took them years to construct and hide this place, under the greatest cloak of secrecy, but their gamble paid off. Emperor Sulachan and his purging armies never discovered the wealth of knowledge those wizards placed here. The camouflage shroud remained in place for centuries, hiding Cliffwall completely from any prying eyes. Only the villagers here in the canyons even remembered it existed."

"Until fifty years ago," Victoria said, with obvious pride in her voice. "And now the preserved knowledge is available to all again."

Nicci turned to look across the canyon as afternoon shadows closed in. Some of the shepherds slept in tents near their flocks in the canyon-floor pastures. In the numerous alcoves studding the opposite cliffs, she saw other dwellings lit by cook fires and lamps, but the imposing Cliffwall complex shone brighter as the gifted scholars used magic to illuminate the library archive.

"And we are studying, and practicing, as quickly as we can." Simon sounded enthusiastic.

The farthest structure at the right side of the alcove caught Nicci's eye. A large tower was damaged, melted as if the stone had become candle wax. The slickrock overhang had folded in, reminding her of a drooping eyelid. The windows were sealed over like an ice sculpture that had thawed, slumped, then frozen in a fresh cold snap.

Before Nicci could ask about the damage, though, scholars opened the towering doors and Simon led them through the main stone gate into the front tower. "This is only the outer fortress, but there's much more to Cliffwall than what you see here. An entire complex of tunnels runs through the heart of the plateau all the way to the cliffs on the other side."

Inside the main library building, the ceilings were high and vaulted, the thick walls made of quarried stone. Their footsteps echoed along the blue-tiled floor of the entry portico, and bright lights glowed from perpetual lamps evenly spaced along the walls, burning with magic. The stone halls were lined with wooden shelves crowded with mismatched volumes, an odd assortment of leather spines or rolled scrolls, even hardened clay tablets with indented symbols that Nicci didn't recognize.

Nathan hungrily ran his gaze along the shelves. "I can't wait to start reading."

Simon chuckled. "These? Just minor overflow volumes that scholars took out because they looked interesting. The main vaults of knowledge are deeper inside the mesa—and much more extensive. All manner of knowledge is preserved here."

Three lovely young acolytes came up to join Victoria, sweet-faced and eager, none of them older than twenty. The matronly woman nodded at them with a gentle smile. "Thank you for joining us, my dears. We can use your help and attention." She introduced them to the visitors. "These are my most dedicated acolytes Audrey, Laurel, and Sage."

The three women wore white shifts, sashed tight around their waists with a fabric belt, and each girl was strikingly beautiful in her own way. Audrey had high cheekbones, full lips, and rich, dark hair, almost a blue-black. Laurel had strawberry-blond hair that hung loose, except for a decorative braid on the side; her eyes were green, her lips were thin, and her white teeth glinted in a ready smile. Sage's deep reddish-brown hair was thick and shining, and her breasts were the most generous of the three.

Nicci and Nathan gave them a polite acknowledgment, but Bannon made a deep bow, his face flushed with embarrassment when the girls fawned over him, paying more attention to the young man than to the others.

Victoria clucked at them. "These strangers must be tired and hungry, so let us eat while we hear more of their story. Go, prepare extra plates. Everyone will be gathering for the midday meal." The older woman smiled. "We have roast antelope and fresh corn, along with honeyed fruits and pine nuts for dessert."

Nicci was startled to realize how hungry she was. "That would be appreciated."

The wizard grinned. "And far better than munching on roasted lizards." When Thistle shot him an annoyed glare, he raised a conciliatory hand. "Not that we didn't appreciate the food, child. I just meant I was up for a bit of variety."

The dining hall held long plank tables covered with flaxen cloths. Men and women of all ages had gathered for the midday meal. Some were engaged in low conversation, exchanging new revelations they had found in forgotten scrolls. Many seemed too preoccupied even to notice the strangers; they wolfed down their meat and vegetables, then went back to their books without waiting for dessert.

After they took seats on the long benches, Simon served himself a hunk of savory meat, then passed the platter to Nicci and Nathan. As he filled his plate, Nathan said, "Please tell us more about Cliffwall, how it was constructed, and what it was for."

Simon accepted his tale-spinning duties as part of his role as scholar-archivist. "Three thousand years ago, at the beginning of the great war, wizards were hunted and killed in the Old World, and all magic was considered suspect. Emperor Sulachan sent teams to scour the land and destroy any magic he could not acquire for himself. He and his predecessors wanted no one else to have the powerful knowledge that had been assembled over generations.

"But the wizards did not surrender so easily, and they spread word from city to city, archive to archive. The emperor's armies were far superior in number, and the wizards knew that when they eventually lost, their vital knowledge would be destroyed. So the greatest gifted scholars gathered all books of magic and prophecy and slipped them out of known libraries, hiding any volumes that could not be copied in time."

Thistle sat propped up on the bench, paying little attention to the conversation. She used her fingers to take a second helping of antelope meat and corn. It was obvious she hadn't eaten a meal like this in some time, perhaps in her entire life.

Simon shifted his gaze from Nathan to Nicci. "The renegade wizards found this place in the maze of canyons up on the plateau, where no one could ever track them down. For years as Sulachan continued his conquests, the desperate wizards smuggled contraband books, scrolls, tablets, and magical artifacts to the new hiding place. They built Cliffwall to hold that knowledge, and many of them gave their lives to protect it, dying under horrible torture without revealing the location of this canyon.

"When every last book and lexicon had been stored inside the warren of chambers and shelves, the wizards knew they couldn't rely even on the isolation of these canyons to keep this knowledge safe. They needed something more powerful."

"More permanent," Victoria added.

Simon's eyes gleamed. "And so, the wizards conjured an impenetrable shield, an undetectable camouflage shroud that walled off the cave grotto. This entire cliffside was *hidden*. No one could see anything but a smooth, natural cliff face."

Victoria didn't seem to like how he was telling the story. "The shroud was more than a hiding spell, but also a physical barrier. No one could find or enter it. Cliffwall was meant to be sealed away—permanently, until those who would eradicate magic were themselves eradicated."

Nicci glanced at Nathan. "Like Baraccus hid the Temple of the Winds, whisking away the most vital magical lore by sending the whole temple to the underworld, where no one could have access to it."

"And that is how so much knowledge was preserved in a time of great turmoil," Simon finished. "Without Cliffwall and the camouflage shroud, everything would have been lost in Sulachan's purges. Instead, it remained intact here for thousands of years."

"Not everything," Victoria said in a crisp voice. "We had our alternative."

Reluctantly conceding, Simon let the matronly woman pick up the story while he chose an ear of roasted corn from a platter. He began to eat noisily.

"The physical documents were sealed in the archives," Victoria explained, "but the ancient wizards had a second plan to guarantee that the knowledge wouldn't be lost. They insured that someone would always remember. Someone special." She had a twinkle in her grandmotherly eyes.

"Among the people who lived quietly here in the canyons, serving as the guardians of Cliffwall, the wizards chose a few who were gifted with special memory abilities, perfect retention. *Memmers,* magically enhanced with a perfect-recall spell, who could memorize and retain all the words of countless documents."

"For what purpose?" Nathan asked.

"Why, to remember, of course," Victoria said. "Before the camouflage shroud was imposed and sealed everything away, the memmers studied the works in the archive, committing every word to memory." A rich undertone of pride suffused her voice. "We *are* the walking manifestation of the archives. For all the years when the archive was sealed, we remembered. Only we retained the knowledge."

Nicci was reminded of how Richard had memorized the entire *Book of Counted Shadows,* line by line, page by page, back when he was just a woods guide in Westland. George Cipher had made him learn the entire book, backward and forward, burning every page after Richard had learned it, so that the evil Darken Rahl could not have access to what it contained. Even though that book had ultimately been a flawed copy, Richard had used that knowledge to defeat both Darken Rahl and Emperor Jagang.

But *The Book of Counted Shadows* was just one book. Each of these memmers had committed hundreds of volumes to memory. Nicci could not comprehend the incredible scope of the memmers' task.

Victoria tapped her fingers on the tabletop. "I am one of the memmers, as are all my acolytes." On cue, Audrey, Laurel, and Sage came into the dining hall carrying bowls of honeyed fruit. The three young women made a point of offering the dessert first to an embarrassed Bannon; then they spread the plates and bowls around so that all could partake of the fruits.

Nathan chose a glistening peach slice, which he savored, then licked the honey from his fingers. He looked at Victoria, his forehead furrowed. "You each committed thousands upon thousands of volumes to your memory? I find that amazing—though somewhat hard to believe, I'm afraid."

Victoria's expression puckered. "No, one person could not hold all that knowledge, even with memory-enhancement spells and our gift. So the wizards divided the task among our ancestors. Each of the original memmers took specific volumes to study. All told, with enough memmers, our predecessors preserved most of the archive, but the books are scattered among many different minds, and those memmers taught the next generation and the next, dispersing all the books further, depending on how many memmer acolytes were available." She tapped the side of her head. "Nevertheless, the knowledge is there."

Nicci had no interest in the sweet fruit and passed the bowl to Thistle, who began to paw through the dessert with her fingers. "So you have taught and recited all these volumes for thousands of years? Losing nothing? Without a mistake?"

Simon said, "An expert memmer drills and practices with several acolytes, teaching them line after line, so that their students remember every word of every spell. In this way, the memmers kept the knowledge alive for centuries, even though the books themselves were locked away behind the permanent barrier. The camouflage shroud kept us all safe."

He paused to drink from a goblet of spring water, then wiped his mouth. He heaved a sigh. "Unfortunately, every wizard who was powerful enough to remove the shroud also died in the ancient wars, and no one could access the knowledge hidden here. It was lost forever, the impenetrable camouflage sealed in place. No one could break through the shroud."

Victoria interrupted him. "Until *I* figured out how to dissolve it, thus opening the archives again for study. Fifty years ago." She chose three fat strawberries and ate them quickly, then wiped her fingers and lips on a cloth napkin. "I was just a young woman at the time, barely seventeen."

Simon looked at the scholars up and down the plank tables, many of whom were buried in books, focusing on the words while they ate.

"Yes, and that changed everything. After guarding the hidden archive for millennia, the canyon dwellers suddenly had access to the vast treasure trove of information. But what were they to do about it? They were simple villagers with quiet untroubled ways. They had known little of the outside world for all this time. And even the memmers—they could recite the words they had memorized, but they didn't necessarily understand what they were saying. Some tomes were in languages no one could understand."

"We understood enough." Victoria picked up the story with an edge in her voice. "But we did recognize we needed help. The canyon dwellers occasionally traded with the towns in the great valley, although we were considered primitive and strange. The wizard wars were long over, and as far as we could tell, the Old World was at peace.

"So, when the camouflage shroud came down, we decided to bring in experts from outside. The best and most studious scholars from the valley, those who showed an aptitude for the gift. We were cautious. We invited only the exceptional ones, and then we guided them here through the maze of canyons, up from the valley and into the plateau."

"All told, this archive now supports a hundred dedicated scholars," Simon interrupted her. "I was one of those who came here long afterward, a gifted scholar—gifted in both senses of the word—summoned when I was young and eager, so that I could devote my life to relearning all the lost knowledge. I was quite skilled at reading and interpreting, and I learned many languages. I was so talented, in fact, that I rose to prominence here." His smile of wonder turned into a troubled frown. "I came twenty years ago, just after the Lifedrinker escaped."

Victoria's mood darkened, too. "For years now we have had no more new scholars. The towns in the valley are gone, swallowed by the growing Scar." Her voice became bleak. "We are all that remains. The Lifedrinker's devastation has not reached us yet, but it is only a matter of time, a few years at most."

Simon nodded somberly. "Our main work in the archive is simply to understand what we have. So much knowledge, but in such disarray! Even after half a century, two-thirds of the books remain to be organized and cataloged."

"All of my memmers recall separate pieces," Victoria said. "We have tried to exchange information so that we can at least refer one another. It is a vast puzzle."

Simon's voice took on a sarcastic edge. "Yes, and what the memmers say they remember cannot always be verified with printed documentation." He picked up a honeyed orange slice and sucked on it. "Thankfully, we can study all of the scrolls and tomes, and specialized memmers are no longer necessary. Entire teams of scholars have been reading tome after tome, studying and translating in order to relearn all that knowledge . . . and make use of it. We will become great wizards someday, but it takes time. We are all self-taught, and some of us have a greater gift than others. We are searching to find a spell powerful enough to fight the Lifedrinker." He swallowed hard and looked away. "If we dared to do so."

"Self-taught wizards?" Nicci was skeptical. "The Sisters of the Light spent years training gifted young men to use their Han, to understand their gift, and now you are attempting to train yourselves? Using old and possibly mistranslated books?"

Nathan's brows drew together in a show of his own concern. "I'm afraid I also have to worry that the memmers must have garbled some lines, misremembered certain words from generation to generation. Such trivial errors might not amount to anything of significance in a legend or a story, but in a powerful spell the consequences could be dire."

While Victoria took quick offense, and Simon mumbled excuses, Nicci suddenly recalled the damaged, half-melted tower in the Cliffwall alcove, and she drew her own conclusions. "You have already made mistakes, haven't you? Dangerous ones."

Simon and Victoria both looked embarrassed. The scholar-archivist admitted, "There was a certain . . . mishap. One of our ambitious students had an accident, an experiment went wrong, and the main library vault holding our prophecy books was forever damaged. We lost much." He swallowed hard. "We don't go there anymore. The walls are collapsed and hardened over."

"The memmers still recall some of those volumes that were lost," Victoria said. "We will do our best to reproduce them."

Nathan exchanged an expression of concern with Nicci, then spoke to the scholars. "I suggest you exercise a great deal of caution. Some things are too dangerous to be dabbled with. Your one 'accident' destroyed a building or two. What if another error causes even greater harm?"

Simon looked away as he stood up from the table. "I'm afraid you are correct. Another one of our scholars already made such a grave mistake and turned himself into the Lifedrinker. Now the whole world may have to bear the consequences."

CHAPTER 42

After the meal, Simon led the companions deeper into Cliffwall through the back of the stone-block buildings and into the warren of excavated tunnels that penetrated the vast plateau. The wide halls were lit with so many magically burning lamps that Nicci hoped this was the extent of their dabbling. Small light spells were one thing, but unleashing larger, uncontrolled magic was far more dangerous.

The main fortress buildings that filled the cave grotto were enormous, but the archive vaults were even more impressive. The spacious, vaulted chambers had walls lined with shelves crammed with books. In room after room, students sat in reading chairs or hunched over tables next to the bright glow of oil lamps. Bins filled with scrolls stood at the end of each long table. Ladders extended to the highest shelves to make hard-to-reach volumes more accessible. An intensity hung in the air, a hush as so many people devoted their full energies to relearning knowledge lost to history.

"Places like this were called central sites," Nathan said, "large caches of books hidden under graveyards, in the catacombs beneath the Palace of the Prophets, or in ancient Caska." He looked around, curious. "This appears to be more extensive than anything I have previously seen."

"And you are only seeing the smallest fraction here," Simon answered. "Remember, these archives have only been open for fifty years, and the wealth of information is daunting, tens of thousands of precious volumes." He spread his hands. "Even after decades, we are still trying to catalog what knowledge we have. That is the first important step. We don't even know what's here."

Victoria added, "When the ancient wizards compiled this archive, they were in a rush and under threat of extermination. They desperately needed to preserve as much knowledge as possible before Sulachan could destroy it. Caravans bearing magical tomes and scrolls came into the hidden canyons to unload, and riders arrived overland with packs of stolen books, half-scorched manuscripts rescued from libraries and universities that were burned by the emperor's hunters. As time ran out, books of all kinds were piled up and sealed away with little attempt at organization."

Victoria brushed a stray wisp of gray-brown hair from her forehead. "The memmers were assigned volumes by level of importance, rather than specific categories. Therefore, certain memmers might know about weather magic and prophecy, along with dire warnings about Subtractive Magic. Another memmer might preserve knowledge of how to manipulate earth, clay, and stone, as well as how to control lightning, and maybe change the currents in the sea, although we are far from the ocean."

"That is quite a jumble," Nathan said. "How does one locate any specific knowledge?"

Simon shrugged. "By searching. That is the life of a scholar. All knowledge is useful."

Nicci's response was harsher. "Some knowledge is more useful than others. Right now we need to know about the Lifedrinker. The Scar continues to grow, and he must be stopped."

Simon wore a troubled expression. "Let me tell you—or better yet, I'll show you, so you can understand."

He led them through passageways like wormholes, deeper into the heart of the huge plateau, and eventually up a winding slope until they reached the opposite side of the mesa. A natural rock window opened out from the cliffs of the plateau's sheer drop-off, which spilled down to hills and the sprawling valley. They stood together at the opening and looked out upon the sickening extent of the Scar, far away.

It was late afternoon, and the sun set in a glowering red blur at the horizon. Nicci could see the spreading desolation that rippled outward from a distant central point. "All of this used to be beautiful," Simon explained with a sigh. "A green, bucolic paradise. Until the Lifedrinker destroyed it."

Nicci frowned, more determined than ever. "Before we can fight him, we need to know who the Lifedrinker is, where he gets his power. Where did he come from?"

Simon sighed. "He was one of Cliffwall's most ambitious scholars. His name was Roland."

Bannon stared out at the desolation. "One of your own people did that?"

"Not intentionally," Victoria said, as if defending the man. "It was an accident. I was a scholar, married, in my middle years. Roland had been studying the archives for a long time. He was one of the first outsiders invited in after I brought down the camouflage shroud."

"Roland was revered among us," Simon interjected with a sigh. "I wanted to be like him—everyone did. He was Cliffwall's first scholar-archivist. But even the greatest scholars suffer human frailties." He shook his head. "Roland was not an old man, but he fell ill with a wasting disease, a terrible sickness that weakened him, made him grow gaunt. Tumors grew inside him like snakes. And the sickness was beyond the skill of our best healers."

Victoria picked up the story. "Roland lived his life in terrible pain, weakening, and he knew he would die before long. We could all see it. His eyes were hollow, his cheeks sunken, his hands trembled. He had such a great mind, and we were all dismayed that we would lose him. There seemed to be nothing we could do.

"But Roland did not accept his weakness. He did not surrender. He was afraid to die, in fact, and he vowed to save himself, at any cost. Roland said he had too much work to do here." Victoria swallowed hard.

"He asked questions, trying to find someone with the knowledge that he sought. He studied scrolls and books, searching desperately for what he needed in order to draw energy that would let him fight the wasting disease. So, he found a spell, a dangerous spell that would allow him to absorb life energy and keep himself alive. One of my memmers recalled it, at least partially, and that gave him a clue for his search of the uncataloged archives. He knew it was unwise, but he told no one. Knowing he would die soon, he worked the life-energy spell without hesitation, even though he didn't really understand what he was doing. He bound it to himself so that he could borrow bits of life from the world and rejuvenate his ailing body."

Victoria pressed her lips together until all the color drained out of them. "And it worked. Roland had been so weak and skeletal, clearly on the edge of death . . . but he grew strong again. The spell worked wonders. It brought back the flush of health. I remember seeing him." Her expression grew more troubled. "But then Roland didn't know how to stop. He couldn't control it."

Simon cut her off. "I recall those days of growing fear—I had just come here as a student. Roland felt guilty, horrified at what was happening to him—and at what he was doing to others. He kept draining more and more of the life around him, whether or not he wanted to. We tried to help him. His friends rushed to his side, offering their assistance, promising that they would help him solve the problem—but anyone who touched him *died*. Roland stole their lives and incorporated them into his own. We all began to weaken."

"He killed my husband," Victoria said. "To protect us, to save us, Roland fled Cliffwall. Unable to control the magic he himself had unleashed, he ran far from the archives and out into the valley wilderness, away from the towns . . . although not far enough. He hoped to live out his days there and harm no one else. But the Lifedrinker spell continued, unstoppable, never satisfied. Roland was like a sponge, absorbing life from the forest, from the grasslands. His very existence killed trees, drained rivers dry. And the desolation around where he had gone to ground spread wider and wider in an ever-expanding scar. He wiped out croplands. He erased entire towns." She straightened and brushed a hand across her eyes. "Roland didn't mean it."

Nicci thought of Thistle's family, of Verdun Springs, how they had clung to their hardscrabble existence, and then died. "His intentions don't matter. Think of all the damage that man has done. He must be stopped, otherwise his bottomless pit of magic will swallow the world."

Simon added, "For years our Cliffwall scholars have been scouring the books, trying any mitigation spell they could find. But no one could even get close to what was needed."

As the night deepened out in the dead valley, Nathan stared out at the Scar, watching the shadows move. "I wouldn't expect you to know how to stop such a powerful enemy. All of you are untrained wizards. You have read books, but you were never *trained* by a wizard, and you have never proved your abilities. Ah, I wish the Prelate Verna were here to help you. Wizardry untested cannot be trusted."

"You tried your best," Nicci said. "Now we will do our own research. If this archive is as vast as you say, it must hold the key, a counterspell. We simply need to find it."

"We would do anything to help you save us," Simon said. "But after the . . . accidents, we are afraid to try extreme measures of our own."

"That is wise," Nathan said. "But something must be done."

"That's why we are here," Nicci said, then finally admitted, "to save the world."

The orphan girl added with deep longing in her voice, "I want to see the valley the way it's supposed to be. I want to see the fertile land, the green fields, the tall forests."

Nicci looked at Thistle. "You will."

CHAPTER 43

Though Nicci wanted to begin her research in how to combat the Lifedrinker, she knew they were all exhausted from their long journey. Deep night had set in outside.

"Let us show you to your rooms," Victoria said. "You must rest." She glanced down at Thistle. "The girl needs her sleep."

"I'm still awake. I'll help." She looked at Nicci, determined. "And tomorrow I can study alongside you."

"Are you able to read?" Nicci asked.

"I know my letters, and I can read a lot of words. I will be much better after you teach me. I learn fast."

Nathan gave a good-natured chuckle. "Dear girl, I appreciate someone so willing to learn, but that is quite an ambitious goal. Some of these languages and alphabets are unknown even to me."

Nicci fixed her gaze on Thistle's dust-smeared skin, her bright and intelligent eyes. "When the Sisters trained me in the Palace of the Prophets, I spent more than forty-five years as an acolyte learning the basics."

The girl looked amazed. "I don't want to wait forty-five years!"

"No one does, but you're an intelligent girl. Since you learn quickly, it might take only forty years." Thistle did not at first realize Nicci was teasing her. Then Nicci continued in a more serious tone, "We need to defeat the Lifedrinker long before that, or there won't be any world left."

Victoria shooed them along. "Rest now, time for a fresh start to-morrow. We have separate quarters for each of you. They are austere, but spacious. We will let you unpack and rest."

"Not much to unpack, since we lost almost everything when the dust people attacked," Bannon said. "We've been living with little more than the clothes on our backs."

With a warm smile, Victoria promised, "We will provide clean clothing from the Cliffwall stores, and we will launder and mend your own garments."

The matronly woman showed them to private chambers deep within the plateau, where the temperature was cool and the air dry. Beeswax candles burned inside small hollows in the stone walls, adding a warm yellow glow and a faint sweet scent. Each room's furnishings consisted of a reading desk, an open floor with a sheepskin to cover the stone, a chamber pot, an urn of water, a washbasin, and a narrow pallet for sleeping. In each room, fresh, loose scholars' clothes had been laid out for them.

Victoria offered the spunky orphan girl a place of her own, but Thistle followed Nicci into her chamber. She bounced up and down on the pallet's straw-filled bedding. "This is soft, but it may be prickly. I'd rather sleep on the floor. You can have the pallet. That sheepskin looks warm enough for me. I'll stay close if you need me."

Even though the girl seemed perfectly satisfied with the arrange-ment, Nicci asked, "Why don't you want your own room? You can sleep as long as you like."

Thistle blinked her honey-brown eyes at Nicci. "I should stay nearby. What if you need protection?"

"I do not need protection. I am a sorceress."

But the girl sat cross-legged on the sheepskin and responded with a bright grin. "It never hurts to have an extra set of eyes. I will keep you safe."

Although she would not admit it, Thistle obviously did not wish to be alone. "Very well, you can guard me if you like," Nicci said, remem-bering all the girl had been through. "But if you are to be effective in protecting me, I'll need you rested as well."

After they had changed into the borrowed clothes, one of the Cliff-wall stewards arrived at their door to gather the bundled-up garments to be laundered and mended. The waifish girl's rags needed a great deal of repair, as did Nicci's black traveling dress. After handing over the old clothes, Nicci sorted through the scanty possessions she had managed to save from Verdun Springs.

Eager to help, Thistle laid out the items on the writing desk—the long sharp knife, some rope, near-empty packets of food. Although exhausted, the young girl kept up a chatter. "I never had any brothers and sisters. Do you have a family?" Her elfin face was filled with questions. "Did you ever have a daughter of your own?"

Nicci arranged the bedding on her pallet, keeping her face turned away so that she could ponder the proper answer. A daughter of her own? Someone, perhaps, like Thistle? The idea had not occurred to her, not for a long time at least. She touched her lower lip, where she had once worn a gold ring.

"No, I never had a daughter." It should have been a simple answer, and Nicci was puzzled as to why she had hesitated. "That was never meant to be part of my life."

After all those times Jagang had sentenced her to serve as a whore, or when he himself had forced himself upon her, Nicci surely had the opportunity to become pregnant, but thanks to her skills as a sorceress, she had never needed to worry about a child. She had always prevented herself from conceiving. Early on, Nicci had learned how not to feel anything—no passion, no love of any kind.

The girl examined the items Nicci had removed from the pockets of her old travel dress, her belt, and her side pouch. She unrolled a cloth-wrapped packet among the paraphernalia. "Oh, a flower!" Thistle said, looking at the violet-and-crimson petals. "You carried a flower all this way?"

Nicci instantly swept up the cloth packet, whisking the dried blossom away from the startled girl. "Don't touch that!" Her pulse raced.

Thistle flinched. "I'm sorry! I didn't mean to do anything wrong. I . . ." She cleared her throat. "It must be very special to you. Is it a pretty keeepsake from a suitor?"

Nicci narrowed her blue eyes, amused by the idea. Bannon had indeed offered the flower as a romantic gesture—a notion she had thoroughly quashed. "No, not that at all. The deathrise flower is deadly poison—one of the most potent toxins ever found, very dangerous." She wrapped it carefully in the cloth again, then placed it in the highest alcove above her sleeping pallet. "It would lead to a long and horrible death. Maybe the most horrible death ever known."

Thistle looked relieved. "So you're protecting me! And I'll be safe, too. Because we protect each other." The girl rearranged the sheepskin on the empty space on the stone floor, ready to curl up and go to sleep.

Nicci blew out one of the candles, but before she could extinguish the other, Thistle asked, "If that poison is so deadly, couldn't you use it to kill the Lifedrinker?"

"No, I don't think it is potent enough for that."

Thistle nodded, then wrapped the sheepskin around her and lay down on the hard stone floor, which she insisted was perfectly comfortable. "Then we'll have to find a different way."

Nicci used magic to snuff out the candle on the opposite wall, plunging the room into darkness.

Though he was anxious to study Cliffwall's wondrous books and scrolls, Nathan slept for many hours that first night. He felt safe, warm, and comfortable for the first time in a long while.

After waking refreshed, he hurried to the dining hall, where he scrounged a few scraps of breakfast, since most of the scholars had eaten much earlier and hurried to work. His borrowed scholar's robe was comfortable, though a bit drab and not at all fashionable. He supposed it would do until his more acceptable clothes came back from the washing and mending teams. For now, he would scour the library in hopes of finding how to stop the Lifedrinker's voracious, out-of-control spell that sucked away all life.

In the first of the library chambers, he considered a wall of fat leather-bound volumes. So many of them! Scrolls lay unfurled on tables as intent scholars discussed the possible meanings of obscure lines;

other readers hunched over open tomes, writing notes with chalk on flat slates.

When he looked at the dizzying number of shelved books in front of him and the other walls with an equal number of shelves—and knowing there were numerous rooms identical to this—the scope of Cliffwall's knowledge felt as intimidating as it was exhilarating.

In the Palace of the Prophets, books had been Nathan's quiet companions for a thousand years, his source of information about the outside world. Recently, Richard Rahl had also granted him access to all of the books in the People's Palace of D'Hara, but most of those works had dealt with prophecy, and so were no longer relevant. Now the world's future might depend on what he read here.

And there was so much more than the witch woman's cryptic line in his life book.

Being surrounded by these works made him feel as if he had come home again—even if it was a huge home and a cluttered mess. "Dear spirits, how can I find any information here, except by accident?" He paced in front of the shelves, pondering, while acolyte archivists rolled scrolls or replaced volumes in their proper spots.

Victoria approached him, accompanied by her three lovely acolytes. "My memmers and I are here to be of assistance, Wizard Nathan. Simon's catalog system is confusing to most, and he is the only one who knows where the volumes are. But I have committed many of these works to memory, and my lovely acolytes each hold more than a hundred volumes in their own minds. I can also bring you Gloria, Franklin, Peretta, and ten more well-trained memmers. You could sit back while we recite our knowledge to you."

Nathan found it amazing that these young women—or any of the memmers—were able to commit thousands of pages of dense and precise magical lore to memory, even if they did not organize or, perhaps, understand the words they could recite.

Audrey, Laurel, and Sage looked at him with such intensity that he felt a warm flush come to his cheeks. He gave Victoria a polite, gentlemanly smile. "I am impressed with your skill, madam, and I would certainly welcome the company of such beautiful ladies, but I'm afraid they would distract me. I've spent years reading books with my own eyes, and that's the way I should search for the information."

Victoria's grandmotherly face wrinkled with disappointment. "Generations of memmers have well-respected skills. We possess the information you need. If you tell us what you are searching for, we can quote the relevant passages for you, if we remember." She waved a hand dismissively. "These books are just the static preservation of words. We would bring those words alive for you. We could tell you everything we know."

The woman's determination made him uncomfortable, and he wanted to get to work in his own way. "It doesn't seem pragmatic, I'm afraid. I can't study so much magical lore if it is locked inside your heads, and I don't have the time to listen to your people speak aloud one book at a time." He traced his fingers along curious symbols on the spine of one black volume. "Some of these tomes are written in languages I don't recognize, but I am fluent in numerous others. I can read quite quickly."

"But not all the books are available to you," Victoria said. "You saw the archive tower that melted in the . . . accident. All those books were wiped out."

"Your memmers can recall the volumes that were lost there?" Nathan asked.

The three young acolytes nodded. Victoria lifted her chin with a measure of pride. "Many of them. We don't exactly know what was lost. For the most part, they were works of prophecy, but many were miscategorized."

Nathan let out a sigh of relief. "Prophecy? Well, then, with the star shift, prophecy is gone and any such volumes would contain little of practical value. Prophecy is of no use to us—and certainly of little interest in our quest to stop the Lifedrinker."

But he did not so easily dismiss the prediction Red had made. *And the Sorceress must save the world.*

Victoria could not hide her indignation at his attitude. "If that is what you truly wish, we will leave you to your studies, then. My memmers are always here to assist. We can recall many things that Simon and his scholars have not yet bothered to read."

Nathan gave the woman his sweetest smile. "I thank you. Everyone at Cliffwall has been so generous. If the knowledge is locked away here, we will find it, and we will use it to defeat the Lifedrinker." He fought back a flush of embarrassment, as he realized that his own unfortunate lack of magic would make him of little use in the actual battle against the evil wizard. "Nicci is a powerful sorceress. Do not underestimate her. She used to be called Death's Mistress, and she struck fear across the land."

Victoria's expression turned sour, unimpressed. She seemed a competitive sort. "Death's Mistress? We have no need of further death. Let us hope she can bring *life* back to our fertile valley."

The woman departed with her acolytes, leaving him alone to face the disorganized books, scrolls, and tomes before him. He didn't know where to begin his search for the original spell that had created the Lifedrinker, or where to find an appropriate counterspell.

But he had other priorities as well. If Nathan could restore his own magic, he could fight beside Nicci against the Lifedrinker. Somewhere in the library must be information about how and why he had lost his gift, or perhaps an accurate map showing how to find Kol Adair. Everything was connected.

He walked along the shelves from one side of the great chamber to the other, running his finger across the spines of the leather-bound volumes. He didn't know where to start.

So he carried a volume at random over to a table and took a seat next to an intense young scholar who didn't even look up from her reading. Nathan opened the book and scanned the handwritten symbols on the page, not certain what he was searching for, but sure he would uncover useful information, nevertheless.

CHAPTER 44

While Nathan assessed Cliffwall's countless volumes of preserved magical lore, Nicci decided she needed first-hand knowledge about the Lifedrinker. While she was an accomplished scholar in her own right, she wanted to investigate the Scar with her own eyes.

Bannon was also restless, wandering the silent halls of the giant archive. He practiced with his sword, prancing about in the open halls, because his mentor was too preoccupied in the library. He would dance, slash, and twirl down the corridors, frightening a few distractible scholars as he fought his own shadow, and usually defeated it.

When Nicci proposed a cautious reconnoitering of the Scar to learn about the Lifedrinker, Bannon jumped at the chance. He raised his sword. "I'll go along, Sorceress. Sturdy and I will be your protectors."

Thistle was always at her side, and she sniffed at the young man's eager bravado. "I am Nicci's protector."

"I need no protector, but you are welcome to come along, Bannon Farmer. There may be more dust people to fight." She turned to the orphan girl. "But you will stay here, where it is safe."

"I don't want to be safe. I am safest when I'm with you."

Nicci shook her head. "Bannon and I will go scout, and we'll be back in a day or two. You stay here." Disappointment flashed in the girl's eyes, but she didn't argue further. She darted off to find Nathan and see if he needed her help.

Nicci once again wore her black travel dress, which had been cleaned and mended. The people of Cliffwall provided packs, water, and food for their scouting expedition.

Before she and Bannon set off into the broad desolation, Simon joined them at the outer wall of the plateau, from which they would climb down into the foothills. "Most of those who go to seek the Lifedrinker never come back," he said.

"We don't intend to fight him now," Nicci said. "We are just investigating, checking to see his defenses. And when I return, armed with the intelligence we've gathered, I can help Nathan look for what we need among all those volumes."

She and Bannon left Cliffwall in the early morning, emerging from the opposite side of the plateau onto a steep, winding path. They picked their way down the sheer slope to the foothills, where the vegetation had begun to wither as the Lifedrinker's desolation expanded. The low mesquite trees and piñon pines had bent over, as if in the agony of a long poisonous death. Thorny weeds tore at their clothes as they walked along, descending through the hills. Black beetles scuttled along the ground, while spiders hung forlorn in empty webs.

Much farther out into the valley, the terrain was cracked, lifeless desert. Nicci tried to imagine that broad expanse filled with croplands, thriving villages, and well-traveled roads, all of which had now been swallowed in the dust over the past twenty years. From the vantage of the foothills, the waves of oncoming desolation were as apparent as ripples in a pond.

She narrowed her eyes as she gazed toward the heart of the crater. "The Lifedrinker will be there. We'll get as close as we can for now, gather information, but I will save the real fight for when I know how to kill him."

Bannon squinted toward their destination, then gave a quick nod.

Before they left the last hills, Nicci heard a rustling of shrubs behind her, a loose stone kicked aside, the crack of a dry mesquite branch. Bannon spun, raising his sword, and Nicci prepared to fight.

When the dry boughs of a dead piñon moved aside, Thistle pushed herself through, looking around. Spotting Nicci, the girl smiled. "I knew I would catch up with you sooner or later. I came to help."

"I told you to stay behind," Nicci said.

"Lots of people tell me things. I make up my own mind."

Nicci placed her hands on her hips. "You should not be out here. Go back to Cliffwall."

"I'm coming with you."

"No, you are not."

Thistle clearly wasn't going to listen. "I know these lands. I've lived here all my life. I led you to Cliffwall, didn't I? You would never have been able to find it without me. I can take care of myself—and I can take care of you." She put her hands on her rag skirt, imitating Nicci's stance. Her lips quirked in a defiant smile. "And if I wanted to keep following you, how would you stop me?"

Nicci gave a quick answer. "With sorcery."

The girl huffed. "You would never use sorcery against me."

Thistle's bold confidence brought a wry smile to Nicci's lips. "No, I probably wouldn't. And I'm fully aware of how useful you can be out in the wild, perhaps even more so than Bannon."

The young man flushed. "But I've proved my usefulness in battle. Think of how many dust people I killed back in Verdun Springs, and all the selka before that."

"And you may need to fight and kill more enemies." Nicci didn't want to waste any more time. "Very well. We will go together, scout the Scar, and return quickly. But stay alert. We don't know what other defenses the Lifedrinker might have."

Descending from the last foothills, they headed along cracked canyons that led into the Scar. The breezes swept up white, salty dust from the dry ground, and Bannon coughed as he wiped bitter white powder from his face. Nicci's eyes stung. Her black dress was also smeared with tan and white from all the blowing alkaline powder. She rationed her water, knowing they would find none in the desolation.

The ruined landscape seemed to grow angrier as they continued. The sun pounded down as they emerged from the widening washes of dry rivers that were now just barren, rocky beds. Salt-encrusted boulders protruded from the ground, and all that remained of round lakes were cracked mosaics of dry mud. Dust devils swirled ghostly curls of powder.

Weary in the oppressive environment, the three engaged in little conversation, and paused to rest infrequently. When they sipped a drink, their water tasted bad from the caustic dust on their lips.

Farther along, the cracks in the ground exhaled fumes where steam rose up from underground vents. Nicci smelled the burnt tang of brimstone. Bubbling mud pots looked like raw wounds; bursting and splattering, they emitted the foul stench of rotten eggs. Thistle sprang from rock to rock, picking out a safe path for them.

The stirred debris in the air made the sun appear swollen in the late afternoon, and Nicci felt uneasy about the prospect of camping in the Scar. "It's been hours since we last saw even a dead tree," Bannon said.

"We can find shelter in the rocks," Nicci said. "Or maybe we should just walk through the night. I can make a hand light to guide us."

The girl looked uneasy. "Dangerous things come out at night."

Bannon looked around warily, but the sulfurous steam from fumaroles and bubbling mud pits made the air thick with haze. The sounds would have masked any stealthy movement.

Nicci said, "We can be attacked just as readily during the day."

As they considered their choices, the dry, caked dirt stirred beneath them. Reacting quickly, Nicci pushed Thistle to safety and she herself sprang back as dark, desiccated hands reached out of the dust. Cracks spread apart in the ground, and dust people crawled up from below. Bannon yelled and raised his sword, running toward the attackers.

Nicci let magic boil into her hand. She had battled these things before. She released a surge of fire, igniting the nearest attacker before it could crawl entirely out of the cracked soil.

Jumping onto a flat rock for stability, Bannon swung his sword with a vicious sweep that decapitated three mummified men clad in dirt-encrusted rags. But even headless, the creatures still lunged forward, blindly grasping for victims. Dodging from rock to rock, Thistle ducked under the outstretched claws, and Bannon cleaved a cadaver's torso in two, then hacked off its brittle legs at the knees.

Nicci released a focused hammer blow of wind that shattered the bones and dried sinews of another emerging creature, leaving it in a pile of broken debris half out of the ground. Another push of air knocked the unsteady dust people backward into the bubbling mud pits. The creatures fell into the roiling, churning cauldrons, where they thrashed and sank.

Thistle sprang onto the back of a desiccated creature that advanced toward Nicci from behind. The girl tugged at its shoulders and battered her fists onto its sticklike ribs, stabbed the dry body repeatedly with her knife. The mummified creature broke and fell to the dust.

As Nicci turned to thank her, another pair of dust people crawled up out of the ground, lunging toward Thistle with a clearly focused intent. One was a shriveled woman with a faded red head scarf wrapped around the tufts of wiry hair on her skull. The other, a man, wore the tattered remnants of a leather vest.

Thistle lifted her knife to swing at the new attack, but then she froze in horrified recognition. The dust people stumbled toward her, much too close, hooked hands grasping for the girl. "Aunt Luna? Uncle Marcus!"

Nicci recognized them as well, and she swept in, placing herself in front of the stunned girl. The creatures that had been her aunt and uncle wanted to drag Thistle back with them, but Nicci stood before them. "You can't have her!" Leathery, cadaverous hands touched her arms, her black dress—and Nicci released a furious surge of magic, sparking fire within the inhuman remnants of Marcus and Luna.

The sudden fire burned a hot, purifying white, consuming the remains of the two in an instant. As they reeled away from Nicci, the pair fell into fine gray ash, dropping with a rushing sound that was almost a sigh. Thistle let out a despairing cry.

Panting heavily, the three stood together, poised for more attackers, but the Lifedrinker sent no more dust people after them. The battle was over as swiftly as it had begun. In the distance, they heard scuttling movement, a clatter of pebbles . . . not reanimated corpses this time, but other creatures—armored things with many legs that kept to the shadows.

Thistle clung to Nicci's waist. "The Lifedrinker knows where we are. He is spying on us."

"Are you sure we should keep going out there in the darkness?" Bannon asked. He could barely keep the quaver from his voice.

"It would be a waste to sacrifice ourselves now," Nicci said. "Until we discover a way to cut off the Lifedrinker's magic, we have seen enough. For now."

They made good time retracing their steps toward the rising land at the north end of the vast dead valley, but it was long after dark when they reached the dying forests and remnants of trees in the foothills. The dry grass, dead weeds, and gnarled, leafless trees seemed welcoming by comparison. They were exhausted by the time they found a place to camp.

"At least we have enough wood to build a fire now," Bannon said. "A very large fire."

Still shaken from seeing the remnants of her aunt and uncle, Thistle brought several armloads of dry mesquite and made a pile at their chosen campsite. "It'll be very bright and warm, but won't the Lifedrinker be able to see such a big fire?"

Nicci used her magic to ignite the pile, and the bright fire crackled with intense flames and ribbons of aromatic smoke. "He knows full well where we are. Now at least we will be able to see any attack that comes."

Bannon and Thistle hunkered close to the comforting flames. "Both of you sleep," Nicci said. "I will keep watch."

They bedded down, though they remained restless for many hours. As she sat alone, Nicci listened for sounds beyond the pop and crackle of the burning wood.

The Scar remained silent, an emptiness in the dark that seemed to swallow up sound as well as life. Nicci sensed some other presence out there, however, something prowling in the dying hills around them. Alert, she peered into the blackness beyond the firelight, but could see nothing, hear nothing. Yet she *felt* it . . . something strong and deadly.

Something hunting them.

CHAPTER 45

Surrounded by gifted scholars, Nathan found their dedication refreshing and inspirational. "If I had a thousand years with this grand library, I'd become the greatest wizard who ever lived," he said with a good-natured but weary smile, as Simon brought him another stack of volumes.

"A thousand years . . ." said the scholar-archivist with a shake of his head. He arranged the selected volumes in careful stacks on Nathan's cluttered study table. "I would like nothing more than to spend centuries reading, studying, and learning . . . but alas, I have only a normal life span."

"That was one of the few advantages of being trapped inside the Palace of the Prophets, the webs and spell-forms that prevented us from aging," Nathan said. He looked at the mountains of books brought to him for his review, stacked by subject, some of the passages marked with colorful strings or feathers to separate the pages. "But if the Scar continues to grow and grow, there may not be more than a normal life span left for any of us."

Intent on searching for any useful information about the Lifedrinker, the Cliffwall students pored through book after book, scroll after scroll, highlighting any writings that might bear relevance. Nathan wanted to find the original spell Roland had used to fight his wasting disease, the spell that had transformed him into the Lifedrinker.

During his years in the palace, Nathan had become an extremely fast reader. Even though he'd had all the time in the world, he also had access to thousands and thousands of books, and even forever hadn't seemed like enough time. He could skim a document as fast as he could turn the pages, and he could absorb several thick volumes in an hour.

In only two days here in Cliffwall, he had already finished reading shelves of books, but it would take so much time to learn it all. So much time . . . He had learned very little about the Lifedrinker's draining spell.

Nathan drew his fingers down his chin. "Remind me, did you say that Roland used a spell that was preserved by the memmers?"

"One of the memmers remembered part of it and made certain suggestions. They gave Roland an idea where to look." Simon frowned at an embossed leather volume and set it aside. "We have not yet been able to recover the original text of the spell to study it ourselves. Therefore, we must rely on Victoria's word." When he frowned, the lines in his face made him look much older. "Memories can be faulty. I would prefer independent text verification."

As if summoned, the memmer leader came up with her three lovely acolytes. As she heard him speak, her face darkened with annoyance. Audrey, Laurel, and Sage crowded close behind her, looking indignant on her behalf.

"The memmers are beyond reproach." Victoria stood before the study table piled high with tomes. "You wouldn't have any of these books to study at all, were it not for me. If I had not discovered how to dissipate the camouflage shroud, no one would have access to the archive."

"Nor would Roland," Nathan pointed out, "and we wouldn't be in quite so much trouble."

Simon gathered his dignity and drew himself taller in an attempt to belittle Victoria. "All of us in Cliffwall appreciate your past service. The memmers were important in their day, but you are obsolete now. Gifted and intelligent people have access to the *entire* library now, not just selected volumes memorized generations ago."

Victoria huffed. "Words written on paper are different from words held in the mind." She tapped her temple and leaned close. "It matters not what is written down, but what we *know*."

Simon plainly disagreed. "Knowledge that is not written down cannot be properly shared. How can I study what is inside your mind? How can our scholars draw insights and conclusions if we can't see your thoughts? How can you share properly with Wizard Nathan right now?"

"We will tell him whatever he needs to know," Victoria said.

Nathan raised his hands I exasperation. "Dear spirits, do not quarrel! Cliffwall is a banquet of special lore, and we have a feast before us. Why quibble over a few tidbits?"

Struggling not to let the argument flare, Simon turned to depart. "I will keep gathering suitable volumes for you and let these women tell you the stories they hold in their heads."

Victoria gave the scholar-archivist a condescending frown as he left. "Don't worry about young Simon, Wizard Nathan. He has reached a level of responsibility beyond his capabilities." She sounded sweet and maternal. "Archiving all the volumes in the library is an immense and overwhelming task, and it will take many generations to do properly. Memmers have dealt with the problem of retaining our information for thousands of years, so it is understandable why Simon feels such urgency."

"But there is genuine urgency, madam," Nathan said. "If the Lifedrinker continues to drain the world, none of us has much time left." He ran his fingers through his shoulder-length white hair. "I do need to know what you have memorized, but, as Simon pointed out, I cannot access what is stored inside your head."

Victoria smiled with a patient warmth. "Then we will lead you through it. We shall recite the books you need to read, because we know them by heart."

Nathan could skim words on paper faster than any memmer could speak, but if Victoria and her acolytes sorted through their memorized knowledge and recited only the relevant portions, perhaps it would be worthwhile.

He regarded Audrey, Laurel, and Sage, saw the three different types of beauty. "They are not your actual daughters, though I see how you care for them. You must be very close."

"These dear girls have spent their lives with me. I consider all of my acolytes to be my surrogate sons and daughters." Sadness washed over Victoria's face like a fog closing in. "I never had children of my own, although my husband and I tried very hard. When we wed, Bertram and I dreamed of having a large family, but . . ." Her expression fell further, and she turned away. "But I was barren. We never had children. Three times I found myself pregnant, and we had such hope. I even started making infant clothes . . . but I lost the baby each time. And then Bertram died."

She closed her eyes and heaved a great breath. She gave the three young acolytes a loving look. "So I poured all my maternal instincts into guiding my acolytes, and over the years I have trained a family larger than Bertram and I ever dreamed we could have.

"I have done my duty to preserve the memmers, so that knowledge is passed on from parent to child, independent from what is written down in the archive." She sounded defensive. "I refuse to let go of our heritage. It is we who kept the lore preserved for the centuries when Cliffwall remained hidden." Audrey, Laurel, and Sage, with tears in their eyes, nodded. Victoria swept the three of them into a hug. "Sometimes I wish I had never remembered the spell that dissolved the camouflage shroud." She shook her head.

"You had to," Laurel said.

"It was time," Sage said.

Intrigued, Nathan pushed the stacked books aside. "And how exactly did you reveal the hidden barrier after thousands of years? I thought no one knew how to counter the camouflage spell."

"It was a rare mistake—for the memmers, and for me."

Nathan folded his hands together, raised his eyebrows. "I am listening."

"As we told you, the camouflage shroud was more than just a disguise. It was a barrier, a preservation spell. Cliffwall was sealed behind a barricade of *time*. Not just hidden—it was *gone*.

"But the first memmers were given the knowledge of how to take down that secret barricade when it was time. If no one remembered how to drop the shroud, then the knowledge might as well have been destroyed. So, the key was passed along in our collective memory, generation to generation." She nodded to herself. "After three thousand years had passed, and the wizard wars were long over, the canyon dwellers considered it safe enough to try. But, alas, the release spell we had memorized millennia ago no longer worked."

Victoria put a hand to the center of her chest and drew a shaky breath. "Somewhere along the line, we had remembered it wrong! We truly could not recall the nuances of phrasing. At some point when passing the knowledge from parent to child, from teacher to student, someone must have made an error." She looked away in embarrassment, as if the revelation shamed all memmers.

"Dear spirits," Nathan muttered.

Victoria continued, "We could admit it to no one, though. The isolated canyon people had devoted their lives to keeping the secret—for millennia! They trusted the memmers, they believed in us. We could not tell them we had forgotten! Some stalled for time, making awkward excuses and saying that it wasn't yet time to reveal the archive. But no one knew how to do so! For more than a century, we held out hope that someone would figure out what had gone wrong. The memmers secretly prayed that someone would correct the spell and reveal the library vaults again."

Victoria looked up, met Nathan's azure gaze. "That person was me . . . and it was a mistake. I memorized a spell incorrectly. I uttered an improper combination of syllables in the ancient tongue of Ildakar." She continued in a breathy voice, "And it worked! I was just a girl of seventeen years, being trained by my parents . . . and I got the spell wrong."

Nathan let out a delighted chuckle. "But, dear madam, you accidentally got it *right*. You made a corresponding error, mistakenly saying the sounds properly. The camouflage shroud fell, and you revealed the hidden archive. That is exactly what you wanted, isn't it?"

"Yes." Victoria sounded disappointed. "For millennia, the memmers were powerful and respected, the keepers of inaccessible knowledge. But by throwing open the floodgates and inviting gifted scholars from the outer towns, I may have made us obsolete."

"Perhaps." Nathan briskly rubbed his hands together. "But now everyone has this knowledge. It may help us defeat the Lifedrinker."

Victoria's face remained lined with concern. "Dangerous information for any fool to use! Giving it to people who were not ready, not trained—that was what created the Lifedrinker in the first place."

She grumbled. "My mother was a harsh teacher. She would make me repeat her words over and over again until each spell became part of my soul, every word imprinted in the marrow of my bones. She beat me with a willow switch every time I made an error. She would shriek warnings at me about the dangers a mistake could unleash on the world."

Victoria lifted her shoulders and let them fall. "I remember my father's smile and his patience, but my mother did not believe he took his role seriously enough. She blamed him for teaching me an incorrect phrase, and he just laughed, delighted that the problem of the shroud had been solved—by his own daughter. It was time for celebration, he said. The camouflage shroud was at last gone."

Victoria leaned closer to Nathan, who was captivated by the story. "My mother killed him for it. She threw him over the cliff before he could believe what she was doing. My mother didn't even bother to watch him fall. I heard him scream—and it stopped when he struck the ground.

"My mother railed at me for making my mistake. 'Do you not know how important this is? Do you not see that every word must be perfect? If you do not revere the words, the dangers could be unimaginable!' I was terrified. All I could hear were shouts down on the canyon floor as people rushed to my father's body. But my mother was intent on me. Her eyes were wild, and I could feel her hot breath on my face. 'I killed your father to protect us all. What if he had misquoted a fire spell? What if he mistakenly taught one of us how to breach the veil and unleash the Keeper upon the world?' I had to nod and admit the depth of my father's error. We never mourned him." Tears filled Victoria's eyes.

"But if your error corrected an error, why should you feel guilty?" Nathan asked.

"Because the error itself showed everyone that our perfect memory might not be perfect."

CHAPTER 46

At their makeshift camp, the hot mesquite campfire died to orange coals before dawn, but Nicci did not wake Bannon to change the watch. She needed little sleep, so she remained alert throughout the night, studying the nightmarish outlines of rock formations at the edge of the waning firelight. As soon as Thistle awoke, the girl crawled over to sit next to her. Neither of them said a word, but both stared into the darkness waiting for sunrise.

Bannon yawned, stretched, and got to his feet, brushing dirt and dried twigs from his clothes. Soon enough, they set off, leaving the comforting glow of their campfire embers behind.

As they made their way back toward the sheer wall of the plateau that rose up above the encroaching Scar, Nicci and Bannon picked their way along a wash, while Thistle scuttled ahead with the grace and agility of a darting lizard. They found a trickle of water and followed it up step after step of ocher slickrock. The trickling sounded like music after the dust devils and chemical haze of the desolation. The three spent long moments cupping their hands, filling their palms with drip after drip of cold water, which they splashed on their faces to wipe away the burning alkaline dust.

"Can the Lifedrinker still be watching us?" Thistle asked. "Even here?"

"He could be. There are other dangers, as well," Nicci said. "Something in this world always wants to kill you. Don't forget that."

They moved on up the canyon. Reptiles darted among the rocks overhead, and Thistle glanced up at the ledges, tempted to hunt them, but she kept moving instead.

Bannon trudged through the rocks of the wash, keeping his sword in hand just in case. All night long, Nicci had sensed that predatory presence circling their camp, but she had heard no sound, seen no flashing eyes in the firelight. Now she again felt that oppressive sense of being watched. Following Bannon, she looked around, stared at the rock formations, and wondered if the evil wizard might stage another ambush. But she saw nothing.

Silent and unexpected, something heavy dropped from above and struck her in the back, an avalanche of tawny fur, slashing claws, and loud snarls. The blow knocked Nicci to the ground before she had a chance to release her magic.

Bannon yelled and spun around. Thistle cried out.

Hidden in the ruddy tan of the slickrock walls, two additional feline shapes sprang—huge sand-colored panthers with curved saber-like fangs and claws, like a fistful of sharp daggers.

When the first panther crashed down on Nicci, the blow knocked the wind out of her. She squirmed, trying to fight back. The beast was a dynamo of muscles, its body an engine of attack. It could kill her in mere seconds.

Nicci dodged the first swipe of its paw, but the other paw raked bloody furrows down her back, slicing open her black dress. The panther let out a roaring yowl and tried to clamp its fangs down on her head. Nicci didn't have time or luxury of concentration to find its heart with her magic and stop it dead.

In a desperate defense, she released an unfocused wave of magic, a rippling shock wave of compressed air in every direction. The invisible explosion flung the feline attacker away from her, but the blast seemed oddly diminished. Bleeding badly, Nicci staggered to her feet.

Bannon had pressed his back against the slickrock wall for protection while he jabbed with his sword. One of his blows scored a bloody gash in the ribs of the second panther. Thistle dodged and darted as the third beast tried to trap her, playing with her like a cat with a mouse. Angry at seeing the girl threatened, Nicci reached out and aimed her gift, intending to burst the heart of the attacking panther.

Nothing happened.

Nicci felt the flow of magic go out of her, but somehow her spell bounced off the sand panther like a stone skimming over the surface of a pond. She tried again, also with no effect. She *had* control of her gift—she had not lost it, like Nathan—but this big panther was impervious to her strike.

As the beast prowled in, Nicci saw that its hide was branded with arcane designs, glyphs that were all angles and swooping curves. She recognized it as a spell-form of some sort, perhaps a kind of magical armor.

These were not merely wild beasts.

Nicci crouched to defend herself as the first panther came back to attack. She hurled fire that should have incinerated the big cat, but the magical flames rolled off of its fur. Undaunted, the snarling cat sprang toward her, and Nicci had no time to consider what alternative magic might be effective.

She pulled the long dagger at her side, ready to fight. She realized the branded arcane symbols might give the sand panthers a kind of protection against magic, but surely a sharp knife would cause damage. She sliced the air with her dagger, then sprang to one side as the lunging cat missed her. She did not have time for finesse, nor did she mean to taunt these creatures. She needed them *dead.*

Thistle ducked behind a fallen slab of slickrock and a twisted piñon. Bannon defended himself, wildly flailing with his sword, forgetting the intricate moves that Nathan had taught him. The panther was also a flurry of feral rage.

Nicci watched the big cats move together in an oddly coordinated attack. The three big cats moved in eerie unison. They had separated their prey, and each panther seemed to know what the other two were doing. Although she couldn't read the symbols branded on their hides, she had heard of spell-bonded animals before. These three panthers were a fighting triad, a *troka,* their minds connected to one another to make them a perfect fighting force.

Nicci wondered if the Lifedrinker had sent these predators to attack them, but that didn't seem right. Sand panthers were not part of the Scar, or the original fertile valley here from years ago. They must have been raised and trained somewhere else, by someone else.

Regardless of their origin, the cats were perfect killing machines. The reasons didn't matter. Not now.

She diverted her attention to see Thistle duck under the piñon boughs and scramble out the other side as the cat lunged into the tangled branches. The girl rolled on her back and came up with her own knife in her hands. She wrapped both hands around the hilt as the panther pounced.

Nicci caught her breath, knowing that she couldn't reach the girl in time—and then she realized that Thistle had intentionally lured the overeager predator. As the cat lunged, Thistle brought the knife up under its chin, driving the blade through its jaws, the roof of its mouth, and into its brain. The panther convulsed and shook, then collapsed on top of the scrawny girl, nearly crushing her.

When the big cat fell dead, the other two panthers shuddered and reeled, as if they, too, had suffered a painful blow. They howled in eerie unison.

Bannon used that moment to charge forward, thrusting his sword straight into the rib cage of the second panther. The tawny predator thrashed and roared, opening its mouth wide, but the sword point had pierced the creature's heart and protruded from the opposite side of its chest.

Nicci raked her own knife across the ribs of the last panther, which was momentarily stunned by the deaths of its two spell-bonded partners. The maddened creature slashed at her with its claws, and Nicci sliced again with her knife. The injured beast thrashed its tail and came back in a wild attack, as if ready to throw away its life. The heavy creature drove her to the ground, but Nicci stabbed upward, deep into its belly.

Soaked with blood, Thistle squirmed out from under the body of the panther she had killed and flew like a demon to Nicci's rescue. The girl stabbed the last panther several times with her own knife, and with a great heave, Nicci pushed the dying beast away. She extricated herself and stood covered in blood, both the panther's and her own. The skin of her back had been torn to ribbons.

Bannon was in shock as he slid his sword from the carcass of the panther he had killed. "I'm surprised the Lifedrinker didn't send giant scorpions or centipedes."

Nicci shook her head as she stood bleeding, beginning to feel the fiery pain of her multiple wounds. "I am not certain the Lifedrinker is the cause of this."

The last sand panther was not dead. It lay on the ground heaving great breaths, rumbling with deep pain and bleeding from numerous wounds.

Bannon stepped up behind her, gasping at the deep bloody furrows in her back. "Sorceress! Those wounds! We have to heal them."

Nicci looked down at her scratched arms. "I can heal myself." She bent next to the dying sand panther. "But this one is nearing its end. I should put it out of its misery." She looked around. "With those spell symbols shielding it from magical attacks, I'll have to use my knife."

The dying panther emitted a loud rumble that sounded more forlorn than threatening. Bannon's face fell and his lip trembled. "Do you have to kill it? Can't you heal it, too?"

Nicci narrowed her eyes. "Why would I tend this creature? It tried to kill us."

"What if it was trained to do that? Shouldn't we know where it came from?" Bannon asked. "We already killed the other two, and it's . . ." The words caught in his throat and he choked out the rest. "It's such a beautiful cat. . . ." He couldn't say any more.

As the adrenaline rush faded, Nicci began to feel the raging pain of her own wounds. This panther's claws had torn her back down to the muscle and bone. "It is not a helpless kitten like the ones your father drowned."

"No it's not." Bannon shook his head. "But it is dying, and you can heal it."

Thistle squatted next to the heaving panther and looked up at Nicci with her honey-brown eyes. "My uncle and aunt said that you shouldn't kill unless it is absolutely necessary." Smeared with blood, she looked waifish and forlorn.

Bannon agreed. "And this isn't necessary. Not now. "

Nicci reached out to touch the heaving female cat, cautiously extending her magic to measure the extent of its injuries. The branded spell symbols did not stop her, so she realized the protection must be specifically designed to deflect an attack. She moved her hand to touch the knife wounds she had inflicted. "I can heal it. I can heal *her*," Nicci said, "but you need to know that these three sand panthers were spellbonded. Her two sister panthers in the *troka* are dead. If we save her to live entirely alone, we may be doing this one no favors."

"Yes we are," Thistle insisted. "Please, Nicci."

Her own wounds and blood loss were making her dizzy, making her weak. She didn't have the strength to argue with the orphan girl.

Nicci touched the panther's deep cuts. As she did so, some of the animal's blood mingled with her own from the gashes in her arms and hands. The blood of two fierce creatures trained and ready to fight . . .

Nicci called up her healing magic, released a flow through her hand into the tawny beast, while also infusing her deepest wounds.

When she did so, Nicci felt a sudden jolt, like the last link being forged in a mysterious chain that connected her with the panther. The chain, the *bond* ran from her heart through her nervous system and her mind, and extended into each of the cat's counterpart systems. Thoughts flooded through her as powerful healing magic surged into both of them, erasing the claw wounds, the knife cuts, the scrapes, the smallest scratches, even the sore muscles.

Yanking her bloody hands away, Nicci staggered backward. Even when she stopped touching the panther, she could sense the animal's presence connected to her. Like a sister. She could not deny it.

"Her name is Mrra," Nicci said in a hushed tone. "I don't know what the word means. It's not really a name, just her self-identity."

The newly healed panther huffed a great breath and rolled over, coiling back onto her feet. The cat's eyes were golden green. The long tail lashed back and forth, in agitation and confusion.

"What just happened?" Bannon asked. "What did you do?"

"My blood mingled with hers. The death of her spell-bonded sisters left a void like a wound inside her. When my magic healed Mrra, it filled that void within me at the same time." Nicci's voice grew breathy, and she was amazed at what she herself had experienced. "Now we are connected, but still independent. Dear spirits!"

The sand panther looked up at her, thick tail thrashing. Nicci looked again at the scarred spell symbols, but in spite of her link to Mrra, she still could not interpret the language. She did, however, understand the residue of pain—the lumpy, waxy scars from when red-hot irons had brutally branded those symbols into the soft tan fur.

Staring at her former prey, Mrra twitched, then dropped her gaze to the bodies of her two sister panthers. With a low growling moan, she turned to pad away, putting distance between herself and the three humans that the *troka* had meant to kill.

Nicci could feel the bond between them stretching, thinning. She couldn't communicate directly, couldn't understand what Mrra might be thinking. She just knew that she, Bannon, and Thistle were safe from further attack. And that Mrra would live now . . . if alone.

But not completely alone: there would always be a shadow of Nicci inside her.

With a thrash of her tail, the sand panther loped into the desolate wilderness, bounding up into the slickrock outcroppings, ledge by ledge.

Thistle stared after the sand panther, while Bannon still held his bloody sword, confused. As Nicci watched the panther go, she felt a strange sense of loss.

In a flash, the beast vanished into the uneven shadows.

CHAPTER 47

As he began to grasp the sheer breadth of the library, Nathan believed the Cliffwall archive might hold the secrets of the entire universe . . . if only he could figure out what he needed and where to find it. He pondered as he nibbled on an oat biscuit that one of the acolytes had brought him from the kitchens.

The problem was, no one understood the entire puzzle. Altogether, the hundreds of archivists and memmers knew only disconnected pieces. It was like trying to find the constellations on a cloudy night when only a few flickers of stars shone through.

Well, the constellations were all wrong now anyway, and everyone had to relearn the universe from scratch.

Nathan finished his biscuit and absently munched on another from the plate. He finished skimming the volume in front of him just as a shy young female scholar delivered more. Mia was one of the students assigned to assist him. About nineteen years old, she had short mouse-brown hair and darting eyes that seemed more accustomed to reading than making contact with other people.

"I found these for you, Wizard Nathan. They might contain viable lines of investigation." She was a daughter of a canyon-dwelling family, and she had grown up learning to read and study. She had been born just after Roland fled Cliffwall and began to drain the life out of the world.

"Thank you, Mia," he said with an appreciative smile. Whenever he asked her to find books or scrolls on a particular subject, she would hurry off and return with possibilities. As he ran his fingers down the words in ancient languages, Mia would often sit quietly beside him, reading books that had captured her own interest, hoping to help.

Now he picked up the top volume and opened the scuffed cover. "Ah, a treatise on enhancing plant growth."

Mia nodded. "I thought it might offer some possible counteraction to the Lifedrinker's magic that drains life. The foundational spell-forms might have some commonalities."

"Excellent suggestion," Nathan said, although he thought it unlikely.

The next volume in the stack was covered in letters he did not recognize, angled symbols and swooping curves of runes. The words seemed to exude a kind of power, and he touched the writing as if he could let the foreign alphabet seep into his fingertips. "Do you recognize this language?" he asked Mia. "It is not High D'Haran, nor any of the languages of the Old World that I know."

The young woman pushed her short hair back from her face and tucked it behind her ears. "Some of our oldest scrolls are written in those letters, but no one can read them anymore. Some say they were part of an ancient library stolen from the city of Ildakar."

Nathan set the volume aside, since the incomprehensible writing rendered it useless to him. He was delighted to see that the next book contained maps of a broad land area, although without any frame of reference. One chart showed a range of mountains extending from rolling foothills to sharp crags. Dotted lines indicated winding, treacherous paths that led up to a summit. The exotic names of peaks and rivers were unfamiliar—until his eyes fixed on a pair of words.

Kol Adair.

He caught his breath. So, his destination truly existed—in that much, at least, the witch woman had been right. He wondered if the broad valley on the map represented the once-fertile basin that had become the Scar.

Nathan felt a desperate longing to have his magic back, if only to help in the fight against the Lifedrinker. Nicci couldn't be required to save the world on her own. Upon beginning this journey, he had not cared overmuch about losing his gift of prophecy, since all the forked paths and dire warnings had caused him nothing but grief. But his gift of magic was such an integral part of him that he had taken it for granted. It made him whole.

He tapped on the map, but his own needs would come later. He set aside the volume and pondered the Lifedrinker's spreading desolation. Nathan went back to his books, still searching for the answer.

Nicci, Bannon, and Thistle reached the sheer rock wall below the mesa, glad to leave the bleak Scar behind. Thistle climbed up the steep slope, easily finding half-hidden trail markers and ledges on the way to the alcove opening high above that led back into the plateau and the archive city.

As she climbed, Nicci looked back the way they had come. The powdery dust whipped across the desolate crater like a miasma. When Bannon stopped beside her at the entry alcove high up on the plateau wall, they all stood together looking out at the devastation. The Lifedrinker was somewhere deep at the center of the crater.

"Are you anxious to go back there, Sorceress?" he asked.

"No," she answered honestly, "but I know we must."

Nicci could still feel a tendril in her mind of a prowling feline presence—a lonely presence. Mrra was out there, roaming the uninhabited wilderness. The spell-bonded cat had spent her life as part of a *troka* with two sister panthers, both now gone. The healing magic had filled that void with Nicci, but she didn't know how to help. . . .

When they returned to the Cliffwall gathering chambers, Nathan hurried out to join them, glad to see them back safe. Hearing about their battles with dust people and sand panthers, he gave Bannon's shoulder a paternal pat. "Did you use the swordcraft I taught you?"

Bannon nodded. "Yes, I remembered everything you showed me."

Nicci remembered how wildly the young man had flailed with his blade, but he had fought the enemies, as needed. She couldn't fault Bannon for that.

"I killed as many as he did," Thistle boasted.

"Of course you did, child," Nathan replied with a wry smile. "And that is exactly what we expect of you. But Bannon is my protégé, and I wanted to make sure he acquitted himself well. As you did."

"Even though you weren't supposed to come along," Nicci said, though her reprimand had no sting. "I'm glad you know how to take care of yourself."

The girl looked up at her. "Am I your protégée, Nicci?"

The idea surprised her. This orphan girl was certainly useful, and eager to help, but Thistle hadn't shown any particular aptitude for the gift. "A protégée in what way? I cannot train you to be a sorceress."

"But my reading is better now. I can help you find books in the library. You said you needed to do a lot of research."

Nicci was surprised to realize she wasn't averse to the idea. "You can help, so long as you don't get in the way."

"I won't!"

When the scholars gathered, Nicci gave a more detailed report of the desolation, the cracked canyons, the fumaroles and mud pots, as well as the Lifedrinker's defenders. She sketched out a map, as best she could remember. "I am sure there will be more powerful guardians closer to the evil wizard's lair. We must be ready." She raised an eyebrow at Nathan and all the eager scholars. "As soon as you find me a weapon I can use to kill him."

Simon lifted his chin. "I am confident the answer resides here in the archives." His fellow scholars gave intent nods and muttered among themselves. "We just have to find the right records."

In the dining hall, they all sat down as servers brought in the evening meal. Thistle ate with her hands—both hands, since she was voraciously hungry. Victoria led her student memmers into the room, taking them to Nathan so they could describe some of the subjects they had committed to memory.

The three beautiful acolytes sat next to Bannon, leaning close and listening to his every word. Audrey, Laurel, and Sage found excuses to feed him morsels of food from his plate: roasted vegetables, freshly baked rolls, skewers of spiced lamb. Warming to his tale, the young man talked with exaggerated gestures. Sage picked up a cloth napkin and dabbed the side of his mouth. His cheeks turned pink.

Audrey giggled. "Look how his freckles stand out when he blushes!"

The comment only made him turn brighter red. "I appreciate your attentions. I don't often have such a . . . beautiful audience." He swallowed hard, then gulped from a goblet of spring water, muttering, "Sweet Sea Mother!"

Victoria stepped up behind Bannon and gave the acolytes an encouraging smile. "I understand your attraction to the young man," she said, as if Bannon weren't there. "I hope you three don't turn out to be barren and childless, as I am."

Bannon blinked. "I—I don't want to stay here and marry anyone." He looked at Nicci as if hoping that she would save him. "We're on a mission."

Nicci regarded him coolly. "After I saved you from the cutthroats in Tanimura, I told you to rescue yourself from then on. You will have to meet this challenge on your own."

Bannon blushed again.

Victoria sounded sad as she stood like a mother hen behind the three young women. "Dry, dusty scrolls cannot possibly make up for carrying a life inside you, or holding a newborn baby. Someday you'll know."

The three acolytes smiled.

Victoria stepped over to Thistle, who was finishing a second handful of grapes. The girl still wore her dusty, raggedy clothes from the journey out into the Scar. "I have good news for you, child." She set a cloth-wrapped parcel onto the table and began to undo the knotted twine that held the edges together. "We have very few young children here in Cliffwall, and certainly no suitable clothes, so therefore I asked a skilled seamstress to make this new for you."

She held up the garment, shaking the fabric to unfold a small, trim dress made to fit Thistle's scrawny form. It had been dyed bright pink.

Thistle stopped chewing a mouthful of grapes. "A new dress?" She frowned uncertainly, not sure how to react. "I've never had a dress like that before."

Victoria continued to smile. "You no longer need to wear rags. You are such a pretty girl, and this will make you even prettier. Do you like the pink? It comes from cliff roses that grow in the canyons."

The dainty dress seemed unsuited for the girl's life of running through the desert and hunting lizards. Thistle looked at Nicci, who responded with a hard honesty. "In general, I dislike the color pink." So much so, in fact, that Nicci had once used Subtractive Magic in a wildly inappropriate fashion just to erase the pink dye from a satiny nightdress she had been made to wear in the Wizard's Keep.

"I think I like my old dress better," Thistle said. "This one is very nice, but I wouldn't want it to get dirty when I follow Nicci on her explorations. We've got the whole world to see after we kill the Life-drinker."

Victoria chuckled. "But, child, you're with us now, here at Cliffwall. You will stay and be one of my acolyes. I will teach you how to read and understand the spells, and soon enough you will be able to memorize hundreds of books. You will become our newest memmer." She patted the girl's arm.

Nicci felt on edge. "But is that what the girl wants?" Thistle looked back and forth from the matronly memmer woman to the sorceress.

"Of course it is," Victoria said. "I will take you under my wing, child, clean you up, and train you."

Thistle squirmed on her bench. "I want to read better, and I want to learn things, but I won't just stay in Cliffwall. Nicci can teach me while we're out exploring the world. For Lord Rahl. It's an important mission."

Victoria gave a dismissive gesture. "Flights of fancy, child. Better to read adventures than have them for yourself. I can protect you." She gripped the girl's bony shoulders, squeezing hard.

Thistle ducked and slid closer to Nicci, leaving the pink dress on the table. Nicci rose to her feet, on her guard. "Enough, Victoria. The girl is with us."

The memmer woman looked angry, as if unaccustomed to anyone defying her wishes. She made a clucking sound with her tongue. "You know the child needs care and an education. We'll train her how to remember."

Nicci's voice was as hard as forged steel. "Thistle must make her own choice. Her life is her own to control."

"I want to hunt lizards and climb the canyon walls," she interjected. "Nicci promised to take me across the Old World."

Nicci assessed the increased level of tension in the room. The scholars had stopped eating, listening to the escalating verbal battle.

Victoria fixed her gaze on the sorceress. "Are you the girl's mother? By what right do you make decisions for her?"

"No, I am not the girl's mother. I was never meant to be a mother. That was a choice *I* made."

Victoria's mood shifted in an unexpected direction. "And have you ever thought it might be the wrong choice? Why would a beautiful, strong, and obviously fertile woman like yourself choose *not* to create life? I wanted so badly to have children but wasn't able to!" Her voice rose as she grew more incensed. "No one has ever denied me an acolyte before. Who are you to deny me?"

Nicci thought of many answers, but chose the one with the most power. "I am Death's Mistress."

CHAPTER 48

After the satisfying meal in the warm banquet hall, Bannon could still taste the sweetness of the honeyed fruit from dessert. He patted his belly on his way back to his quarters. After sleeping outside in the dying foothills the previous night, he found the simple stone-walled room with its sleeping pallet wonderfully safe and homey. It reminded him of his own room back on Chiriya, when he'd been a young man, when he and his best friend Ian had talked about their dreams . . . before his father had started beating him, before the Norukai slavers took Ian, before the world fell apart.

Bannon closed his eyes and blocked those thoughts. He cleared his mind, breathed in and out, and repainted his memories with bright, if false, colors. Ready for a good night's sleep, he dropped the fabric door curtain for privacy and removed his homespun shirt, which was still encrusted with harsh white powder and dried sand-panther blood. Humming to himself, he tossed the shirt to the side of the room; tomorrow, he would take it to the Cliffwall laundry. In the meantime, he had a spare shirt and trousers, neatly folded on the unused writing desk.

Someone had delivered a fresh basin of water for him, along with a soft rag he could use as a washcloth. It was the sort of thing his mother would have done to take care of him. He dipped the rag in the water and used it to scrub his face. It felt refreshing and wonderful. Someone had even put herbs in the wash water to make his skin tingle. He soaked the rag in the basin again, rinsing out the grit and grime. He squeezed out the excess water, then looked up, startled as the hanging cloth moved aside from the door.

Audrey slipped in, her dark brown eyes glittering. She did not knock or ask to enter. Shirtless, Bannon was instantly embarrassed. He dropped the rag back into the basin. "I'm sorry—" he said, then wondered what he was apologizing for. "I was just washing up."

"I've come to help you," Audrey said with a smile and let the cloth hanging fall back into place.

As she moved toward him, her deep brunette hair was long, loose, and lush. Unlike the white woolen gown she usually wore, her dress seemed tighter than usual, its bodice cinched at her narrow waist and below her breasts to emphasize their swell. "After all you've been through, Bannon Farmer, you shouldn't have to wash yourself."

"I—I'm fine." He felt his cheeks grow warm again. "I've been washing myself all my life. It's not . . . usually a job that requires more than one person."

"Maybe you don't require it," Audrey said, taking the wet rag and dipping it into the herbed water, "but why turn down help? This is a much more pleasurable way to bathe."

All arguments vanished from his mind, and he realized he had no worthwhile objections anyway.

Audrey drew the moist cloth across his chest to wipe away the grit. She moved more slowly than necessary, but her intention was not merely to clean him. She wet the rag again and used it to caress his chest, then down along his flat stomach.

Bannon realized his throat had gone entirely dry. He bent away in further awkwardness as he realized that he had become aroused, prominently pressing out from his canvas trousers.

Audrey discovered it as well. She pressed her hand against his trousers, and a low groan came out of his throat without him even realizing it. He quickly touched her wrist. "There's no need—"

"I insist. I want to make sure you're thoroughly bathed." She undid the rope at his waist to loosen his pants, which had become remarkably tight.

Bannon squirmed. "Please, I—" He stopped and swallowed again.

If anything, his throat had become drier. He wasn't sure whether he was asking her to please stop, or please continue. Audrey reached into his loose pants and used the washcloth to stroke him with its moist softness.

"I want you completely clean," she said, then pushed him back to the pallet, but Bannon's knees were weak and he was ready to collapse anyway. As he lay there looking up at her with shining eyes, Audrey loosened the laces of her bodice, removed it, then slipped out of her white shift, letting the soft wool slide away from her creamy shoulders to expose her ample breasts. The dark circles of her nipples reminded him of the berries she had fed him at the banquet table not long before.

He gasped with wonder at the sight, and she turned to him let him admire the curve of her back, the gentle swell of her perfect buttocks. But Audrey wasn't going away from him. She just wanted to snuff one of the candles, leaving only a single orange flame flickering in its pot. It was enough light for them to see, but most of the time Bannon had his eyes closed. He gasped many more times as she joined him on the pallet, pressing him down on his back. She slid one leg over his waist and straddled him.

When returning to his quarters, Bannon had been exhausted and sleepy, but now sleep was the farthest thing from his mind.

He touched Audrey's skin, felt its warmth, then reached up as she leaned forward, inviting him to cup her breasts. When she shifted her hips to settle on top of him and he slid inside her, he felt as if he had fallen into the embrace of paradise. And it was.

Bannon lost all sense of time, hypnotized by the sensations that Audrey showed him. And when she was done and climbed off of him, she leaned forward to kiss him long and full on the lips, then trailed her lips down his cheek, and his neck. He let out a long, shuddering sigh of ecstasy. He was even more exhausted now and not at all tired. His entire world had changed.

As Audrey picked up the supple white shift and pulled it over her head, his heart already ached for her. "I . . . I don't know what to say."

She giggled. "At least you knew what to do."

"Does this mean that you—you've chosen me? I'm sure I'd be a good husband. I didn't know that I wanted to get married, but you've made me—"

She laughed again. "Don't be silly. You can't marry all of us."

"All?" he asked, not understanding.

After Audrey finished dressing, she came back to his pallet, where he lay drifting and happy, his entire body tingling. She kissed him again. "Thank you," she said, then slipped out of his chambers, darting silently into the corridors.

Bannon's head was spinning. He was sure he would have a foolish grin on his face for days, if not months. He closed his eyes, let out a long sigh, and tried to sleep, but his body was still on fire. He had heard many love poems before, minstrels singing about the yearning of romance, and had not quite understood it. Of course, Bannon remembered his foolish attraction for Nicci, his inept flirtation in giving her the deathrise flower, but he had never dreamed of anything like Audrey. Perfect, beautiful, and *hungry* Audrey.

He lay for an hour, wanting to sleep, but not wanting to let go of a single moment of these cherished memories. He relived in his mind her every touch, imagining the feel of her lips on his cheek, on his mouth, on his chest—everywhere.

He heard a rustle of the fabric door hanging and didn't at first understand what it was, until he raised his head, blinking. Had Audrey come back?

Laurel stood just inside the doorway, her strawberry-blond hair brushed and shining in the faint light of the remaining candle, adorned with a single decorative braid. She responded with a seductive smile, and her green eyes sparkled. Her tongue flicked around the corner of her mouth, and she showed perfect white teeth.

"I see you're still awake." She glided closer to his sleeping pallet as Bannon struggled to sit up. "I hope I'm not disturbing you." As Laurel moved toward him, her hands worked at the tie at her waist, and she slid out of her acolyte's gown like a beautiful naked butterfly emerging from a chrysalis.

Bannon drew in a quick breath. He was alarmed, confused—and aroused again. "Audrey was just—" he said, reaching up, but instead of being pushed away, she met him, took his left hand, and placed it against her breast. It was smaller and firmer than Audrey's. Her nipples were erect.

"Audrey has already had her turn," Laurel said with a smile. "I hope you're not too tired." She reached down, ran her fingers along his belly, then farther down to stroke the corn silk there. She grinned with delight. "I see you're not tired at all." She started kissing him, and now that Bannon knew exactly what to do, he responded with increasing enthusiasm. Given his earlier practice, Bannon decided he might be getting good at this after all.

Laurel was slower and gentler than Audrey, but more intense. She caressed him and showed him how to caress her, wanting to enjoy his entire body, and Bannon proved to be an avid student again. When he tried to rush, feeling the passion build within him, she held him back, strung him along, teased him. Then she rolled him over, slid beneath him on the narrow pallet, drew him down on top of her, and wrapped her arms around his back.

She whispered hotly in his ear, "It's all right. There's no hurry. Sage won't be here until closer to dawn."

CHAPTER 49

After seeing the desolation of the Scar firsthand, Nicci immersed herself in the lore in the wizards' archive, devoting every hour to the piles of old books. And although Thistle tried to help in every way, fetching books she thought looked interesting, bringing food from the kitchens, she was bored.

The girl wished she could offer some assistance, but her skills as a scholar were minimal. When she had helped her friends survive in the wilderness, she'd felt important, useful to be catching lizards, finding water. But, books . . . Thistle didn't know enough about magical lore or ancient languages.

Her aunt and uncle had taught her letters, so she knew how to read some basic words. She took it upon herself to memorize certain key terms that Nicci was interested in—"life," "energy," "Han," "diminish," "drain"—and she would stand in front of the shelves in the great reading rooms, going from spine to spine, book after book, scroll after scroll. Each time she found a likely prospect, she would hurry with it over to Nicci, adding it to the sorceress's reading stack. Nicci always took her offerings seriously, but so far no one had found any revelation about the Lifedrinker's possible weaknesses.

Thistle had always been independent, able to take care of herself. She sensed that Nicci valued her in part because the sorceress appreciated someone who could handle her own problems. Thistle wanted to prove that she could be a valuable member of their group, but she felt left out, without a purpose to serve.

So, she explored the great stone buildings and the tunnels that ran through the heart of the plateau like the worm tracks in a rotting tree. Absorbed in their research, the Cliffwall scholars paid little attention to Thistle.

She avoided Victoria, not wanting to be indoctrinated as a memmer to memorize old books. Once, she came upon one of their rote-memorization sessions, with young men and women sitting cross-legged on the stone floor while Victoria read a paragraph aloud and then had them all repeat it word for word. Spotting her, the matronly woman gestured for Thistle to join them, but she ducked away. The older woman's intensity made her uneasy. She didn't want to be locked up here poring over dusty old books all her life. She wanted to stay with Nicci instead. She wanted to share in her adventures.

Thistle found a restless Bannon prowling the tunnels as well, carrying his sword. He commiserated with her. "I wish we could just *do* something." He swung his sword at invisible opponents, though there was little room in the passageway for a satisfying imaginary battle.

"We should go out and fight the evil wizard together," Thistle said.

"You're just a girl."

Thistle scowled. "And you're just a boy."

Bannon huffed. "I'm a man, and I'm a swordfighter. You should have seen how many selka I killed when they attacked the *Wavewalker*."

"You saw me fight the sand panthers," Thistle said, "and the dust people."

With a sigh, he rested his sword on the stone floor of the tunnel. "Neither of us poses much of a threat to the Lifedrinker. We have to wait until someone learns how to destroy him."

Thistle frowned. "The waiting is driving me crazy."

Bannon went off down the tunnel battling imaginary foes with his sword, but when he came upon Victoria's three beautiful acolytes, he awkwardly stumbled to a halt. As opponents, Audrey, Laurel, and Sage could have hamstrung him with a flirtatious glance. Thistle rolled her eyes.

She made her way through the tunnels to the window on the outer steep slope of the plateau. As she gazed out on the Scar, Thistle's heart ached to see the sweeping devastation and the distant heat shimmer. She longed to know what this beautiful valley must have looked like at one time.

The scholar-archivist Simon found her standing there. "I stare out at it every day," he said. "Each morning I watch the Lifedrinker expand his terrain and suck more and more life out of the world. If you've been here as long as I, you know just how much we've lost."

Thistle looked up at him. "What was it like?"

Simon gestured out the opening. "From here, you could see lakes and rivers. The hills were thick with forests, and the sky was blue, not this dusty gray. There were roads from one end of the valley to the other, connecting the villages. Pastures and crops dotted the countryside." He blew a soft whistle through his teeth. "Sometimes it seems I'm just remembering a dream. But I know it was true."

Thistle felt a tingle of warmth and determination. "We can make it that way again. I know we can."

Simon's voice took on a harder edge. "It should never have happened in the first place—one of our scholars unleashing a spell he couldn't control. Now the valley is gone, the towns dried up—including my old home. The people are all dead." A low groan came out of his throat. "And it's our fault. We have to find some way to fix it."

"I want to help," Thistle said. "There must be something I could do."

He gave her a patronizing smile. "I'm afraid this is a problem best left to the scholars."

Stung, Thistle turned away, muttering a quiet vow that she would help make the world right again. Even after she left, the scholar-archivist continued to stare out at the far-off wasteland.

Forgoing sleep, Nicci read the words of tome after tome until her eyes ached and her skull throbbed from trying to take in so much information. Although she learned a great deal, including many derivations of spells she had used in the past, she did not find the answers she sought. She set aside another volume in impatient disgust.

Now she had a greater grasp of just how dangerous, how devastating the Lifedrinker was, and if she did not stop him, then the world was indeed at stake—she did not underestimate the threat. The Scar would grow and grow, eventually drowning the Old World, then D'Hara.

Now she knew full well why she was here.

During the day, sunshine streamed in through the lensed windows of the towering stone buildings to illuminate the document rooms. During the night she read by the warm yellow light of candles or oil lamps. Nicci turned pages, studied the cryptic ancient languages, and dismissed ten more volumes by morning.

Absorbed in his own research, Nathan could skim and grasp the contents with ease, and he had always been more studious than Nicci. She was a woman of action, trying to save the world. She *had* in fact saved the world by helping Richard Rahl, and saving the world from the Lifedrinker's debilitating spell was exactly what she needed to do next.

Her eyes burned, and her neck and shoulders ached. Needing to clear her head and breathe the open air, Nicci left the archive rooms and emerged from the highest stone tower in the sheltered cave grotto. She looked across the narrow inner canyon, thinking of the people who had lived there undisturbed for centuries. Although it was midmorning, the sun had not yet risen high enough to remove the dark cloak of shadows in the narrow canyons.

She saw sheep grazing near the central stream flanked by blossoming trees in the nut orchards. Nicci inhaled, enjoyed the cool bite of the morning air. A faint breeze blew stray wisps of blond hair around her face.

Nathan stepped out into the open to join her. "Out for a breath of fresh air, Sorceress? Ah, when you look out at the sheltered settlement here, you can almost forget the Scar and the Lifedrinker on the other side of the plateau."

"I can't forget." She glanced over at him. "I need to consider what we should do. I found many tangential spells, but nothing good enough. This morning I've been studying how one might kill a succubus, on the off chance it might prove useful."

Nathan stroked his hands over his white hair. "How does a succubus relate to the Lifedrinker?"

"Both of them drain life. A succubus is a kind of witch woman who has the power to absorb vitality through sex. Men find her irresistible, and she tempts them with physical pleasure, trapping them as she drains them to nothing more than a husk." Nicci added with skeptical sarcasm, "The men supposedly die with smiles on their lips, even as their faces shrivel away."

Nathan laughed uneasily. "It would not be wise for a woman as beautiful as yourself to have such magic, Sorceress."

Nicci lifted her chin. "I already have more powerful magic than that. It is all a matter of control—and I do have control. The Lifedrinker, however, does not. He drains the vitality of his victim, and in this case his victim is the whole world. In that sense, he is like a succubus."

"Quite extraordinary. And how is a succubus killed, then? What did the old document say?"

"The succubus is responsible for her own demise . . . in a way," Nicci said. "In each of the countless times she lies with a man, there is a very small chance she will get pregnant. If that happens, the succubus is doomed. The child itself, always a daughter, is a powerful entity that gestates and grows, until it absorbs the life from its own succubus mother—doing the same thing to her as she does to men, draining the mother dry until she is nothing but a husk. Then the baby claws its way out of her womb . . . to become the next deadly succubus."

Nathan pursed his lips. "That does not sound like a practical method of killing a succubus if we were to encounter one. There is no other way?"

"According to the legend, the newborn succubus is weak. If one times an attack properly, the baby can be killed, thus terminating the line of succubi."

Nathan looked across the quiet, narrow canyon at a shepherd guiding his small flock to a flower-strewn patch of grass. "Although that tale is delightful and fascinating, I fail to see how it can be useful in our situation."

"I don't see how it can help either." She sighed.

Victoria emerged from the tower library with a determined look on her face. Seeing them, she hurried forward. "In our communal discussions, my memmers recalled something important." She focused on Nathan. For the past two days, since Nicci had refused to let her take Thistle as a new acolyte, the matronly woman had given her a cold shoulder. "Because each of us remembers different books, the memmers compared notes, made suggestions."

"And you have remembered something useful?" Nicci asked. "That would be a welcome change."

Victoria's eyes flashed with annoyance, and the wizard quickly broke in, "What is it? The original Lifedrinker's spell?"

Victoria rocked back, lifting her chin. "It is a story about the original primeval forest that once covered the Old World, the pristine wilderness that thrived in perfect harmony with nature. The Eldertree was the first tree in the first forest—a towering and titanic oak that was the most powerful living thing in the entire world. It is a story of creation."

Nicci did not try to hide her disappointment. "How does an ancient myth about a tree help us against the Lifedrinker? He is a present threat, not an old fable."

Victoria's expression darkened. "Because all strands of life are connected, Sorceress. When the primeval forest covered the land, the world had great power and great magic." She addressed her story to Nathan, finding him a more receptive audience. "Even before the wizard wars three thousand years ago, devastating armies swept across the Old World, cutting down trees, razing the last remnants of the original forests. Those evil men cut down the original Eldertree, a task so difficult that it required a hundred powerful wizards and even more laborers. And when the great tree fell, a vital part of the world died.

"But one acorn was saved, one last seed from the Eldertree. As the armies cut down the sweeping forests, they drove all the energy of life back into the Eldertree until at last it was condensed into this single acorn, the final spark of the primeval forest. All the energy of the Eldertree and all its offspring concentrated into that single acorn, stored there, where it could someday be released in an explosion of incomprehensibly powerful life itself."

Nathan sucked in a quick breath of air. "And you think that might be powerful enough to kill the Lifedrinker?"

"It must be," Victoria insisted. "But the more powerful he becomes, the more difficult the task will be. Soon it will be too late. At the moment, I believe that Roland, or what is left of Roland, will be no match for the last spark of the Eldertree."

"Again, how does this help us?" Nicci said. "Do you believe the acorn truly exists? If so, where can we find it? I have read many books and found no mention of the legend or the seed itself."

Nathan also shook his head. "Nothing in my studies either."

"But I *remember*," Victoria said. "It is in one of my memorized books. The acorn of the Eldertree was locked away here in Cliffwall, deep in a vault . . . somewhere over there." She indicated the misshapen tower that was partially melted into a glassy lump at the side of the alcove. "It is still here."

CHAPTER 50

Under Simon's guidance, workers from the other canyon settlements brought their tools to Cliffwall and set to work trying to reach the lower levels of the damaged tower, hoping to find where the Eldertree acorn had been stored. In the cool, dusty underground, some of the access passages had slumped, the stone melting like wax to clog shut the openings, but the determined laborers used hammers and chisels to penetrate the hard slickrock.

A solid wall of vitreous rock had flowed over the opening, sealing off an entire basement level. Laborers were already hard at work, hammering and hauling away the rubble of broken rock. A grime-streaked stonecutter groaned and turned to Simon. "It'll take many days to carve even a small hole through that, sir."

After they followed the workers down into the deep underground passages, ducking and crawling into the damaged vaults, Nathan looked at Nicci. "Sorceress, surely a barricade of solid stone is not too great a challenge for you?"

"No, it is not. Allow me—we are in a hurry." The workers backed away, curious, and Nicci reached out to touch the smooth wall of melted rock. When she released her magic, the stone that had flowed once, now flowed again. She did not need to resort to Subtractive Magic, but was able to work the material like clay, not destroying the rock but simply moving it. She lifted handfuls of fluid stone like a ditch digger slogging through mud. Although she expended a great effort, Nicci succeeded in carving out a tunnel, widening it, lifting the ceiling, and burrowing farther ahead.

After using her magic to move aside ten feet of stone blockage, Nicci began to doubt there truly was another chamber on the other side of the rock. What if the clumsy and untrained wizard had solidified the entire archive with his disastrous accident? Soon, though, she felt the stone grow thin in front of her, then break like an eggshell, and she pushed her way into a dark, claustrophobic vault, exactly where the plans suggested they look. Inside, the air was thick and stale, sealed away for years.

Cupping her hand, Nicci ignited a light spell so she could see the walls dotted with cubbyholes carved into the slickrock. She shone the diffuse glow around the chamber, seeing shadows dance around reverent display shelves that were filled with valuable, mysterious objects, artifacts, sculptures, amulets, all of them covered with dust.

Nathan pushed in behind her, and he straightened, fastidiously brushing stone dust from his borrowed scholar robes. "Dear spirits, this is exactly what we were looking for. Is the Eldertree acorn here?"

Simon and Victoria followed him, and they stared in amazement. "Exactly where my memmers said it would be." She flashed a sharp glance at Nicci. "You should have believed me, Sorceress."

"I prefer to have proof," Nicci said, not responding to the other woman's edgy tone. "Now that I have proof, I believe you."

Impatient, they moved around the museum vault, inspecting the marvelous items that had been sealed away for millennia. They searched among the exotic artifacts, carved vases and small marble figurines, bright glass vials, amulets worked in gold and jewels, fired-clay medallions covered with a jade-green glaze—and a wooden chest no wider than Nicci's hand. She felt drawn to it, sensing an energy in the air, a power barely contained within the small box. When she removed it from the alcove, she felt a warm pulse through her palm. "This holds something very important."

"That is it," Victoria said, pushing closer. "I remember the descriptions from the original writings."

Nicci opened the lid and looked at cushioned folds of purple velvet, which embraced a single acorn that seemed to be made of gold.

Nathan grinned like a young boy. "Quite extraordinary. The Lifedrinker will be no match for that. Now we have the weapon we need."

"Yes." Nicci closed the small chest. "I do."

N icci was impatient to leave immediately. "The Lifedrinker's power grows every day. This mission will be more dangerous than our last expedition, but I will go." The scholars could study the other artifacts down in the vault in due time; if she defeated the evil wizard, they would have all the time in the world. Nicci removed the acorn from its ornate chest, wrapping it in the scraps of purple velvet so she could tuck it into the pocket of her black dress.

As they returned to the main buildings of the archive, Nicci considered what she would need to do before departure. Aside from packing food and water, she didn't need to make other preparations. Bannon and Thistle joined her, as curious scholars gathered around, eager to see the Eldertree acorn.

Victoria looked at Nicci, both stern and uneasy. Her brow furrowed as she spoke to the rest of the scholars. "I know she is the most powerful sorceress among us, but I am reluctant to give such a sacred treasure—the essence of life itself—to a woman who calls herself Death's Mistress."

Nicci continued her preparations, ignoring the memmer woman's objection. "It must be done, and I am the one to do it."

With a sidelong glance at Victoria, Simon suggested, "Every person in Cliffwall knows that this is a great battle. We can send scholars and trainee wizards to accompany you. We can be your army against the Lifedrinker."

Nicci looked at the too-young scholar-archivist. "You would all be slaughtered. None of you here is fully trained in magic. The risk is far too great."

Thistle ran up, excited. She had stars in her honey-brown eyes.

"Nicci will do it, I know she will. Do you think it will restore the valley to the way it was?"

"Killing the Lifedrinker will end the spreading blight," she said. She did not want to give the girl unrealistic hopes. "But the wound in the world is severe. It will take some time to recover, even after he is defeated."

"I need to go with you," the girl insisted. "I have to help restore the valley."

Nicci would hear none of it. "Too dangerous. I cannot defend myself and finish my mission if I'm worried about you."

"But you don't need to worry. I *want* to go. I want to help—just like last time."

Nicci crossed her arms. "No, and you will not slip out to follow me. I may have Nathan tie your arms and legs and lock you in a room until I'm gone."

"You wouldn't," the girl said.

"Correct, I wouldn't—but only if you promise me you'll stay behind. That is what I need you to do, because it is the only way I can complete my mission. This is deadly serious."

The girl fumed. "But—"

Nicci raised a hand, leaving no room for doubt. "Or would you rather I blanketed you with a sleep spell, so you do not awake for days?"

"No," the girl mumbled. "I promise I'll stay here." Her voice was low and glum.

"And do you break your promises?"

Thistle seemed insulted. "Never."

Nicci looked long and hard at her, and she believed the girl. "Then I will trust you."

"That child must stay safe, of course," Nathan agreed, "but in a great battle like this, you need someone to fight beside you. The Lifedrinker is an evil wizard, perhaps one of the most powerful you have ever encountered."

"I have killed wizards before," she said.

"Indeed you have, but not a wizard like this. We cannot guess how the Lifedrinker will try to block you. I should come with you, for whatever assistance I can provide."

Nicci raised her eyebrows. "How could you help? Your gift is gone."

He touched the hilt of his ornate sword. "I am an adventurer as well. Magic still resides within me, whether or not I can use it. Maybe if I encounter the Lifedrinker, it will help me to release my powers again."

A chill went through Nicci. "That is what I fear, Nathan Rahl. I know how formidable a wizard you can be, but we cannot risk it."

The old man huffed. "I insist—"

She shook her head. "Think about it. When you tried to heal that victim in Renda Bay, what did your magic do? The wild backlash tore him apart. And when you fought the Adjudicator, the magic backfired again, but fortunately for us, it folded that man's own evil magic back upon himself. But the Lifedrinker is already out of control. If he encounters your wild, chaotic power and it twists further, just imagine the possible consequences." She watched his eyes widen as the realization struck him. She continued, "When I unleash the Eldertree acorn, with so much magic surging through the air, blasting into the Earth—what happens if there is a backlash from your powers? The repercussions could tear you apart . . . or tear the world apart. We dare not risk it."

Nathan gave a reluctant nod and said in a small voice, "I fear you may be right, Sorceress. If I somehow twisted the Lifedrinker's magic and turned it against us but a thousand times worse, there would be no way I could place it back under control. Dear spirits, the damage I could cause . . ."

Nicci squared her shoulders, straightened her back. "I must depend on my own magic, and I can travel quickly." She touched the folds of cloth that wrapped the throbbing golden acorn in her pocket. "Your sword would be welcome, Nathan, but I already have my weapon."

Setting his jaw, Bannon stepped forward. "Then *I* am the one to go along. If you need a sword, you can have mine." He gave her a cocky grin, mostly for the benefit of Audrey, Laurel, and Sage, who also stood listening. "And you already admitted that you never worry about me at all, Sorceress."

Nicci gave him a skeptical frown. "You should not make such a brash offer simply to impress your lovers."

He turned as red as beet soup. "But, I can help! Sweet Sea Mother, you saw how I fought the dust people and the sand panthers. If we are attacked as we approach the Lifedrinker's lair, what if I can buy you the seconds you need to complete your mission? That might mean the difference between success and failure."

Nicci pressed her lips together, assessing the young man. In their battles against seemingly insurmountable enemies, he had indeed killed more than his share of opponents. "I admit, you can sometimes be useful. But know that if you go with me to fight the Lifedrinker, you could face certain death. I will not be able to save you."

"I accept those terms, Sorceress." He swallowed hard, struggling to hide his fear, since he clearly understood the risk in what he was suggesting. "I'm ready to face the danger."

Victoria's acolytes watched him with admiration, which only seemed to increase Bannon's eager determination. Nicci doubted she could change his mind, and she admitted she might need him. "Very well. If nothing else, you may be able to distract a monster at a key moment so that I can keep going."

Audrey, Sage, and Laurel hurried to give Bannon their farewells, and Thistle threw herself against Nicci in a furious hug. "Come back to me. I want to see the world the way it was supposed to be, but I want to see it with you."

Nicci felt awkward, not knowing how to respond to the girl's enthusiastic embrace. "I will restore the world if I can, and then I will come back to you." The next words came out of her mouth before she could think better of it. "I promise."

Thistle looked up at her with her large eyes. "And do you break your promises?"

Nicci gritted her teeth and answered, "Never."

CHAPTER 51

After climbing down the outer wall of the plateau on their way to the Scar, Nicci and Bannon made good time even across the rugged, dead terrain. During their earlier scouting expedition, they had cautiously picked their way, exploring, but now that she possessed the right weapon, Nicci had a clear, firm goal. With the Eldertree acorn, she was on her way to kill the misguided wizard who had caused such appalling damage, had sacrificed countless lives, all because he feared his own death.

Nicci considered the Lifedrinker a monster, an enemy to be defeated at any cost; she did not think of him as a sick and frightened man, a naive scholar playing with dangerous magic. He was not *Roland* in her mind. He was a toxin spreading in every direction. He was a scourge who could destroy the world.

And this was the reason Red had sent her on this journey, accompanying Nathan to find Kol Adair. *Save the world.* She would do her part.

Bannon kept up with her without complaint as they crossed the worsening landscape, and Nicci was impressed with the young man's dogged determination. After emerging from the dying foothills, they made their way on an arrow-straight path across the cracked and rocky Scar. Wind whipped the powdery dust of dry lakes into a salty chemical haze in the air.

Nicci focused ahead. She did not run; she simply did not rest. The barren landscape sparked anger and impatience in her. She picked up the pace, covering miles at a steady clip. Bannon kept looking from side to side, wrinkling his nose in the bitter air. They passed under the shadow of a goblin-shaped pinnacle. Spiky branches of a dead piñon pine protruded from a crack in the rock formation.

Without stopping, Bannon took a cautious sip from his waterskin. A worried frown crossed his face. "Sorceress, is it wise to travel out in the open? Maybe we should try to hide our path so the Lifedrinker doesn't know we are coming for him?"

She shook her head. "He knows where we are. I'm certain he can sense my magic. Skulking in the shadows would only slow us down."

When Bannon offered the waterskin to Nicci, she realized her throat was parched. She drank. The water felt warm, flat, and slippery on her tongue. She handed the waterskin back, and Bannon fastened it at his side, then touched his sword and turned slowly. "I sense that something is watching us."

Extending her gift, Nicci could detect that this desolate place festered with twisted life, the few surviving creatures that had adapted to the Lifedrinker's evil taint. "Many things are watching us, but they don't interest me unless they interfere with our mission." Her lips curled in a hard smile. "If they do, then we will show them their mistake."

Nicci intended to press forward without rest, without making camp, until they reached the heart of the Scar. They had left Cliffwall with the first glimmerings of dawn, and after they had trudged through midday and into the dry afternoon, their pace began to falter. She and Bannon perspired in the relentless heat, and white alkaline dust clung to them, making both of them look white as stone.

Nicci brushed the powder from her face and arms. Her black travel dress was now crusted with the harsh chemical residue.

After the sun set, thermal currents skirled up dust devils, blowing sand and grit into howling veils. As darkness fell, the building dust storm masked the strange stars overhead, but the two plodded on through the night. Near midnight, the raging winds had reached such a crescendo that she could barely hear Bannon behind her, and they grudgingly stopped in the lee of a tall rock. Nicci said, "Rest while you can. We'll stop for no more than an hour."

"I could keep going," he insisted. His lips were cracked, his eyes swollen and red, nearly puffed shut.

"We are too vulnerable if we continue in this blowing storm," Nicci said. "If we can't see, we might fall into a pit, or the Lifedrinker could send dust people to attack us. We will stay here until it calms. It is not my preference, but necessary."

During the brief respite, she released some of her magic to dispel the gritty residue from their chafed faces and burning eyes, but as she used her gift, Nicci felt the magic thrum and recoil inside her. Something else had detected it, tried to grasp it. This deep into the Scar, the Lifedrinker's vitality-sucking power grew more oppressive. She immediately felt him struggling to gain a hold on her, to sap her strength and draw away her powers. Her small use of magic had triggered his response.

The howling wind and whipping sand diminished only slightly after midnight, but Nicci decided they had waited long enough. "We need to go."

Bannon stumbled after her across the parched open terrain. The young man's determined energy had flagged, and it was more than just weariness after the day's long, rugged journey. Nicci could not deny what they saw. The closer they came to the Lifedrinker, the more they both began to weaken from his dark and oppressive thirst. He was draining them as well.

Hours later, the sky became a red haze as the bloated sun rose above the mountains like fire from the funeral pyre of slaughtered victims. Far ahead, Nicci spotted the black center of the crater, a vortex into which the Lifedrinker's potent magic swirled.

"Sweet Sea Mother, we're almost there," Bannon said in a raspy voice. He sounded more relieved than frightened.

"Not close enough." Nicci tried to put on a burst of speed, which only showed her how much the wizard's relentless drain had diminished her. If they didn't confront the enemy soon, she feared she wouldn't have the strength to destroy him, even with the powerful talisman of the Eldertree.

Ahead, the ground became uneven. Slabs of rock tilted at shallow angles, as if restless upheavals continued to stir beneath the surface of the dead valley. Fissures sketched across the land like dark lightning bolts, and tall boulders lay strewn about as if the Lifedrinker's rage of magic had scattered game pieces.

Nicci and Bannon climbed over the sharp rocks, tottering on un-stable slabs and leaping across the fissures, from which foul fumes ema-nated. Even as they journeyed into the increasing heat of the day, the dark lair shimmered like a mirage in the distance. Nicci sensed a prowl-ing presence watching them, closing in, though not yet ready to attack. Although she remained alert, the Lifedrinker was her real enemy, and everything else was just a distraction.

Though her irritated eyes were blurred from the dust, she saw a large shape move across the ground ahead of her, brown and angular. A hissing sound scratched through the air, and a well-camouflaged scaly figure scuttled toward them among the rocks. The creature opened its mouth to reveal moist pink flesh, rows of jagged white fangs, and a forked black tongue: a huge lizard armored with pointed scales, its back crested with a dark sawblade fin. The reptile moved forward on four legs, thrashing a long tail. The creature's hide was mangy with oozing, red sores.

Nicci backed away, and Bannon held up his sword to face the liz-ard. As it charged at them with a swift skittering gait, Nicci caught more movement to her left and her right. Three more of the giant rep-tiles emerged from behind rocks or beneath the broken slabs. She had seen the dust-colored lizards that Thistle hunted in the desert, but these were each the size of a warhorse. All were scarred with countless lesions and festering sores.

Bracing himself for the fight, Bannon let out a low whistle. "I always wanted to see a dragon. I've heard legends but—these are real!"

"Not dragons," Nicci said with scorn. "Just lizards." But as the rep-tiles came closer, flicking their forked tongues and snapping their jaws, she added, "Big lizards."

Beside Nicci, Bannon planted his boots in the dust and held Sturdy in front of him. Two of the lizards stampeded forward, focused on their prey, while the other two crawled on the rock formations around them, flanking Nicci and Bannon. The reptiles moved with a swift grace, warmed by the baking sun and driven by bloodlust.

Nicci held out her hand, curled her fingers. She concentrated on the lizard's chest, found its heart, and as the nearest one bounded toward her, she released a burst of fire. In other battles, she had used her magic to increase the heat inside a tree, flash-boiling the sap and causing the entire trunk to explode. Now she did the same, heating the lizard's heart until the blood burst into steam. The monster staggered and collapsed forward, ploughing a furrow in the rocky sand at Nicci's feet. She knew she could make swift work of all four lizard attackers.

But after killing the first one, she felt a wave of dizziness. By releasing her gift, it was as if she had opened a floodgate to the Lifedrinker. Even from afar, he began to steal her magic, siphoning off her strength.

Long ago, Nicci herself had assimilated the powers of other wizards she had killed, and now the same thing was happening to her. Roland was stealing her life. In a reflexive survival measure, she wove shields to stop the bleeding rupture of power, but she realized she could no longer fight the lizards with magic. She reeled and slumped back against the nearby boulder.

Bannon was busy blocking the second lizard and did not see her stagger. Holding the grip with both hands, he swung his sword with all his weight and strength behind it. When the edge of his blade struck the scaly hide, the sound that rang out was like the tongs and hammer in a blacksmith's shop. He wavered as the blade ricocheted off the lizard's armor, leaving no obvious injury.

The reptile lunged back toward him. Bannon recovered and spun, clattering his sword across the scales, to little effect. When he finally pierced one of the oozing, mangy patches, the lizard did recoil and squirm, but then it kept coming.

Bannon smashed its head so hard that sparks flew. When the lizard opened wide its fang-filled mouth, he pulled back the sword and thrust forward with all of his strength, stabbing Sturdy's tip into the soft pink flesh. He shoved harder, twisting the blade and digging it into the creature's soft palate until it broke through the thin bone and pierced the small brain. As the monster perished, Bannon tore the sword back out, severing the black forked tongue, which fell out and flopped like a dying snake in the blood-soaked dust. The enormous beast twitched and thrashed in a thunderstorm of last nerve impulses.

Bannon spun as the third giant lizard approached from the left, climbing over one of the boulders. Sparing a glance for Nicci, he gasped to see her slumped against the rock as she attempted to recover. "Sorceress!"

Rallying herself, she released a small burst of magic, hoping to stop the creature's heart, but the moment she made the attempt, Nicci felt the voracious Lifedrinker snatch at her magic and her strength like a hunting dog clamping its jaws around a hare. Before it was too late, she cast her protective webs again and closed off the attempt. Dark static swirled around her vision, and she fell against the boulder, but vowed not to give up. She slid the dagger from her side and clutched it in a shaking hand, determined to fight with whatever weapon she had—even teeth and nails if necessary.

"I'll take care of the other two, Sorceress." Bannon charged toward the oncoming lizard, yelling with wordless fury. Again his sword struck sparks from the armored hide. He hammered and hammered with his blade, chipping scales and digging into the lizard's flesh, and he twisted into one of the crusted, patchy sores. When the lizard hissed and snapped at him, Bannon responded with a primal roar of his own.

Nicci had not seen him release such blind rage since battling the Norukai slavers, but something had unleashed his fighting reactions. He was more calculating than a mindless dervish, though. Even if the edge of his blade caused little harm, he raised the sword above his shoulder and drove the point straight into the lizard's eye.

With a gurgling hiss, the monster tried to squirm away, but Bannon pushed forward, driving his sword harder, pushing it in farther. He twisted and screwed the tip so that it turned the creature's eye into a soupy splash of gore. It wasn't enough.

Throwing his full weight into the thrust, he slammed the sword through the bone of the lizard's eye socket and into its head. The monster collapsed. Bannon heaved great breaths and struggled to wrench Sturdy free, but the sword was stuck in the lizard's cranial cavity. He grunted and cursed. "Come on!"

The last of the attacking lizards crawled toward Nicci, cautious. She held out her long dagger, ready for the attack. The monster prepared to spring. She knew its weight and momentum would drive her backward. And she also knew she was too weak to kill it.

Just then she sensed a feral presence, *felt* the ripple of muscles like an echo inside her, experienced the anticipated joy of the attack and the kill. Before the giant lizard could crash down on her, a tawny feline shape bounded from the boulders above. The great cat hurled herself down in a mass of claws and curved fangs and slammed into the distorted lizard, knocking it off balance.

Nicci felt a surge of excitement and relief as she dragged herself to her feet. "Mrra!"

The sand panther mauled the lizard with her long claws, ripping loose mangy patches of scales, exposing open sores. The monster writhed and bucked, but Mrra would not let go. Saberlike fangs chomped down, working into weak spots in the reptile's armor.

Inside her mind, thanks to her connection to the spell-bonded panther, Nicci could feel the bloodlust, the energy, the need to kill this threat . . . this threat to *Nicci*. Mrra was born as a fighter, trained as a fighter, as a killer.

Because she was joined to Mrra, Nicci wanted to tear this monster apart with her bare hands. A feral blood rage sang through her, as it sang through the sand panther. She bounded forward to join the attack. She didn't need magic, just her knife.

Mrra pushed over the thrashing lizard to expose the softer scales in its underbelly just as Nicci reached its head. They seemed to be coordinated, synchronized. The monster clamped its fanged jaws shut, and Nicci drove her sharp dagger beneath the reptile's chin, piercing the thinner skin of its wattled throat. She drove the blade into its head again and again while Mrra tore open the thing's belly and hauled out its flopping entrails. The lizard's gushing blood washed away the caked white powder on Nicci's skin and hands, but she did not feel clean.

Instead, she felt invigorated.

By the time the fourth monster was dead, Nicci shook with exhaustion, but was also afire with the need to go on.

Bannon looked ready to collapse, but he managed an odd grin, giving a respectful look to Mrra. "Good thing I convinced you not to kill the panther, Sorceress."

"I agree." Nicci looked down at Mrra, feeling the powerful inexplicable threads binding them. Her sister panther growled deep in her throat.

Bannon added, "And I told you I could be useful. You need me."

"There are few things I need." Nicci shaded her eyes as she scanned ahead, looking toward the dark vortex still miles away. "Right now, we need to get to the Lifedrinker." She touched the pouch at her side that held the Eldertree acorn. "Before it's too late."

CHAPTER 52

They trudged forward. The Lifedrinker's presence dragged at their bodies like tar, making their movements sluggish, their bodies weak, but Nicci pushed ahead toward the center of the Scar, and the wizard she needed to kill. For Thistle, for this once-fertile valley, for Richard, the D'Haran Empire, and the whole world . . .

"We're almost there, Sorceress," Bannon said in a voice as thin as old paper. "My sword isn't dull yet."

"He will keep trying to stop us, but we don't know how he will attack us next," Nicci said. "Be wary."

The young man managed a hint of cheer in his tone. "And I'll be useful." When she made a noncommittal response, Bannon acted as if she had given him a great compliment.

Mrra stayed with them. The sand panther loped ahead, her tan fur blending into the dusty wasteland. The debris around them turned darker, sharper. The boulders were made of shattered volcanic glass, with every angle as sharp as a knife edge. Sulfurous steam made the air thick and nearly unbreathable, and each step sapped more of their strength.

But as they descended the crumbling, uncertain slope at the heart of the dead valley, Nicci could see their destination ahead. Her target.

The evil wizard's lair resembled an amphitheater with black stelae, spires of rock reaching upward like desperate claws that encircled a central pit. Waves of the Lifedrinker's appetite had frozen into ripples preserved in the blasted stone.

Overhead, thunderclouds strangled the sky, and a web of tortured lightning skittered around—electric whips that cracked across the sky, then stung the tops of the high stelae surrounding the amphitheater. The wind rose to a keening whistle, accompanied by a basso undercurrent of perpetual thunder.

On the ground to their left, a slab of black rock split off to reveal a raw flow of lava beneath. Molten rock like the blood of the world spilled out from a cracked, festering scab.

Bannon staggered back from the furnace air. More obsidian rocks shattered and thrust upward, shifting, twisting. Mrra picked her steps with great caution, her muzzle curled back in a snarl as more lightning flashed overhead. She prowled along, close to Nicci.

Bannon gasped, brushing loose ginger hair out of his eyes. "How can we go on?"

Nicci chose her footsteps carefully as the ground grew more unstable. She climbed over the sharp edges as she pressed toward the Lifedrinker's pit, knowing she would find him there. "How can we not?"

She felt the throbbing, desperate presence ahead, and she wrestled to build shields around her, calling upon her knowledge to protect herself with both Additive and Subtractive Magic. She could not let the Lifedrinker seize her gift, her life. Nicci made use of new spells that she had learned only recently while poring over volume after volume in the Cliffwall archives. It didn't make her entirely safe, but it let her keep moving.

Plodding along in a determined trance, Bannon followed her, step by step. When Nicci turned to encourage him, she was astonished to see his face seamed with wrinkles. His long reddish hair was shot through with streaks of gray. He looked at her in turn, and his hazel eyes went wide with alarm. "Sorceress, you look . . . old!"

Nicci touched her face, and felt wrinkles in her dry skin as if all the years of her long life were catching up with her. The Lifedrinker was stealing the time they had left. "We must hurry," she said. She needed to use the Eldertree acorn before it was too late, before the evil wizard grew any stronger.

Dread built inside her, but it was not a fear for her own life, not despair at the thought that she might be growing old: for Nicci, the greatest fear was that she might *fail* on a quest to which she had given her heart and soul, that she might fail Richard's dreams of a hopeful new order. "I am Death's Mistress," she muttered in a grim whisper. "The Lifedrinker is no match for me."

Mrra hobbled along, and Nicci saw that the cat's big paws left blood smears on the sharp obsidian rocks as she padded forward. But Mrra remained close at hand, ready to fight alongside her surrogate sister panther.

The static in the air thickened, and the background sound near the amphitheater increased to a crackling hiss. Nicci's blond hair rose in a charged corona around her head.

The obsidian rocks ground together, and a belching gasp of brimstone steam coughed upward, nearly choking her. Nicci fixed her gaze to where the circle of ominous sharp spires cast dust-blurred shadows on the ground.

Nicci knew the powerful wizard was inside there. She would stand before him, and she would kill him, even if it cost her last spark of energy.

"Lifedrinker!" she shouted, listening to the deep pervasive thunder in the air. Slashes of lightning whipped through the thunderheads. In a lower voice, she said, "*Roland.* Face me."

The ground shuddered and cracked, and scuttling forms emerged, black-armored creatures with multiple legs, glittering eyes, and segmented front limbs that ended in clacking pincers. Scorpions, each the size of a dog, emerged from underground nests to stand as guardians on top of the black boulders. Each long tail was capped with a wicked stinger that dripped venom.

Beside her, Bannon gave an audible gulp. Nicci recalled that Thistle's parents had been killed by similar creatures.

She stepped forward, remembering her main enemy. She shouted a challenge. "Lifedrinker!"

Suddenly, she remembered what the witch woman had written in the life book: *Future and Fate depend on both the journey and the destination.*

More rocks shifted as the ground convulsed within the circle of towering stelae, and the blackness from the central pit seemed to deepen. Hulking shapes emerged from beneath the ground, withered and desiccated human forms, black with dust. Their sinewy bodies were covered with festering boils, sick open sores that dotted arms and necks, bulges that pushed out the sides of their faces. These horrors were worse than the previous dust people. They stood in a line, blocking Nicci from going closer to the Lifedrinker's lair.

Mrra growled. Bannon raised his sword. "We can cut through them, Sorceress."

The blighted human forms lurched forward, and Nicci drew her knife, careful to restrain her magic, but knowing she might have to use it. With clacking pincers, the scorpions scuttled closer, weaving in and around the desiccated dust people.

Mrra bared her long fangs, and her tail thrashed. Bannon stood at her side. "I'll fight them so you can get close enough, Sorceress." He gulped.

Finally, with a swirl of black static and a slash of angry lightning all around them, the Lifedrinker himself emerged from the darkness.

CHAPTER 53

The ring of distorted pillars surrounded an empty pit like the gullet of a giant buried serpent, a well that sank into the coldest depths of eternity. From this sunken hole, the Lifedrinker's unchecked magic continued to absorb the life from the world.

Climbing out of the inky emptiness from below, the thing that had been Roland emerged. The evil wizard hobbled and lurched, swelled and shrank, a tangled construction of incredible power intertwined with desperate weakness. He had been human once, but very little evidence of his humanity remained.

He stepped out into the crackling air illuminated by slashes of blue-white lightning that racked the thunderheads above. Dust swirled and howled, as if the wind itself were gasping in awe at the Lifedrinker's presence.

He wore what had been the robes of a Cliffwall scholar, but they had frayed and extended into long flapping shrouds that trailed behind him into the deep pit. Dark ripples flowed from his body as his magic stole light itself from the air, drinking, absorbing, draining everything down into the black well. It seemed as if a powerful life lodestone lay at the bottom of the depths—a magical force so great that even the Lifedrinker could not escape its pull.

When the wizard spoke, the words were sucked out of the air along with all other sound, taking Nicci's breath away, stealing more of her energy. "Few come to see me," Roland said. He loomed up, his tattered robes whipping about in the storm of his own energy.

She touched the pocket of her black dress, felt the hard kernel of the Eldertree acorn. She took a step closer, remembering many other terrible foes she had faced, and defeated. "I came to destroy you."

"Yes . . . I know," said the wizard. "Others have tried."

Nicci heard no defiance or arrogance in his voice, just an odd undertone of despair.

His face was long and gaunt, the cheeks sunken, his large eyes red with sickness. Roland's neck was so thin that the tendons stood out like ropes. As the fabric of his flapping robes exposed his bare chest, Nicci was appalled to see his ribs laced with a tangle of swollen growths, as if his torso were composed entirely of tumors. The chaotic protrusions pulsed and throbbed, reservoirs of misdirected life energy that had grown within him and kept growing, desperate for nourishment. The wasting disease had extinguished everything that had been the weak-willed wizard, and controlled him.

His legs were bent, his spine twisted. The Lifedrinker lived because he was a structure of stolen life, a jumble of patched-together flesh, muscle, organs. "Please . . ." he said, in a much quieter voice that surged to a roar. "I hunger . . . I thirst . . . I *need*!" He swayed.

The dust people around the circle of obsidian pillars stood motionless.

Bannon held his sword, but could not conceal that his hands were shaking.

Mrra crouched, growling, but did not move.

The Lifedrinker raised his hands. His fingers were mere sticks covered with a film of skin—no matter how much life he drained from the world, it was not enough, never enough. He curled his hands in a beseeching gesture. "I did not intend this. I don't want this." He heaved a deep breath, and lightning skirled all around them, striking the tops of the obsidian stelae. "I cannot stop this!" the Lifedrinker moaned.

Even as she felt the years and the life draining away from her in the inexorable tug of the evil wizard, Nicci stepped across the uneven ground. "Then I will stop you." She would fight him, hurl him back into the endless pit. The Eldertree acorn might be the most powerful weapon she'd ever held.

But the terrible drain wrung vitality from her muscles and made her thoughts fuzzy.

An uncanny flash flickered in the Lifedrinker's sunken eyes. The tumors that comprised his body writhed like a nest of vipers ready to strike. "No," he said, "I must survive. I have to."

An army of unwieldy but deadly marionettes, the dust people began to move. More than a hundred of them lurched into motion, ready to attack.

Nicci forced herself to move three more steps, and the Lifedrinker did not retreat. He seemed to grow larger, swollen with dark energy, like a man-shaped pustule about to burst from its own evil.

The twisted, festering dust people surged closer. Bannon threw himself between Nicci and the mummified attackers. "I'll clear the way!" He lopped off a desiccated arm at its elbow, then sliced off the head of a second creature. The skin-covered skull rattled onto the blasted ground, its bared teeth still clacking and snapping.

With the oustretched palm of his other hand, the young man shoved another grasping creature, knocking it back into two oncoming foes. Though by now he looked like a greatly aged man himself, Bannon swung and chopped with his sword, splintering ribs, separating shoulders, cleaving body cores. "Complete your mission, Sorceress! Kill the Lifedrinker!"

Nicci could feel herself withering with age and weakness, second by second. She remembered an old crone she had seen long ago in Tanimura hobbling through a market at a snail's pace, as if each step required careful planning and then a rest afterward. Now, Nicci understood how that felt. Her bones were brittle, her joints swollen and aching, the skin on her arms dry and shriveled.

With a snarl, the sand panther also threw herself upon the dust people, shredding the husks of the Lifedrinker's victims as if they were no more than straw and kindling. Mrra's curved fangs ripped the reanimated corpses into scraps of bone and dried flesh.

Behind the dust people, enlarged scorpions moved with angular arachnid speed. In a flash of tawny fur, the big cat dodged the venomous stingers, then bounded onto a rock, leading several scorpions away.

When one of the lashing stingers was about to pierce Mrra's hide, Bannon swung his sword to amputate the segmented tail. Then he skewered the scorpion's hard shell and flung the dying creature into two oncoming dust people.

Snarling, Mrra lunged back into the fray as more desiccated corpses closed in on Nicci, who was fighting her way closer to the Lifedrinker.

The evil wizard jerked his hands, guiding his minions. More dust people crawled up from hiding places beneath the seared ground. For all the attackers that Bannon and Mrra had already savaged, twice as many now joined the fight.

Nicci didn't have much time.

The Lifedrinker's sunken gaze met her cold blue eyes. "Please . . ." he said. "I know I have caused so much harm. I see what I have done, but I *cannot* make it stop! I just wanted to live, wanted to stop the wasting disease from stealing the life inside me. I never wanted this curse."

He raised both of his hands, clenched his clawlike fingers into hard, bony fists. His body swelled with dark ripples of energy, and Nicci felt a sudden flood of debilitating weakness that nearly drove her to her knees.

"I don't know how to shut it off!"

Nicci said in a hoarse voice, "If you found the power within yourself to cause this, then you can find a way to stanch the flow, tie off the wound that is bleeding the world to death. Find it within your own soul."

His voice was hollow with despair. "I drank my own soul long ago. All that remains of me is the *need*!" When he surged again, Nicci knew that the magic had entirely possessed him. The spell had become a living thing in its own right.

An overwhelming army of dust people closed in. More venomous scorpions clattered over the boulders, rushing toward Nicci.

Bannon fought with wild abandon. By now he was an old man with sparse gray hair, yet he still defended her with all his strength, giving the sorceress a chance to make her move. The sand panther also looked old, her fur showing spots of mange, but the branded spell-forms seemed to protect Mrra from the Lifedrinker's deadly appetite.

Nicci herself exhibited many signs of age. The backs of her hands were a tangled map of veins marked with liver spots on skin that had been so creamy and perfect not long ago. Each step she took felt as if she were fighting against a wind of time, age, and weakness.

Behind her, dust people closed around Bannon, but he kept fighting, hacking, chopping them to pieces, even though there were too many. Mrra dove into the fray, trying to protect the swordsman, but a new army of scorpions flowed in, stingers poised and dripping.

Nicci took the final step and reached into her pocket. The Lifedrinker kept draining her magic, and she could not unleash wizard's fire, could not so much as attempt any of her spells. He would only absorb them and then engulf her.

Nicci pulled out the throbbing Eldertree acorn and spoke through gritted teeth. "You. Will. Stop!"

The Lifedrinker swelled even more, looking at his creatures around him. Oddly, he cried as well, "It must stop!" With a surge of his magic, he stole more life from the world, squeezing last drops out of the air, out of the dust—out of the dust people. As he drained his own servants, ten of the mummified corpses twitched and then crumbled into blackened bone powder. The scorpions cracked, shattered, and fell into dust.

The Lifedrinker howled, squirming in the air, raising his hands, as if by triggering this last great call, he had accelerated a magical wildfire, and now a cyclone began to draw down into the endless pit that formed his lair. "Save me," he begged.

Nicci took advantage of that one second of respite. "No. No one can save you, Lifedrinker."

He whispered, "I . . . am . . . *Roland*."

Nicci held out her palm, cupping the last acorn of the Eldertree, and released a simple burst of magic, gathering the air around her in what would otherwise have been a trivial effort. Instead of manipulating the wind to create fists of solid air against an opponent, she used the air to accelerate the acorn forward. The life-infused projectile sped through the air like a quarrel fired from a tightly wound crossbow.

The Lifedrinker screamed, and the acorn plunged into his cavernous mouth, down his throat.

Contained within its hard shell, the last seed of the Eldertree held the concentrated life of the once vast primeval forest. Deep inside the evil wizard, the hard nut cracked and released a flood of life, like a dam bursting in an enormous reservoir. Resurgent energy flared out in an unstoppable explosion of vitality, of renewal, of rejuvenation.

Roland let loose a shriek that seemed to tear open the Scar itself. The evil wizard was an empty pit, an endless appetite that demanded all life, all energy—and the seed from the Eldertree *contained* all life, all energy. The thrashing tumor-strangled wizard was like a man dying of thirst who now found himself drowning in a flash flood.

His evil spell tried to absorb the limitless power geysering from the acorn. The dust storms howled around the curved black pillars; tornadoes of unleashed fury whipped the dry ground, flinging sharp obsidian projectiles in all directions.

Spent, Nicci collapsed mere feet from the edge of the Lifedrinker's pit, unable to move. The battle within the evil wizard continued to build, and he howled with agony. The acorn that had embedded itself inside him blazed and brightened into an inferno of life.

While the Lifedrinker attempted to smother it with ripples of hungry shadows, the remaining dust people collapsed in a rattle of bones and dried skin. The last of the scorpions fell dead, their segmented limbs curling up tight against their armored bodies; their stingers went limp.

Bannon threw the bodies off of him and climbed forward to try to rescue Nicci. He tottered like an ancient man, barely able to survive another hour. Mrra, too, pushed forward, close to the sorceress. Although Nicci was wrung dry and utterly exhausted, she felt the touch of her sister panther in her mind.

The ground shook and rumbled. Stones cracked. Huge boulders fell into the Lifedrinker's pit. The towering stelae creaked, then toppled like felled trees into the hole. The avalanche continued, and the sinkhole slumped, filling with debris. Lightning struck all around.

The raging battle of life continued. The remnant of the Eldertree struggled to produce new life faster than the Lifedrinker could drain it. The bright flare that surged out from the acorn dimmed and flickered away as dark magic continued to fight, but the shadows faded as well, grew patchier, like a mist burning off under a morning sun.

Finally, the evil wizard, the Lifedrinker—Roland—disintegrated, his body gone. All of his death and emptiness turned to dust, and a last bright echo coughed out of the Eldertree acorn, washing over them.

Nicci staggered backward, feeling the warmth like a summer breeze reviving her. Life. Energy. Restoration.

Her joints eased and loosened. Her throat grew less constricted, and when she gasped in a long breath, she smelled a sweetness in the air that she had not experienced since she had first seen the Scar. Nicci raised a hand to her face as the dazzle cleared from her vision, and her skin felt smooth and supple again.

Bannon picked himself up, coughing and shaking. When he turned toward her, Nicci saw that his hair was again thick and red. The wrinkles that had covered his face were gone, leaving only his usual spatter of freckles.

She brushed herself off, and her eyes searched for the place where the Lifedrinker had collapsed, where Roland had lost his battle with the last seed of the original forest.

There, in the middle of the vast dead Scar, stood a sprig of green, the only thing left from all the exuberant power of the Eldertree acorn. A single spindly sapling.

CHAPTER 54

On their long return trek across the desolation, the ominous tension lifted from the air as if the world had heaved a nervous sigh of relief. Though the Scar still remained bleak and desolate, the Lifedrinker's corruption was gone, and his blight would fade from the once-fertile soil. The valley would return, just as Nicci had promised Thistle.

The haze of blown dust and salty powder dissipated, leaving a blue sky scudded with clouds. Bannon looked up with a smile. "I think it might even rain within a day or two, wash the valley clean again." He walked with a jaunty step, obviously proud of himself. He was battered and bruised, with numerous cuts from his last battle, but none the worse for it. "I fought well, didn't I? Made myself worthwhile?"

Though she was not one to shower unnecessary compliments, Nicci did acknowledge the fact. "Yes, you were rather useful when I needed it most."

He beamed.

Mrra stayed with them, ranging widely, wandering out of sight in the rocky canyons, exploring the foothills, and then returning as if to acknowledge her bond with Nicci. The sand panther was a wild creature, though, and as they approached the uplift of the Cliffwall plateau, she seemed restless, sniffing the air. Looking up the striated cliff, Mrra growled; her long tail thrashed.

Nicci gave a brusque nod, which the sand panther seemed to understand. "You can't go in there with us. That is a human place."

Judging by the branded spell markings on her hide, Mrra's previous captivity among humans had not been a pleasant one. With a flick of her tail, the big cat bounded off to vanish into the dry scrub oak and piñon pines.

Nicci and Bannon began the long climb up.

T he people of Cliffwall welcomed them as heroes, which Bannon enjoyed and Nicci tolerated. With a broad grin, the young man patted the sword at his side. "I handled myself well enough. I saved the sorceress too many times to recount."

Nicci was sure he would recount them anyway.

Bannon accepted the fawning attentions of Victoria's three acolytes, who took turns fussing over the scabs and scratches on his cheek, his arms, his hands. They dabbed at the wounds with wet cloths, then cleaned the dust from his forehead, wiping his hair. Bannon touched a cut on his face. "Do you think this one will leave a scar?" he asked, sounding hopeful.

Laurel kissed it. "Maybe so."

Laughing, Thistle ran forward and threw herself on Nicci. "I knew you would survive! I knew you'd save the world."

"And I'm glad you stayed behind, as you promised," Nicci said.

Pleased to hear of their adventure, Nathan stroked his chin. "I wish I had been there, though. It would have been quite a tale to include in my life book."

"We will find other tales, Wizard," Nicci said. "We have a long journey ahead of us yet. Our work here is done."

"Yes, your work is done." He smiled and nodded. "And now that the Lifedrinker has been dispatched, our focus should be on finding Kol Adair, so I can be made whole again—it is quite inconvenient to feel useless! The Cliffwall archives have maps and charts of the world, and Mia will help me sort them right away."

As the ostensible leader of the Cliffwall scholars, Simon was grateful for what Nicci had accomplished. "Even from here, we could feel when the Lifedrinker was defeated. The weight of the world seemed lifted, as if something fundamental had changed." He led the gathered scholars in a loud cheer to thank Nicci and Bannon. "Before we devote our full attentions to learning and cataloging, we should make an expedition to the site of the battle and see this new Eldertree sapling."

Victoria and her memmers nodded in grudging admiration. "Yes, we should all see what remains."

The following day, nearly fifty people made their way down the narrow, hidden trail from the mesa cliff into the now-quiet Scar.

Full of energy, Thistle trotted along as the group worked their way through the foothills and out into the devastation. The girl was eager to guide them along the easiest path, scouting ahead. "Now I know I'm going to see this valley the way it was meant to be! Someday, I can have my world back, green and growing."

"Maybe even with flower gardens," Nicci said.

She felt that the shadows were lifting from the Scar. They walked at an easy pace all that day, camped for the night, and then set off again the next morning, heading toward the heart of the devastation. Mounds of obsidian glass still protruded from the ground, but the stinking fumaroles had sealed over and the exposed lava hardened. It was only the faintest, first step in the long, painful process of healing.

Finally, near the end of the second day of travel from the Cliffwall plateau, the group of eager travelers gathered at what had been the lair of the Lifedrinker. Nicci and her companions stood with the group, cautiously approaching the crumbling debris that filled the crater.

They paid no attention to the shattered remnants of dust people, the cracked scorpions. Instead, the amazed scholars gathered around the single oak sapling, a delicate tree no taller than Nicci's waist.

"If that is the sapling from the Eldertree, I don't sense any magic from it," Nicci said. "It seems like a normal young tree."

Nathan said, "All of its magic must have burned out in the final battle with the Lifedrinker. This is all that remains, just an oak sapling, but it is alive. That is the important part."

Thistle nudged her way through the crowd so she could look at the spindly little tree that stood so defiant in the desolation.

Victoria seemed disappointed. "That's all? It was . . . the Eldertree!"

"The acorn's outpouring of life was just barely sufficient to win the battle," Nicci said. "The power of life versus the power of death. It was a very close thing. It gave all of its magic to destroy the Lifedrinker—another week or month would have been too late."

While Victoria and her memmers crowded close, the matronly woman let out a sigh. "It is a good thing our memmers recalled the story. Without us, we would not have found the seed of the Eldertree at all, and Roland would still be alive and dangerous."

A flicker of annoyance crossed Simon's face. "Yes, Cliffwall provided the necessary weapon to defeat him, and now we must make up for all the suffering." He raised his voice to address those gathered at the site. "It will be a great deal of work, but we can reclaim this land. The streams and rivers will flow again. With rainfall, we can plant crops and orchards. Many of our scholars came from the towns in this valley, and we can rebuild and replant it."

Understanding the enormity of the problem they faced, the people muttered their agreement.

Nathan placed his hands on his hips, stretching his back. "The Scar can heal. Now that the blight has been eliminated, the natural beauty of the valley will return. It'll just take time." He smiled optimistically. "Maybe only a century or two."

"A century?" Thistle's expression fell. "I'll never see it, then!"

Victoria was grim and determined. She muttered so quietly that only Nicci heard, "It will need to go faster."

CHAPTER 55

The land was dead and desperate. Victoria knew that the harm would take decades, maybe even centuries, to restore . . . if left on its own. That was unforgivable. She could not forget what the self-centered, shortsighted Roland had done, how that pathetic man had killed the land . . . and murdered her dear husband.

But Victoria knew magic, had memorized countless secrets of arcane lore. As the most prominent memmer, she held a wealth of magical information in her mind, and now she searched for a faster solution to revitalize the great valley. The answer was within her—she knew it!

Simon and his scholars could fool themselves that they were experts. They could read books and study spells, but that didn't mean they understood that knowledge. Just because a starving man looked at a pantry filled with food, he did not have the nourishment he required. The memmers, though, had all that information *inside* them, part of their being, their heart, their soul.

Ancient wizards had built this hidden archive to preserve history and lore for all future generations to use. Everything a powerful gifted person could imagine was inside these vaults, written down in volumes, stored on shelves . . . and locked in the minds of the memmers.

That knowledge was part of Victoria.

After the group visited the site of the final battle, the sorceress had seemed so smug, so triumphant about what she had done. Death's

Mistress! Yes, Nicci might have killed the Lifedrinker's ravenous need, but she had not restored life by any means. That was a much more difficult and time-consuming task.

Victoria found the spindly sapling deeply disappointing, even pathetic. Such a small thing, without any magic? She had hoped for much more from the Eldertree. From when she was a young woman, she recalled the rolling hills covered with thick forests, the fertile basin with sweeping croplands and thriving towns. Though the isolated inhabitants of Cliffwall had only rarely left their hidden canyons, they knew the way the real world was supposed to be.

One of the first outsiders brought back to the archive after Victoria had dispelled the camouflage shroud, Roland had been an intense and nervous researcher, an innocuous scholar who read volumes of spells and dabbled with minor magic. He had been quiet and good-natured, and Victoria's husband had considered him a friend.

Early on, Bertram had noticed that Roland was growing gaunt and thin. Victoria now realized those were signs of the wasting disease devouring him from within. But Roland had refused to accept his fate; he had made a bargain with magic he did not comprehend. Without understanding what he was about to unleash, he had turned himself into a bottomless pit of need that siphoned away all life, not just his own.

Victoria winced as she remembered the fateful day she had come upon Roland after he met her husband in the corridor. Desperate, begging for help, he had clasped Bertram's hand, but was unable to control what he unleashed, and the magic kept stealing more and *more* from her poor husband. Bertram could not pull away, could not escape no matter how hard he struggled . . . and the monster Roland purloined his entire life, gorged himself on Bertram's essence.

By the time Victoria saw them, it was too late. Roland fled in terror, and she rushed forward to catch her husband as he collapsed in the corridor. She held him, pressing him against her breast and rocking him back and forth as he faded swiftly. Bertram's skin turned as gray and dry as the old parchments in the archive. His cheeks sank into dark hollows, his eyes shriveled into puckered knots of flesh, his hair fell out in wispy clumps. In her arms, her husband turned into nothing more than a mummified corpse.

From where he had retreated down the corridor, Roland had watched in horror and revulsion. He held up his hands, denying his own deadly touch. "No, no, no!" he screamed.

But after draining all the life energy from Bertram, he did indeed seem stronger, invigorated by what he had stolen. Roland, fast becoming the Lifedrinker, had fled Cliffwall, running into the vast valley. Only later did Victoria learn that he had killed ten other scholars in his frantic, blundering attempts to keep himself strong, trying to get away from the isolated archive.

Now the Lifedrinker was dead, but that was not enough for Victoria. She could not bring Bertram back, but she needed to restore the fertile valley and reawaken life, and she was sure she had the power to do so. Unlike the deluded, inept Roland, she would not make any mistakes. . . .

By the time the expedition returned to the plateau two days later, Victoria knew what she had to do. Sage, Laurel, and Audrey were her three best memmers, but she also had Franklin, Gloria, Peretta, and dozens more students, all of whom were repositories of knowledge. Even now that she had brought down the camouflage shroud and made the wealth of knowledge available to any student who could read, Victoria insisted on keeping the memmer tradition alive. Maybe her acolytes would remember something even more important.

Back inside the great Cliffwall library, Simon insisted on holding a celebration feast, but Victoria could not pretend to be as overjoyed as the others. There was still so much work to do, centuries of work—and that was much too long to wait.

Much as the researchers had scoured the archive for a way to destroy the Lifedrinker, Victoria now sought a *fecundity* spell, some powerful magic to restore everything the evil wizard had taken. If a corrupted spell could steal life away, could not another spell bring it all flooding back? Victoria needed to find that type of magic. Surely some solution lay among all the wisdom preserved here from the ancient wizards.

She spread the word among her memmers, who pondered and sifted through the countless books they had committed to memory. They talked to additional scholars, who combed through now-forgotten volumes from the deepest vaults and dustiest shelves, incorporating that knowledge into their own memory archives.

There had to be a way!

Victoria met privately with her trusted acolytes, keeping her voice low as if they had started a conspiracy. "You are all fertile, all throbbing with life. I can sense it in you. You must create life." She smiled at them, feeling the warmth within her. "And you have gone to Bannon Farmer?"

The three young women looked both eager and embarrassed. "Yes, Victoria," Sage said. "Many times."

"We are trying," Laurel said.

Audrey smiled. "Trying as often as possible."

Sage said, "But none of us is pregnant. Yet."

Victoria sighed and shook her head. "The seed sometimes goes astray, but it will happen in the normal course of things. It is not enough, though. We will have to try something else. The ancient wizards must have known a spell to restore life, magic to encourage growth and rebirth."

"Restore life?" Laurel was astonished by the idea. "You want to bring back the dead?"

"I want to bring back the *world*," Victoria said. "A fertility spell to remove the blight and corruption out in that desolation. I want to bring back the forests and rivers, the meadows and croplands. I want to fill the streams with fish. I want to summon flowers and then bees to pollinate them and make honey. I want the land to thrive again." She drew a breath and looked at her followers. "I refuse to wait decades for that to happen."

While Cliffwall scholars as well as the other canyon villagers engaged in giddy revelry to celebrate the end of the Lifedrinker, Victoria's special memmers meditated, sifting through the vital information in their perfectly preserved memories, searching for some way to accelerate the process.

Victoria spent her every waking moment wrestling with the mountains of words she had locked inside herself. Her head pounded, as if the proper spells were struggling to break free, but she did not have the key to release them. Not yet.

Standing outside under the great cliff overhang in the gathering dusk, she watched shadows fill the finger canyons. Evening lights glimmered from the windows of other alcove settlements across the canyon. Insects buzzed in a low contented music, and she heard the whisper of wings as two night birds swooped by. The world seemed at peace, awakening.

Victoria reflected on the damaged tower that had held the prophecy library. She could remember the terrible day when an inadvertent spell had liquefied the structure and drowned the hapless but foolish apprentice wizard in a flood of stone. Such incidents, even though they were rare, frightened the other scholars from attempting major spells.

Now, standing in the cliff grotto, she looked at the damaged tower with scorn. She had no respect for the clumsy student who had failed to understand the power he unleashed. Another disaster, just like Roland.

Victoria would never allow such a thing. She had higher standards.

As she thought of the mistake that had been made here, something clicked in her mind and she remembered part of an old fertility spell, not just for a woman to have children—perhaps to reawaken the womb of a barren woman, like Victoria herself—but a *creation* spell, a fecundity rite tied to deeper magic that could increase crops, expand herds, rejuvenate forests. She felt the tickle of faint memory, a spell buried deep among so much other knowledge. Victoria tried to sharpen the arcane thoughts at the distant edge of her mind.

She remembered her stern mother, whose angular face looked like the wedge of a hatchet. While her mother had forced Victoria to memorize the lore word for word, she had never bothered to make sure young Victoria *comprehended* what she knew; her mother cared only that she could accurately repeat every line, even if it was in a language neither of them understood. The woman had repeatedly whipped Victoria with a willow switch, raising red welts, spilling blood. Sometimes, she had cuffed her daughter across the face, boxed her ears, or made her bleed from the nose in an attempt to make her try harder to remember, to use her gift and make no mistakes.

Mistakes caused harm. People suffered when an error was made, even an innocent error. Weeping with sincerity, young Victoria had promised her mother she would make no errors. And she had watched that woman shove her good-natured father out of the cliff overhang to his death—a deserved fate, according to her mother, since he had made a mistake, a potentially dangerous mistake.

Victoria could make no mistakes. . . .

Now, once she touched the scattered, ancient spell and followed the memories buried in her past, Victoria could see the words unfurling in her mind. The arcane language, the unfamiliar phrasings, couplets with pronunciations that seemed to defy the letters with which they were written. Victoria remembered the fecundity spell, repeated from generation to generation, passed from memmer to memmer. The thoughts were faint and wispy, frayed from disuse, but she possessed the knowledge. She could use it.

Satisfied, Victoria reentered the main library fortress and hurried to her quarters. Though she had committed everything to memory, she lit her lamp and bent over the low writing desk. On a scrap of paper she began to write, preserving the words she had brought to the forefront of her mind, rolling them over in her mouth, making sure each detail was correct. She spoke the sounds carefully aloud to be sure she got every nuance correct. After she wrote down the fecundity spell, she read it and read it again until she was sure she was right.

Victoria braced herself. She knew what she had to do, and she understood the instructions perfectly.

The land had already been bled dry. What did a little more blood matter?

CHAPTER 56

Cliffwall served its purpose, exactly as the ancient wizards intended," Simon told Nicci and Nathan, still looking very pleased with himself. After the defeat of the Lifedrinker he seemed more relaxed and focused in his role, back to what he believed his true work should be, though he still looked too young to be the senior scholar-archivist. "Now, at last, our scholars can continue their cataloging and their pure research. There is so much to learn."

The teams of dedicated researchers returned to their everyday work of listing the countless tomes, reshelving volumes by subject, and noting the type of knowledge contained in various disorganized sections. Obviously, decades of work still remained.

Simon looked around with giddy wonder as he tried to encompass the thousands of books shelved haphazardly in the vast library rooms. "The project seems overwhelming, yet for some reason, I feel energized now, more hopeful than I've been in twenty years."

"And well you should feel that way, truth be told," Nathan said. "Simply rediscovering the potential wonders in this library will be an adventure in itself, however. Besides, as you know, all the rules just changed with the star shift. We don't yet understand how much of this information is still accurate, or if everything needs to be relearned, retested, rediscovered."

Simon seemed content. "We are ready, whatever the answer. If your Lord Rahl intends to create a new golden age, then all of this magic can serve humanity."

* * *

Bannon basked in the attention, although one person could handle only so much feasting and dancing. He took a moment to marvel at all that had happened to him in the past month. Despite the horrific ordeals he had endured, the young man realized he now had the life he always wanted.

While battling the selka or the dust people, even facing the Life-drinker himself, he had been sure he would die. But afterward, the colors of those memories shone bright and vibrant—and they were stories that he could tell until he was a gray-bearded old man, preferably with a wife, many children, and many more grandchildren. In fact, he already wished he could relive some of those adventures.

And love! Here at Cliffwall he had discovered the joys of three beautiful women who adored him and schooled him in the ways of physical pleasure. Though at first Bannon had been embarrassed and awkward, he was an eager student, and now his nights were filled with warm skin and sensuous caresses, whispered laughter and shining eyes. How could he choose a favorite among them? Fortunately, Audrey, Laurel, and Sage were happy to share.

For so many years, he had been trapped in a nightmare, and now he lived a dream that he could never have imagined.

After the late celebrations, Bannon wandered through the Cliff-wall complex, searching for the three young women. They had re-warded him most enthusiastically after his triumphant return, but now Victoria had gathered all of her memmers, giving them some very important task that took all of their attention and energy. The lovely young women had expressed their sadness that they couldn't tend to Bannon, claiming other urgent priorities. He hadn't seen them in two days.

Missing Audrey, Laurel, and Sage, Bannon searched the library rooms, the dining hall, and the acolytes' quarters, casually looking for them. He found one of the other memmers, a middle-aged man named Franklin with large, owlish eyes and a square chin. "Victoria took them outside, somewhere in the Scar," Franklin explained. "I think she found the answer they were looking for, something to help the valley return to life."

Bannon gave a solemn nod, not wanting to seem desperate. "It must be important work, then. I'll leave them to it." He went off to his own quarters, hoping they would come back soon.

Thistle was still content to sleep curled on the sheepskin on the floor in Nicci's chamber. "I was worried about you out there," she said. "I didn't want to lose you. I already lost everyone else."

Nicci's brow furrowed. "I promised I'd come back. You should have believed me." While the seamstresses repaired her black travel dress, yet again, she had changed into a comfortable linen gown.

"I did believe you," the girl said, her eyes bright. "I knew you would kill the Lifedrinker. And now I'm ready to go see the rest of the world with you. Will we leave soon?"

Nicci considered the long journey ahead, the unknown lands and the many possible hazards. "You have been through a lot already, and our journey will be full of hardships. Are you sure you want to go?"

On the sheepskin, Thistle sat up in alarm, drawing her scuffed knees to her chest. "Yes! I can hunt, I can help you find the trail, and you know I can fight."

"Someday, people will rebuild Verdun Springs," Nicci said. "Don't you want to go back there? It's your home."

"It's not my home. I lost my home a long time ago. I won't live long enough to see the valley green and lush again, so I want to see what other places are like. You're my new home now." She scratched her mop of hair. "When you leave, I'm going with you again."

Amused by her determination, Nicci readied herself for bed and lay back on her own blanket. "Then I don't think I could stop you." She pulled the blanket over herself, released a hint of magic to snuff out the lamp, and went to sleep.

CHAPTER 57

After the draining, skeletal touch of the Lifedrinker, Nicci slept deeply, plunging into odd dreams.

Though asleep, she ranged far . . . and she wasn't herself. Her mind and her life rode in another body, traveling along on powerful, padded paws. Her muscles thrummed like braided wires as she raced through the night, her long tail lashing behind her, pointed ears cocked and alert for the faintest sounds of prey. The slitted pupils of her gold-green eyes drank in the starlight.

She was Mrra. They were bonded on a deep inner level. Panther sisters. Their blood had intermingled. Nicci had not sought this strange contact in her dreams, but neither did she fear it. She prowled the night, part sorceress, part sand panther. And more.

Lying on the hard pallet inside her chambers, Nicci stirred, twitched, then dropped into a deeper sleep.

Mrra was out hunting, and Nicci hunted with her. They roamed together, and joy sang through her powerful feline body. They raced along for the sheer pleasure of it, not because they were in a hurry. Although hunger gnawed at her belly, she was not starving and she knew she would find food. She always did. With her panther senses, Mrra could catch any scent of prey on the wind, hear the movement of a rodent, see any flicker in the deepest shadows.

And she was free! No longer a prisoner of the handlers. She was wild, as a sand panther was meant to be.

Mrra flowed through the night, exploring the edge of the Scar, which no longer smelled of the festering blight, sour and bitter magic, such as what she had experienced in the great city. This night, the Scar was quiet and Mrra sensed death and silence, but there would also be prey as creatures ventured back into the crumbling wasteland.

Mrra clung to her connection with Nicci. Throughout her life, the sand panther had been spell-bonded with her two sisters, cubs from the same litter, bound inexorably together by the wizard commander, and then turned over to the handlers for training.

Now Mrra's sister panthers were dead, slain in combat—as they were meant to die. Nicci and her companions had killed them, the girl and the young male warrior, but Mrra held no hatred for what the others had done. In the *troka*, the spell-bonded panthers were meant to fight, just as they were meant to eat, breathe, and mate.

The big cat could not think far ahead, did not plan or envision things that might be. Nicci was her bonded partner now. A longing growl rumbled through her chest, and she hoped that she and Nicci could fight together again, side by side. They could tear apart many enemies, just as they had fought the giant lizards or against the Life-drinker.

Mrra bounded onto a slickrock outcropping, where she sat on her haunches under the moonlight, staring across the landscape. Narrowing her golden eyes, twitching her tail, she sniffed the air. Her whiskers vibrated. The hunt was just like a battle, and every day was a battle. Her *troka* had escaped from the great city after killing their handlers, and then the three sister panthers raced into the expansive wilderness and the life they were meant to have.

All three of them had been free, for a time.

As Nicci stirred in her sleep, the dreams became more vivid, the memories more precise. . . .

Violent experiences, razor-sharp recollections of razor-sharp pain. She had been young, and her life was full of mirth and joy as she played with her sister cubs. Then the wizard commander had seized them, forcibly holding the young cubs down while he brought out white-hot irons tipped with spell symbols. Mrra had thrashed, and raked the handlers with her claws, but the leering wizard commander had thrust the searing brand against her hide, burning the symbols into her skin, sizzling the tawny fur. The smoke of burned flesh and hair rose up in a thick cloud, stirred by her feline shriek.

The agony had been unforgettable, and Mrra's pain resonated with the pain of her sister panthers bonded to her, as the spells braided the three into a *troka* so that they shared their minds, their thoughts, and their blood.

That was just the beginning. Once the three panthers were linked by the first blazing symbol, the wizard commander branded more spells into their flesh. And because the three panthers were connected, each one experienced the hideous pain again and again, until their minds were as marred as their beautiful bodies.

After the cats recovered, the handlers began to train them, using hard and painful lessons that involved blood, prey, fear—and more blood. As she and her sister panthers grew stronger, though, Mrra learned to enjoy the tasks. She became faster, deadlier. Her *troka* became the best killers the great city had ever seen.

Mrra's existence became the hunt and the kill. She learned to attack and slay humans inside a gladiatorial coliseum. Some of the prey were terrified and helpless: they ran, but to no avail. Others fell to their knees, weeping and shuddering as the panther claws tore them apart. Some victims were fearsome human warriors, and those provided the best sport, the most challenging battles. Other prey wielded magic, but the symbols branded onto Mrra and her sister panthers deflected the magical attacks.

She remembered the roar of the crowd, the cheers, the howls of bloodlust. With blood-spattered fur, Mrra would lift her head up to the bright sun, and glare at the stands teeming with spectators. She flashed her long, curved fangs and let out her own victorious roar. She remembered the heat of the sun and sand, the taste of the hot blood as it gushed out of a torn throat. Mrra remembered killing victims. Killing warriors. Just *killing*.

Because if she didn't do as she was told, the handlers would cause them pain.

Now free, she prowled around the desolate valley, venturing back to where they had fought and killed the evil wizard. She saw human figures there in the moonlight, four of them, all females who had come out to the lone oak sapling that had grown up at the site of the battle. Sniffing the air, Mrra recognized them as people from the city inside the cliff. An older woman and three young ones.

They were not prey, and therefore held no interest for her.

Mrra ran on into the night, hunting. She picked up the scent of a scrawny antelope that had ventured out of the foothills. The big cat loped onward, picking up speed. Even though the antelope was nearly invisible against the dusty brown landscape, her sharp eyes detected the movement. With a burst of speed and fire through her muscles, she bounded forward.

Even though the panicked antelope tried to run, hooves clattering over the loose rocks, Mrra ran it down and knocked it into the dust. In a flash of fangs, she tore out its throat, then ripped open the antelope's guts while the hooves and the head kept twitching.

The warm blood was delicious, magnificent! She began to feed with a contented, rumbling purr. . . .

In bed, far away, Nicci let out a long satisfied sigh in her sleep.

CHAPTER 58

The great dry valley was intensely silent in the night, brittle with lingering death when it should have been teeming with life. Victoria was offended just to be here. This place should be lush with vegetation, tall grasses, thick forests, and fields of waving grain.

Roland had caused this—stolen all the life, sterilized the land. Even though Nicci had stopped him, that was only part of the solution, and Victoria would not settle for half measures. The others at Cliffwall could congratulate one another, but there was far too much work to do. She would not rest until the job was done, and she could trust no one else to take the necessary measures.

Accompanied by the three loyal young women, she left Cliffwall in the gathering darkness, and together they made their swift expedition across the wasteland out to the site of the Lifedrinker's lair. Laurel, Audrey, and Sage were eager to help, their shining eyes filled with hope. Though the journey took them nearly two days, Victoria had revealed only part of what she intended to do, but these were her acolytes and they would submit to the world's need.

"Our work here is not for personal gain," she said to them. "It will be a triumph for every living man, woman, and child."

At last, at nightfall of the second day, they reached the silent and shuddering area surrounded by fallen obsidian blocks, cluttered with the broken carcasses of giant scorpions and the bony husks of dust people. It was a frightening place, and also a sacred place.

Victoria led them to the lone oak sapling, the frail and fragile tree that had grown from the Eldertree's last acorn.

"It looks so small and weak," Sage said.

"But it has the power of the Eldertree," Laurel said.

"It has the power of the *world*," Victoria corrected. "But its special magic burned away in the battle, and it seems to be just a normal tree now. Nevertheless, it is a tiny spark, a symbol—and we have the power, you three and I, to fan this small flame into a bonfire of life. Are you willing to help?" She looked at the acolytes in turn. "Are you willing to invoke the necessary magic?"

The women nodded without hesitation. Victoria had never had any doubt.

Standing under the moonlight near the thin gray sapling, Victoria loosened the lacings of her dress, then pulled open the collar so that she could remove the garment. She pulled off the drab gown over her head and tossed it aside. The garment fell onto one of the jagged obsidian blocks, and she stood naked in the moonlight, smelling the dusty breezes, experiencing the chill of the darkness.

She turned to her acolytes. "You three must disrobe. You are life. You are pure and fertile. And you must stand as you were born for this sacred process of creation."

The women did as she asked, pulling off their white woolen shifts so that they all stood nude, regal and flawless. Creamy skin glowed in the starlight, their breasts full, their hips rounded. They let their hair flow loose and free.

Audrey's raven locks flowed back like a deeper part of the night, matched by the dark thatch between her legs, while Laurel's strawberry-blond hair looked like gold burning in a slow fire. Sage's nipples were dark and erect in the chill; her breasts were perfectly rounded, flush with the need to create new life.

The power of their beauty took Victoria's words away. These acolytes were the purest personification of female energy, of life itself.

A long time ago, Victoria herself had been just as beautiful. Men had lusted after her, but she had given herself only to Bertram. With a long sigh, she recalled that first time when he had taken her in an orchard on a night with no moon, while the canyon brook made trick-ling music, but not loud enough to drown out her gasps of pleasure. As Bertram stole a kiss, then stole her virginity, they had lain entan-gled under the soft, fallen leaves, exploring each other. It had been perfect.

After that night, Victoria had never imagined being satisfied with any other man. She had found herself pregnant a month later, which was no surprise since she and Bertram had enjoyed each other many more times. They spoke the ancient marriage rituals to each other, re-citing the words that memmers kept in their minds. But only two months into their marriage, Victoria lost the baby after hours of ago-nizing cramps and a gush of blood that produced a small fetus about the size of her finger. It didn't even look human. And there had been so much blood.

In her misery, Bertram held her, promised that they would have many more children. But that had never happened. Discovering that she was barren had devastated Victoria, one of her greatest disappoint-ments, one of her greatest failures. She had never given birth to a single son or daughter, no matter how much she longed for it, no matter how often she and Bertram tried.

She loved her husband very much, but eventually their physical pleasure had become more of a duty, and a hopeless one at that. So Victoria became a surrogate mother to her acolytes and especially these three perfect, beautiful young women. Victoria claimed that she was now the true mother to so many more children than she could ever have had on her own, but she did not convince even herself.

After invoking tonight's ancient, powerful spell, however, she would be mother to the entire world. Even with the price to be paid, how could Victoria have any second thoughts?

"Male magic is the magic of conquest and death, of hunting and killing," she said. Her voice sounded very loud in the silent, secret place. "Female magic is the magic of life—and our magic is stronger." She smiled at the three.

Audrey, Laurel, and Sage were flushed as they stood naked to-gether, breathing hard with anticipation. They moved slowly, swaying their hips, shifting from one foot to the other. Victoria could see that they were aroused. Perhaps enhanced by magic, their own sweat, scent, and inner heat filled the air. Audrey reached down to touch herself and let out a small gasp. Tempted, Laurel and Sage did the same. The night itself was charged with potential, with *life*. Even the oak sapling seemed to tremble.

Victoria's heart ached, and she drove away her growing dread, refusing to let it delay her work, her vital work.

As the three young women stood ready, their eyes half closed, soft groans of pleasure came from deep in their throats. Victoria rummaged in the wadded fabric of her dress and removed the vial she had brought. It was a tincture bottle filled with a deep blue liquid. "You must each drink of this. One swallow should be enough."

Audrey reached out to take it. Her fingers were moist as she removed the cap. "What is it?"

"A vital part of the spell. Drink."

Audrey took a cautious swallow, then passed the bottle on to Laurel, who looked at it. "If you are certain, Victoria . . ."

"I am certain. I have pondered long and hard. We must bring life back to the land, and this is the way we can do it."

Laurel drank without further question; then Sage drained the last of the dark liquid from the bottle.

With a heavy heart, Victoria watched her three acolytes sway, then go limp and collapse to the ground. They were so trusting. . . .

Working quickly, she pulled their naked forms together, propping them up near the Eldertree sapling. Now she could let herself weep, because the girls were unconscious. Hidden in folds of her dress, she had brought strong leather bindings, and she lashed their wrists together, as well as their feet.

The naked young women breathed heavily in their deep drugged sleep, but they would awaken soon, and Victoria had many preparations to make.

Copying what she had memorized in the ancient book and what she had drawn on her scrap of paper for absolute certainty, Victoria scribed a complex spell-form on the ground, etching out the angles and curves of symbols in a long-forgotten language so that the pattern surrounded her acolytes. They were her seeds now; they were the start of new life, the power of which could not be measured.

But there was a cost—there was always a cost. Life required life. Blood required blood.

Victoria shuddered as she finished the pattern, telling herself repeatedly that the benefit was worth the cost. The fecundity spell left no doubt: these three droplets of life would unleash a vivifying downpour. They would restore this verdant valley and heal the wound in the world.

But, oh, Audrey, Laurel, and Sage . . .

Victoria paused to suck in a long shaking breath, and then she let herself sob. Tears flowed down her cheeks. But it had to be done.

When she looked up many minutes later, Victoria saw that the three acolytes had awakened, sooner than expected. Their eyes were still groggy and confused, but the spell required that they had to be conscious, had to be willing. They had already given Victoria their permission.

"What are you doing?" asked Laurel. "What's happening?"

"You're saving us all." With tears pouring down her face, the matronly woman took the knife from her wadded dress and knelt beside the first acolyte.

Sage's eyes went wide, and she squirmed in fear as Victoria drew the razor edge across her throat, spilling a river of blood down her neck and over the swell of her perfect breasts. Her heart kept pumping, gushing out her life's blood onto the achingly sterile ground.

"I'm sorry," Victoria said as she moved to Audrey. Gathering the girl's long dark hair in one hand, she pulled back Audrey's head and slashed her throat.

Laurel looked up at her in defiance, her jaws clenched. She struggled against the leather bonds for just a moment, but her shoulders slumped as she felt her two companions sag in death against her, still bubbling blood across the ground. In a quavering voice, Laurel said, "Tell me it is necessary."

"There is no other way," Victoria answered.

Then Laurel lifted her chin, and Victoria slashed for the third and final time.

When the girls had finished their long wet dying, Victoria wailed with grief. These had been like her daughters, her perfect followers . . . and she'd killed them. But she had done it to bring life.

Now, Victoria worked the spell. The restoration magic unleashed a flood of fecundity strong enough to bring back the forests, the meadows, the grassy plains, the croplands.

Rich blood poured out of the three sacrifices, and Victoria spoke the incantation that she had so perfectly memorized and practiced. The blood flowed like runnels of melted candle wax into the spellforms she had etched there. The liquid glowed a deep red like lava . . . and then the blood changed, darkened, freshened. It turned green and bright as it seeped into the devastated soil, which began to awaken.

Tiny shoots appeared in the brown dust; blades of grass, wide-leaved weeds, tangled green branches, bushes, and flowers sprang up.

Victoria stood back and gasped in wonder. The Eldertree sapling grew upward and outward, and more branches unfurled as it rose taller and spread itself. Ferns uncurled like bullwhips and expanded into fan-like fronds. Colorful mushrooms boiled out of the ground, swelled, and burst in an eruption of spores that led to another generation of furiously growing fungi. The ground simmered and crackled as it awakened.

Newborn insects scuttled around, and the night was abuzz with flying creatures—moths with bright feathery wings, beetles with iridescent carapaces.

Victoria stepped back and listened to the rush of life. Inhaling deeply, she smelled moisture, pollen, the perfume of flowers, the resinous scent of fresh trees, the waxy green aroma of leaves. Vines scrambled out of the ground like serpents, following the lines of spilled blood. Roots expanded and thrashed, knitting the broken soil together, raising woody stems and bunches of leaves. Tendrils coiled around the bloodstained bodies of the sacrifices, engulfing the three young women as fertilizer, as trophies.

Victoria stared around herself with wonder. She had never felt so much life before, and she had created this! She had sparked this rebirth. Her rejuvenation spell was powerful enough to overwhelm the damage done by the Lifedrinker.

The verdant forest seemed manic, exploding with life, desperate to reclaim lost territory. Victoria stepped back, proud of what she had done. The scholars at Cliffwall would see the rebirth here, and they would know that Victoria was responsible for it. She stood there naked and pleased, satisfied with her accomplishment. She closed her eyes and let out a sigh of gratitude.

Something seized her ankle. Her eyes flew open and she saw a writhing vine coiling upward, touching her calf. With the speed of a striking viper, it wrapped around her knee and held tight.

She cried out and tried to pull back, but the vine was as unyielding as an iron spring. It tugged in response, dragging her back. Ferns uncurled, bowing over her, closing in. Branches extended toward her, and she struggled to push them away. A curling twig caught her wrist. Vines erupted from the ground, like a swarm of thrashing tentacles that seized her legs. More writhed up to encircle her waist and then tightened.

Victoria screamed and tried to pull away. Roots grabbed her feet, anchoring her. "No! I didn't—!"

As she shouted, a leafy branch thrust into her mouth and pushed into her throat. She gagged and coughed. Fresh green fronds wrapped around her eyes, blindfolding her. She thrashed her head from side to side, choking.

Tendrils thrust into her nostrils, growing deep into her head, while others poked into her ears and explored deeper. She couldn't scream, couldn't see, couldn't breathe. Victoria fought as the vines squeezed tighter.

Then, like the arms of a mighty muscled warrior, the vines pulled her legs apart. She writhed, twisting her hips in a desperate attempt to get away. She felt another vine rising up along her legs, gliding against the side of her thigh, then, with only the slightest hesitation, it plunged between her legs and thrust upward, swelling there, filling her.

The agony throughout her body lasted a long, long time, before the tendrils finally pierced her brain, and her soul was swallowed up in a green darkness.

CHAPTER 59

As Cliffwall stirred with morning activity, Nicci awoke with the taste of blood in her mouth, a delicious coppery flavor that felt warm and hot, but soon faded with the dream memory. She blinked and sat up.

Thistle was beside her, shaking her shoulders. "I was worried about you. You were sleeping so deeply."

Nicci brushed a hand over her eyes, stretched her arms. Her body felt strange. "I am awake now."

"You growled and twitched in your sleep. You must have been having a nightmare."

Flashes of feral memory rose up like tantalizing mist-echoes. "A nightmare, of sorts." She frowned as she tried to remember. "But it wasn't all a nightmare." In fact, the dream in which she hunted with Mrra, in which she had been *part* of Mrra, held a great deal of pleasure. Nicci was strong and exuberant, her instincts singing, every muscle alive as she bounded along, free in the world. Her human lips quirked in a smile.

Thistle knelt beside her pallet with a look of grave concern. "I thought maybe you were dying. I've been trying to wake you up. Your eyes were open, but they were all white, as if you weren't there . . . as if you were somewhere else."

"I was somewhere else," Nicci said. "Gone on a journey. I was with the sand panther, and we were hunting." She lowered her voice, quiet with wonder. "I didn't remember my body here at all."

She went to the low table and splashed her face with water from the basin while she recalled riding inside the sand panther's mind, as if she were an animal dream walker, like Jagang. But while she had dreamed with Mrra, her body here had remained in a deep trance, completely helpless—and that concerned her. Nicci did not like to be vulnerable. She could never allow that to happen again unless she was in a sheltered place, watched over by a guardian.

She straightened her soft shift and combed her blond hair. "If Nathan has found his maps, we will prepare to leave today," she said, hoping to distract the orphan girl. "We have done all we can at Cliffwall."

The girl nodded. "With the Lifedrinker dead, the valley is safe. Someday, I'll return." She flashed a bright, optimistic smile. "The people of Cliffwall will write about this in legends, won't they?"

"I have no wish to be a legend," Nicci said.

They would need packs filled with supplies, fresh travel garments, mended boots. Nicci was still uneasy about having the girl accompany them into unknown dangers, but Thistle certainly was resourceful, fast, clever, independent. Her loyalty and dedication made her a worthy companion, and good companions could be an asset when traveling.

Nicci thought about the great unexplored continent of the Old World, where there were new cities and cultures . . . perhaps with oppressed people, enslaved lands, or ruthless rulers who would need to be brought into line for Lord Rahl's golden age. With a twinge and a shudder, she saw the vivid images from Mrra's mind: the searing white-hot pain as the handlers branded spell symbols into her hide, the great city, the huge coliseum, the wizard commander, the bloodshed.

The great city . . . *Ildakar.* The word came to her, but she couldn't be sure. Was it a name that Mrra had heard but not understood? The sand panther did not comprehend the handlers' speech, only the pain they inflicted. Ildakar . . .

She and Thistle went together to the dining hall, where breakfast was being served as the scholars gathered, ready to dive into another day of research. Simon consulted with two other researchers, comparing notes on an old volume with faded letters. Nathan and Bannon were there already at the morning meal, chatting together.

Seeing Nicci, the wizard gestured them over. "We have what we need, Sorceress. Mia has found ancient maps, which show the landscape as it was three thousand years ago when the documents were hidden behind the camouflage shroud."

"The roads will have fallen away, by now," Nicci said. "Armies swept across the landscape, kingdoms rose and fell. Cities were abandoned, while new ones were built."

Nathan shrugged. "True, but cities are cities, generally built on crossroads and waterways, near productive mines or fertile farmlands. If there was a reason for a city thousands of years ago, the reason is likely still valid." He reached over to tousle Thistle's curly nest of hair, and the girl grinned and reached up to muss his white hair in return, which startled him. He laughed and said to the group, "And if the cities are different and the land has changed, then that is what exploring is all about. Besides, I need my magic back."

"We all need you to have your magic back," Nicci said. "We'll leave as soon as possible. The Lifedrinker is dead, and I have saved the world, so I have fulfilled the witch woman's prediction. Now we go to Kol Adair."

Nathan could barely contain his eagerness. "True, true, my dear sorceress—but what makes you think you will be required to save the world only once?"

With an embarrassed frown, Bannon ate his oat porridge. "Before we go, I really want to say good-bye to Audrey, Laurel, and Sage. We've become very good friends."

The wizard had a twinkle in his azure eyes. "Yes, I suspect very good friends indeed."

Bannon flushed. "But I can't find them. They went away somewhere with Victoria."

Nicci vaguely remembered seeing the group of women through Mrra's eyes in the dream hunting the night before, but she had not seen them since. She said, "If you find them in time, you can say your farewells. But we are leaving." She felt restless, determined to find Kol Adair for Nathan, but also to continue her mission for Lord Rahl, to move on to other kingdoms, provinces, cities, and towns, all of which needed to know they were now part of the expanded D'Haran Empire.

A mousy young woman dashed into the dining hall, her short brown hair windblown as if she had just run a great distance. Sweat glistened on her forehead. The young scholar, Mia, had often helped Nathan find required tomes in his search for defenses against the Lifedrinker. Now she ran up to the scholar-archivist. "Master Simon, something's happened out in the Scar! I can't even begin to explain it. You must come and see." She looked around the room and also spotted Nathan. "Nathan, you have to see. It's a miracle!"

Simon ran his hands through his mussed brown hair. "What is it?"

In response, Mia led them all into the tunnels through the heart of the plateau, jabbering. "Who could ever have expected this? Wait until you look through the window alcoves. It's remarkable."

The crowds grew larger as they moved through the corridors, following Mia. Simon asked, "Where is Victoria? If it's so important, the memmers should see this as well." He seemed to be trying hard to include them, but no one could remember seeing the matronly woman or her three acolytes. Finally, they reached the window wall that looked out upon the vast valley. From here, they had viewed the extent of the Lifedrinker's spreading devastation, but now they stared out at something exceedingly strange.

Nicci came forward, focused on the sudden, dramatic changes that had occurred overnight.

In the center of the vast, dead valley where the evil wizard had dwelled, the dusty brown had changed. The sandstorms and dust devils were gone, replaced by a green haze over an area of new growth—a burgeoning jungle that arose in the Scar. The vegetation was much more than the lone and defiant Eldertree oak sapling they had left behind. It looked like a storm of plant growth.

And it was clearly spreading.

CHAPTER 60

When the magic revived her, penetrated her, and jolted her, Victoria found herself alive . . . and more than just alive. She was *exploding* with life, seething with an energy that surged through her veins like the runoff from mountain snowmelt. Her muscles writhed, teeming with new creatures. Every droplet of blood, every scrap of skin, every splinter of bone, each hair on her head was alive. She felt as if thousands of swarming bees or termites were energizing her while countless strands of plants bound her together.

Victoria drew an astonished breath. As she inhaled, a furious gale rippled through a dense forest, leaves rushing and rattling, thick boughs swaying against each other, bending in reverence . . . to *her*. She opened her eyes, and light surged in with all the green of the forest, the power of the soil.

By shedding the blood of her sacrificial acolytes, Victoria had worked that ancient spell and unleashed a magic powerful enough to counteract the deadly blight caused by the Lifedrinker. The destructive, selfish fool had brought untold harm to the world, and now Victoria accepted the task of repairing the damage he had done. She was strong enough. Roland had been an embarrassment and a failure because of his improper understanding of powerful spells that he had no business even contemplating.

Victoria could fix it. It was her duty to fix it.

Precious Audrey, Laurel, and Sage had given their lives for the cause, and Victoria realized that she herself had given even more than that. When the awakening forest seized her, co-opted her, she had not understood its intent. She had struggled and screamed, terrified that the writhing explosion of life wanted to kill her. But no, that hadn't been correct at all.

Her spell had awakened an avalanche of exuberant, uncontrollable life, replenishing all that the Lifedrinker had taken, and the magic needed Victoria as a conduit. Even as the vines wrapped around her, plunged into her mouth, and nose, and ears . . . after the writhing plants held her open and assaulted her, the surge of magic was merely trying to make her something *more*, to build her into a woman so filled with the energy of life that she could guide the whole world's reawakening. She would let it flow like a flash flood of fresh growth bursting from the broken dam of Roland's evil sorcery.

When Victoria stood up in the heart of the primeval jungle and extended her arms, she saw that her skin was the mottled green of countless leaves. Her hands were large and powerful, the fingers like small branches. Her muscles were coiled and twisted like sturdy wind-lashed trees. Rising taller, she could feel her limbs creaking as if she were a redwood that towered over the forest. Her vision was shattered and dizzying, as if she saw through countless eyes. She heard the loud hum of bees, saw the colorful flurry of birds, swarms of bright butterflies, fresh blossoms bursting open like a magician's celebratory trick at a wedding party.

Victoria was the embodiment of all this life energy, but she still remained *herself*. With the release of the fecundity spell and the sacrifices she had made, the price she had paid, Victoria contained the sum of fertility—green, vibrant, and feminine. Through her own body and her own soul, she had given birth to life everywhere. In the new forest, she could feel the trees growing and spreading, the perimeter of her reclaimed green territory expanding like a bold army that meant to conquer the Scar, and much more.

This was just the beginning of her work. Victoria would do more than restore the world to the way it had been. Why stop there? Why limit herself at all? After the parade of armies and warlords, after thousands of years of bloody history, mankind had caused tremendous damage.

The spell she had unleashed was extremely powerful, and the magic was as wild and unpredictable as life itself, but for so great a task, Victoria required lieutenants. And she knew exactly where to find them.

Her three acolytes had already given everything. They had believed in her dream and had never questioned her instructions. Even though Simon had insulted her memmers and tried to make her feel irrelevant to the work of Cliffwall, those girls had been utterly loyal. Victoria would reward them now. With the rejuvenated gift so strong within her, she had the power to do anything.

In the swarming, boiling army of life that arose from the desolation, she reached out with her mind and her magic, searching in the dense underbrush, the swelling weeds and shrubbery, the vines that tilled the soil. She found long-forgotten seeds and sparked them awake.

The bodies of Audrey, Laurel, and Sage had become a matrix for the regrowth. Their blood had spilled into the channels Victoria carved in the barren ground, where now the thickest roots and vines swelled, building and strengthening that spell-form. But her acolytes' bodies were more than just fertilizer—they were catalysts.

Victoria found the remains of the young women and rebuilt them, pulling together the strands of their bones, reweaving their muscles, using soft plant tissue to re-create their flesh. She did not intend just to restore the three as they were, however. She would make Audrey, Laurel, and Sage into forest guardians as well. They needed to be strong enough to combat those who would inevitably try to stop her miraculous work.

After she re-created the bodies of the three women as constructs of the living forest, Victoria bent close to the figures and exhaled, blowing the tingle of irresistible life force into the parted lips of first Sage, then Audrey, then Laurel.

The bodies roused, and moved. When their eyes opened, the irises sparkled green as if made from the overlapped carapaces of jewel beetles. The young women breathed hard; they opened their new lips and flicked out pink tongues, exposing sharp white teeth. Their matted hair was lush, like Spanish moss, and they extended their arms and flexed their muscles to show off astonishingly beautiful forms, the perfect embodiments of femininity, of life magic, of the energy of lust and creation.

Awake and aware now, the acolytes looked at Victoria with wonder, admiring what she had become. Victoria could not see her own body, but she felt its power, its ominous beauty, and the potential she contained.

"Victoria," said Sage, but she was no longer Sage; she was but one component of the three-part manifestation of the unstoppable spell.

"Mother," echoed Laurel and Audrey.

Yes, Victoria thought, I am the mother now. The mother of all things.

"We have great work to accomplish. We have the power, the magic, and the will to do what must be done. My original intent was just to restore this valley, make it as fertile and pristine as it once was. Now I know that my ambitions were too limited. I have been given a gift, and I now bear a tremendous responsibility. Through me, you all have the same duty."

She looked at them. "With the acorn from the Eldertree, we have the magic and the spark. It is time to restore the original primeval forest across the Scar and spread it throughout the land, so that the whole world can once again be perfect, as it was when the Creator first manifested his vision."

Victoria's dark green lips curved in a smile. Her three beautiful acolytes nodded. She added, "A world lush and untouched. And without humans to sully it."

CHAPTER 61

After seeing the burgeoning area of growth at the heart of the Scar, a curious and awestruck Simon led another expedition from Cliffwall, rushing out to see what had happened. The people were guardedly optimistic. Life was returning to the great valley.

Simon made his best effort to find Victoria and invite her to join them, but when no one could find her, he heaved a sigh. "We cannot wait. Let us go see this miracle."

As the group descended the plateau wall and headed out across the still-barren landscape, the glimpse of green in the distance made Thistle chatter with excitement. She walked close beside Nicci. "Maybe it won't take so long! Maybe the valley will be green again, just like I dreamed, and I'll have a chance to see it in my lifetime."

"The sorceress gave you all a second chance." Nathan tossed his straight white hair and strode along beside Bannon, who kept his hand near the pommel of his sword, pretending to be alert for dangers.

Nicci glanced back to Nathan. "I helped kill the evil wizard, but do not credit me with this rebirth. It was not my doing."

Nathan said, "Perhaps the Eldertree still had a remnant of energy that the Lifedrinker did not quench after all. That might have triggered this reawakening."

Nicci regarded the verdant haze of forest that had already spread across the desolation. Even from a distance, she could hear a stir of plants and branches, the buzz of life. "So much growth . . ." She frowned at the swell of green ahead of them. "I am concerned unless I understand it."

Nathan raised an eyebrow. "You find fault in an overabundance of life, Sorceress? After so much desolation, this is a good thing, is it not?"

Her eyes narrowed. "Is it?"

Sooner than expected, they reached the edge of the lush vegetation, as if the swath of growth had moved outward at great speed to meet them. The air was humid with vegetation, thick with the smell of grasses, leaves, pollen, and the sickly sweet odor of explosive blossoms.

Thistle gaped. "I've never seen anything like this."

Simon stretched his arms outward to welcome the furiously insistent jungle. "It's marvelous!" Towering ferns unfurled, and trees stretched and cracked, rising impossibly high in such a short period, as if time itself had accelerated to let the forest catch up for all that had been lost to the Lifedrinker.

Branches stretched and strained, unfurling countless leaves. Twigs rustled as they proliferated. Vines swirled back and forth like twitching tentacles. To Nicci's ears, the stir of rampant fertility sounded sinister, restless . . . even dangerous.

The tree trunks enlarged as they grew at a manic pace, groaning with the agony of too much life. The stirring branches sounded like slashing blades. The plants spread a blur of pollen throughout the air. Shrubs and flowers spat seeds, and mushrooms flung spores in all directions. Grasses rose up whispering and hissing.

As the group from Cliffwall stood marveling at the unexpected sight, more shoots sprang up, grasses and weeds extending from the perimeter to reclaim more of the parched desolation. This primeval jungle expanded at a tremendous pace.

"Sweet Sea Mother!" At first, Bannon grinned in amazement, but the awestruck wonder on his face shifted to an expression of concern. "Isn't that a little too fast?"

Bees and beetles hummed and whirred through the air. A dark mist of gnats rose up like a wave.

Simon shouted into the forest, as if he could summon a greater presence. "Thank you! We are grateful for the return of life."

A stirring occurred among the trees and branches, and larger shapes flitted through the green angled shadows: human figures, *female* figures—naked, shapely women whose mottled skin provided perfect camouflage among the leaves. The branches and vines parted to reveal the three women standing before the gathered scholars.

The young women were as lush as the forest itself, their breasts and hips swollen with life, their hair a tangle of matted leaves and moss. They looked alien, their transformed bodies more forest than human. Their features were still recognizable, still familiar.

Bannon gasped. His lips curled in an uncertain smile. "Laurel? Audrey? Sage?"

When the three figures moved forward, the undergrowth flowed along with them. Their eyes flashed an iridescent green. Victoria's acolytes throbbed with fertility, the essence of the forest and life itself. They exuded a wafting and irresistible pull of attractive scent, like an animal in heat. Even Nathan seemed affected by their presence, along with Simon and all the other men in the group. The sexual shimmer pervaded the air.

Bannon breathed heavily. Perspiration covered his skin, and he flushed with longing. The look on his face was one of yearning and impossible separation. "You were gone," he said. "I didn't know where you went. I looked for you."

Laurel said with a vibrant giggle, "We waited for you, Bannon." The other two young women echoed her sentiment.

"We wanted you here."

"With us."

Simon was even more insistent. His mouth was drawn back with male need, his eyes shining, even glazed. At the front of the group, he pushed forward, blocking the others. "So much life, so much hope," he said. "We want you. *I* want you!"

"Yes, come closer," said Sage, fixing her attention on him. "We want you too. We want you all."

Bannon tried to join him, but the scholar-archivist pushed him aside, raising his hands. He didn't even seem aware of what he was doing. "You brought back the forest," Simon cried. "You counteracted the Lifedrinker's curse. It is wondrous!"

The three green forest women reached out to welcome him. "There is enough, enough for all," said Audrey. Their soft and yearning fingers suddenly transformed into pointed wooden spikes. Their nails curved and became the sharpest of thorns.

Drunk on the thick, seductive scent in the air, Simon didn't notice. His eyes were heavy-lidded, his mouth open in a gasp of a smile. When the forest women tore him apart, he didn't even have time to scream. They stabbed him with wooden-spike fingers, raked him open with thorn claws. They sliced and unwrapped his flesh, peeling it away as if stripping the bark from a fallen tree.

Several scholars screamed as they scrambled back. Some let out moans of disbelief. "Simon!" cried Mia.

Releasing a burst of defensive magic, Nicci knocked the rest of her companions away, sweeping them out of reach of the grasping, deadly women.

Bannon shouted in dismay. "Laurel, no! Audrey, Sage!"

Astonishingly, when the forest women tossed Simon's butchered corpse onto the barren ground beyond the fringe of the expanding forest, his blood was like a magical elixir, a potent life-giving spell. As the red droplets soaked into the dead soil, new roots writhed about like earthworms. Shoots of green grass and unfurling leaves lifted upward to form a carpet in the fading shape of a man.

When the young women laughed, it came as the sound of a storm in thick trees.

Nathan and Bannon drew their swords. Nicci stood ready to release her magic if the vicious women lunged after them. "Beware, the attack could come from anywhere." But the three acolytes did not step beyond the edge of the growing forest.

Even Nicci did not expect what they all saw next. Weeds, vines, and thorny brambles continued to erupt from the spilled blood in the pattern of Simon's body, but in the thicker jungle, trees rustled, and the undergrowth backed away as if bowing to a powerful lord. The three deadly forest women respectfully moved apart as a larger form emerged from the forest: a throbbing female titan with skin like bark, leaves, and moss, a naked body with enormous swaying breasts, the broad waist and hips of a gigantic oak, and hair made of vines and ferns. Her face no longer carried even a hint of matronly kindness.

Victoria . . . or, what had once been Victoria.

The fearsome forest woman towered above the gathered people from Cliffwall, and her voice boomed out. "This is my forest, and you are no longer welcome here—nor in this world." She focused her startling, burning eyes on Nicci, who returned the gaze defiantly, not backing down. Victoria added in a mocking tone, "For I am *Life's* Mistress."

Branches cracked. Leaves and branches swelled, and the explosive outpouring of growth continued to spread.

CHAPTER 62

Nicci did not like to retreat under any circumstances, but the insane jungle was too unpredictable and could easily tear the Cliffwall scholars to pieces. As well as Thistle.

She pulled the girl to safety, away from the thrashing forest. The scholars' faces were filled with despair after the slaughter of Simon and the monstrous appearance of Victoria and her acolytes, but she shouted, driving them into action, "Get back!"

Nathan and Bannon helped to herd the Cliffwall people away from the boundary of the deadly jungle, and the others needed little encouragement to run.

Nicci glared at the swollen, transformed figure of Victoria. The green female *thing* had an uncontrolled, hungry magic similar to Roland's—and just like Roland, Victoria would have to be stopped. For this, Nicci suspected they might need a weapon even more powerful than the Eldertree acorn.

And the Sorceress must save the world. Maybe she wasn't done here yet after all.

As the panicked scholars fled back to the uplift of the plateau, Bannon withdrew into a sense of sick denial after what he had seen the three young women do to Simon. "Sweet Sea Mother, they were so beautiful, so loving and kind. I loved them, and they loved me."

"They loved you so much, they wanted your blood," Nicci said. "They would have torn you apart, but Simon paid the price for you."

Bannon shook his head. "We have to save them! They're entangled in an evil spell, but I know their hearts are good. We can bring them back, I know it."

Nicci frowned at him. "Don't delude yourself with unrealistic hopes, Bannon Farmer. Those things are no longer the women you knew. We will certainly have to kill them."

The young man stared at her, his mouth open in disbelief. "No, it can't be. My life was happy, almost perfect for once. . . ."

With an understanding nod, the wizard squeezed his shoulder. "Sometimes outward beauty only masks a darkness inside."

When they finally climbed back up the slope and returned to the hidden archive inside the plateau, Nathan strode directly toward the large library chambers, wasting no time. "Once again, we need to learn about a corrupt, uncontrolled spell," he said, "so we can fight it."

Nicci turned Thistle about, leading her toward their quarters. "I will destroy her, just as I destroyed the Lifedrinker."

The girl hung her head, sniffling. "I just wanted to see my valley restored, but that jungle is almost as bad as the Scar." Her voice hitched as if her throat were full of tears.

"We must eradicate both threats and help the valley return to normal, without being crushed by evil masters," Nicci said. "That is what Lord Rahl stands for." She touched the girl's curly mass of hair, and Thistle looked up at her with complete faith. "That is precisely why we are here."

"I know," Thistle said.

With no clear leaders, the people of Cliffwall turned desperately to Nathan and Nicci for answers. The old wizard buried himself in the archives again, absorbing volume after volume, scroll after scroll, so that he could counteract the dark fecundity that "Life's Mistress" had clumsily unleashed.

Mousy, dedicated Mia hovered by Nathan's side, reading documents with lightning speed, tracing her fingertips over the handwritten lines. She could take in the gist of the text and cull out the important books she felt Nathan should read.

Nicci, though, decided to seek information in a more direct fashion. Because the memmers held the knowledge within their minds, she interrogated Victoria's people face-to-face.

Marching into one of the classroom chambers where the memmers would recite their lessons, she faced them with her hands planted on the curve of her hips. "Victoria commanded you to search for fertility spells, horticulture magic, even restorative lore that could be applied to wildfire damage in forests. One of you must have recalled the dark spell that she used." She narrowed her eyes, looking for an unexpected flush or a wary flinch among the memmers. "Someone pointed her to whatever incantation or blood magic she invoked. I need to know what it was."

"Victoria wanted to save the valley and save us all," said Franklin, blinking his owlish eyes. "She had only the best of intentions. We all wanted to help."

"Best of intentions?" Nicci's glare froze them as if she were a predator about to pounce. "You never learned the Wizard's Second Rule."

Gloria, a plump and earnest young memmer, frowned. Her lower lip trembled. "The Wizard's Second Rule? What is that? Is it in the archives?"

"Any student of magical lore should know it. *The greatest harm can result from the best intentions.* Victoria proved exactly that. Rather than patiently waiting for nature to reclaim the valley, she unleashed even more dangerous magic, and now it is out of control. With her good intentions, Victoria may well have doomed us all, unless we can find a way to stop her."

Gloria swallowed hard. "But how can we undo what she's done?"

"First, we must understand the magic she used, the exact spell she triggered. Did one of you help her to find it?"

The memmers fidgeted uncomfortably in their memorization room. Franklin said, "She hoped one of us might recall something that we had committed to memory, but there were so many possibilities, none of them clear. She wanted to help the valley grow back faster."

Nicci's voice was sharp. "I can tell when you are lying." They feared she was using some rare truth-sensing magic, but she did not need that. She could see their nervous twitches, their averted eyes, the sweat sparkling on their skin. She raised her voice into loud command. "Which spell did Victoria use? Tell me what blood magic she invoked to trigger that wild growth."

Gloria flinched. "It was an ancient fecundity spell, one that could awaken the earth. It was in an obscure language we didn't exactly know how to pronounce or interpret."

Nicci straightened her back. "So she unleashed such a terrible spell without recalling how to say the words?"

"She knew," Franklin said defensively. "We all knew. Memmers remember perfectly from generation to generation."

Nicci pressed harder. "You are saying that what we saw out there in the Scar, that explosive deadly growth, was exactly what Victoria *intended*?"

The memmers were embarrassed. Franklin finally gathered the courage to answer. "We do remember some fertility spells, but we don't know how to counteract them. Very few ancient wizards ever wanted to *stop* life, growth, and prosperity."

"There were some reciprocal spells," Gloria admitted, "but they are dim in our minds, relegated to minutiae. The details were not considered useful, and our ancestors already had so much to remember and preserve."

"Write down whatever you remember, and I will study the information," Nicci said.

Gloria went to a podium in their memorization room, on which an open tome rested on display. During their daily lessons, the acolytes often listened to a speaker, committing line by line to memory. Instead of reading aloud now, Gloria picked up a quill pen, dipped the sharpened end into an inkpot, and began to scratch out words on a scrap of paper. She paused, closed her eyes to summon the details, then wrote more words. She kept her hand on the paper. "This is the spell that Victoria used. I think."

Franklin came forward to study Gloria's letters, corrected one piece of punctuation, altered one word. The memmers gathered around, nodding as they proofread. Once they all agreed on the precise formula and the arcane words, they handed the paper to Nicci.

As she scanned the spell, most of the words were mere gibberish to her. "Nathan might be better informed than I." She tucked the paper into the fold pocket of her dress, then extended a finger, scolding the memmers. "Ransack all the knowledge inside you. Find some way that we can fix the damage Victoria has caused."

From the window alcove on the outer side of the plateau wall, Nicci gazed across the tortured valley, where a crimson sunset deepened like the blood of the sacrifices Victoria had shed. She had given the written spell to Nathan, who read with great eagerness, then deep concern.

"This is every bit as bad as I anticipated. Perhaps worse. The power invoked comes from a language even older than High D'Haran. It will be difficult for us to find a magic powerful enough to overturn it."

"Richard did not send us out to solve simple problems," Nicci pointed out.

"Of course. I just wanted you to appreciate the magnitude of the challenge."

As the red-gold rays of dusk fell over the broad valley, she concentrated on the swarming forest at its core, the primeval jungle that glowed an unhealthy green.

Drawn by the view as well, Bannon joined her, gazing out with a forlorn expression. "First, all life was draining away in the world, and now there's an unstoppable *flood* of life. How do we fight it?"

"We will find a way," Nicci said. "And then I myself will destroy the woman who calls herself Life's Mistress."

"I want to do something, too," Bannon said. "You and Nathan can study all the books to look for a solution. You both understand the magic and can read mysterious languages, but I'm just waiting here, feeling useless. Like I was when we waited for a weapon against the Lifedrinker." He sighed in obvious frustration. "You admitted that I *can* be useful, Sorceress. Isn't there something I could do?"

"Help the farmers harvest crops. Tend the flocks, work the orchards," Nicci suggested. "Learn a skill, perhaps as a carpenter."

Anger flashed across his face. "That's not what I mean! There's got to be some way to save Audrey, Laurel, and Sage." His face was wrenched with helplessness. "I love them."

"And they are hungry for you. Remember what they did to Simon."

His expression grew steely. "We need to understand what is happening out there, Sorceress. You know I can handle myself. I'm going to go on a scout, and I'll come back and tell you what I see."

"That's a foolish risk," Nicci said.

"You've called me a fool before! I want to do this. Don't try to stop me."

"I cannot stop you, Bannon Farmer, but if you are going to expose yourself to such great and unnecessary danger, at least make certain you return with valuable information."

He lifted his chin, relieved that she didn't argue with him further. "I will."

Looking long and hard at him, Nicci added in a softer voice, "And be careful."

CHAPTER 63

Being surrounded by so many books and so much knowledge usually exhilarated Nathan. The secrets and stories contained in those soft, well-worn volumes had made his centuries of captivity a little more tolerable in the Palace of the Prophets. The Sisters' huge library held countless tomes describing magic that Nathan could never use, thanks to the wards, webs, and shields woven throughout the palace architecture, not to mention the iron collar of his Rada'Han. Still, reading the legends, histories, even folktales had brought joy to his tedious existence.

When Lord Rahl's star shift had made all books on prophecy useless and irrelevant, he had offered to let Nathan keep one small library for his own entertainment, perhaps even out of nostalgia, but the wizard soon decided that what he really wanted was not to bury himself in old archives but to go out and live his life, to write his own story. And that was exactly what he did.

He patted the mysterious leather-bound life book the witch woman had given him. Now he had other reading to do. Vital reading.

He let out a weary sigh as dutiful Mia brought him a new stack of volumes. "I have no idea what these contain, Wizard Rahl, but they look interesting." Mia got directly to work, showing him a tome at random. Many of these new books looked waterlogged, scuffed, or tattered. "Somewhere in our archive we'll find a way to stop Victoria. Cliffwall has every answer, if only we can find it."

Nathan chuckled. "Are you suggesting the ancient wizards in the time of Baraccus and Merritt knew all there is to know?"

The studious woman's brow furrowed as if he had questioned her reason for existence. "Why, of course! This is *Cliffwall*. All knowledge was placed here for safekeeping. *All* knowledge."

He drew two fingers down his chin and gave her an indulgent look. "I'm glad you have such faith in the ancients."

Mia nodded. "They were much more powerful than anyone alive now."

"But if they had all that knowledge, then why did they fail?"

She responded with a stern look. "Just because knowledge exists, doesn't mean people know how to *use it*."

"Well, I wish I had your confidence, young woman." Nathan peeled open the cover of the book he had chosen, frowning to see that the pages were swollen and rippled, as if they had been soaked in water and improperly dried. Some of the pages were torn, the ink smudged and unreadable. He brushed clumpy dust off the cover of the next book in the stack. "Where did these volumes come from? Did you dig them out of a hole?"

Mia looked embarrassed. "After the sorceress opened the sealed vault beneath the damaged tower, our laborers used picks and chisels to break into other previously inaccessible chambers. Some of the books had been partly fused into walls, others buried under rubble. No one has looked at them yet, but I wanted you to see them right away, in case they were important."

He picked up a third book, trying to decipher the embossed symbols on the cover. "I thought the damaged tower contained only books on prophecy. I doubt they will help."

"No, the prophecy sections were in the upper levels. In the final days of building Cliffwall, the ancient wizards were in a panic to finish, being hunted down by the forces of Emperor Sulachan. The lower vaults were piled with last-minute additions. No one has seen them except you, Wizard Rahl."

"Then I am absolutely delighted by the opportunity, my dear." He patted the empty chair beside him. "Would you help me study them? I only have two eyes, and together we could read twice as fast."

Mia beamed. "I'd like that." She sat beside him, chose a book at random, and began working her way through the smudged and faded letters.

Deep within the resurgent forest—which was her heart, her very soul—Victoria felt the magic of reawakened life pulsing through her . . . and, by extension, through everything she had made, the burgeoning life that came from the stillborn ground. The tortured Scar had been as painful to her as the stillborn baby that she and Bertram had so wanted to have.

But unlike her bloody and painful miscarriages, Victoria now had the power she had always longed to have: a woman's power to create and nurture life. As proof, she needed only to look out at the flourishing new jungle she had created. The growth charged forth like a wild stampede, but Victoria didn't want to control it, not at all. She wanted it to fill the valley, roll over the mountains, and sweep across the continent, pristine, primeval, and unstoppable.

Life would triumph over death. Her unquenchable victory would overtake all efforts to stop it. "Victory" . . . the very word was in her name. She was Victoria. She was Life's Mistress. Within her, she had a power to rival the Creator Himself.

As she pondered her new role, thickets rose and swirled around her body. Thorny vines and flowers exuded a heady, hypnotic perfume. The trees grew so swiftly they swelled, shattered, and toppled over. And then even the splintered trunks hosted swarming worms and beetle grubs, as well as fungi and molds that churned the fallen tree into mulch, which became fertilizer for more life.

And yet more life.

Her acolytes, who wielded the same energy of vibrant fertility, had gone separately across the primeval jungle. They were stewards of the reawakened life now, nurturing the trees, the insects, the birds, and more. Victoria would see to that. The world would once again be pristine.

As Life's Mistress, she would never be satisfied to merely return this valley to its former baseline, an exploited landscape with enslaved herds and rigidly defined croplands. Victoria understood now what her true role in the world was. All the generations of memmers and their preserved ancient lore had led to this. Victoria could not be content with memorization for its own sake; she had to find those powerful spell-forms, the maps of magic that would let her accomplish what was necessary.

As her unnatural body thrived and the tendrils of her forest conquered the barren territory, her mind unlocked more of what it remembered, revealing esoteric and deadly magic that she could use.

The wizard Nathan and the sorceress Nicci had searched for a way to destroy the Lifedrinker, and she had no doubt they were applying themselves with as much determination to eliminate *her*—and Victoria would not stand for it. She felt the power of life, the power of the Creator, and knew she was stronger than any magic those two adversaries could hurl against her.

Even so, she did not underestimate their abilities.

Although Nicci claimed credit for killing the evil Lifedrinker, Victoria knew that the Eldertree acorn was truly responsible for that triumph. The sorceress was undeniably powerful, nevertheless, and Victoria did not want to be hindered in her sacred work. She already knew that Nicci was a nuisance, interfering where she was not wanted.

Although Nathan Rahl's ability to use magic was minimal, perhaps even imaginary, he was a man with great knowledge and experience, and thus a threat to her as well. There was something about the man, and Victoria did not wish to be sanguine about him, either.

They both must be stopped.

In the thriving thickets, trees, vines, and mushrooms swelled around her like a bubbling life spring. The buzz of swarming flies, bees, and beetles hummed an intense lullaby. As her wisdom and power expanded, Victoria recalled forgotten methods and incantations that the ancient wizards had sealed behind the camouflage shroud, preserved for millennia among the memmers.

With that knowledge, Victoria understood how to create a weapon to eradicate both Nicci and Nathan, perhaps a weapon strong enough to tear down Cliffwall, stone by stone. To activate the magic, Victoria didn't even need to move, because she *was* the forest, all the stirrings within, all the leaves and branches, the wings of insects, the flutter of birds. Everything belonged to her, was part of her.

She released the magic to create her emissary, an assassin, a manifestation of the jungle's primeval power: a *shaksis*. A *shaksis* was a creature molded entirely of debris, the detritus of the forest.

With her mind and her magic, Victoria gathered up fallen branches and gnarled twigs to serve as the bones and framework for the *shaksis*. She wove them together, building a wooden skeleton around which, with whiplike speed, she wound grass blades and dry leaves, forest mulch, and thorny twigs. Fungi inflated to fill out the muscles.

Victoria summoned an army of worms, beetles, maggots, and other crawling creatures to expand the creature's body. By the time the magical construct extended its arms and took tentative steps, its entire form boiled with a thousand points of life.

Two iridescent beetles, each as large as a fist, scuttled along the forest floor and crawled up the thing's body framework. Its rounded head was woven of bent twigs and supple willow, skinned with bark, thatched with dry grasses. Two hollows formed in what should have been its face, and the beetles crawled up the construct's head and nestled into the sockets to serve as surrogate eyes. A splintered branch across its lower face made a gash of a mouth. It clacked and chewed, broken spikes grinding together.

Pale green vines looped around its legs, winding and weaving into its flesh, like blood vessels filled with sap. The *shaksis* creaked as it stepped forward. It folded and unfolded its sharp branchlet fingers, while the two beetles inside its eye sockets stared out with a faceted, malevolent gaze.

Made of the jungle itself, the *shaksis* was Victoria's puppet, her surrogate, her killer, a soulless thing that was merely an extension of the primeval forest.

Victoria flashed it a warm and welcoming smile, a maternal smile. She stroked the uneven chest, feeling the life she had deposited there, a new child she had created. Into its hollow mind, she placed the details of its mission—images of the blond sorceress and the pompous old wizard with straight white hair.

"Find them and kill them," Victoria said. "Go with my blessing."

The animated construct turned and, with a rustle of brittle limbs, stalked out of the forest toward Cliffwall.

CHAPTER 64

As he scouted through the gathering darkness, Bannon felt brave and important. After all his ordeals, he no longer hid from his past, no longer pretended that those dark memories didn't exist. He was not just Bannon, the son of a man who drank himself into blind violence and abused his family, a bitter man who drowned helpless kittens and beat his own wife to death. No, Bannon was no longer defined by his father.

Standing tall, he marched into the moonlit night on his scouting mission, wending his way through the still-dead foothills. Though the grasses and scrub trees were dry and brittle, he no longer felt the Lifedrinker's poison oozing from the hillsides. This was more like a normal landscape after a long winter: not dead but dormant, waiting to reawaken with spring. Now that the evil wizard was defeated, seeds would germinate, shoots would arise, meadows and forests would creep back.

But Victoria had been too impatient for that natural process. With a sick feeling in the pit of his stomach, Bannon considered the harm she had done with her explosive fecundity spell. Rather than letting the Scar awaken of its own accord, Victoria had effectively dashed icy water into the face of a deeply ill person.

He gritted his teeth as he trudged into the night, making his way toward the expanding jungle boundary. He paused to rest near a moonlit boulder and took out his waterskin to drink while he listened to the vast starlit darkness. He could sense the vibrating power of the proliferating forest and could hear the inevitable sounds of cracking, straining branches, growing trunks, writhing vines, stirring leaves. Combined, it sounded like evil laughter.

A sad shiver ran down his spine. He knew that Audrey, Laurel, and Sage were there in that mass of wild growth, corrupted by Victoria's out-of-control magic. His heart ached for them. He remembered their touch, their kisses, their laughter. He smiled to think of their warm breath in his ears, how he had loved to stroke their hair, touch their bodies. They couldn't be gone now! They were beautiful, wonderful, loving.

Then he fought back a wave of nausea as he recalled what they had done to Simon. If the scholar-archivist had not shoved him out of the way in his eagerness to go forward, *Bannon* would have been the one ripped into ribbons of meat, his blood spilled onto the soil to spawn more of their awful magic.

He pressed his knuckles hard into his eyes, wanting that memory to be just a dream, a nightmare . . . but it was real, in exactly the way his mother's murder had been real, the way he had abandoned Ian to the slavers. It was not a memory he could pretend would ever go away.

Feeling the hairs tingle on the back of his neck, he stepped away from the boulder, alert, sniffing the air. He whirled and looked above him to see Mrra crouched on the rock outcropping, her feline form sandy gold in the moonlight. The big cat let out a growling purr, but Bannon did not feel threatened. The sand panther knew who he was, possibly even understood that he was the one who had begged Nicci to heal her wounds, rather than kill her.

Mrra just sat there watching the night. As Bannon studied the powerful tawny form and the ugly symbols branded onto her hide, he was no longer reminded of the helpless drowned kittens. He was glad he had saved her, and in a sense, he had saved part of himself as well. Those limp, dead kittens had been a symbol of grief and guilt. The Adjudicator had found that agonizing experience inside him and dragged it to the front of Bannon's mind as his damnation.

Running away from Chiriya Island, he had sought a life for himself, not just for adventure but for self-preservation. Since then, he had found all he could have hoped for by joining Nathan and Nicci. He had discovered not just exciting adventures, but friendship, acceptance, and inner strength.

He realized that he had been fooling himself with the illusion of a perfect life, but the things he had discovered since venturing out into the world were so much more. More than anything, he remembered the look of respect and appreciation that Nicci had given him after he helped her kill the Lifedrinker. He had risked his life, given his all, and they had been victorious together. He didn't think his life could get better than that moment. Such thoughts eased his heavy memories of the bad things that had happened to him.

With a swish of her tail, Mrra vanished like a moon shadow into the night. After taking another swig of water, Bannon made his way onward, still hoping against hope that he could save the young acolytes who had so captured his heart, although he feared it might be too late.

The moon had set, and the night held its breath while waiting for the dawn. When Bannon finally reached the edge of the ever-spreading jungle, the demarcation was abrupt, with desolation on one side and a madness of foliage on the other. He could smell the leaves and the resinous wood, the potent aromas of wild vegetation.

Sword raised, Bannon faced the primeval forest, hoping he would not have to go inside. The twitching branches and gnarled, spasming vines unsettled him, but he shored up his courage. Drawing a deep breath, he called out, "I've come for you!" He meant to shout, but it came out as no more than a whisper. His voice cracked.

The vegetation snaked and curled. In the starlight, as his pupils dilated with fear, he spotted more movement, heard a stirring that was more than frenetically growing plants. They had heard him.

Beautiful feminine forms glided between the trunks, branches, and undulating vines. Even with the camouflage of their mottled skin, he could make out the beautiful bodies that were so familiar to him.

He said, "I came to save you."

Though the young women were fundamentally transformed, he still recognized Audrey, Laurel, and Sage. His breath was hot in his mouth, and his pulse raced. He had seen what these forest women could do, and he knew they were monsters . . . yet still he wanted them. Their enhanced scent was thick in the air, making him dizzy.

"Come with me," he begged. "We can go back to Cliffwall. We'll find a spell to make you normal again. Don't you want to be with me?"

They laughed in unison, a musical sound that made all the branches stir. "Don't be silly," said the thing that had been Sage. "We are so much more now. Why don't you come with us? Think of how we could pleasure you with all of our new skills."

Bannon could barely breathe. His vision blurred. They seemed more intensely lovely than he remembered them, more than anyone he'd ever seen, any woman he could imagine. Something about their scent . . .

Flowers suddenly sprang up all around them, a spray of intense violet-and-crimson blossoms that he recognized with a shudder. The deathrise flower! The smell made him dizzy, and in the back of his mind he knew that Nicci must have been wrong about these blossoms, because surely this was the most beautiful, exquisite poison in the world!

Unbidden, he took a step forward. The three young women extended their emerald arms, exuding a mist of attracting chemicals. The lovely, but deadly, flowers bloomed around them.

Tears filled Bannon's eyes, because he *wanted* them so much. He remembered how wonderful they were, how sweet and caring, how innocent, and yet how skilled when they had made love to him.

"We can be together," he said, "if only you'll just—"

Laurel interrupted him. "Yes, we can be together. Always."

"We want you now more than ever," said Audrey. "We are more fertile, more filled with desire."

"We can be everything you want," Sage added. "And you will give us everything we need."

They spread their arms, and their breasts beckoned him. Their dark green nipples looked like flower buds. Bannon yearned for them. He had meant to come and argue, to fight to take them back. The sword felt slick in his hand. Even with its leather grip, his palms were so sweaty, he could barely hold on.

"Come to us, Bannon," said Laurel.

The other two echoed the invitation.

He could not resist. He succumbed, gliding toward the edge of the jungle.

With a great blow, a growling, furred form crashed into him. The full weight of a sand panther knocked him off his feet and tumbled him out of the reach of the vicious forest girls.

The beautiful apparitions snarled, their mouths opening to reveal long woody fangs. Their arms stretched out, coiled with vines, corded muscles, and tendons. Their fingers reached out for him, tipped with hooked thorns. The smooth, perfect green skin on their arms became studded with deadly barbs that dripped with milky venom.

Gasping, Bannon rolled over and tried to catch his breath. The spell was broken. Mrra bounded away, then circled back, snarling. The forest women reached out with a thorn-studded embrace, trying to catch Bannon before he got out of reach.

He instinctively slashed with Sturdy, lopping off one of Audrey's arms. It dropped to the ground, and its severed stump twitched, extended, and grew roots, digging deep into the ground while the arm continued to grope upward for him.

Howling, Audrey raised the stump of her arm, and a new limb grew from the severed end, a tangle of vines, muscles, and blood vessels re-emerging to restore her.

Bannon hacked at them, swinging his sword sideways, then up, then back down, splintering the female forms. They did not bleed red, but spilled oozing green sap.

"I wanted to save you," he cried.

The three just laughed as they regrew into contorted new forms with additional branchlike arms that sprang from their shoulders and torsos. Their hair became a wild, marshy tangle of strands.

The sand panther retreated, growling to Bannon. He backed away onto the rocky, desolate ground where the forest avatars could not yet go. From their verdant refuge, they simply glared at him, and Bannon stared back, sobbing. Tears ran down his cheeks. "I thought I loved you."

"We will have you again," the women said in a single rasping voice like dry leaves crackling in a fire. "We will have you forever."

CHAPTER 65

The broad grin on Nathan's face made Nicci immediately suspicious. "I may just know where to find the answer, Sorceress!" The old wizard stopped her in the hallway as she made her way to her chambers, where Thistle was already asleep.

She allowed herself a moment of hope. "You are certain of this spell?"

Nathan's smile faltered. "'Certainty' is an overused term, to be sure. I am confident, let us leave it at that. See here." He set the thick volume on a bench in one of the corridors.

He opened the pages, drew his fingers down a line of archaic text. "It is just a clue, but the best clue we've had. You already gave me the incantation and the spell-form that the memmers think Victoria used, and that provided some excellent parameters for a counterspell or a weapon. We knew the essence of what we were fighting, but not how to do so."

He tapped a stained page where tight handwriting had run together as the ink dissolved. "This gives us somewhere to look, a listing of other books that also shed more light about the Lifedrinker."

"He is no longer a concern," Nicci said. "I killed him."

"Yes, yes, but think of how they are connected. Roland's spell stole too much from the world, and now Victoria's will restore too much. It is all a matter of control, finding a way to modulate the flow of hungry magic, the power of giving and taking."

"Like a valve," Nicci said, unconsciously biting her lower lip. "The

Lifedrinker said he had opened up the magic with his spell, but the flow was too strong. He could not stop himself."

"And neither can Victoria," Nathan said. "Both Roland and Victoria were conduits for the magic. When you destroyed the Lifedrinker, you shut off his flow of death. Now we must destroy Victoria and stop the flow in the opposite direction."

"I couldn't agree more," Nicci said. She looked up as three scholars hurried past them, eager for their dinner. Another middle-aged man strolled by, holding an open book in his hands, reading as he walked. She continued, "I simply need to know how to do it."

Nathan pointed at the stained pages again. "This listing identifies a volume we need to find, and I have reason to believe it is buried in the vault beneath the damaged tower, where those other scattered books were hidden. It is very late now, but we can try to excavate tomorrow."

"And you know where to look?" Nicci asked, thinking of the unexplored maze of damaged rooms and passages underground. "Exactly?"

Nathan smiled. "Mia does."

Though it had left the riotous fecundity of the primeval jungle behind, the *shaksis* could still feel the power of Life's Mistress driving its mission. As the creature walked across the desolate ground on limbs made of twisted vines and leaves, motivated by swarms of worms, spiders, and insects, the *shaksis* kept drawing energy from a distance.

It continued across the desolate Scar through the night. Though parts broke off in the dry rocks and jagged uplifts, the *shaksis* replenished itself with plant matter once it reached the foothills and walked through scrub brush and tangled grasses. The dead vegetation came alive again, whipping around its body, strengthening its limbs, winding like armor around its body core.

Finally, in the darkest hour before dawn, the creature faced the sheer cliff of the plateau uplift. The *shaksis* knew that its two victims were inside the hidden enclave high above.

Because Victoria knew all about Cliffwall, the *shaksis* remembered how to ascend that sheer rock, using the hidden handholds and the faint trail that had isolated the great archive for millennia. The golem of reanimated twigs and vines turned its hollow head upward and stared at the cliff with living-beetle eyes.

An agile person could climb the path to reach the hooded overhang above, but the *shaksis* did not need agility; it had a different kind of power. It reached out with the splayed branches of its hands and touched the stone. With a surge of vibrant life, the fingers grew. Vine tendrils extended and worked their way into the rock, like the roots of a clinging windswept tree. The *shaksis* reached with a branchy arm, slapped its hand higher up, and fastened with root tendrils. Its bulging wooden muscles groaned. The vermin infesting its hollow body skittered around, adding energy, squirming.

The *shaksis* pulled itself upward.

A wooden foot found a notch in the rocks and anchored there, while the tendrils released from the first hand, and it climbed higher, stretching and cracking. The insects and grubs made a simmering, humming sound that was lost in the silent gulf of the night.

Staring through scarab eyes, the *shaksis* ascended. It had little room for thoughts in the dried leaves that filled its head. But it held a vivid image of Nicci, of Nathan.

Its targets.

Shouts awakened Nicci from a deep sleep, and she rolled off her pallet into a fighting crouch, instantly alert and aware. Fortunately, tonight her dreams had not entangled with the sand panther's mind; otherwise she might not have been able to extricate herself quickly enough.

Thistle sprang from her warm sheepskin on the floor and pulled aside the door hanging as more shouts echoed down the corridor, which was lined with shelves of disorganized books. Even where the scholars slept, wall shelves were crammed with old volumes, stacks of scrolls, folded parchments, and documents the students had taken out to read, but not yet reshelved.

Nathan Rahl, exhausted from his studies and eager to ransack the underground vaults the following morning, emerged in rumpled sleeping robes. He fumbled for his ornate sword and drew it from its scabbard, ready to fight, but he had not found the source of the shouting. Nicci joined him.

Then they saw the thing coming toward them, an inhuman soldier made of brambles, wicker, and tangled thorns. It strode forward with a crackle of limbs and an aura of buzzing noises.

One unfortunate scholar emerged from his quarters just as the creature passed. Reacting to a potential target, the thing lashed out. In an instant, its arm grew long spiky thorns, and the limb curved around and impaled the young scholar, whose mouth opened, gaping, then gasping, and finally spurting a gush of blood as the long wooden spikes found his organs. The stalking creature tossed the dead man aside.

Other horrified scholars in the halls screamed; some remained frozen in place, while others fled.

Thistle clung close to Nicci. "What is that monster?"

"I believe it is a *shaksis*," Nathan said. "Made from the detritus of the forest, castaway items from the underbrush."

"What does it want?" cried one of the scholars, dismayed to see the bloody corpse of his comrade still twitching on the floor.

The *shaksis* lurched forward. The buzzing around its body grew louder.

Nicci knew. "Victoria sent the thing. It wants us."

Two bright beetles nestled in the creature's eye sockets turned toward Nicci's voice. Seeing her, the *shaksis* became animated and began to run toward them down the hall.

Turning to face the attacker, Nicci pushed the orphan girl behind her, while Nathan raised his sword. The frightened scholars ducked into their alcoves.

The *shaksis* surged closer, extending arms like wildly growing vines. Its entire body seemed to swarm with small moving bugs and grubs. The reanimated forest creature drove straight toward Nathan and Nicci.

The wizard hacked at the *shaksis* with his sword, as if he were a woodcutter felling an unruly sapling. One of the creature's wooden arms snapped and shattered, then dropped to the stone floor. Insects and worms spilled out like a spray of bizarre, festering blood. The *shaksis* drew back its stump. Twigs, vines, and grasses curled around, extending outward as the limb regrew.

Nathan hacked off its other arm, again wielding his sword like an axe, but this time the *shaksis* regrew even faster. The severed vegetation lashed and whipped, then sprang back into place.

"This will require more than a sword, Wizard." Nicci raised a hand and released a blast of air that rattled into the creature, but it anchored itself, reaching out its branchy arms. It was hollow, woven of wicker, and the breezes whipped and whistled through it. More writhing bugs scuttled across the floor.

"I can't unleash my black lightning or wizard's fire in here," Nicci said. "It would destroy all of the books and the people trapped in the corridor."

The *shaksis* lunged forward, extending its sharp hands. Nathan swept his sword again, letting out a loud grunt with the effort. "There's barely room to swing my blade."

Nicci hammered at the thing with another fist of air. The creature staggered. Books tumbled off the shelves, their pages flapping. In response, the *shaksis* stretched out tangled limbs and seized another scholar who tried to slip away to safety. Vines and thorns curled around the young man, snapped his neck, then tossed his discarded body up against the wall, knocking down an entire shelf of books.

Struggling to control the level of destruction, Nicci called a single bolt of lightning that struck and splintered the thing's thick left leg, rendering it unbalanced. Even though it smoked and smoldered, the tottering creature regrew itself.

Nicci and Nathan stood shoulder-to-shoulder as a barricade, refusing to let the creature past—but it did not want to pass. It wanted to kill them. With a thrashing of uncontrolled branches and dry leaves, along with a buzzing of hungry insects, it pushed back against Nicci's blasts of air. Nathan hacked again, splintering the encroaching branches.

From behind her, Thistle said, "I'll get a torch to light that monster on fire." She darted away, but she didn't get far.

The *shaksis* reacted to her movement, and a long whip of its thorny arm extended. Even though Nicci's magic shoved against the thing's body core, the deadly elongated arm seized Thistle. Sharp finger-thorns pierced the girl's skinny leg and drew blood. She kicked and fought, trying to pull away.

Rage rose within Nicci. She didn't hesitate, did not exercise caution in the confined corridor. This monster had to be stopped. She summoned a ball of flame—normal flame, since wizard's fire could have been catastrophic—and exploded the blaze into the *shaksis*.

Flames immediately caught inside its torso, raging through its skeleton of bent branches and dried vegetation. Roasting insects burst or fled. Worms squirmed out, sizzling. Even as the *shaksis* burned, in a surge of desperation it plodded forward and extended its blazing arms toward Nicci. She shoved back with a blow of solid air and knocked the living inferno against the wall. Some splintered, charred pieces of the forest golem still clattered and twitched, grasping out for any victim.

The forest construct broke into flaming ashes, finally dead. But the embers scattered among the clustered books and stacked scrolls. Because of the speed of her attack and the rush of the air she had unleashed, the volumes quickly caught fire, their pages blackened and curled. Flames raged along the shelves, spreading from one to the next. The fabric door hangings in front of the private quarters also ignited.

Despite her bleeding leg, Thistle ran to their quarters and yanked down the door hanging and tried to put out the spreading fire. Nathan did the same as they yelled for more scholars to help, and they all worked together to stop the inferno.

Nicci released more magic, calling upon the air again, summoning moisture to douse the larger flames. She stole air away to starve the fire until it guttered down to a low smolder.

Cliffwall scholars rushed from other chambers and corridors to aid in quenching the blaze before it could spread to the larger libraries and vaults of books. Seeing their murdered comrades, some of them gasped, halted in their efforts to fight the insidious fire, but others swallowed hard, faced the crisis, and turned their attention to saving the books, the scrolls, the library itself.

One woman, sniffling, struggling to control her weeping, knelt by the first dead and broken scholar. She adjusted his body, his head, and began to pick up the blood-spattered books strewn on the floor from the splintered shelf.

When they had the fire under control, Nicci turned her attention to Thistle and saw that her thigh was bleeding heavily. Without asking, Nicci pressed her palms hard against the deep wound, and released magic to heal the girl and remove the pain.

Thistle laughed with relief. "I knew you'd save me."

The wizard shook his head. His face was smudged with soot. He plucked a squirming beetle grub out of his white hair and crushed it between his fingertips.

Then, just after the ruckus died down, Bannon returned to Cliffwall, gasping and disheveled, weary from an ordeal of his own. His eyes shone with excitement as he pushed his way through the crowded corridor.

"I just got back. Sweet Sea Mother, you won't believe the night I've had!" He ran his hands through his bedraggled red hair, and he finally noticed the destruction and turmoil around him for the first time. "Oh! What happened here?"

CHAPTER 66

The attack of the *shaksis* made clear Victoria's ruthless intent. The next morning, with an odd smile, Nicci nodded with satisfaction. "That means she is afraid of us."

"And well she should be, my dear sorceress," Nathan said as they worked their way into the tunnels beneath the damaged prophecy tower. "I would feel much more confident, though, if we can find the hidden volume that holds the means to destroy her."

"It's down here," Mia said, winding them through the twisted, claustrophobic tunnels.

Down in the dusty vault, where the damaged ceilings were slumped and alarmingly uneven, Mia brought them to a small room where stone walls had melted like candle wax over stacks of books. With an intent expression, the mousy researcher pointed to one thick tome fused partway into the rock. She couldn't hide her excitement. "This one! See the spine? It is exactly the book we're looking for. It matches what was on the list."

Nicci touched the volume and felt its extreme age. "The pages will be difficult to read," she said, "since it is part of the wall."

Nathan gave a futile tug, but could not break the grip of the stone. He looked at her. "Mia has a small amount of the gift, and I would generally encourage her to practice. In fact, under normal circumstances I would just do this myself." He frowned at the trapped book. "But because of the importance, Sorceress, and since you are the only one with the proper control of magic, could you manipulate the stone and release the volume for us?"

"Agreed. This is not an instance where one should resort to dabbling." Nicci ran her fingers over the binding, touched where the pages had seamlessly blended into the stone, and released her magic. A small flow pushed aside the rock, but did not separate the paper and the leather-bound cover from the stone matrix. She concentrated harder, working to extricate the fused elements. "The bond is not easily separable."

"You never shy from difficult things," Nathan said. "You can do it."

"Yes, I can. Just not perfectly."

She moved the fundamental grains of rock and released the locked pages, but some of the fibers remained intertwined. When she finally withdrew the damaged book from its rock prison, some of the pages were still stiff and powdery, as if the last reader had been a sloppy bricklayer with mortar on his hands. Nevertheless, Nathan took the volume from her and pored over the words with an eager Mia close beside him, under the glow of a flickering hand light.

"This is it. This is the deep life spell!" Mia grinned. "Just what we were looking for."

"Good," Nicci said. "Now tell me how we can neutralize Victoria."

Nathan looked at her in alarm. "Dear spirits, it is not so simple as that!"

"It never is. Just tell me what to do."

"This will require some study." Nathan and Mia conferred over the damaged words on the brittle pages. "Ah, yes, that seems clear enough." He looked up at Nicci, explaining, "What Victoria used was a deeply bound life spell, drawn from the bones of the world. That is where Life's Mistress receives her energy, and that is the only way we can stop her." He looked up. "The only way to shut off the valve from her uncontrollable flow of magic."

Mia pulled the book closer to herself and pointed excitedly. "Some words on the bottom of the page are damaged, but the answer is clear." She drew a quick breath. "It's the way we can defeat Victoria."

"I'm pleased to have a clear answer for once." Nicci crossed her arms over her chest. "And what is the weapon?"

"A special bow," Nathan said. "Such an enemy can be destroyed with an arrow, and the archer must be someone with a great command of the gift, a powerful wizard or sorceress."

"That would be me," Nicci said, already anticipating the task. "And I know how to use a bow."

The wizard shook his head. "Alas, it is not so simple as that, Sorceress. The life spell itself is intertwined with the most ancient creatures, the very structure of the world. The arrow must be shot from a special bow—a bow made from the rib bone of a dragon."

Nicci drew in a quick breath of the dusty, still air in the newly opened vault. The magical fire in her hand light flickered. "The rib of a dragon?"

Nathan's voice became troubled as the excitement faded. "Indeed. I can see how that poses a problem."

Mia's disappointment was clear. "Dragons are extinct."

Now that she had a potential answer, though, Nicci refused to give up hope. "*Nearly* extinct."

The scholars gathered in one of the large meeting rooms. A fire of mesquite wood burned in the hearth, sending a warm, savory fragrance into the chamber. Nathan had shown the ancient volume to the intent researchers, and they were all abuzz with the possibility.

"We must take action, and soon." The wizard spoke in a firm, serious tone. "The *shaksis* was only Victoria's first foray against us. I think she meant to catch us in our sleep, but she may also have been testing us. The next attack will certainly be more dangerous."

"And she grows stronger with every inch of territory she claims with that monstrous jungle," Nicci said.

Bannon sat near the hearth, sharpening his sword and brooding. His face was grave. "After what I saw last night, I am convinced there is no other way. Those poor girls . . ." He swallowed hard. "There was no saving them. We have to do what's right. If we don't stop that rampant growth, Victoria will cause as much destruction as the Lifedrinker."

"We have to protect Cliffwall." Franklin sounded alarmed. "Should we block off the other side of the plateau? Seal the window alcoves? How do we make sure nothing can get in from the Scar? Like the *shaksis*."

"We know she is coming for us," Mia said.

Nicci nodded. "Blocking the openings would help, but only as a temporary measure. Once Victoria's jungle reaches the cliffs, her vines and heavy tree roots will crack open the mesa itself. We have to stop her before then." She raked her gaze over them. "I don't care how difficult it is. We must kill her."

"And now we know how to do that," Nathan said, "thanks to the lost volume that dear Mia and I found." He smiled over at the attentive female scholar. The other memmers and scholars muttered uncertainly. Having lost both Simon and Victoria, their two factions were adrift, leaderless. "Our powerful sorceress needs to shoot Life's Mistress with an arrow, using a bow made out of a dragon's rib." His voice faltered. "We only need to find a dragon."

Most dragons had been gone for many years, especially in the Old World, and the devastating Chainfire spell had erased even the memory of dragons from humanity for a time, but they still existed. They had to exist.

Bannon let out a sad laugh. "Of course! It's so simple. And once we find a dragon, we just have to slay it and cut a rib from its carcass." He sat down heavily on the hearth. "Sweet Sea Mother, I don't suppose that would take more than a day or two. What are we waiting for?"

"In the last days of the war against the Imperial Order, the witch woman Six flew on a great red dragon in her attacks on the D'Haran army," Nicci said. "The dragon's name was Gregory, but he is far away now, and we would never find him."

Thistle had taken one of the large chairs, curling her knees up on the seat in an awkward but oddly flexible position. She scoffed at the young man, teasing him like a little sister. "We don't need to find and kill a dragon. We just need a dragon *rib*."

Nathan spoke in a professorial tone. "Dear child, dragon ribs come from dragons. How do you expect us to find a rib bone without finding a dragon?"

Thistle gave a groan of frustration. "I mean we don't have to find a live dragon and kill it. We just need to find a rib *bone*. That means we're looking for a dragon *skeleton*."

Bannon looked annoyed. "Sure. That's much easier. They must be lying all over the place."

Nicci had a sudden memory of when she and her hostage Richard had crossed the Midlands as they made their way down to Altur'Rang. On their journey they had found the rotting carcass of a dragon. "I've seen such a skeleton, but it was far up in the Midlands."

"Even if we could find it again, the journey alone would take months, if not years," Nathan said.

The girl groaned again. "That isn't where you'd look for dragon skeletons." She gave an exasperated sigh.

"Where would you propose we look?" Bannon asked.

"Kuloth Vale, of course," she replied, as if he were the uneducated child. "Everyone knows that."

"We are not from here," Nicci said. "What is Kuloth Vale?"

"In my village I grew up hearing stories about the great graveyard of dragons. Kuloth Vale." Thistle looked around the room, and the scholars muttered, clearly expressing concern. Some of them, though, seemed familiar with the tale. Among the memmers, Gloria nodded.

"Kuloth Vale is far away," said Mia, "a sheltered hanging valley in the mountains to the north, and it's a dangerous place. That is where the dragons go to die."

The scholars consulted among themselves. Franklin spoke with his eyes half closed, reciting from memory: "'All dragons have an instinctive bond to the magical place of Kuloth Vale. The bones of hundreds of dragons lie there at rest.'" His voice became ominous. "'No human has ever gone there and returned to tell the tale.'"

"Then how was the tale ever recorded?" Nathan asked.

Gloria nodded gravely. "That is a mystery yet to be explained."

Nicci said, "If you know of this graveyard of dragons, then surely we can find a rib bone and come back swiftly."

Though always eager for an adventure, even Bannon looked doubtful. "Sounds like chasing mist dancers on a foggy night."

But Nicci had heard all she needed to hear. "Our alternative is to wait here while Victoria's jungle keeps spreading, and hope that a dragon happens to fly by so we can kill it and take a rib."

"I see. When you frame the debate in that way, Sorceress, even Kuloth Vale sounds like a preferable alternative," Nathan said.

Thistle looked up at her with an intent gaze. "Kuloth Vale is real. I've heard stories all my life."

Bannon rolled his eyes. "You're not even twelve years old."

Nicci turned to the gathered scholars. "You've been gathering maps to help us on our journey, Wizard. Have you found any that show the location of Kuloth Vale?"

"If no one has ever seen the graveyard of dragons, how could they make a map?" Bannon asked.

"Another unexplained mystery," Franklin said.

Nicci did not give in to frustration. She would follow this lead, knowing it was their best chance. "While we are gone, the rest of you must shore up the defenses of Cliffwall in case Victoria sends more attackers against you." Thistle slid off the chair, stretched her legs, and moved to stand by Nicci.

"The journey to Kuloth Vale will take many days," Mia said, "across unknown terrain."

"We have done that before," Nicci said. "The sooner we leave, the sooner we will return. With a dragon rib."

CHAPTER 67

The sketchy maps from the Cliffwall archives gave them a starting point in their search for the legendary graveyard of dragons, and Nicci and her companions set off with confidence. With full packs and fresh traveling clothes, they moved up through isolated canyons, climbing into the desert highlands, away from the great valley.

Full of energy, Thistle took point as they headed north toward a distant line of rugged gray mountains that looked volcanic in origin. The air was clear and the terrain expansive, which made the distances uncertain.

"Those mountains are many days away," Nathan said, "even if we keep up a good pace."

Nicci kept moving. "Then we should not slow."

The wizard paused to wipe his brow. He withdrew a white kerchief that Mia had shyly given him before their departure, and he looked at it with a curious smile. "Let's see if that dear girl's spell worked." He wiped the cloth across his face, then brightened. "Ah yes, moist and cool and refreshing. She promised me it was a simple, innocuous spell, but I find it quite effective."

Nicci had been there when the quiet young scholar had given Nathan the white rag. Mia promised that the spell would always keep the kerchief cool and moist to ease a traveler's burden. "Simple and innocuous," Nicci agreed. "But no matter how gifted the scholars may be, I am reluctant to see them dabbling with any sort of magic. They are all untrained. Think of the damage they have already done, unaware of what they were doing . . . the melted archive tower, the Lifedrinker, now Victoria and her mad jungle."

"It is just a kerchief, Sorceress . . ." Nathan said.

"And that is how it begins."

Embarrassed, he tucked it away in his pocket, but she did see him using it often during the heat of the afternoon, especially in steep terrain.

They walked all day, taking only brief rests for water and a quick meal. Ranging ahead, Thistle killed several plump lizards to supplement their meals, not because they needed the food, but because she enjoyed the hunt.

By the second day, they left the high desert, and the terrain grew more forested. In the rolling hills they found brooks to refill their waterskins and even a grove of wild plum trees. With the simple joy of finding plentiful fresh fruit, they ate far too many plums, particularly Bannon. That evening, they all suffered from stomach cramps and knotted intestines.

The following day Nicci sensed an animal presence watching them, and she realized that Mrra had trailed them up from the valley. She caught a flash of tawny fur gliding among the low trees in the distance, staying close. Still spell-bonded with Nicci, the big cat followed wherever her sister panther traveled, but maintained her independence.

Nicci was pleased just to know of the animal's presence. She sensed the big cat's need to hunt, and with a distant thrill in her veins, she felt Mrra on the chase, the pounding heart, the taste of iron-hot blood, and the squeal and twitch of fresh prey brought down.

When Nicci led them into a small meadow in late afternoon, they found a bloody deer carcass, freshly slaughtered. Its guts were torn open and the liver had been devoured, but the rest of the meat remained intact. Nathan and Bannon were immediately wary that the predator was still nearby, but Nicci dropped to her knees next to the deer. "Mrra hunted for us. She's had her fill and left the rest for our supper."

The wizard brightened. "Dear spirits, now that's a different story. Let's have a good meal."

While Nicci prepared a fire, Thistle and Bannon worked together to carve out strips of venison to roast over the flames. The girl admitted that it tasted better than her lizards. After the feast, they bedded down on the soft meadow grass, satisfied. The next morning, they wrapped some of the steaks in fresh green leaves, and Nicci worked a simple preservative spell to keep the meat from going bad. They carried the meat in their packs.

Over the next several days they wound through trackless areas and ascended sheer gorges that rose into more rugged terrain, but the sharp, volcanic mountains remained very far away.

"I don't recall hearing of Kuloth Vale in my histories," Nathan mused. He enjoyed talking to Bannon as they walked, although the others listened as well. "But I did read many tales of the Midwar, records of when Emperor Kurgan conquered the south of the continent. General Utros and his invincible armies swept across the land, and city after city fell. He had wizard warriors, as well as hordes of expendable soldiers.

"When he set off to lay siege to the remarkable city of Ildakar, Utros knew he would face extraordinarily powerful magic, so he needed a special weapon." Nathan looked down at Thistle and dropped his voice into a dramatic whisper. "They captured a dragon—a silver dragon." The girl's eyes widened.

"I've never heard of a silver dragon," Bannon said. "Are they special?"

"All dragons are special, my boy—and they have always been rare. Angry red dragons, aloof green dragons, wise gray dragons, evil black dragons. But, General Utros wanted a *silver* dragon."

"Why?" Thistle asked.

"Because silver dragons are the best fighters." Nathan waved a persistent white butterfly away from his face, which fluttered off to seek flowers instead. "But they are not easily tamed or controlled. Utros's warriors did manage to capture one such beast, and they kept it chained and harnessed. The army intended to turn it loose once they reached Ildakar.

"But one night the dragon snapped its bonds and broke free, devouring the harness and then the handlers. It could simply have flown away, but instead the dragon took vengeance. The silver monster ripped through the army camp and slaughtered hundreds of the Iron Fang's soldiers. General Utros barely escaped with his life, though the side of his face was burned, scarred from dragon fire. The silver dragon flew away, leaving his army a shambles, but General Utros would never go back to Emperor Kurgan and admit failure. So he pressed on, hoping to find some other way to conquer Ildakar."

Nathan continued his story as they moved through the forest until they reached the crest of a hill, where they could see the towering black mountains rising closer at last. "But when his armies arrived at Ildakar, Utros found that the entire city had vanished! One of the greatest cities in the Old World, entirely gone."

"How? Where did it go?" Thistle asked.

The wizard shrugged. "No one knows. The legend is fifteen centuries old, so it could just be a story."

"Let's hope that Kuloth Vale is more than just a story," Nicci said.

That night they slept next to a roaring campfire as the winds picked up through the thin trees. Nathan agreed to stand first watch while the rest of them bedded down. Thistle curled up in her blanket, as comfortable on the hard forest floor as she had been in the stone chamber at Cliffwall, although she missed her soft sheepskin.

Nicci lay near the girl. Listening to the crackle of the fire with her eyes closed, she extended her senses, but picked up no immediate danger in the nearby forests. Her mind touched the sand panther, however, and from a distance, Mrra felt the bond as well. The big cat affirmed that they were safe from any threats, so Nicci let herself fall into a deep sleep. . . .

While her body rested, her dreams ranged far, once again inside the mind of her sister panther. Mrra was more content in this sort of terrain than in either the desolate Scar or the unsettling primeval jungle. Here, the hills felt normal, and she experienced true freedom.

As the cat loped along in the night, Mrra's mind was attuned to the world, while also in touch with pristine memories, which Nicci experienced. Mrra remembered her spell-bonded *troka* mates, who would romp together, biting, clawing, pretending to hurt but causing no real damage.

The handlers soon forced stricter, deadlier training upon them. At first, the wild sand panthers resisted, but then they learned to enjoy the fight, the kill. In her dream state, Nicci also experienced the remembered pleasure of clawing her victims, from terrified humans who offered little fight, to horrific monsters created by the fleshmancers for the combat arena.

With singing adrenaline, Mrra remembered a particular beast she and her sister panthers had fought in the gladiator arena before shouting crowds, spectators who demanded blood, demanded death—though Mrra did not understand whose blood they wanted. Under the guidance of the wizard commander, the fleshmancers had altered, manipulated, and *twisted* a powerful bull into a fighting beast with a rack of four sharp, curved horns, a flat armored head, and steel-hard bony hooves that struck sparks from the arena gravel. The monster bull was far more massive than the three cats combined, but the *troka* had to fight it. Mrra and her sister panthers understood that.

As the demon bull charged forward with an ear-shattering bellow that overwhelmed the giddy roar of the crowd, the sand panthers had split apart, each knowing what her sisters were doing. Coordinating their attack, the *troka* circled the giant snorting beast.

The bull lumbered forward, picking up momentum, and Mrra sprang to one side while her sister panthers circled and struck from behind. One raked the beast's left haunch, leaving parallel bloody gouges down its hide. The other cat sprang for the demon bull's throat, but the creature's muscles were like corded steel, and her curved fangs could make only shallow bites.

Mrra stood her ground as the monster thundered forward, too heavy and too swift to stop. She leaped for its head, clawed at its eyes, but the bull knocked her to the ground, nearly crushing her. She felt her ribs crack. Blood burst inside of her. Pain exploded in her mind at the same time that the bull's hot blood poured down upon her from the deep wounds.

Through the spell bond, she experienced her two sister panthers leaping onto the bull's back, using claws and saber teeth to tear deep wounds. With a great bellow, the beast threw them off, striking more sparks with its enhanced hooves as it lashed out in search of a target.

Mrra rolled in the dusty sand, listened to the roaring cheers, ignoring the pain of her broken ribs. *This* was what the handlers wanted her to do. *This* was why she and the entire *troka* existed. Moving as one being, the three panthers attacked again. Even though the bull charged, even though the panthers were already injured, eventually they wore the monster down.

The fleshmancers watched from the stands, scowling with displeasure to see that the specialized combat monster they had created could be defeated by three panthers.

Mrra and her sisters tore the twisted bull into tatters of gore. Its entrails dangled from its stomach, but like a great senseless machine, it still lumbered and charged until it collapsed with a grunt and a spray of dark blood. Its thick pink tongue gasped out of its mouth, and the beast died with a rattling exhale.

Mrra and her sisters stood together, bloody and in pain, their tails thrashing. They looked up, waiting for the handlers to come and retrieve them. Even with the deep-seated agony from her broken bones and gashed hide, Mrra had felt content. The sound that bubbled from her chest was more a purr than a growl, because she had done what the handlers had trained her to do.

She had killed. She had defeated the enemy.

During the late part of the night, while Nathan curled up near the fire and went to sleep, Bannon took second watch. He sat on a fallen log, his sword ready, looking out for his friends and listening for any threats out in the forest.

Nicci slept soundly, lost in dreams. She twitched, and a low sound came from her throat, something like a feline growl. The sorceress was so deep in the dream, she was vulnerable. Nicci had warned them about this, and Bannon did not intend to let her down.

He sat alert, guarding her until Nicci finally awoke at dawn.

CHAPTER 68

After days of hard travel, they finally reached the volcanic mountains. Very little vegetation poked through the crumbly rust-brown soil, and the boulders were porous pumice, honeycombed with fossilized air pockets. Lichen and moss mottled the lava boulders.

Standing on a high ridge, Nathan studied the crude charts from Cliffwall so he could get his bearings. "This way. Almost there." No one questioned his definition of "almost." He wiped his brow with Mia's special kerchief, then tucked it away before setting off, refreshed.

"I hope you're correct," Nicci replied. "We have been gone for too long already, and Life's Mistress will keep growing more powerful back there in the valley." Seeing the breathtaking sweep of the rampant growth, she had no doubt this scourge would grow even faster than the Lifedrinker's desolation. Yet again, she would have to stop an enemy that would threaten Lord Rahl, the D'Haran Empire, the Old World and the New.

After pushing through the untracked mountains, they finally arrived at a saddle that overlooked a stark and secluded hanging valley. The rocky bowl below was guarded by sharp volcanic barricades and towering rock spires, like a walled-off preserve skirted with glaciers and broken cliffs. The black-rock basin held patches of snow and a partially frozen lake among the giant boulders and pinnacles of solidified ash.

Nicci recognized the place instinctively, and she could feel in her heart that this was where they needed to be. "Kuloth Vale," she whispered.

Thistle pointed eagerly. "Look! See the bones?"

Looking closer, Nicci could discern the scattered white skeletons of enormous creatures—dozens of them, lying stark against the desolation.

The sharp breezes blew Nathan's white hair into his face. He wore a satisfied smile. "Dragon bones, all right," he said, as if he were particularly familiar with such things.

Bannon craned his head upward and peered into the sky as if expecting to see the angular silhouette of a circling dragon.

"We have to get down there," Nicci said. She paused to assess the difficult route down into the rocky valley, but Thistle set off like a mountain goat, making her way down the loose rocks. When the scree slid beneath her, she merely hopped to a more stable boulder, and kept descending into the bleak basin.

With the goal finally in sight, Nicci picked her way down the slope without dwelling on the spectacular scenery. Bannon and Nathan followed close behind them, the wizard toiling with great care and the young man offering unwanted help. Behind them, Mrra remained at the top of the ridge, a silhouette in the afternoon light; the panther did not go farther, refusing to enter Kuloth Vale. Nicci knew the big cat would make her own choices.

Among the broken black rocks at the bottom of the bowl, they came upon the first dragon skeleton. Its rib bones had collapsed in like the legs of a dead spider. Time and weather had twisted the vertebrae. Its skull was hollow, and many of its long fangs had fallen loose. Its empty eye sockets stared upward at eternity.

Nathan went to the skeleton and tugged on a curved rib. "Should we just take the first one and go?" He rapped his knuckles on the hollow-sounding ivory. "You could fashion one of these into a bow."

Bannon looked at the wizard in disbelief. "We can't leave yet! We have to explore. This is the lost graveyard of dragons—think of the stories!"

"We need to choose the right bone," Nicci said. "I want to test the size and resiliency of the ribs."

They moved among the grim clutter, exploring the wealth of ribs, vertebrae, and skulls in the final resting place of the last dragons.

The wizard paused beside a towering skeleton to which some shreds of scaled hide still clung. Nicci examined the enormous skull, which was as large as an oxcart. Its long fangs were pitted, possibly rotten with age. The rib bones that curved majestically up from the skeleton were twice her height. Even in this faint remnant, Nicci could feel the power still resident in this great creature. She understood the closely bonded life magic throbbing within the bones. Yes, a bow made from such a rib could hold enough power to quench Victoria's rampant spell.

"This one looks like a black dragon," Nathan said. Each ebony scale was the size of his outstretched hand. "A great dragon, possibly a king among his kind."

Nicci was more pragmatic. "Perhaps so, but this rib is far too large for me to use. We need to find a more appropriate skeleton."

Moving around the upthrust volcanic rock, Bannon paused to inspect another set of collapsed bones. Nathan came up beside him, nodding. "Look there, see the slight differences in the shape of the head and the structure of the wing bones? This was a green dragon, I believe. Note the horn protrusions on its snout? That is how one can identify a green dragon."

Bannon frowned. "Wouldn't you know it's a *green* dragon by the color of its scales?"

"Yes, my boy—but once you are that close, then you face troubles far more pressing than scientific classification."

As they worked their way deeper into the valley, clouds scudded across the sky. They walked among the skeletons, piles of them, as if at one time there had been a great die-off of dragons.

"I wonder when the last one came here." Bannon bent down at another skull, a small one, perhaps that of a young dragon that had perished beside its mother. Even the young dragon was larger than a draft horse.

Thistle scampered ahead to explore among the rocks. She climbed out of sight as she found more and more cluttered bones, ancient generations of fallen dragons.

"Over here, Sorceress!" Nathan called. "Perhaps this one? It's a silver dragon, based on the configuration of its skull and the bony back ridges there. Metaphorically, at least, this one might be best for fighting."

Joining him at the skeleton he had found, Nicci assessed the length and curvature of the rib, extended her arms as if holding an imaginary bow. "A good possibility."

Bannon stepped up with his sword. "If that's the one you want, Sorceress, I can cut the bone free. We'll shape it into a bow when we get back to Cliffwall."

Thistle screamed.

Nicci moved in a flash, bounding over the pitted volcanic rock and dodging the jumbled skeletons. She reached a pumice outcropping from which she could see the girl racing away in terror. Something stirred among the rocks and bones—something enormous.

A pair of angular wings unfolded, and leathery gray skin stretched taut. With a hiss, a serpentine neck scattered the rocks and heaved itself up in a spray of dust and gravel. The piled bones clattered and tumbled away from the half-buried form. It was a reptilian beast with wattled skin at its throat and tendrils drooping from fang-filled jaws. Many of its pewter-colored scales were missing, leaving exposed sections of wrinkled skin.

With the sound of blacksmith's bellows, the dragon inhaled air into its lungs, flapped its broad wings, and lifted itself up. Fire lit its golden eyes. The creature seemed incredibly ancient, but not at all weak.

As it rose up, the gray dragon scattered debris, looming over them. Thistle cringed, directly in its line of sight. She had nowhere to run.

The beast spoke with loud thunder that caused more rocks to tumble from the steep slopes of the vale. "I am Brom!" He flapped his wings backward, making a stir of wind. "I am the guardian. I am the last." The ancient gray dragon snorted, inhaling again to fill his withered, wrinkled hide. "And you are intruders."

CHAPTER 69

As Brom heaved himself up from a pile of bones and volcanic rock, Thistle backed away, her eyes darting, searching for shelter. Throwing herself forward to face the gray dragon, Nicci dug within herself to find magic she could use against the huge beast, sure the girl would be incinerated any moment.

Bannon and Nathan both drew their swords and stood ready, as if they might terrify or intimidate Brom. The wizard seemed defiant, but Bannon was clearly awestruck and terrified.

The gray dragon kept rising from the rubble of skeletons. Dust, boulders, and bones pattered off of his wrinkled hide. Smoke and sparks curled from his mouth as his jaws yawned wide. "I thought I was at my end," Brom rumbled, "but I am still the protector of this place." The great wings flapped back and forth; the thin membranes were blotchy and discolored, and small rips gave the wings a tattered appearance. Nicci doubted the beast could fly anymore.

Brom was unspeakably ancient. Scales fell like loose coins from his hide. Summoning a roar from a bottomless pit of great weariness, the dragon bellowed at them. "Thieves! I must guard the bones of my kind."

When Nathan raised his ornate blade in challenge, he looked laughably insignificant. "We meant no harm to you, dragon, but we will defend ourselves." He swept his sword high, cutting through the air. Bannon followed his mentor's lead, waving Sturdy in an attempt to scare the huge creature.

The gray dragon turned his head and squinted, as if he had trouble seeing. "You are not like other dragon slayers I have encountered. You are much punier. Easy to kill." His serpentine throat swelled like pumping bellows as he coughed gouts of smoke, cinders, and sparks at them.

Just in time, Nicci released a wave of wind that deflected the dragon's sputtering exhalations. She reached the terrified girl and pushed Thistle away from Brom. "Run—find shelter!"

The gray dragon lunged toward them on unsteady limbs.

Foolishly, Bannon leaped forward, and with a great yell, swung his sword down on Brom's foreleg. Sturdy's keen edge cut through the loose, displaced scales and the parchment-thin hide, sinking in to the bone, as if the reptilian leg were nothing more than a fallen log.

Brom let out a roar, sparking more fire from his throat. The ancient dragon thrashed his barbed tail and knocked bones and volcanic rock aside in an explosion of anger and pain. He thrust his long neck forward, questing and snarling, as he squinted his slitted eyes.

Nicci pushed the girl along as they ran, ducking behind pumice towers and huge bones. Even a feeble, decrepit dragon was a formidable opponent. Rattling dry ivory bones around her as she climbed, Thistle reached the giant skeleton of another black dragon just as Brom came up behind her and Nicci.

The beast heaved back his long head and inhaled, building up smoke and cinders. Knowing she had to protect the girl and herself, Nicci tossed Thistle inside the petrified dome of the black dragon's skull and dove in beside the girl.

The gray dragon's blast of smoke and flickering fire pelted the skull, and Nicci felt the shudder of the impact, the wave of forceful wind rocking their shelter, a throb of intense heat. Thistle curled up against her, holding tight as they weathered the attack.

As soon as Brom's blast was over, Nicci heard Nathan call out, "Fight someone your own size, dragon!" He let out a rude laugh. "But since no such opponent is available, you will have to battle us. Today, Bannon and I will become dragon slayers after all."

The young man added his shout, deliriously and foolishly brave. "Come on, old thing—or are you too weary? Is it time for your nap?"

Snorting at the insult, Brom wheeled about, sprinting away from the blackened skull that still sheltered Nicci and the girl. With a roar that sounded more like a trembling sigh, the gray dragon staggered after the two swordsmen. Nathan and Bannon darted about, hacking and hammering at Brom's hind legs and tail, gouging the scales and skin. Thick, dark blood oozed out of the wounds.

Brom snapped his jaws, but Nathan rolled out of the way amid a clatter of long-dried vertebrae. Though the ancient guardian dragon seemed intimidating, many of his teeth had fallen out. Because of his titanic size, Brom toppled rock spires and struck Bannon a glancing blow, knocking him among the debris.

As soon as the dragon had turned away, Nicci pressed Thistle down. "Stay here. You're sheltered, at least for now. You'll be safe enough." Then she emerged to face the ancient dragon herself.

"Be careful, Nicci!" Thistle called after her.

Her normal magic would not be enough against even this weak and decrepit behemoth, and she was forced to draw upon elements of both Additive and Subtractive Magic. In the gray smear of clouds that had closed over the high valley, thunder cracked like an explosion. Nicci pulled down skittering lashes of blue-black lightning. The jagged bolts were wild and rampant. One crashed into the curved rib cage of a sprawling skeleton, but two other branches of lightning struck Brom, ripping through the membrane of his right wing and scoring a deep black wound along his side.

The old dragon let out a smoke-filled roar and thrashed his head from side to side. "No! I am the guardian." Brom stormed toward Nicci, though he could barely see.

Nicci held both hands out in front of her, curling her fingers. She could unleash a ball of wizard's fire and throw it at the dragon, but she had another idea. Better to summon fire *within* the dragon, burn it from the inside out. She could find Brom's heart, and explode it.

In previous battles, she would summon heat and dramatically raise the internal temperature of an object, as she had done with the giant lizards near the lair of the Lifedrinker. Now, searching with her mind, she found the dragon's heart. She could burn it to a cinder.

Facing the giant beast, she remained calm, focused. When Brom lunged, Nicci released her magic, filling the dragon's heart with fire. She would give the ancient beast a swift and merciful death.

Her magical blaze ignited Brom's heart into a furnace—but still the dragon didn't stop.

Instead, as the fire continued to rage within him, building inside his chest cavity, Brom actually flourished, grew, swelled. Losing control of the magic she had triggered, Nicci realized her terrible mistake.

Fire would not burn a dragon's heart to ash. Fire was intrinsic to the very being of such a creature. The intense heat had reignited Brom's heart—not killing him, but *rejuvenating* him, infusing the dragon with a renewed power. His thin skin and rows of ribs became flush again. His wing membranes crackled and healed. His enormous reptilian body grew more threatening.

Fully alive again, Brom flapped his wings to create a gale of wind that knocked Nicci backward. Bannon and Nathan scrambled out of the way, diving for shelter among the volcanic boulders.

The gray dragon turned his head to the sky, spread wide his jaws, and let out a river of bright, intense fire. When Brom swung his head around, his eyes, which had been previously dimmed with age, blazed with a golden intensity.

"Now you have made me strong enough to defeat you!"

CHAPTER 70

As the dragon turned its newly bright-eyed gaze toward them and let out a blast of flames, Bannon dove for shelter behind the tall pumice boulder, dragging a startled Nathan along with him. The roar of heat slammed against the pocked volcanic surface, blackening it.

While a rejuvenated Brom attacked her companions, Nicci summoned lightning again, a blast three times as strong as her first barrage, but now the dragon's pewter scales were like thick armor, and the lightning skittered harmlessly off his back. Full of energy, the guardian dragon coiled his leg muscles, and sprang into the air, creating a great gust with his restored wings.

"This is a sacred place to dragons! You are thieves."

He vomited a wave of fire toward Nicci, and she cast out her hands, releasing magic in a shield of air and mist that deflected the flames. But she staggered under the incinerating onslaught, reinforcing her barrier, straining as the avalanche of flames pounded and pounded. That one defense nearly drained her, and when the fire subsided, she staggered back.

"Grave robbers!" Brom roared from the sky. "You must die."

"No!" Thistle's voice rang out in the odd silence that filled the gap between the dragon's bellow and the blast of his flames. "Brom, listen! That's not why we're here."

Nicci whirled to see that the scrawny girl had climbed on top of the giant dragon skull and now stood waving her hands to draw Brom's attention. "We came because we have to!" Thistle looked tiny and vulnerable out in the open.

The gray dragon swooped above the girl and curled his serpentine neck in preparation for another fire blast.

Nicci screamed, "Thistle! Take cover!"

The girl looked so waifish, so brave, so impossible, that even Brom hesitated. Thistle stood on top of the curve of the monstrous blackened skull, defiant and angry. "We're trying to save the world! My friends and I made a long journey to come here. It's important!"

The dragon's eyes were bright, reflecting a sharp mind now, his full faculties reawakened with the supercharged fire that Nicci had pumped into his heart. "You are a strange creature, tiny one," Brom rumbled. "Very brave and very foolish."

Thistle put her hands on her narrow hips and her raggedy skirt. "I am determined. And I was told that gray dragons are wise." She shot a quick glance over to Nathan, then back to Brom. "You should listen to reason. Don't you want to know why we came here? Aren't you curious?" She huffed, then answered without waiting to hear a response. "An evil woman has unleashed a terrible magic that could swallow up the whole land. It will destroy Kuloth Vale before long . . . and there's only one way to stop it. We need a bone—a dragon's rib." She glared at the gray-scaled beast. "That's why we came here. We'll kill you if we have to. We don't *want* to, but we mean to take what we need. We are trying to save the world."

Intrigued, Brom backflapped his wings and settled his great bulk among the graveyard rubble, close to Thistle. Bannon and Nathan emerged from where they had taken shelter. Their hair was streaked with sweat, their faces smeared with soot and dust.

Nicci held the magic within her, barely restraining herself from releasing another barrage of lightning, though she was not sure it would do any good. She was still weary from her previous defense and doubted she could kill or even stun the reenergized dragon. She realized that attacking now would only put Thistle in greater danger. If gray dragons were the most intelligent of the species, maybe Brom would listen before he lashed out again.

The dragon settled back, extending his wedge-shaped head forward. Smoke curled out of his nostrils as he regarded the spunky girl. Thistle faced him without flinching, even though Brom's hot breath blew back her tangled curls of hair. "Explain yourself, tiny one."

Still standing as tall as she could on top of the scorched dragon skull, Thistle said, "I just want to save my land. First, the Lifedrinker killed my parents, my aunt and uncle, my village, and everything in my valley—and we destroyed him. But now there's an even worse threat, a sorceress who unleashed an explosion of life, and now *that* is taking over the valley. It will destroy everything!" Her voice became a desperate shout. "I just want a normal world. I want the beautiful valley back, the one everyone talks about."

Brom snorted smoke. "A sorceress created *too much* life?" He lifted a now-healed forelimb and used an enormous claw to scratch between his tusk-sized teeth. "I marvel at the concept. Too much life . . ."

He turned his blazing gaze to where Nicci, Bannon, and Nathan stood ready to fight. The dragon addressed them. "I came here to die, as all dragons do at Kuloth Vale . . . but it has been so long. I was the guardian, and I remember their lives. Now you have restored my life." Smoke and cinders curled from his mouth as the gray dragon let out an odd, growling chuckle. "Although I do not believe you meant to." He turned back to Thistle, leaning forward. The dragon's head was so close that she could have reached out and touched his scaled snout. "Now, brave tiny one, what does this have to do with me?"

"Not with you," Thistle said. "But with the bones . . . or just one bone. The only way we can kill the evil woman and stop that flood of life is with a bow made from a dragon's rib. That's why we came here. We mean to take one!"

Nicci carefully edged her way closer to Thistle. She wanted to be in a position to shield the girl with magic if Brom became enraged. Nicci spoke up, in a firm but reasonable tone. "Just one rib, noble dragon. That is all we ask—and it is also what we require."

Bannon spoke up. "There are plenty of bones here, dragon. You won't miss one."

Brom lifted his huge head and flexed his wide leathery wings. "These are the remains of my kind. These are my ancestors."

"The spell is very specific and powerful," Nathan explained. "We would not have come to Kuloth Vale unless we had no choice. Gray dragons are wise, are they not? If we don't stop Life's Mistress, eventually her wave of rampant growth will cover the world, even these high mountains."

Brom simmered for a long moment, pondering deeply. "I understand that it must seem a small thing to you, considering all these bones here, but I must revere the remains of the dragons and do what I have sworn to do. Dragons are honorable creatures." He paused, regarding them one by one with his reptilian gaze. "*I* am an honorable creature."

Now he faced Nicci, his eyes a molten gold. "However, I must acknowledge what you did for me, Sorceress. You gave me life. I was about to perish and become the last set of bones here, and then no dragon would have guarded Kuloth Vale. But with the fire that you placed in my heart, I am alive and powerful again. You have added centuries to my life and purpose." He huffed and seemed to relax. "Perhaps a single rib bone is not an excessive price to ask."

As dusk swallowed Kuloth Vale, the gray creature watched their every move while the companions searched through the graveyard of dragons. Nicci assessed each rib for its suitability. When she found exactly the right one, she ran her fingers along the smooth, ivory surface, bent it slightly, felt it spring back.

Nathan studied the head, the structure of the skull. "That skeleton belonged to a blue dragon. A medium-size one. The bones look undamaged."

Brom loomed above them. A thick membrane flickered across his golden eyes, then slid back beneath the lids. His voice was somber. "Not just any blue dragon, that was Grimney. I remember him well. We were young together, hatched only a century apart. He was always a reckless adventurer, wanting to fly across the seas or soar off to the frozen wastes. He would play in the updrafts of the mountains, taking foolish risks." He snorted a curl of smoke. "Once, Grimney crashed down in a thick forest and became so tangled in tree limbs that he bellowed there for days until other dragons arrived to extricate him. I helped burn the forest to ash so Grimney could pull himself free."

Brom shook his heavy head from side to side. "Another time he flew high, high enough that he hoped to taste the fire of the sun. He came back long afterward, spiraling and flying unevenly. He was never right in the head after that." The gray dragon flapped his wings, then folded them neatly against his back. "I believe it fitting that you use his rib for your quest. Take what you need. Grimney would approve."

Nicci assessed the rib bone one last time to convince herself that it would make the perfect bow to kill Life's Mistress. She used a line of magic to cut the rib free, and the long, curved arc came loose in her hands. "Thank you, Brom."

"Now, leave this place," said the gray dragon. "Much as I enjoy the conversation, it breaks my rules. Take Grimney's rib and do what you must. Honor him—give him one last adventure."

As darkness fell, they climbed up the rocky slopes to get past the wall that bounded the valley, so they could camp outside of Kuloth Vale. When they crossed the pass and began the rugged descent into the thickening darkness, Nicci stopped and turned back to look.

The gray dragon stood on the ridge, spreading his wings. Brom called after them in a loud thrumming voice. "I am the Guardian of the Vale. Do not think we are friends. I will kill you all if you ever intrude again."

Nicci hoped they would never need to return.

CHAPTER 71

It was a long journey back to Cliffwall, but the terrain and the route were familiar to them now. During the initial trip to Kuloth Vale, Nathan had annotated the ancient charts, marking their way and identifying landforms, and also updating his life book.

Determined to get back to the archive, Nicci pressed them to their best possible speed, dreading what damage Victoria had caused while they were away from the isolated canyons. Now, she had the weapon she needed to destroy Life's Mistress. She carried Grimney's curved rib lashed across her shoulders, and she felt the faint tingling power intrinsic to the bone of the magnificent creature, a power resident in life, connected to the world itself.

Leaving the volcanic mountains behind and descending into the gradually opening terrain, she could sense Mrra out in the distance again, watching over them. The sand panther had been unwilling to enter the place of dead dragons, but now she was there to guard them, ranging ahead and scouting, keeping them safe on the way back to Cliffwall.

Knowing they had no time to lose, the companions walked for many miles until the terrain was too dark to see, and even then Nicci was not ready to stop. She would ignite a hand light to lead their way for a few hours longer. They slept when they could, and always set off into the first light of dawn.

When the hills finally gave way to high desert and red-rock canyons, the clear arid air carried the hint of a miasma. Even from a distance, Nicci could see a moist greenish haze beyond the plateau, simmering with primeval forest energy as it spread across the valley toward the cliffs.

Mrra left them again when they entered the network of canyons, not wanting to come too close to people, but Nicci could still feel the big cat out there, watching. Farmers and workers from the outlying settlements in the canyon-wall alcoves welcomed them back while sending runners to report to Cliffwall. When the companions reached the overarching cave grotto that held the primary archive buildings, anxious scholars rushed out to meet them. In the late-afternoon shadows, they gathered to welcome the weary but triumphant travelers as they climbed the steep cliff trail.

"Look, she has the dragon rib!" Gloria called, waving down at them. Beside her, Franklin was relieved. The mousy scholar Mia happily welcomed Nathan, helping him as he climbed up to the cave overhang, followed by Bannon. She chattered about the fascinating and useful books she had read in his absence, and the wizard gave her a warm, paternal pat on the back. "By the way, I used your kerchief while we were traveling, my dear. The spell worked quite well. It was very refreshing and restorative." Mia responded with a glow of pride as he held out the perpetually cool, moist cloth to show her. "A remarkable and useful bit of magic."

Inside the archive complex, a determined Nicci led the way into the main hall, where she unslung the large rib bone and dropped it onto the first table she found, moving aside other books that had been piled there by distracted scholars. "We can now make the weapon we need." She ran her hand over the smooth ivory surface, studying it by the light of the magical torches burning in the main entry hall. The scholars gathered around, breathless and eager to see.

Nicci straightened her shoulders and explained. "This rib belonged to a blue dragon named Grimney. With this bone, I will fashion a powerful bow, and I will be the archer to stop Victoria. We have a chance to stop a scourge that I believe is even greater than the Life-drinker." She saw the hope in their eyes. "I just have to get ready. Ask the hunters among the canyon dwellers to bring me their best arrows and bowstring. I will prepare everything else here."

Nathan ran his fingers through his pale hair, looking at the scholars, and Mia in particular. "Did you have any troubles while we were away? Did Victoria and her wild jungle attack Cliffwall? Another *shaksis*?"

Franklin's words gushed out, as if he couldn't contain them. "We erected a barricade at the outer wall of the plateau to keep us safe, just as you instructed. For defenses, we built wooden bars and planks across the cliff openings to block any other attacks. We tried to make this place impregnable."

"But that horrendous jungle kept spreading," Gloria added. "It filled the valley, and now even the foothills are exploding with life. Some of her thorn vines reached as far as the plateau wall, and they're climbing the cliffs."

"It keeps spreading and spreading," Franklin said. "Nothing can stop it."

Mia nodded, her forehead furrowed with concern. "All those wooden barricades and bars—we didn't think anything could break through our defenses. But when Victoria's magic touched them, the wood itself burst into life again! It sprouted, then kept growing. Soon, the chamber behind the window alcove was an impenetrable thicket. We tried to cut it back, but there was nothing we could do. It grew too fast."

"When wood didn't work, we used stone bricks to wall off that passage," said Franklin. "It is secure now, unless Victoria can find a way to make the stone come alive."

"That's a good solution," Bannon said.

"But only a *temporary* solution," Nicci said, shaking her head. "Given time, vines and roots can break through even the strongest stone." She stroked the curved dragon rib, imagining how she would use it. "But I will not give Victoria that time."

Mia came up to the wizard, holding a charred book in her hands. The pages were curled and blackened, the cover scorched. "Nathan, I've wanted to show you. We salvaged this volume after the fire from the *shaksis*. I was putting the books away when I found a reference in here to a dragon-bone bow, so I knew it was relevant to the spells we need. Would you help me study them? See if we can make out the words, even though the pages are damaged?" She lowered her head. "I didn't want to use my gift to restore the ink and the paper unless you were here to help me."

"Why, I'd be delighted to supervise, my dear," Nathan said, turning to follow the young scholar. "Do you think we could have some tea while we read? And something to eat?"

Gloria shouted for food and drink to be summoned for all of them. "Where is our hospitality? These people have had a long journey! Victoria never would have—" She cut off her words in embarrassment, realizing what she had said.

Though she was tired and dirty, her black dress tattered, her boots scuffed, Nicci refused to rest. "I have to get to work. I am going back to my quarters to fashion the bow we need."

"I'll help," Thistle said, tagging along. "Show me what to do."

Seeing the eagerness in the girl's eyes, Nicci gestured down the corridor. "Come with me. This requires my magic, but you can watch and be ready to help if I think of anything." Thistle readily agreed and accompanied her with a jaunty step through the stone tunnels until they reached their shared room.

The girl poured water into the washbasin and let Nicci refresh herself by wiping a damp rag over her face and her tired eyes. When she was done, Nicci rinsed the rag and handed it to Thistle. "Now you scrub, at least enough so I can see your face."

"You've seen my face."

"I'd like to see more of it. You may well be a pretty girl, but I have yet to see complete proof."

Thistle gave her a teasing frown. "As long as you don't make me wear a pink dress."

"Never."

Dutifully, Thistle washed her cheeks, forehead, eyes, and nose, scrubbing hard. "Clean enough?"

Nicci saw that the girl had indeed exposed some patches of clean skin, and smeared dust around others. The water in the washbasin was brown with grit. "Clean enough for now. You can sit on your sheepskin and watch me, but quietly. I need to concentrate."

The girl acted as if Nicci had given her a solemn mission. She found a comfortable spot on the sheepskin, tucking her knees under her. When one of the archive workers hurried in with a tray of tea, biscuits, and fruit, Thistle served Nicci, who ate distractedly. The girl, on the other hand, devoured everything that remained.

Laying the long bone across her lap, Nicci sat on her pallet and considered how she would fashion the bow. She ran her palm along the curve of Grimney's rib, found the structure of the bone, and released her magic to reshape it. She softened and then hardened the marrow. She felt the great power already contained in the stiff, curved rib, but added even more power to it.

Working carefully, cautiously, she adjusted the arc, then fashioned a recurve on each end, added flexibility where it was needed, reinforced cracks in the bone structure, sealed the porosity. She concentrated tirelessly, consumed with the task.

Looking up, she saw that Thistle was sound asleep, curled up on the sheepskin. Nicci watched the sleeping girl, noting the relaxed expression on her elfin face, her smooth brow now that she felt safe and at peace.

Nicci knew she needed to kill Life's Mistress, so that she could *keep* the girl safe.

While Thistle dozed, Nicci finished her work. She felt the rib trembling with energy and anger, ready to complete its mission. In his life, the blue dragon Grimney had wanted excitement, had wanted to accomplish great things. Now he would do that.

Touching the new weapon, Nicci thought of how she would bring much-needed death back to the throbbing evil of the primeval forest.

Leaving the other scholars behind, Mia led Nathan into a small, well-lit study room. She carried the burned, damaged book she had found among the volumes salvaged from the *shaksis* fire.

Nathan took a seat and patted the bench beside him. "Now, let's study those records you found. The more we understand, the better chance Nicci has." He knew they could never go back to Kuloth Vale and demand another rib bone from the gray dragon if this one failed. "We'll only have one chance."

He and Mia sat in a small alcove lit by bright candles, leaning close to study the blackened, curled pages of the volume. "I don't know if this is anything significant," she said as she flattened the pages and pointed out lines written in an eclectic dialect. "But it does mention a bow made of a dragon's rib."

"That can't be a coincidence. I never heard that dragon skeletons were particularly useful." He touched his lips. "Though I admit they are certainly impressive."

The young woman frowned at the smudged writing, the scorched paper. "No one noticed this spell before, because we were looking for a spell to block the outpouring of life." She gave him a faint smile. "After you left, I searched for such documents, and another scholar referred me to this book. He was actually researching a cure for impotence." She lowered her voice to a conspiratorial whisper. "It took some doing to get him to admit that."

"A cure for impotence? I suppose that fits with the restoration of life," Nathan quipped. "And is there a counter to it?"

"For his purposes, he did not find the spell he needed, so he placed the book back in the corridor shelves to be returned to the archives in the normal course of work. As it happens, the *shaksis* attacked before the book could be reshelved, and it went missing. Some of these pages are damaged, but I noticed a mention of the dragon-rib bow, and I knew you would want to see it." She pointed to a deep brown spot on the paper. "Look here."

"Indeed. We already knew the power of the bones, my dear girl. It references the weapon we want?"

"Yes, the bow itself and the powerful gifted person required to be the archer. But that is only part of the spell! This section, the damaged part, mentions requirements for the *arrow* as well. We didn't have all the information before."

Nathan's brows pulled together in a troubled frown as a chill ran down his back. "You're certain the arrow has to be special, too? The bow doesn't impart the required magic? I hadn't considered that. How discouraging. What more do we have to do?" He squinted, but the blackened char on the edges had destroyed the ink. He knew Nicci would certainly not want to be delayed. "It's too damaged to read."

"I can attempt to fix that," Mia said, smiling. "I found a trick when I was studying the old books, but I didn't want to try unless you were here. I've never done it before, but I think I understand the magic involved." She traced her fingers along the outside of the pages, then released a tiny trickle of her own gift. To Nathan's delight, the edges of the paper became white again, then tan. The damaged page healed and stiffened, clarifying the ends of sentences that had previously been obscured.

Marveling at what she had done, and how easily, Nathan let out a sigh. "I forgot how many people here are gifted, even if they are untrained." He sniffed. "And *I'm* supposedly the great wizard and prophet."

"It's a simple spell, really," Mia said, embarrassed. "Nothing dangerous."

"Starting a fire is also simple if you have a spark. But without the spark . . ." He shook his head, and focused on the newly restored writing. "Never mind. Now, what does it say?"

Mia concentrated on the words she had just restored. "Hmm, the couplet only refers to a 'properly prepared arrow.' And this section here"—she tapped with a finger—"says, 'Only one kind of poison is appropriate.'"

"Dear spirits, a poison? What kind of poison is it?" Nathan groaned, fearing they would be faced with some other lengthy and difficult quest before they could fight Victoria. "And where are we supposed to find it?"

Mia turned the pages and they scanned the other spells, including the most effective cure for impotence, though they needed the opposite sort of magic to stop Victoria. "In this next line it refers back to the original spell book, and we didn't read all of that, either. I thought we had all the information we needed, but some of those pages were damaged when it was fused with the stone wall."

Nathan gave her an encouraging smile. "You've just demonstrated your proficiency with the new restoration spell. Maybe you can fix those pages, too?"

Mia stood from her seat, ready to do whatever he asked. "Perhaps I can."

Still weary from the journey, he sipped his tea and pondered while the young librarian ran into the archives. She knew where to find what she was looking for and soon returned with the damaged book that Nicci had extracted from the melted stone wall.

Together, they turned the pages, assessing the smears of dust that obscured the ancient writing. Using her gift, Mia held her hands over the pages, squeezed her eyes shut in deep concentration, and worked her fingers over the smeared writing. Some of the stone powder flaked off like dried mud and lifted free in tiny specks of dust, floating away to expose words that had previously been damaged and lumped together.

"I thought we had read the whole spell before," Nathan said, "but this section on the next page . . ." He leaned closer to read what she revealed.

Mia cleared away and freshened the distorted ink, pleased to use her newfound skill. When the letters became dark and clear, Nathan read the precise instruction for preparing the arrow to be shot from a dragon-rib bow, an arrow that could kill the wielder of the uncontrolled fecundity spell.

It was the key to defeating Life's Mistress, the poison that they needed to accomplish their task.

In a long, hoarse whisper, Nathan said, "Oh no."

CHAPTER 72

When she was finished, Nicci considered the dragon-bone bow a work of art, a work of death. The surface of the magic-infused ivory was veined with lines of faint gold that were intrinsic to the dragon itself, threads connected to the world and life.

She couldn't wait to use it against Victoria.

In the Cliffwall canyons, the isolated settlers often hunted with bows of their own making, and the best archers had already provided sturdy bowstrings made of woven sheep gut. At Nicci's request, they had also offered a selection of long arrows fletched with crow's feathers and tipped with splayed iron heads, their razor edges sharpened to a bright silver edge.

After she strung the graceful recurved bow, it thrummed with the energy of one of the world's most magnificent creatures, a dragon tied to the source of life deep within the earth—likely the same source of power that the Eldertree had drawn upon. The bow vibrated in her hand, as if Grimney's spirit was eager to be released for one last quest.

Nicci was ready. The arrows were ready.

She took her weapon and headed through the winding tunnels until she reached a gathering hall for the Cliffwall scholars, deep in the heart of the plateau. She found Nathan already there, his face stricken, his skin ashen. Beside him, the young scholar Mia looked terrified.

She immediately sensed something terribly wrong. Her hand tensed around the bow. "What is it, Wizard?" Nathan opened his mouth, closed it, as if he couldn't find the words. "Tell me." The sharpness in her tone startled the answer out of him.

"The bow isn't enough," Nathan said.

Just then, Bannon entered the room with a jaunty step, full of energy. Thistle accompanied him like a little sister, washed, dressed, and rested now. Bannon's eyes sparkled in anticipation of the great battle that was to come. He seemed too naive to be afraid. "I am ready to fight Victoria! Just like when we destroyed the Lifedrinker together. Will I join you, Sorceress?"

Nicci raised a hand so abruptly that she cut off his words as surely as if she had released a silencing spell.

Thistle's honey-brown eyes went wide at her reaction. Bannon looked around in confusion and saw the expression on Nathan's face. "W-What happened? What's the matter?"

Nathan slid one of the old, damaged books across the table toward them. "A bow made from a dragon's rib is an extremely potent weapon, and you are indeed a powerful sorceress to wield it, but that is only part of what the magic requires to destroy Victoria. There is more . . ." He slowly shook his head. "The price is much greater than we knew."

He opened the stained volume to the pages that Mia had restored with magic. He touched the words with his extended finger. "Read the ancient text yourself, Sorceress. Draw your conclusions." His voice grew much quieter. "The words leave no room for interpretation."

Mia stared at the lines, as if she hoped the letters would change. She slumped heavily into a chair.

Bannon stood straight and determined. "No matter the price, we have to stop Victoria," he blurted out. "After what she did to those poor girls . . ."

Nathan's azure eyes bored into Nicci as he explained. "In order to kill Life's Mistress, not only must you use a bow made of dragon bone, but the arrow itself has to be tipped with the necessary poison—a poison that can sap all vitality from life."

"What poison?" Thistle asked.

Nicci looked down at the page and read the words herself even as the wizard recited, *"The loss of a loved one."* He drew a deep breath. "No matter how sharp the arrow is, or how strong the bow might be, in order to kill Victoria, the arrowhead must be coated with the heart's blood of someone that the archer loves, someone the archer kills. And we have already established that *you* must be the archer, Sorceress."

Bannon and Thistle both gasped, and Mia slumped in her seat, her shoulders shaking. Nicci felt deep cold rush through her as she read the spell again, grasped what it said. "This is not acceptable."

Before she could respond, a distant crack resonated through the stone-walled chamber and rumbled through the corridors. Cliffwall scholars hurried down the hall, running to investigate. An old librarian with a long white beard scuttled past the chamber door, his eyes wide with alarm. "The outer wall! Victoria's vines are attacking the plateau defenses."

Followed by the others, Nicci bolted out of the chamber and rushed among the panicked scholars through passageways to the outer wall of the plateau. Thistle ran faster, racing ahead to where a frantic crowd tried to barricade the opening that had been breached by writhing, murderous vegetation. Men and women frantically hauled crates and stone blocks from other rooms, any obstacle to block the passage from the intrusion.

Outside, thick, thorny vines from the explosive primeval jungle had climbed the cliff like an invading army. Tendrils and tentacles thrust into cracks in the rock, pushing, prying, breaking open the defenses. The vines had now burst through the outer chambers previously sealed with stone blocks. The wooden bars the defenders had initially mounted in place had now grown into huge writhing thickets that shoved open the temporary barricade, and the broken stone blocks lay strewn in the hall. Wild vegetation spewed into the formerly impervious archive complex.

Mia cried out in dismay when she saw the infestation of dangerous growth. Thistle dodged and danced away from the grasping vines and branches that surged into the corridor. A whipping tendril scratched her skin, but she slapped it away and scuttled out of reach.

Nathan had not brought his own sword, but Bannon leaped to the attack, using his blade to hack the whipping vines and branches. One woody appendage snapped back and slammed hard against the side of his head, stunning him. The young man reeled and his knees began to buckle.

Nathan rushed in to grab his protégé, and pulled him to safety before the vines could lunge for him. Bleeding from the side of his head, Bannon groaned and dropped his sword with a metallic clatter on the stone floor. Nathan dragged him farther out of reach so that he could check his injury.

Mia, left staring appalled at the horrific growth, did not move quickly enough. Before she could dodge out of the way, a thorn-studded vine lashed around her neck, coiled, and tightened. The sharp spikes plunged into her throat, digging through flesh and blood vessels. Gouts of crimson sprayed out as she screamed and struggled.

Whirling, Nathan howled, "No!" He lunged toward Mia to save her, instinctively lashing out with his hand to summon a blast of magic . . . but nothing happened, not even a flicker. He was helpless.

With an additional jerk and twist, the malicious vine snapped the young woman's neck, then discarded her body against the curved wall.

Nicci knocked the frightened scholars away as she pushed forward, desperate to find something powerful enough to block this incursion. Ignoring Bannon's groans and the wizard's outcry of grief and fury, Nicci thought of how she had manipulated the fused stone down in the vaults, reshaping and moving the rock. Now she called upon the structure of the plateau walls, reshaped the stone as if it were soft candle wax to create an impenetrable curtain across the opening the plants had broken through. Under her guidance, the re-formed slickrock flowed down and severed the writhing vines and branches, sealing off the outer wall of the plateau. The stone solidified, restoring the integrity of the cliff, walling off the incursion of deadly plants. They were safe. For now.

Sobbing, Nathan had dropped to the floor, pulling the dead young scholar against him. Mia bled from the brutal gashes in her neck, soaking the wizard's borrowed robes with red, and her head lolled. He groaned. "She was so smart, so loyal. Dear spirits, if not for Mia we wouldn't have found the other part of the spell. Otherwise, all our efforts would have failed. It's because of her that we have a chance." He looked up at Nicci with reddened eyes. "We have a chance."

Nicci assessed the shocked and frightened scholars. She had no illusions about how difficult this terrible enemy would be. "We need the necessary poison for the arrow." But the task seemed impossible, and dread weighed heavily in the pit of her stomach. The heart's blood of someone she loved? Her voice was cold. "But I love no one."

It was a bleak statement, but true. Her one true love, the only man she would ever love, was Richard Rahl. She had given him her heart with a passion that had now transformed, but had never waned. At first, that love had been dark—the wrong kind of love—but Nicci had an epiphany. She had grown and learned her lesson, eventually accepting that Richard would only ever love Kahlan. Those two belonged together in a special way and could never be separated, *should* never be separated.

Nicci had come to that realization long ago. She still loved Richard with all her heart, but in a different way. Nicci had gone to the Old World to serve him, to explore his new empire, to lay the groundwork for a new golden age . . . even if it meant she had to be far away from him.

She had not believed the words Red had written, about saving the world—for Richard—but now she saw it was true. First the Lifedrinker and now mad Victoria would have swallowed up the world, devastated the D'Haran Empire. Nicci had to do everything necessary to defeat the enemy, but in order to do so she needed the heart's blood of someone she loved.

And it was Richard she loved. She could think of no one else.

Nicci had to be the archer. No one else had the necessary power to face Victoria. Nathan had lost control of his gift, and none of these amateur scholars and dabblers here in Cliffwall even approached Nicci's skill. It must be her.

But . . . someone she loved? Truly loved? Richard . . .

That solution was not possible. She couldn't save the world for Richard, if she had to kill Richard to do so. Oh, if he knew the situation, truly understood what was at stake, Nicci was sure he would immediately agree to the terms—he would offer himself, tear open his shirt to expose his chest so that she could take his heart's blood. He would willingly give Nicci what she needed, the blood poison that would stop Life's Mistress.

But he was on the other side of the world.

And Nicci would never kill Richard, *could* never kill him. The very thought filled her with horror. She remembered how it had destroyed her to stop his heart, to send him to the underworld, so he could rescue Kahlan. He had begged her, and Nicci could not refuse him.

But now . . . Would she sacrifice the world itself, just to keep Richard alive a little longer? It sounded foolish, but she knew she would. Her stomach knotted.

Somewhere, far up in the Dark Lands, Red must be laughing.

The heart's blood of a loved one.

As she listened to the moans of the gathered scholars, she knew they were all terrified, but not as despairing as Nicci was. After the difficult quest to obtain the dragon's rib, and with her own powers as a sorceress, she had expected to have the weapon to kill Victoria.

But it was not enough, and now the last component simply did not seem achievable. She didn't know what to do.

Nathan sat on the floor, staring at Mia's pale, lifeless face. He stroked the mousy brown hair from her forehead. "I am so sorry, my dear." Wearing a stricken expression, he wiped her brow with the always moist, always cool kerchief that she had given him before their journey to Kuloth Vale.

Nicci looked down at Thistle, who was thankfully unharmed from the attack, other than a scratch on her leg.

Suddenly Bannon stood before Nicci, still bleeding from his forehead. He rested the point of his lackluster sword on the floor in front of him. He reached up to wipe a smear of blood from his wound, obviously drawing on his courage. He raised his chin and looked at her. "I am the one, Sorceress." He drew a ragged breath. "It has to be me."

He hooked his fingers in the opening of his shirt and tore it open to expose his chest. "I know you care for me. I saw how you looked at me after we fought the Lifedrinker together. You praised me for how useful

I was. And I have seen what Victoria is doing . . . what she already did to Audrey, Laurel, and Sage." Sad determination filled his eyes. "If I can save the world by giving my life, then I'll gladly do so. Draw your knife, take my heart's blood." He swallowed hard. "It belongs to you anyway." He lifted his head back and closed his eyes, as if bracing himself for a deathblow.

Taken aback, Nicci scowled. "Don't be a fool." She pushed him aside. "That would never work. I have no time for this."

Leaving the crestfallen Bannon behind, she stalked away to the archive chambers, hoping to find a different answer, some other way in one of the spell books. She felt a terrible dread inside.

After all Nicci had endured in her life, what if there was no one she loved?

CHAPTER 73

With the full intensity of a dedicated memmer, Nicci mulled over all the knowledge she possessed, the spells she had been taught, the powers she had stolen from the wizards she killed. There had to be another solution.

Wanting to be alone as she grappled with her thoughts, she went to stand outside under the great overhang of the main cliff grotto. She looked across the hidden, protected canyons to the clustered dwellings in the smaller alcoves scattered up and down the opposite cliffs. All these people had lived sheltered for millennia, guarding this secret archive. They had seemed safe, untouched by the outside world until young Victoria had accidentally brought down the camouflage shroud and revealed the great library after thousands of years.

The knowledge contained in the archive was dangerous enough, Nicci knew, but far worse were those amateur would-be wizards who did not understand the powers they foolishly unleashed.

Now, late in the afternoon, the secluded canyons felt peaceful and quiet, as if unaware of the monstrous flood of life that approached like a destructive wave from the opposite side of the plateau. Nicci had to stop Victoria, who had transformed herself into a monster. She knew how to accomplish the task, how to defeat Life's Mistress, but whether or not the price was too high, Nicci didn't know how to pay it. The answer seemed impossible.

Nicci, a gifted sorceress, had the dragon-rib bow, she had arrows, and she had the will. She was ready to face Life's Mistress and kill her.

But she did not have the necessary poison.

Nevertheless, Nicci refused to accept the impossible. She never had.

Tension filled the halls of Cliffwall as the scholars tried to find some way to help. Nathan mourned the death of Mia, and Nicci knew he would do anything to destroy Victoria and her rampaging fecundity, but he had no magic to offer . . . or if he did, the wild and uncontrolled backlash might cause even more destruction than Victoria.

There had to be something else. . . .

Lost in thoughts, Nicci stared into the brooding canyon silence, where shepherds, farmers, and orchard tenders went about their business as they waited for what came next. Sheltered, peaceful, oblivious . . . A grim weight pressed down on her shoulders. These people all counted on her to save them, because no one else had the ability.

Yet Nicci wasn't sure she had the ability either—the ability to love.

It seemed laughable and tragic that, for all her knowledge, for all the great magic she possessed—and every skill she had learned or power she had stolen—Nicci's great failing was a simple human emotion that any child could produce at will.

Her eyes stung as she looked at the secret canyon where so many people had lived undisturbed for generations. She wanted to preserve this peaceful home for the inhabitants of Cliffwall—and especially for Thistle, who had already endured so much, lost so much.

As a child, Nicci had loved her father, although she had been convinced otherwise. Without understanding the depth of his devotion to his employees, his business, his future, Nicci had watched her father work in the armory. She had observed the workers' respect for him, but she gave him no credit for his skills, thanks to her mother's corrupt influence.

Her mother had made Nicci feel worthless, feeding her the debilitating philosophy of the Order until Nicci choked on it, all the while believing she was being fed a fine feast. Only after Richard pulled the blindfold from her eyes and showed her how to break those lifelong chains had Nicci understood her father's devotion and exactly how much harm the Order had done to him, as well as what they had stolen from her with their twisted philosophy.

But Nicci's father was long gone and the Order defeated, Jagang dead by her own hands, and she could not make up for the past. Instead, she had to look to the future. Now, as part of the new task for Richard that she had taken into her heart, she could save the world from Life's Mistress . . . if only she could find a way to use the weapon she had.

Looking nervous, the memmer Gloria emerged from the front stone gates of the main tower, waving to Nicci. "Sorceress! We've been looking for you."

Nicci felt a tiny spark of hope, ready to grasp at any straw. "Did you find another solution?"

Gloria's round cheeks puffed out as she blew air through her lips. "Why, no, Sorceress. It's just that the orphan girl asked us to look for you, says it's extremely important."

Nicci was instantly alert. "Is Thistle all right?"

"She's waiting in your quarters to talk with you. She said it was urgent, but wouldn't tell any of us, only that we had to find you right away."

Leaving Gloria behind, Nicci rushed back inside the main buildings, hurrying along the corridors. She was worried about the girl. Thistle had watched her village collapse, fought dust people, sand panthers, and a dragon, and if *she* claimed that something was urgent . . .

Or maybe she had remembered some detail that they could use?

Thistle was waiting for her inside their quarters, sitting on the sleeping pallet, her scuffed knees drawn up against her chest. Her body was shaking. When she saw Nicci, her large honey-brown eyes filled with relief, but also fear.

Before Nicci could speak, the girl said, "I've already eaten the seeds. I knew you would try to stop me, but now you can't. It was the only way I could be sure, so now you have to do it."

A chill like a trickle of ice sliced down Nicci's back. She stepped forward. "What do you mean?"

Thistle clutched dried petals and leaves in her hands. Nicci instantly recognized the shriveled plant, the distinctive violet-and-crimson flower, the crumbled stem. The girl held it out to show her. The deathrise flower, the poisonous bloom that Bannon had clumsily given her, not knowing its awful potency. As a sorceress, Nicci had kept it because she knew that such powerful tools were not to be wasted.

Thistle's eyes flashed. Even as Nicci lunged toward her, the girl shoved the rest of the dried petals into her mouth.

Nicci threw herself upon the girl. "Stop!"

Thistle swallowed.

Nicci grabbed the girl's chin and tugged at her jaw, trying to remove any remnants from her mouth, but Thistle kept her teeth clenched together.

"Too late," she mumbled. She was already starting to convulse.

Nicci summoned her magic. Maybe she could force the girl to purge herself. Maybe she could find some way to neutralize the deadly substance.

But Nicci knew that no healing spell could cure the deathrise poison. She remembered Emperor Jagang's tortures, how he had tested variations of the deadly plant in camps that he called Places of Screaming. This was no chilling tale to be whispered over ale in an inn. The deathrise flower was truly the worst possible poison in existence.

If Nicci could kill Jagang all over again, she would.

"There is no cure," Thistle said defiantly. "You told me so yourself." Her mouth was empty now. She had swallowed every bit of the deadly flower.

In anger and despair, Nicci shook the girl's narrow shoulders. "What are you thinking? Why would you do that?"

"To give you no choice," Thistle said. A vicious shudder racked her body, and her voice came out in a gasp. "To make the valley beautiful again, so everyone can live their lives . . . just like I always wished for."

Nicci wrapped her arms around Thistle, as if afraid the girl would try to escape. "That was a stupid, useless gesture. It won't help."

An image flashed through Nicci's mind of Jagang sitting outside his tent to listen to the prolonged agony of the test subjects after they consumed the poison. Some took hours to die, some took days. Even the mildest dose caused eyes to hemorrhage and made blood ooze from ears and nostrils. Some victims writhed so wildly that their convulsions cracked their spines. They screamed until they coughed up their vocal cords in bloody strands. Their skin would swell, their joints burst. Some clawed off their own faces trying to escape the pain.

The orphan girl shuddered in Nicci's arms, and she began to cough. Her skin was already chalky, her lips bloodless. Her mournful honey-brown eyes were bloodshot.

Nicci knew what was going to happen to the poor girl. "There is no cure, child. Why would you do this to yourself?"

"For you," Thistle choked out. "To give you what you need. To make the choice for you." She squirmed and thrashed, and Nicci tried to hold her tight to keep her still. "What you can do—is give me a quick and painless death. End that for me." She looked up. "Take one of the arrows, pierce me through the heart, quick and clean. Before it's too late."

"No!" Nicci called up her magic, tried to find healing spells. She sent power into the girl to keep her strong, but the deathrise poison raged like a wildfire through her body. "I can't!"

"Take my heart's blood. You need it against Victoria."

Nicci glanced over at the razor-sharp, iron-tipped arrows she had left on the writing desk.

"If you love me, you'll save me from what you know is coming," Thistle said. "Kill me. Use the arrow to stab me through the heart."

"No!"

The girl continued in a hoarse voice. "You'll have the blood you need. The necessary poison." As she began convulsing, her small hands clutched Nicci's black dress. "Stop Victoria and save my land."

Nicci was torn, her heart broken. She held the orphan girl, felt her spasms grow worse. She knew the pain was only the start of what would be long hours, possibly even days as Thistle slowly tore herself apart, screaming the whole time.

"I know you love me," Thistle murmured, lifting a trembling hand to touch Nicci's cheek just for a moment.

"No . . ." Nicci whispered, and she wasn't sure the girl even heard her.

Thistle coughed and shuddered, pressing her face against Nicci.

Not wanting to release her hold on the dying girl, Nicci extended her other hand and reached out with magic to pull one of the arrows from its resting place. It slid through the air, across the room, and landed in Nicci's palm. She wrapped her fingers around the shaft, saw the silver sheen of the sharpened edge, the pointed tip.

Thistle could no longer hold back her pain. She convulsed and cried out.

Nicci squeezed her tight, knowing the agony would only grow worse. She held the arrow in her right hand, turning Thistle just slightly with her left arm, finding a vulnerable place in the girl's chest. As tears came to Nicci's deep blue eyes, she drove the arrow forward, taking away the pain as gently as she could.

And when she pulled the arrow out, its tip and the end of its shaft were red with a thick layer of blood from Thistle's heart. The necessary poison.

Nicci bowed her head and unwittingly added even more poison to the bloody arrow—a single tear. The first tear that Nicci had shed in a long time.

CHAPTER 74

As she stalked through Cliffwall preparing to kill Life's Mistress, Nicci felt like a black shadow filled with razors. Hollow inside, her heart a bottomless pit like what she had seen at the center of the Scar, she clutched the bloody arrow, its sharp tip not at all blunted by the sticky coating. The necessary poison was based on dangerous love, a love that Nicci had never admitted existed.

Now her heart was just a hot wound.

The spunky orphan girl had surrendered her very life, had forced Nicci to do such a terrible thing in order to achieve the victory they all needed. Thistle had seen something in Nicci's heart that the sorceress did not even know she had. She squeezed the arrow tighter, but she forced her muscles to relax, so that her anger would not snap the shaft. She dared not waste this weapon she had acquired at a great, impossible price.

Thistle's blood.

Her normal reaction would have been to deny such feelings, to burn them away or wall them off, but she needed that emotion now because love was the vital component. Love was the poison. In this case, as Victoria would soon discover, love was deadly.

As she prepared to make her way out into the primeval jungle, Nicci saw that she had stained her black dress with the innocent girl's blood. More poison.

She paid no attention to other tense, frightened scholars who huddled in Cliffwall, looking at her as a savior to stop Life's Mistress. Poor Thistle had already paid the price.

Victoria would pay a higher one.

Future and Fate depend on both the journey and the destination.

Bannon met her in the wide hallway, dressed in fresh traveling clothes and carrying his unimpressive sword. His face looked drawn and pale. "I am ready to go with you, Sorceress."

Nathan stood beside him, haggard and distraught, but he had a fire in his azure eyes. "Even if I can't use my magic, Bannon and I are deadly fighters. You know it. We're going with you."

The young man swallowed hard. "Thistle made it possible. We should all do it together."

She looked at them for a long, silent moment, then shook her head. "No, I go alone. This is my battle. Thistle did her part. Now I will do mine." Nicci didn't *dare* need them. She slung the dragon-bone bow over her shoulder, and carried her one blood-tipped arrow. She did not bring spares. This one would be deadly enough. It had to be. "I have everything I need."

After a long, solemn moment, Nathan seemed to understand. He reached out to clasp Bannon's shoulder before the young man could say anything else. "It's not about us, my boy. You've proved yourself over and over. The sorceress needs to do this alone."

Bannon looked helplessly at his sword, as if it had become useless in his hands. When he glanced up and met her eyes, his expression froze at what he saw on her face. He stepped back, swallowing hard. "Our hearts go with you, Sorceress. I know you will succeed."

Nathan drew in a deep breath, let it out slowly. "Nicci herself is the deadliest of weapons."

Traveling through the tunnels, she reached the wall on the far side of the plateau. She had remolded the rock to seal Cliffwall's defenses against the intrusion of the madly growing jungle, but even stone walls could not stop her. Releasing her magic, she shifted the slickrock and shoved it out of her way like soft clay, opening the wall to the outside.

She looked out upon a primeval disaster, an encroaching wall of twisted, thrashing greenery, tangled vines, fungi that grew as tall as houses before exploding into a blizzard of spores. Thunderheads of gnats and flies buzzed around the fetid forest. In order to solve an extreme problem, Victoria had unleashed an even more extreme solution.

Branches stretched out, vines writhed, ferns uncoiled. A haze of pollen and spores thickened the air into a choking miasma. The rustle, crackle, and hiss of all that growth battering against the mesa cliff sounded like an unstoppable army of life. Too much life.

But Nicci was Death's Mistress.

"Make way," she said. She held out both hands and released her magic in a thunderclap of devastation, clearing the path. Wizard's fire rolled out, unquenchable, unstoppable, and the flames charred the grasping branches and thorny vines into ash. Under the onslaught of heat, massive tree trunks exploded and the storm of splinters shredded adjacent monstrous plants.

Once she had blasted a path, Nicci stepped out into the wreckage and made her way across blackened ground, descending the steep slope. In only moments, the scorched earth already stirred and simmered with new shoots bursting forth. Grass blades and vine tendrils whipped up to grasp at Nicci's feet, trying to hold her back or take her prisoner. She sent a thought toward them, the merest taste of vengeful anger, and the new growth shriveled and died.

Then she went hunting.

Victoria would not hide from her. The memmer sorceress, swollen with lush fertility, wanted to kill Nicci. She had already sent the *shaksis* to attack them, and now Nicci would go to the heart of this primeval jungle. She knew what lurked there.

She adjusted the dragon-bone bow on her shoulders and walked forward, her blue eyes focused ahead. Dead things crunched under her boots. The writhing jungle reached out to seize her with clawlike branches and lashing fronds. Nicci summoned the winds, bringing great raging storms of air that blasted the vegetation, snapped trees, stripped leaves off of branches, exploded mushrooms, uprooted ferns. She tore open a path to insure that her progress would be unhindered. Nicci was the eye of a walking storm.

The distance did not matter. She knew her destination, her target.

Expending so much magic should have weakened Nicci, but the anger and hurt inside her were a rejuvenating force. When she had cleared the way far ahead, she stopped the winds and continued deeper into the mad infestation of life. The plants themselves seemed cowed after what she had inflicted upon them.

In that momentary respite, the insects came, a cloud of black, biting gnats, a swarm of stinging wasps, and a thundercloud of dark beetles, tens of thousands of them.

Nicci spared them barely a glance. As the swarms descended upon her, swirling in the air, she released a thought. She did not even need to gesture with her hands as she stopped tens of thousands of minuscule insect hearts. Gnats, wasps, and beetles fell to the ground like a pattering black rain.

Nicci stepped forward, and the jungle fell into a hush. But she knew she wasn't finished. She had not yet won.

Ahead of her, branches and leaves stirred, and three figures emerged, figures that had once been lovely young women. Audrey, Laurel, and Sage. Now they had been possessed and transformed by the forest. Their skin was the mottled green of mixed leaves, their eyes fractured and glinting with many shades of emerald, their mouths filled with sharp white fangs. Their hair was a stir of moss about their heads.

The women closed in to stand in front of Nicci and block her way. She regarded them with a withering stare. "Victoria sent you to stop me? She fears to face me herself?"

The thing that had been Laurel chuckled. "It is not because she fears you. It's because she rewards *us*."

When the forest women spread their arms, long thorns sprouted from their skin. Glistening sap oozed from the thorn tips as if they had become scorpion tails.

"This is a chance for us to test our powers," said Sage.

"And we'll have fun," Audrey said.

Nicci did not touch her dragon-bone bow, leaving her single poisoned arrow in its quiver as the deadly forest women approached. "I don't have time to play," she said.

She unleashed the still-seething magic inside her, manifesting

three writhing spheres of wizard's fire. They rolled forward like miniature suns. Audrey, Laurel, and Sage had time only to reel backward and
throw out their hands in desperate defensive spasms before the trio of
suns exploded, one for each of them. Unstoppable flames engulfed their
green-infested bodies, closing tight, crushing the inhuman women
with incinerating fire. The female figures crumbled to ash that smelled
more like burning wood than burning flesh.

"Death is stronger than life," Nicci said.

She stepped over the ashes of their bones and made her way to the
heart of the forest.

CHAPTER 75

The jungle stopped fighting back, as if it had accepted its own doom, and instead the writhing, simmering forest welcomed her, lured her ahead. Trees bent out of the way, and vines curled aside to clear a path for her. Weeds and spiky shrubs bowed down before Nicci. She walked forward, dressed in black, her blond hair flowing behind her.

She knew Victoria had not surrendered. The open way before her was a green tunnel surrounded by drooping ferns and low, twitching willows. It reminded her of a spiderweb . . . a trap. Nicci's lips curved in a thin smile. Yes, it was a trap—but it was *her* trap, and Victoria would learn the truth soon enough.

The terrain that had been the Scar was unrecognizable, but after a long journey she realized she had reached the center. Twisted obsidian pillars and broken black rock had once risen up from the Lifedrinker's lair here, but now Nicci saw a glade of lush, suffocating green. Trees stretched high overhead, their boughs arching inward like hands clasped in prayer—a prayer directed toward the vicious green *thing* that grew at the center of the glade.

Victoria was no longer the matronly woman who had instructed the memmers, a mentor who took young acolytes under her wing and taught them everything she knew. Victoria was no longer human. She still possessed the knowledge, the tangled spells, the lore that filled all the magic preserved by generations of memory-enhanced people, but she had become something so much more.

The skin of Victoria's naked body was encrusted with a lumpy excrescence of bark. Her legs had planted into the ground, taking root as twin trunks, twisting and coiling with bright green vines gathered into a burgeoning nest of growth where the two legs fused into a single torso-trunk with rounded wooden breasts. Victoria's arms stretched out as thick curved boughs, her fingers a myriad of branches. Her hair spread outward in a panoply of twigs, a thicket of tangled brush. But Victoria's face was still recognizable, if awful, her skin not just wood but suffused with green. Pulsing lines of dark sap ran up her cheeks and along her ears.

Seeing Nicci, Life's Mistress preened like a bird displaying its feathers. Victoria drew strength, pulling energy from the ground where her roots had spread throughout the primeval jungle, where the growth had built up enormous spell-forms to enhance and reinforce the magic. Her mouth opened in a loud, sharp-edged laugh.

Neither showing nor feeling fear, Nicci stepped into the glade, paying no heed to the rustle and whisper of angry branches, of slithering undergrowth. Her enemy was here. Victoria had sent the three forest women to block her, but now she would face Nicci herself.

Nicci stopped in front of Life's Mistress and planted her boots in the soft forest loam. Her black dress clung to her with perspiration, and Nicci touched the drying bloodstain on the fabric. *Thistle's* blood. A reminder.

She spoke in a haughty challenge. "For a woman who wanted to restore life and make the land thrive, you have caused far too much pain and destruction, Victoria."

As her huge trunk body writhed, the layers of thick bark cracked. A bellow came out of the forest woman's mouth. *"I am Life's Mistress!"*

Nicci was unimpressed. "And I cannot let you live."

She unslung the ivory bow from her shoulder and calmly, without taking her eyes from Victoria's monstrous face, bent the curved rib of Grimney, the blue dragon. The bone thrummed with energy, the magic of the earth, the source of creation. The string itself came from the people of Cliffwall, and although it had no magic, it did have the power of human creation, stretched taut, ready for what the weapon had to do. Ready to use life to destroy life.

Victoria's laughter stirred the crouching trees and angry under-brush. "One insignificant sorceress? One bow? One arrow?"

"It will be sufficient," Nicci said. "We found the spell, a magic that draws upon the very power of life. A bone of creation . . . the bone of a dragon." She held the bow, grasped the tense string, and felt Grimney's rib vibrate.

"The bones of the earth," Victoria said, her boughs creaking, her body bending. "The magic inside a dragon's rib?" Her face folded and shifted, as if her mind sorted through all the ancient knowledge of thousands upon thousands of arcane tomes that she and many genera-tions before her had memorized.

Nicci pulled out the arrow, looked at its sharp end and the thick red coating, still sticky. Her throat had gone dry. "And I have an arrow tipped with the necessary poison. The heart's blood of one that I loved, one that I killed." She knocked it on the string. "Thistle's blood."

Victoria suddenly jerked back as Nicci provided the last clue. In her vast mental library of ancient lore, the other woman recalled the spell. One of her trunklike legs ripped itself out of the ground. The boughs whipped, branches cracked.

Nicci did not flinch. "You remember. I wanted you to remember. Thistle deserves that."

A desperate Victoria rallied the primeval jungle to attack. The for-est closed in, the ferns, vines, and wildly growing trees lunging toward Nicci. Thorns, branches, stinging insects swept to the attack, rushing in a desperate last attempt to stop her.

But Nicci had only one thing left to do. She drew back the string of the dragon-bone bow and aligned the arrow. She aimed its blood-dipped point directly between the large rounded growths of Victoria's breasts.

As branches, vines, and thorns thundered down upon her, Nicci loosed the arrow.

She didn't need to use magic to guide the shaft as it flew. The air whistled and sang like a last keening cry, and the razor-sharp point struck home with a loud thump. Poisoned with an innocent girl's blood, the arrow sank into the flesh of the transformed woman.

In Nicci's hands, unable to bear the tension of the bowstring, the dragon's rib snapped in half. It had released its magic, the last energy, the final gift of the blue dragon who had sought adventure in his life long ago. As the attacking jungle froze and quivered, Nicci dropped the now-useless weapon to the ground. It had served its purpose.

The Victoria thing howled with screams so loud that her mouth cracked open. Her head splintered; her branch-limbs writhed in pain, broke, and fell like dead wood to the floor of the glade.

Death spread outward from the center of the arrowhead like a blight of revenge, reclaiming the life that Victoria had stolen. The necessary poison had swiftly penetrated her heart, and the green sorceress crumbled. The bark cracked and festered. Smoking sap-blood oozed out of the wound, spilling in thick, stinking gouts down her rough body.

Victoria had uprooted one of her thick legs, but now the rooted leg shattered like a tree felled in a windstorm. She toppled in a long, slow collapse as her branches tangled in the encroaching trees. Vines whipped up as if to cushion her fall, but instead turned brown and withered.

Around the glade, the supercharged jungle that had swarmed across the open terrain began to shrivel. Trees collapsed, rotted, fell apart. All the extra life—the enforced growth and tortured fecundity that never should have existed—dissolved.

Nicci turned away. The corpse of Life's Mistress had already rotted into mulch, returning to the soil. The balance of magic would be restored and the unnatural forest would die back to its former levels, its *natural* levels.

Nicci had accomplished what she needed to. She had completed her mission, and she had paid the price. There was no reason for her to stay any longer.

She strode back toward Cliffwall as the seething jungle collapsed around her. She didn't give it a second thought.

CHAPTER 76

By the time Nicci returned to the steep uplift at the edge of the plateau, the unnatural jungle had already begun to retreat, a mere shadow of itself—a proper level of vegetation that did not strain the very foundations of life itself.

She felt no joy over her victory, *Thistle's* victory. Nicci had done what was required. Her duty was discharged. She had paid the cost in blood and unexpected love.

She was done.

As the once-burgeoning trees sloughed into rotting vegetation, she saw a dart of movement ahead of her, a tawny shape. Mrra came to join her. Gliding out of the falling trees and collapsing ferns, the sand panther paced alongside, not close enough for Nicci to touch her fur, but she was there, and that was what mattered. Nicci drew strength from their spell bond, and the big cat seemed to need reassurance as well.

When the two reached the sheer mesa wall, Nicci saw that the steep slope had broken and eroded away. The gnarled brown strands of dead vines still clung to the rocks, but Nicci found a way up to the alcoves and the tunnels high above. At the base of the cliff, Mrra let out a low growl, a temporary farewell, and loped off into the foothills. She would be back.

Nicci climbed back up the steep wall, using magic when necessary to move aside crumbling blocks that the aggressive vegetation had broken away from the cliff.

Nathan and Bannon met her as soon as she reentered the tunnels. Crowds from inside Cliffwall also came, excited and amazed. While watching from the alcove windows, they had seen the festering jungle die away.

"We must have a celebration!" someone called.

Nicci didn't see who spoke, didn't even bother to turn in the direction of the voice. "Celebrate among yourselves," she said gruffly. "Do not make me a hero."

Life's Mistress was dead, the enemy vanquished, the blight of twisted life now disappearing. Yes, there was good reason to cheer, but Nicci did not feel like rejoicing. Rather, she found a hard core inside her and held on to that.

She would never be Death's Mistress again. She had left that dark part of her life in the past, and she had promised Richard. She had learned from the terrible things she'd done for Emperor Jagang. Though Thistle's blood had provided the necessary poison to destroy Life's Mistress, Nicci herself did not want to be that vulnerable.

Never again. She had saved the world, and that was enough. Even if Thistle could never see it, the girl would have her beautiful valley back.

The Cliffwall scholars were unsettled by Nicci's response, and Nathan looked at her with a concerned expression. He gave her a slow nod, then lowered his voice. "You don't need to dance and sing, Sorceress, but you did defeat Victoria and stop that terrible threat. You can feel satisfied."

She looked at him for a long moment and then said, "I would rather not allow myself to feel anything at all."

At Nicci's suggestion, although it was obvious to anyone who considered it, they buried the girl out on the edge of the valley where the fresh vegetation, the *healthy* shrubs and plants, had begun to grow again.

It was a somber procession as they wrapped Thistle's small body in the soft sheepskin rug she had loved so much when she slept on the floor in Nicci's quarters. Nicci carried the body herself, and although her heart was heavy as a stone, the girl seemed to weigh almost nothing.

Franklin, Gloria, and many of the other remaining memmers and scholars left Cliffwall, emerging along the steep side of the plateau. They walked until they reached a spot just on the foothills overlooking the valley, which Thistle had so longed to see fertile again.

Nicci halted. "This is the place. This the view Thistle would want. From here, she would have been able to see the restoration of life that she made possible."

As hot tears stung her eyes, Nicci caught a glimpse of Bannon and Nathan, their faces also flooded with grief. Bannon's hazel eyes welled with unshed tears, and even Nathan, who had seen so much sadness and lost so many people during his centuries of life, was deeply affected by the loss of this one spunky and determined little girl.

"Her spirit can tell the Creator how she would like the valley to be," Nathan said. "I'm sure she will make herself heard."

Bannon nodded. "Thistle could be very convincing." His voice cracked.

Nicci could only nod. She felt so full of words, emotions, and ideas that she wanted to express, but they only simmered within her. Thistle would know. That was all Nicci cared about.

With a gesture from her hand, she released a flow of magic that moved the dirt and rocks on the chosen patch of ground. As she had done at the village of Renda Bay, Nicci created a grave, carving out a perfect, comfortable last bed to embrace Thistle's remains.

As the scholars watched solemnly, Nicci laid the girl wrapped in the sheepskin into the open grave. "This is as far as you can go with us," Nicci said. "I know you wanted to travel to see all the new lands we intend to explore, but from here you can watch the valley. I hope it becomes all you ever wanted to see."

Her arms and shoulders felt stiff, and it was because she had forced such tight control on her muscles to keep herself from trembling. Nicci drew a deep breath. She, Bannon, and Nathan looked down at the wrapped form in the grave. With a gesture, Nicci brought the soft loamy dirt back into place, filling it perfectly, leaving an open patch of naked brown earth on top.

"Should we mark the grave somehow?" Gloria asked. "Is there a stone or a wooden post you'd like us to use?"

Nicci thought of what Thistle had said, how she had laughed at the frivolous but wondrous thought. The girl had grown up without seeing anything of natural beauty, watching her aunt and uncle eke out a living in Verdun Springs, trying to grow stunted plants for food.

"Flowers," Nicci said. "Plant beautiful flowers. That's what Thistle would want to mark her grave."

Before she and her companions departed again, Nicci called a gathering inside Cliffwall, speaking to the workers, farmers, and canyon dwellers as well as the memmers and scholars. In a stern voice, she said, "We have only been here for a few weeks, but already we have saved the world—twice! Both times the disasters were caused by your own clumsy ignorance. And, oh, the consequences . . . the price that had to be paid."

She swept her blue-eyed gaze over the gifted researchers, and they trembled with guilt and shame.

She continued, "You are untrained. Thousands of years ago, your people were entrusted to guard this storehouse of knowledge. Dangerous knowledge. Do not consider it a library, but an *armory*—all the books and scrolls here are weapons, and you have seen how easily they can be misused."

"With disastrous results," Nathan said. "For all my objections to the Sisters and their iron collars, at least they devoted themselves to training new wizards back at the Palace of the Prophets. With the lore stored here, you cannot just willy-nilly dabble with spells as if they were toys."

Franklin hung his head. "Perhaps we should devote ourselves only to the work of cataloging, exactly as Simon wanted us to do. That is enough to keep us busy for decades."

Gloria wiped a small tear from the side of her eye. "The memmers can help to match what we know with the volumes we find on the shelves." She drew a deep breath, let it out slowly. "But who will teach us?" She looked hopefully at Nicci and Nathan. "Will you stay?"

Nicci shook her head. "We will depart soon. I have my own mission for Lord Rahl, and the wizard has an important destination." She spoke in a tone of command, the same tone she had used to send tens of thousands of Emperor Jagang's soldiers off to certain death. "But after we go, you must do one thing for me. An important task."

Franklin spread his hands, then gave a respectful bow. "Of course, Sorceress. Cliffwall is in your debt."

"Send emissaries north to D'Hara and tell Lord Rahl about this archive, and about what we have done here. That is knowledge he needs. Once he learns what is here, he will send his own wizards, scholars, experts. They will help you."

"I'm sure Verna would delight in the challenge," Nathan said. "Dear spirits, imagine what the Prelate would do with so much unexplored lore! She needs something to do, now that prophecy is gone. She could bring many Sisters with her." He nodded slowly. "Yes, indeed, you would be in good hands." He narrowed his eyes and added in a scolding tone, "But in the meantime, no more dabbling with spells."

Gloria agreed. "We will put in checks and balances to insure that no disaster like Roland or Victoria ever happens again."

One of the scholars fidgeted, looking at the rest of the uneasy audience. "But how will we find D'Hara?" He was a thin and rabbity young man named Oliver who had a habit of squinting, as if his eyesight had already waned from too much reading by dim candlelight. "I will volunteer to go, to accept the quest . . . so long as I know where I'm going."

Nicci had little patience for the details. "Follow the old imperial roads. Head north. Make your way beyond the Phantom Coast to the main port cities of the Old World. Ask about the Lord Rahl."

"That will be an arduous expedition, Oliver." Franklin sounded uncertain.

"Yes, it will be," Nicci said. "And we require it of you. Sometimes you must do things even though they are hard."

"I will go with Oliver," said a thin young memmer woman, Peretta, with tight ringlets of dark hair. "Not only is it an important mission, but every person here in Cliffwall, whether memmer or traditional scholar, has a mission to gather knowledge. And what could be a better way to seek knowledge than to explore the rest of the world?" She blinked her large brown eyes.

Oliver smiled and nodded at her. "I will be happy to have you."

"You'll both learn much. You'll be great explorers." Nathan patted the leather pouch at his side, which still carried his life book. "I will also want Cliffwall scholars to copy the maps I've drawn along the way, and take a summary of our expedition so far. The people of D'Hara need to know everything they can of the Old World."

Franklin looked at the memmers, then at the rest of the scholars, and he gave a confident nod. "Do you think you can do this, Oliver and Peretta? Will you be ambitious enough to undertake this quest?"

Like a slowly exhaled breath, the audience began nodding and talking. Peretta sniffed. "Of course we will."

Ready to go, Nathan had dressed in fine travel clothes again, his ornate scabbard belted at his waist, his brown cape from Renda Bay, a dark vest and ruffled shirt taken from Cliffwall stores. "After years of reading dusty old legends, some of you must want to become adventurers yourselves." He laughed. "When you return from D'Hara, you will have earned your own place in history."

Before her unexpected death, Mia had found for Nathan an old chart that clearly showed a place marked *Kol Adair* on the far eastern side of the great valley, over several lines of stark mountains.

Looking at the ancient map, Nathan was concerned at the prospect of crossing over such sheer and jagged crags. "Maybe it won't be so bad. The cartographer could have exaggerated the extremity of the terrain."

"We will know when we get there," Nicci said.

"And we know where we need to go," Bannon added.

The two men bade farewell to the people of Cliffwall, but Nicci said

CHAPTER 77

Leaving Cliffwall behind them, they crossed the wide, wounded valley for days before reaching the eastern foothills. The hills rose toward distant and far more rugged mountains that looked like the ridges on a dragon's spine.

As they traveled, they found the remnants of old roads that had been all but erased by the life-absorbing Roland and by Victoria's raging fecundity. They crossed terrain where once-thriving towns had been emptied and swallowed up. Now, the uninhabited wilderness was breathtaking in its sheer, empty silence.

Although Nicci didn't feel like engaging in conversation, the silence and constant walking gave her too much time for internal reflection. There wasn't a moment when she did not feel the loss of Thistle, but she tried to build up her inner walls and harden the scar. She had lost many people before, others she cared about, especially in the recent battles with Emperor Sulachan and his bloodthirsty, soulless hordes. Cara . . . Zedd . . .

Nicci had killed countless people herself. She was familiar with death, untroubled by blood on her hands. Her conscience was not heavy. She tried to convince herself that the orphan girl was just another death.

Just another death . . .

Topping a sparsely wooded ridge, Nicci, Bannon, and Nathan turned to look behind them. The vast valley now showed patches of healthy green growth and the flowing silver ribbons of streams. But it was neither a madness of life, nor a cracked desolation of death.

Nathan drew a satisfied breath. "You see? That is what we did, Sorceress."

"It is what we set out to do. Now I'm done with the witch woman's prediction." Nicci turned and continued into the hills before she could think about the price they had paid for that achievement.

"Ah, but Sorceress, on such a journey as ours, is one ever truly done with saving the world?"

When they made camp that night, Mrra dragged a mountain-goat carcass into the meadow and dropped it there for their dinner. The sand panther had already fed, and she sat on the fringes of the clearing, watching Bannon cut fresh meat while Nathan built a campfire. "I want to prove I can do this without magic, though the process is certainly a lot less convenient." He sighed. "Soon, though, I will be whole again."

They contoured along streams through the hills, picking the best path that would keep them moving into the rising mountains. Since Bannon had grown up on an island and sailed the ocean, he had little instinct for finding a route through hilly terrain. Nicci led the way.

She scanned the rugged landscape and picked a switchbacked path up the slopes, across open parks, then into thick pine forests. As they gained altitude, the trees became sparser, then stunted. After thrashing through thickets of knee-high alpine willows, the three emerged into open windswept tundra with whistling grasses and low cushions of wildflowers. Mrra bounded on the rocks, ranging ahead to chase waddling marmots.

Bannon was out of breath, panting hard. He bent over, resting his palms on his knees. "The trail is steep, and the air is thin."

Nathan did not commiserate. "I am a thousand years old, my boy, and I'm keeping up with you. Come, Kol Adair is ahead."

"The air will grow thinner still," said Nicci. "Our destination is much higher."

Bannon squinted as the wind whipped his ginger hair like crackling flames around his head. "When I grew up on Chiriya, I never imagined this." He looked in curious amazement at the rugged lichen-covered rocks as they picked their way toward a steep pass ahead. "I've come so far from that place and from that life, not just in the miles I've traveled but in the things we've seen and done." He gave his mentor a wan smile. "All the things you've taught me and all the experiences I've had, Nathan. Maybe this isn't the perfect life that I dreamed about, but I am happy with it."

He turned to Nicci, pressing her for a response. "Do you think I'll ever see the D'Haran Empire for myself? You've told stories about those lands. Could I even meet Lord Rahl someday?"

"D'Hara is a long way from here," Nicci said, pushing toward the top of the steep ridge ahead. "And we are heading in a different direction."

Nathan was more encouraging. "Maybe you'll see it someday, my boy, but why be in a hurry? This world has many lands, many people, and many sights to see." He smiled and quoted what Red had shown him in the life book: "Future and Fate depend on both the journey and the destination."

Because the slope was so steep, they stopped to catch their breath before reaching the summit of the pass. Nathan took out the Cliffwall charts, studied them again, and looked back at the mountains they had just crossed. "We should be close to our destination," he said. "Very close."

When Nicci set off again, her gaze fixed ahead, Bannon and Nathan hurried after her. Mrra ranged among the rocks, frustrated that the fat, furry marmots always managed to duck into shelter before the cat could catch them. Then one of the animals let out a high-pitched squeal as Mrra killed it for a snack.

The ground was hard and packed under Nicci's boots while she worked her way up to the pass, leading the way, steeper and steeper. Finally, when she climbed her last steps to the top, the grand vista opened up before her, and even she stopped in her tracks, awestruck.

They had reached Kol Adair.

CHAPTER 78

Panting and weary, Nathan came to stand at the top of the pass and inhaled a deep breath of the cold, thin air. The splendor of the view struck him like a physical blow. "Kol Adair—dear spirits, it's magnificent!"

Since escaping from the Palace of the Prophets, he had witnessed many sights, experienced grand and dramatic events, but he had never before beheld a panorama that inspired in him such absolute awe. From here, they could see forever.

The sun shone down upon the high mountain valley through the lens of a perfectly transparent blue sky. Regimented black crags spread out in a fiercely beautiful barrier, their peaks capped with snow. Dramatic couloirs cradled glaciers that dispatched pearly white ribbons of meltwater over cliffs in a chain of thundering waterfalls. The cascades sent up a wondrous spray that spawned rainbows. Mountain lakes in hanging valleys glittered like jewels, the purest turquoise blue, some crusted with broken white ice still unmelted in midsummer.

Bannon plodded up beside him, wheezing, too weary to do anything but stare at his boots. When he lifted his head to take in the view, though, he gasped.

Nathan continued to drink in the visceral beauty around him. The sweeping meadows were lush and green, spangled with so many bright and colorful alpine flowers it looked like a meteor shower of blossoms. Even from this distance, he could hear the soothing roar of the waterfalls that tumbled down the black cliff faces. Bluebirds darted about in the spray or swooped down to snatch insects among the wildflowers.

On the saddle, Mrra paced around the open terrain, staying close to Nicci. None of the three spoke as they absorbed the sight.

Nathan filled his lungs with the brisk air and extended his arms to his sides, just reveling in the beauty, the uplifting spectacle. Was this what the witch woman Red had wanted him to see? Although he gloried in the vista, Nathan wondered if this very place was supposed to restore his gift. He stretched out his arms, flexed his fingers, wondered if he felt whole again.

Restless and not sure what they were supposed to do now that they had arrived, Nicci wandered across the open, flat area. She explored the low grasses, pincushion mounds of pink flowers, and lichen-spattered boulders.

Nathan knew there had to be something more if the witch woman had sent them here, if the command had been written in an old life book and chiseled in the stones of a cairn a continent away. He had to have come here to Kol Adair for a reason.

Nathan could survive just fine without his gift of prophetic misery, but living without his *magic* was different. He had drawn great satisfaction from the spells he could work, the magical weapons he could wield—and he could have been a valuable asset in fighting both the Lifedrinker and Victoria. When he and Nicci had begun their journey, leaving the People's Palace and heading into the Dark Lands, Nathan had believed that the two of them would be invincible, a wizard and a powerful sorceress. He needed to be able to do his part again. He needed his magic back.

And this was the place he should be. But he felt no different.

"Look, another cairn!" Bannon said. To mark the top of the pass, some other traveler had piled up a tall cairn of stones, even more imposing than the one they had seen on the windswept Phantom Coast. He set off, but plodded slowly because he was out of breath.

Nicci reached the rocks first. She circled slowly, searching for a message such as what they had found before. She stopped, looked at the rocks, and frowned. "Nathan, come here."

Hurrying up to her, he felt a surge of hope, longing to feel his Han again, to control his gift and become a useful wizard once more. He needed to be made whole again!

Nathan looked down at the base of the cairn. Among the stacked rocks, like a grave marker, was a flat stone tablet devoid of pervasive lichens. Words had been chiseled into the flat granite surface: *Wizard, behold what you need to make yourself whole again.*

Nathan felt a surge of delight. He had seen that phrase before. "So the witch woman was here. Red communicated those words. And they're written in my life book . . . just as they were engraved on that other cairn."

"Either Red was here in person, or she foresaw it," Nicci said. "Someone left these words, and the witch woman *knew* about this from the time before prophecy was banished from the world. Kol Adair has been waiting for you for some time, Nathan Rahl."

"But what does it mean?" Bannon asked. "How will you get your magic back?" He turned a hopeful look to the wizard.

Nathan didn't want to admit that he had no idea of the answer. His brows knitted in concentration, and he made a grandiose gesture to indicate the astonishing vista, trying to convince himself. "Perhaps it is something about this place. Look around you, a sight so marvelous that it's enough to wash away the darkness in the world." He gave Nicci a meaningful look. "After killing the Lifedrinker and Victoria, and after the tragic loss of that poor little Thistle, maybe this is what we *all* need to restore ourselves." He closed his eyes and drew in another deep, satisfied breath of the clear air.

Nicci turned from the cairn. "I need more than a pretty view to heal the darkness inside me. I am strong enough to do that for myself. I already have a strong purpose."

Nathan swept his gaze across the waterfalls, hanging valleys, snow-capped peaks. His skin tingled, his pulse raced, and he felt a wondrous energy that he drew from the earth itself.

"This must be a magical place, a nexus of power springing from the world, just as the bones of a dragon carry a certain kind of power,"

Nathan said. "Simply by being here, I do feel myself restored! Yes, dear spirits, this is what I needed. It was worth the entire journey."

He stretched out his palm, cupped his fingers, and concentrated, remembering what it felt like. He reached for his Han and released a flow of magic, intending to call up a ball of flame. He remembered the last time he had attempted such a spell, on the windswept deck of the *Wavewalker*, manifesting only feathery flickers that had scattered away in the breeze. Now, he meant to produce a bright blaze cupped in his hand.

He had reached Kol Adair. His powers should be back.

Nothing happened.

He concentrated harder. Nicci and Bannon watched him. But although he strained, he felt no response from his gift. Nothing.

His heart, which had felt so uplifted in this magnificent place, now sank into dismay. His magic was gone, unraveled and untangled, stripped from him just as his ability of prophecy had gone away.

"What did I do wrong?" he demanded. "Why haven't I been restored? I should be made whole here—look at the words on the cairn! What else do I need to do?" He raised his voice in desperation, knowing that neither Nicci nor Bannon would have an answer for him.

He hung his head. The foundations of the world had changed, and the stars had shifted overhead. "Maybe with the loss of prophecy, Red's prediction is no longer true after all."

CHAPTER 79

Nicci watched the wizard withdraw into disappointment and defeat. His expression looked as bleak as the patches of glaciers across the mountain valley. "Nothing," he said, flexing his fingers.

Nathan Rahl had always been personable, confident, intelligent—a perfect roving ambassador for D'Hara. Nicci had accompanied him on the journey for her own purposes, but along the way she had come to value the wizard's abilities and knowledge. There was more to the former prophet than was immediately obvious from his demeanor and his personal façade.

Together, they had come a great distance and endured many hardships to find Kol Adair, all based on the whim of a witch woman. Yes, this immense, virgin land must be filled with resources, incredible wealth to whet the appetite of any ambitious ruler. But there was no magic here for Nathan. He had not found what Red promised.

Intensely weary, the old wizard folded his legs and sat on the tundra next to the cairn's piled stones. He opened the leather pouch at his side and sadly removed his new life book. "I wonder if she left me another message." When he turned back the cover, he saw only the sketches and journal entries that he himself had written. Hoping for answers, he skimmed the lines, but the words offered no surprises.

Future and Fate depend on both the journey and the destination.

Kol Adair lies far to the south in the Old World. From there, the Wizard will behold what he needs to make himself whole again. And the Sorceress must save the world.

He closed the cover and tucked it away again. "What should I do and where should I go now? I came to Kol Adair. Why haven't I been made whole?" Now he only frowned at the spectacular view. "What more am I supposed to behold?"

Nicci said, "We have the rest of the Old World to explore. Maybe someone else can tell you the answer."

Bannon looked down at the carved words in the granite tablet again, as if he had somehow misread the simple sentence. "'Behold what you need to make yourself whole again.'" He stood up quickly. "Wait, listen to what it says! The witch woman didn't claim you would *be restored* just by coming to Kol Adair. She said this is where you would *see* what you need." The young man's freckled face flushed with excitement. "Maybe we just haven't seen it yet."

Nathan struggled to his feet. "That means we have to look for whatever it is I need, my boy." He pursed his lips. "Maybe some magical artifact, or a spell-form laid out in the rocks here on the pass. The witch woman wouldn't be so obvious."

"A witch woman rarely is," Nicci said.

Nathan was grinning with renewed hope. "Dear spirits, there's still a chance . . . but what are we even looking for?"

Bannon bent down to the large cairn and began searching among the mottled rocks, looking for answers. "Maybe something is hidden here. It's the most obvious thing." He found a loose stone at the base and rolled it aside, surprised to find a second flat slab with more engraved words. "I don't think you're finished yet, Nicci."

She felt a chill as she saw the ominous statement carved years—or centuries—ago, but she already guessed what it would say. *Sorceress, save the world.* "I don't need some ancient writing to tell me what to do," she grumbled.

The cairn held no other messages, no artifacts, no clues. At a loss, standing on the high mountain pass, the companions searched the distance. The grand view encompassed countless miles of breathtakingly beautiful terrain, but nothing at all that might help the wizard regain his magic.

The wind whistled around them, mocking. Nathan's azure eyes sparkled with a hint of desperate tears, and he stared as if the very intensity could make his need come true. "We've come a very long and difficult way to reach this place." He shouted, "I would appreciate instructions that are a little less obtuse!"

Just then the sun shone at an angle from a precise spot up in the sky. The air shimmered on the far side of the mountains like a curtain opening, a veil pulled away—to reveal a sudden, startling vision of a distant plain beyond the mountains.

Catching a quick breath, Nicci thrust out her arm. "Look there! It's a . . . city!"

Nathan and Bannon turned. The sand panther let out a low growl.

Bannon cried, "That looks even bigger than Tanimura. It wasn't there before!"

Nathan looked giddy with excitement. "No, my boy. No, it wasn't. Why didn't we see it?"

Nicci drank in the unbelievable details. The far-off city was a magnificent metropolis, perhaps greater even than Aydindril and Altur'Rang combined. The skyline was a forest of fantastic construction, exotic architecture with high temples and civic buildings, crowded dwellings and elaborate villas. The tall buildings stretched upward, soaring towers built of white stone. Their roofs shone with vibrant enamel tiles; windows flashed with jewel colors of extensive glass mosaics.

The air around the whole city flickered and blurred, seen through a viewing lens that sharpened details into amazing clarity before they grew fuzzy again. It was as if a huge dome shielded the strange metropolis, hiding it—and for just a brief moment, the magic and the vantage from Kol Adair had revealed it to them. The dome was crumbling, fading.

"We are seeing it from here, for the first time." Nathan was breathing hard. "That must be what Red meant! We reached Kol Adair, and from this exact viewpoint, we can see that city. 'Behold what you need to make yourself whole again.'" He turned to Nicci, his smile bright. "We need to go to that city. The answer lies there. It has to."

Nicci had spent most of her time in crowded civilization, and she much preferred a city to the austerities of life on the trail. The flickering mirage intrigued her with its possibilities. "I agree."

Before they set off, the air shimmered again—and the entire majestic metropolis simply vanished. On the other side of the mountains, the land appeared completely empty.

Bannon yelped. "Was it just an illusion?"

"Not an illusion," Nathan insisted. "It can't be an illusion. Maybe the city is hiding itself somehow, camouflaged by a shroud similar to the one that hid Cliffwall for so many centuries." He nodded, convincing himself as much as the others. "But now we know it's there. Come, Sorceress! We still have a long journey ahead of us, but at least we realize where we have to go."

Mrra continued to rumble with an uneasy growl at the sight, but the wizard would not be deterred. He set off, picking his way down the slope from the pass. They would have to cross many mountain valleys and work their way through the stark snowcapped crags before they reached the site of the mysterious vanishing city.

As they came over the next ridge, they found a prominent trail from the south, a clear footpath that wound through the mountains. "This is not a game trail," Nicci said. In one section, the path widened to reveal moss-covered paving stones, an ancient thoroughfare that had been laid down for traffic. But it had obviously been used in recent days.

"A road!" Nathan could not suppress his optimism. "We are on our way now, Sorceress. That was the sign we needed."

Tall, black rocks blocked their view as they descended another convoluted ridge. When they rounded a barren swell, following the narrow road, Nicci stopped as they beheld a startling and repulsive sight. Bannon gasped, sickened.

Set upon tall spikes on either side of the path were four severed heads, the faces partially crow-pecked, but otherwise preserved by an anti-decay spell. The skin on the faces had slackened in death, but their mouths had been horrifically and distinctively scarred—sliced from the corners of the lips all the way back to the hinge of the jaw, then sewn up and healed. Their cheeks were tattooed with scales to give them the appearance of serpent men.

Nicci recognized them from their attack on the poor people of Renda Bay.

Bannon flushed with anger. "Norukai slavers."

"It appears they must have offended someone," Nathan said.

Nicci stepped forward to scrutinize the appalling heads. "The preservation spell masks how long they've been here."

Beneath the first stake rested a blood-spattered placard written in strange symbols that Nicci couldn't read. She did, however, recognize the arcane letters as similar to those branded onto Mrra's hide.

The sand panther growled again, long and low.

Nicci flashed a hard smile and looked along the winding trail that led toward the vanished city. "Yes, that place might be very interesting indeed."